ESCAPE

ETHEL VANCE

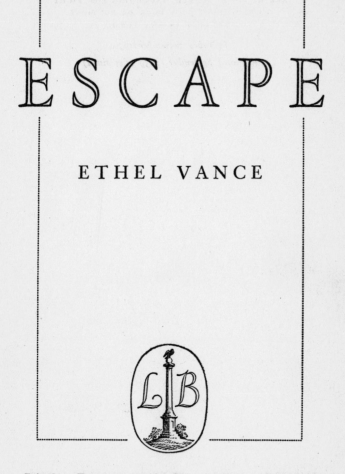

Little, Brown and Company · Boston

1939

Published September 1939

Reprinted September 1939 (five times)

PRINTED AND BOUND IN THE UNITED STATES OF AMERICA
BY THE HADDON CRAFTSMEN, INC., CAMDEN, N. J.

ESCAPE

Chapter I

THE doctor took out the stitches, swabbed the scar with a disinfectant, and then made an examination of his patient. He felt carefully around the region of the abdomen, put a stethoscope to her heart and lungs. He put a clinical thermometer into her mouth. There was no chart, so he made methodical notes for his own use in a little book he carried.

A large woman with straw-colored hair cut short like a man's stood in the doorway. She wore a rough gray cotton uniform and carried a little, chipped, enamel dish of discarded dressings and stitches. Another woman, also lying on an iron cot, had turned on her side to see what was going on.

The doctor folded up his stethoscope and put it in his bag, took the thermometer out of the patient's mouth and went over to the narrow window to read it.

The woman in the doorway said in a hoarse voice, "What a fuss, what a fuss over nothing!"

The doctor frowned. He was a tall, roughly built young man with a bony red face and pointed cheekbones; his eyes were small and intensely blue. Only his thin, red wrists, too long for the sleeves of his black uniform, had a sensitive look.

"Temperature thirty-seven," he read. He shook the thermometer down, put it in its case and came back to the iron cot. He opened his bag again to put the thermometer away and as he rearranged some bottles he said, "I have never seen a quicker recovery. You have a very remarkable constitution."

The patient had been obedient, moving as he told her, turning on her back or her side. Now she lay on her back, her hands clasped on her chest, and two long braids coiled like dark rivers in the gaunt little winter landscape of the blanket. Her dark eyes looked up at him attentively. She was about to say something and was gathering her breath for it. He felt it coming and braced himself, standing very erect. He fixed his eyes on the card at the head of the bed. EMMY RITTER, he read, EMMY RITTER, — feeling some of the same shock as when he had first read it.

"Emmy Ritter!" his father used to say, his voice turning portentous, full of eagerness and disapproval. That was very long ago, in the country house striped with tree shadows. Every Sunday they drove along behind the bobbing tails of horses to visit "the dear Countess" who gave them coffee and sweet cakes. "Emmy Ritter?" he would say. "Oh, yes, I saw her in town last week. They say that fellow Schnitzler is going to write a comedy for her. . . . Really for such a young actress — but they say she's phenomenal. . . ." "I saw Emmy Ritter in a café. She was with some acquaintances of mine and there was a blond young man with them: Preysing, the actor. They say she is going to marry him. That will finish her career. No, I wasn't presented to her. . . ." "They say the Grand Duke gave her his smallest Altdorfer as a wedding present — No, no, they say he sold it to her, he is hard up for cash. . . ." "They say Emmy Ritter has gone to America. . . . They say . . ."

This Emmy Ritter . . . Perhaps the name wouldn't have clung to him if it hadn't been for the photograph. It had slipped between his father's desk and the wall, and he took it and put it under the paper lining of his dresser drawer. It was the picture of a queen, the bad queen of a Grimm fairy tale. He especially didn't want his mother to see it, though he was not sure why. He was a little afraid of it. For a long time he forgot it. Then one summer he came on it again. She wore a crown and a mediaeval robe, and her hair exactly as now in long braids. In her hands a basket. Saint Elisabeth of course. He had forgotten Grimm. People had stopped talking about her by then, and he could make her anything he wanted. He knew a few big-boned girls and never noticed one of them. This was his "Ideal," this heroic, tender figure, charged with life, vibrating with his wildest hopes and surmises.

To think of it now disgusted him. Such a little fool! All that romantic, sickly adolescence! He remembered how completely she had been discredited, diminishing into a mere furnishing of the country house and the time spent there, shrinking again to a photograph left in a drawer, a name spoken by his father's voice.

For years he had never thought of her. Only once did someone say, "Whatever became of that Emmy Ritter?" and someone answered, "Why, she went to America." He didn't know what had become of the photograph.

Then suddenly he read the name on a white card over an iron prison cot. In the crowded prison late one night . . . After the first shock, he had no time to think of photographs or voices, for here was something he recognized, directly before him, waiting for him, a territory very precise and demanding of him exact knowledge, a territory where organs functioned and blood circulated, a human body in fact, remarkable, as he had just told her. Forty, or even forty-five, he thought, if she's a day, but she might be thirty.

"So, I'm getting well?" she said.

He nodded, hoping she would say no more.

[5]

"But when can I walk?" she insisted.

He hesitated and cleared his throat. "Well, perhaps in a week," he said.

"Oh!" she exclaimed, throwing all her power into her voice. "Just in time for my execution."

She raised herself suddenly on her elbows toward him and he thought she was going to throw herself from the bed. The woman in the doorway thought so too. She started forward, but the doctor motioned her back.

"Lie down, Madame Ritter," he cried peremptorily. He saw both terror and mockery in her eyes. She only wants to point up her bravado, he thought, and to shame me once more.

She settled back on her pillow, clasping her hands again. She closed her eyes slowly, smiling as though it had been a good joke, a little, nervous twitch forming at one corner of her mouth.

He turned from her to the woman on the other bed.

This woman was equally condemned to die, but it was impossible for him, even as a doctor, to be interested in her. She was dying of tuberculosis and undernourishment, and there was no will to live left in her. Her name — Anna Hoffman — said nothing to him. She was not in his care; one of the regular camp doctors, himself a prisoner, came to see her every other day or so, and once when the two doctors met in the corridor the camp doctor asked him if he remembered those remarkable cherry tarts that used to be sold at Hoffman's pastry shop: "It was her husband," he said, jerking his thumb toward the doorway, "but I think she was the one who made them."

"I've never eaten them," the young doctor said. "I'm new to this part of the country."

"Well, someone else has the shop now," the camp doctor said. "The tarts are not as good."

[6]

The young doctor said a few words to Anna and then came back to get his black bag that he'd left at Emmy's feet. He looked down at her and saw her eyes were still closed, but she was not smiling.

Yes, in the photograph her braids were exactly as now. She was Saint Elisabeth of Hungary certainly, carrying bread that turned into roses. That was what started him off. If she had been dressed as Maria Theresia for instance, or Marie Antoinette perhaps, he wouldn't have given her a second look.

It's my tough luck, he thought, that we had to meet here. I'd certainly forgotten you. I thought you'd faded off into America. I thought you'd died in my bureau drawer. And I should have let you die there again, up in that crowded prison, before I had any time to think about it. You didn't matter to anyone there. You didn't matter to me. I didn't believe in bad queens or in good queens any more, or in jaded and luxurious actresses, fatal to country squires and their small boys. But no. I had to save you — for a reason that had nothing to do with old photographs or country houses or what the Countess said or what my father said or what I used to think. I wish you'd understand that but I can't tell you that without telling you the other too. It was simply because my skill rose up in me and recognized a complementary skill in you, one I never thought of you as having: a skill to live. It recognized at once the urge that was in all your organs, glistening and elastic with life, and in your blood hammering along in perfect equilibrium, the red corpuscles balancing the white. Yes, after all this time it was our two skills that met, not like lovers, but like, say, a flute player and an Italian tenor; and we did a duet together. That's all. And that is the true and only reason why I saved you, Emmy Ritter. Damn you, he thought, why did you have to get caught?

[7]

He cleared his throat and stared at her with his sharp blue eyes. Then he closed his bag with a click and went out. The woman who had waited in the doorway followed him carrying her little tray of dressings.

Chapter II

IN THE great camp, which had formerly been a munitions factory, there were normally no women. At the moment there were three: Emmy Ritter, Anna Hoffman, and the one who acted as their nurse.

The camp was a world of its own. The men, who came from every walk of life, slept in barracks, ate in a common room, worked in the workshops, the kitchens, or outside the walls under guard, clearing swamps and building roads. The life was hard and many of them when they came were already sick and undernourished. There was a hospital for the worst cases and most of the doctors were prisoners themselves, and some of them were very good doctors.

There was a canteen where any prisoner with money could buy himself sausages, bread, and tobacco. Anna's husband, himself a prisoner, had been in charge of the canteen for two years. During that time she had been allowed to live here with him, and in the long winters, breathing the damp air of the swampy ground, living in an unheated room, she had developed tuberculosis. She got worse and worse. She could have gone away if she'd had any money to go with, but all the money they had saved had to be used in taking care of her mother and sister during this time when her husband could no longer earn any. Then one day her husband disappeared.

Anna never knew how — escapes from here were almost unheard-of. He had a position of some trust, but even so it was impossible for her to imagine how he had managed it; and no one would tell her. It was such a shock to her that she had a bad hemorrhage and couldn't get out of bed.

No one knew exactly what to do with Anna. She had no place to go: her mother and sister had finally left the country, having spent all her remaining savings. The prison doctor said Anna would only live a few weeks. And so the commandant of the camp let them put Anna in a little room of the hospital, and another man was put in charge of the canteen.

He himself had been a Secret Police guard at one of the town jails, but now he was under "honor arrest." He had, it seemed, fraternized a bit with the prisoners and this was to teach him his place, so to speak. His wife was the big woman with straw-colored hair, and if her husband had been tempted to any kindness she was heartily sorry for it and made up for it as best she could.

The room where the two women lay was the smallest one in the hospital, and the walls were covered with lime wash on which other prisoners had scratched with their spoons. It was furnished by the two iron beds with straw mattresses and a rough wooden stand on which were two used cakes of soap, two toothbrushes and a can of tooth powder, two rough brown towels, and two forks and spoons. As they were both too sick to get up and go to the latrine there was a covered iron pail in the corner. This pail was scrupulously emptied and the room was kept very clean. There were no chairs and the single window was not barred. It wasn't necessary. Just outside was a wooden fence, beyond that another fence, and still beyond was a fence of barbed wire charged with electricity; beyond that was a masonry wall studded at intervals with machine-gun towers.

During the three weeks that the two women had shared

this room they had also, lately, shared a few faint whispered jokes, and one of them was that the wife of the new canteen keeper was not a woman at all but a man. They called her "Hermann" and insisted that she shaved every morning and that by evening you could see a faint fair bristle on her chin. They didn't trust her. Sometimes when Emmy and Anna had been talking they heard her tip-toeing away in her creaky boots. And it might be only natural curiosity. They couldn't be sure.

Now that they were alone Anna wanted to talk, but she was embarrassed because Emmy had just spoken about death. The two women had always talked as if it were certain they would some day be well and out of here. This was a sort of politeness they kept up with each other, the only politeness really that was left for them. Anna waited, and Emmy lay with her hands rigid on her chest. Presently she opened her eyes and looked around as though to be sure they were alone.

"What day is this?" she asked in a low voice.

"I don't know. Isn't it Wednesday?"

"I don't know. I should have asked him." She lifted her hand slowly and ran her fingers along her throat. "I suppose it's better than hanging," she said.

"It's quicker," Anna said.

"I wonder. They say now in hanging the neck breaks right away."

"Perhaps they're both quicker than we think. Perhaps the doctor will give you some drug to make it easier. He's been very kind to you, hasn't he?"

"He's never insulted me nor handled me roughly, and I suppose this operation saved my life. I don't think he did that from kindness though."

"Perhaps he's seen you on the stage. Young men often admire actresses. Could it be that?"

[11]

"No, he's never seen me. I asked him. When I left this country he was a child."

"How old would you say he is?"

"Oh, twenty-five, twenty-eight, perhaps even thirty."

They spoke in low despondent voices with no hurry. They had all day to talk and it wasn't noon yet. They could take no part in the routine of the camp except by the sounds that came to them, the bugle early in the morning before daylight, the roll call and the sharp, staccato calling of names and answers, the march of feet outward, and then the marching back again. In the afternoon more marching in the exercise grounds, a quick pattering sound as though a large herd of cattle were trotting over a paddock. Orders. Sometimes a distant voice haranguing. They guessed by the noise of the motor what sort of car was coming into the compound. A big car, some official probably. Or a truck, more prisoners. Early in the evening a bugle sounded again, all lights were out. Sometimes in the night a white searchlight swung in a flash across their beds. Once Emmy heard an owl hooting. During the day there would be a great twittering of sparrows.

Into this dim somnambulistic world the doctor came every morning. He stayed a few moments and said a few words. He was neither kind nor unkind. He showed no interest in them and asked no questions, other than medical ones. Both women watched him closely. His uniform made him like all the rest and his face and body were rude and elementary like a wooden Gothic figure made in a remote village. Only his wrists, so thin and red and clean and always too far below his sleeves, made his gestures seem delicate and incongruous to what he was and to what he did in this chilly room.

"No, I don't think he's a kind man," Emmy said bitterly.

"He only operated on me for the practice. I heard him say that. . . . I was sick all the last day of the trial, you know. Such a terrible stomachache I had, and my head bursting, and nausea! I thought it was fright. But then the night after the trial I couldn't stand it. This doctor came with an older man, a man whose face looked somehow familiar. He called him 'Uncle.' I heard him explaining that I had appendicitis and that at any moment my appendix would rupture. As it did of course. He went over all the symptoms. The pain was dancing in me like a rocket and the other fellow stood there wagging his head at each word he spoke. 'Let me take her to the hospital,' he said, 'let me operate. You know I'm rotting with idleness.' He spoke as passionately as though he were begging for a rendezvous. These doctors! 'There's no room,' the other man said, 'every hospital is filled.' 'How about the camp?' the doctor said. I don't remember what they said after that, but they must have decided to bring me here."

"The other man must have been important. Did he wear a uniform?"

"I don't remember. But the doctor wasn't kind, I can tell you that. It was simply that he'd got tired for the moment of his own system. You've no idea, Anna, how tired they get every now and then. Especially the young ones. Whatever is still growing, still pushing and thrusting in them, won't let them rest in it."

"Yes," said Anna, "I've seen children get sick under too strict a rule."

"Well, children show what's wrong more cleanly. Crush them down and they'll take to Saint Vitus' Dance, to throwing up their food and wetting their beds. The things men sometimes do, we don't talk about. But a man like the doctor can escape for a time by using the special skill he has, his own private, personal knowledge. He does a thing that maybe he's the only one to do, and that makes him feel separate and alive again."

"Perhaps that's so," Anna admitted. "Still, I think he's a good fellow underneath."

Poor Anna, Emmy thought. To be grateful for a problematical goodness so deep underneath showed a humble spirit. She hoped her husband had been nice to her. But she was afraid from little things Anna had told her that he hadn't been.

They had talked a good deal about themselves — a little at a time, for they were both weak — through the long hours of the day, and sometimes even at night in the dark when they couldn't sleep. Anna was a woman of the simplest education and had spent most of her life over a big stove; but that didn't mean she had nothing to talk about. She had had a husband and a child, who died in infancy. Her father died when she was a baby, but there had been her mother and sister and there had been friends. She knew how to cook good food and she knew what badly prepared food will do to the stomach. She had been once in a long while to the opera. Her favorite was "*Der Freischütz,*" because it made her feel so romantic, and every Sunday of her life she'd gone to mass, and she had had money in the bank and knew by just what hard work and what economy it had got there. Anna knew a great many things that are necessary to know. Emmy sometimes grew angry at those women who said they couldn't stand other women because of the poverty of their minds and experience. Emmy liked all women like Anna who had kept their true quality and efficacy as women.

Anna would have said more about the doctor but she was interrupted by a fit of coughing. She had a little carton for sputum at the top of her cot. She reached for it and coughed into it. When she lay back sweat was streaming down her face.

Emmy closed her eyes and wished she might close her ears also to shut out the sound of Anna's cough. All the sounds of the camp had an eerie, hypnotic remoteness, they came from a world of men invisible and unknown, but Anna's cough echoed from Emmy's own life. For it might be Sabina's cough, that cough which had grown lately worse instead of better. It made her see Sabina as she might be at this moment, wearing a costly thin dress or a sable jacket, walking slowly across a room before the hard, curious eyes of women in deep chairs. It made her see the lift of Sabina's thin arms; her much-admired, too-narrow hipbones; and her air of devitalized distinction.

What will become of her? she thought; she doesn't eat enough when I'm not there.

In her little flat were already two refugees, an old woman and her grandchild. The woman was the widow of Jacoby, the great surgeon of Vienna who committed suicide, the grandchild was a chubby boy of ten who practised the violin all day. But *he* ate enough, enough for two.

Anna, having rested a moment, looked over at Emma. She saw that her heavy eyebrows were drawn in a frown and she was tapping the tips of her fingers together nervously. Anna knew she must be worrying about her children again and it would be better for her to be able to talk about them. Anna knew a good deal about them already. But she could never get over being surprised that a woman whose name she had sometimes heard and who had lived the exciting, worldly life of the stage should have also had such a close, personal, even secret life with two children.

This was the life Anna could understand best and liked best to hear about. She liked to hear about the rooms they'd had here and there, filled with pictures and books and signed photographs of celebrated people and friends, and children's toys on the floor, and the warm wet odor of the children's laundry drying in the bathrooms. She liked to hear of their teas of jam and cakes and sandwiches and the stories that Emmy managed to tell them before she went to the theater. The illnesses they had, croup and measles and stomachache and the tonsil operation on Mark in Chicago, and how Sabina nearly died once on a train in Oklahoma. She liked to hear what the children had said, those bright sayings that are treasured in a family, and she knew how they'd looked, with their long spindle legs and their big eyes and pale faces, their ridiculously expensive clothes with real lace collars, and how Sabina was always melancholy and intelligent and how Mark had such excitable nerves and such energy that each time Emmy came home she said first, "What's Mark been doing?"

All this she knew, and as she had an aptitude herself for family life she began to recognize here the family character, the special traits such as the shape of eyebrows and a way of speaking, a certain line of behavior, the special quality of the atmosphere they created, so that when a new thing was told her about one of them she could say to herself, "How like them!"

"How old is Mark now?" she asked. She had been told before but she could never remember. She thought of him mostly, in the easiest way, as a little boy.

"Twenty-three," said Emmy. She turned a deep frightened look but she was grateful to Anna for letting her talk. "He's tall and thin now," she added, "and he looks a little like me."

"Is he handsome?" Anna asked.

"Not exactly. No, not really handsome. The best thing about him is the way he moves. If he were a woman I'd say he had elegance. Men used to like to be thought elegant.

Perhaps they still do, but they like another word for it."

"Does he dress well?"

"Oh, no. It's not that. It's a matter entirely of movement. A man must know how to use his body. To use the hands with fitness and economy is a good beginning. That's why the doctor, grotesque as he is, sometimes has elegance, and a garage mechanic was the most elegant man I ever saw."

"Ah, so," said Anna, doubtful. "Then perhaps it's because he's a painter. Is he a good painter?"

"Yes, he's a good painter. Later he'll be better than good."

"But does everyone say so?"

"A few people say so even now. He's very young still. But I know."

"How can you know? You're his mother."

"Because I've known so many bad painters."

"But your father — he was a great painter. Everyone has heard of Richard Ritter."

"My father? Oh, no. He was very talented and very fashionable. He certainly wasn't a great painter."

He was a painter who made a lot of money, Anna thought. And what, by the way, became of all the money? Painters and actors, she thought, can make a lot of money. But it was a long time, Emmy said, since she had earned enough to speak about, and money that isn't constantly augmented melts away. Yes, Anna knew that very well.

"Does Mark know about you?" Anna asked.

"I don't know," said Emmy. "I thought it better he shouldn't. You see, at first I hadn't been able to take the trial very seriously. Perhaps because I've read too much and been in too many plays. It was terribly familiar and yet it wasn't. And then too, at first I thought it was only a question of the house. They wouldn't tell me anything, not even what I was charged with. They talked about a lot of

[17]

things in what seemed an aimless way: You have lived in America and done so-and-so, you have come back here to sell your house. They asked all about that."

"Did you have a lawyer?"

"I had a lawyer but I never had a chance to talk with him alone. And before all those other people I wasn't going to give away what they might not know."

"Oh," said Anna, nodding her head.

"They kept asking me where I had put the money for the house," Emmy said. "I said here, of course. I thought they were only worried about that. They even let me have a witness. Yes, they let Fritz testify for me."

Anna knew about Fritz too. His was a name that cropped up continually in the family stories. It seemed that at first, when they were rich, when they went to America, he was the butler. He had been a young footman of Emmy's mother. As Emmy's fortunes declined he became still something else, Anna couldn't quite make out what. Emmy would say, "So I sent Fritz to Mark's school and he brought him to spend Christmas with me in Chicago," or "Fritz knew how to make a wonderful, sour cream sauce for venison," or "I borrowed fifty dollars from Fritz." But finally even Fritz had to leave them. He opened a little restaurant, failed at it, and then came back to his own country.

"So Fritz testified," she said. "What did he say?"

Emmy smiled. "He told them I had to his knowledge sold my house for a sum deposited in this country. He had witnessed the sale. The sum was small, he admitted, but he said I had no idea of the value of money. He went on to describe how easily I made it — merely for appearing on the stage! And how easily I spent it. He had often advised me, he told them, to put some by but I wouldn't listen to him. I was an artist, he said, irresponsible, kind-hearted, a little weak in the head. He was what is known as a character witness!"

Anna gave a little laugh which turned into a cough and they were silent again. Anna was wondering what Emmy had really done to be given a death sentence. Anna's questions were always hesitating, and when she had asked them she felt very daring. Emmy was a grander person than herself. She knew that. It seemed strange to her that Emmy was willing to talk so much. It seemed strange she wasn't more haughty and secret. If they hadn't talked about Emmy's trial before it was only because Emmy in her weakness thought most about her children. Now she was getting stronger and she had only a week to live. Anna could see that the stronger she got the less she wanted to die.

Emmy listened to be sure no one was just outside. She listened for the creak of Hermann's boots or the steps of the other doctor coming to see Anna.

No one was outside. Suddenly Emmy said quickly, "All the time I was in America I tried to keep out of it, I tried to close my mind, to say it can't all be true, or it will soon end. But I couldn't. I thought that if I didn't do something I would turn into corruption, I would die horribly, much more horribly than I shall die now."

"Yes, it's been bad over here," Anna said. "Times have been bad. But it seems there's nothing can be done about it."

"Plenty of people try," said Emmy. "Not enough, perhaps. And what they do is so small and so weak. Who really read those pamphlets, for instance? I mailed hundreds."

"Pamphlets?" Anna said.

"Yes, when they finally came to the matter of the pamphlets my lawyer refused to go on with the case. Those poor, feeble pamphlets! He said I had deceived him and he hadn't expected to have to defend a traitor. Then they said to me, 'You see, we can't even get anyone to defend you.'"

They heard the tramp of men coming back from building the road across the swampy land. They knew it must be near noon and that presently their soup and black bread would be brought to them. This they looked forward to, it meant something to do, and they felt the cold a little less with food in the stomach. They had only a thin blanket each and the March days were cold. After that they would take a nap, but today they both felt restless. They couldn't stop talking, and these forbidden things made a flickering warmth in the room.

"But how did you dare to come back?" Anna whispered.

"I came because I had to have money. I had spent everything and Sabina was sick. I'd put up all I could to help people who were coming out and wanted to get into America. I was broke."

"But you knew they might get you if you came back."

"No, I didn't. I thought they had nothing on me. Besides, I only expected to come as far as Belgium."

"Brussels?"

"Yes. It was the ad column of a New York paper that started it. It said: *If the dictators have tied up your property and investments in their countries it is possible to exchange other properties with incomes up to fifty thousand dollars for same.* Then it gave a number to write to. That gave me the idea. But I should have known there was something phony about that advertisement."

Anna would have liked to hear more of this too but it often happened that their most revealing conversations would break off abruptly. They would hear a sound outside, or they would be too tired. Anna would cough, or sometimes just the weight and sadness of their words would stop them. Emmy's brows drew in a frown again as she thought over the things that had gone wrong since she saw that advertisement in the paper.

She sighed impatiently. "I ought to have asked more questions," she said, as if she were explaining it to herself. "If I'd had anyone here to write to I would have. But there was only Fritz. I was rather ashamed to ask Fritz."

"You didn't have any friends here?" Anna asked.

Emmy thought in silence for a moment. "I'm afraid the best friend I had is dead," she said. "It's been six months since I heard from him. Yes, he must be dead. He and Fritz were the only two I ever wrote to. Think how long I've been gone!"

"You were lucky to have Fritz," Anna said.

"He was furious with me," Emmy said. "The first thing he said was, 'My God, Madame Ritter, you oughtn't to have come back.' I said, 'I had to, Fritz. I'm broke.' He raised his eyebrows and said very coldly, 'Naturally.' Then he took me to his niece's to board, and all the way there he scolded me for managing so badly. Still, I knew he'd do what he could."

"But you did sell it," Anna said. "Did you get the money?" She knew there are few things worse than losing money, no matter what high-flown things people like to say on the subject.

Emmy didn't answer. She wondered herself day and night whether perhaps Rieger, too, had got into trouble over the sale, whether he had been arrested, whether the money was deposited, whether Mark now had a fat check book in his hands and whether he and Sabina and the widow of the physician and the little boy who played the violin were having steaks and milk and cake made with six eggs.

She was exhausted with so much talking and her head throbbed, but she couldn't stop now.

"I hope Mark doesn't know," she said. "Nor Sabina. It would kill them."

"But what will they think?"

"I don't know. In the end they'll have to know, but when it's over it will be easier for them."

"Perhaps it will be like that."

"I hope so."

"Still," Anna persisted, "if they knew they might help you."

"Oh, no, I've thought of all that. What could they do? Write letters. Make protests. No. I did what I thought right to do and I must take what comes, and I want them out of it, Mark especially. He's the one who would do the foolish things. Make trouble for everyone, beat his head against a hundred iron walls. You will think I'm exaggerating but I believe Mark is less fitted than anyone I know to help me now, and the truth is I don't want him to be fitted. Sabina is different. Yes, given time it is within the realm of possibility she might do something. But not now. She's too sick. And Mark would only get into dreadful trouble."

"After all, he's an artist," said Anna, accepting the family standard. But it would be useful, she thought, if an artist could stop being one when necessary long enough to do what was required. After all, she thought, he's a man, isn't he? She began to feel drowsy and closed her eyes for a nap.

Emmy lay staring at the white ceiling. How do I know what Mark is capable of? she thought. I've spoiled him perhaps. I've thought that unless he keeps to his own intense, original life, the virtue will go out of him. Apart from that life he's a helpless boy with a bad temper, a boy who sometimes drinks too much, who once wanted to marry that awful girl. What was her name?

No, but I'm right. His mind has its secret balance. Everything he sees and knows, every sensation, must be turned into the maximum of a painter's comprehension. That's his job and that's his secret. Can he write protests, see lawyers, pick locks? No, it's always dangerous to be an artist, but it's more dangerous to stop being one.

But then how could he avoid guessing what's happened? The house sold and perhaps the money deposited. The long silence. He knew, too, about the pamphlets, not much but a little. And then if Fritz mailed the letter —

"Oh, I wish I hadn't written that letter!" she said despairingly.

"What letter?" Anna's eyes came open suddenly.

"The one I gave Fritz. Just after he had testified for me. It happened I had a moment's talk with him in a little waiting room off the court. It happened too that, for about five minutes before, I was sitting with no one watching me. I had a scrap of paper that had come around an aspirin bottle and on my wrist a little gold pencil on a chain that hadn't been taken away from me yet. My lawyer was protesting to some other man that the case was about to take a turn he hadn't expected and that he couldn't defend me any longer. It would get him into trouble, he said. I was beginning to be frightened. I wrote a note to Mark. When Fritz came in I took his hand and slipped the note up his cuff."

"Do you think he mailed it?"

"I don't know. He looked stupefied and angry too. Perhaps he was listening to the lawyer. Perhaps he thought I oughtn't to have endangered him."

"But he's faithful, isn't he?"

"Yes, he is. But in all these years I've never known whether he really likes me. I know he doesn't approve of me. He may not have approved of the note. If he didn't he'd destroy it. Fritz can be terribly ruthless."

She smiled, perplexed and rueful, thinking of Fritz, but her face quickly clouded. "He was right," she said, "I oughtn't to have written it. It showed I was afraid. When Mark and Sabina know it at least they mustn't think I was afraid. I shouldn't have written it. I can't bear to think of it."

Anna had a bad coughing fit and had to grope for the little carton for sputum. When it was over she lay back speechless. So many forbidden things they'd talked about! Their words were so full of danger they were exhausting. She was prostrated with fatigue. It would be better for both of them to take a nap now before their soup came.

But Emmy couldn't stop talking. She said, "When I talk about it, it seems as though I hadn't known very clearly what I was doing, as though I began one thing and ended up doing another. I wanted most of all to help these people here, but how could I keep just to that with other things pressing against me, Sabina's cough and money that we had to have, and even a hundred little daily happenings I haven't told you?"

Anna heard Emmy's quick, excited breathing, and knew she had what she called "worked herself up." She heard her turn on her side, lying so she could see the window. She glanced over and saw her looking at the gray sky, heavy with rain clouds.

"Don't think, Emmy," Anna whispered. "It makes it so much worse."

Emmy didn't answer and Anna sighed and closed her eyes again.

A gust of smoke blew past the window, perhaps from the camp kitchens.

Suddenly Emmy said, "But I will think. It's too easy to stop. Too many people have stopped. How long do you suppose the young doctor will keep his power to think? He's been allowed to keep a spark of it alive. But he can't go on cutting out gall bladders forever with nothing to go on but a mystic obedience and someone else's formula. It's a pity there are so many leftovers, isn't it? So much machinery lying around. Men can still build houses on a plan someone else thought of. You and I know every woman can fry an egg. We can exist on a minimum. It would be a good thing if every time an egg were fried the formula was lost."

"Most of us would be dead," said Anna drowsily, not opening her eyes.

"Maybe most of us would be more alive."

On the window ledge a sparrow with a small, bright fixed eye lighted and drank a drop of water from a hollow in the stone.

A sparrow had come on the edge of the window the last morning in New York. Mark was showing her his lithographs, the etchings and the wood blocks. He couldn't decide which medium to use. The series was to be his own "Disasters of War." Emmy saw at once that they were done with such intense passion, such fury, that in spite of the dense, modulated blacks, the powerful volumes, they had almost a phantom quality. In the tortured writhing of the forms moved a strange figure, a Parsifal among the shades, subhuman and superhuman, clownish, paranoiac, idiotically pure indeed of all that man has known how to want and to command. Mark's hands shook as he held the sheets.

"This," he said, "I engraved with a burin. I shaded it with a rasp and emery paper. And this," he held up a lithograph, "I brushed first on the stone with lithotint, but the medium won't hold what I mean. There is nothing precise enough."

Later he said suddenly, "Do be careful what you do over there, won't you? They've probably got enough on you to hang you, if you ever get in reach."

[25]

"I will," she said, "I'll be careful."

He had looked at her with gray eyes under black lashes, alert and undefended. Then back to his sheaf. He flung them onto the table.

"There's too much pity in them," he said. "Pity today is an insult. It stinks. It's only a softer form of hate. You and I are always pitying people."

But then the phone rang and it was a friend telling him Marie had said she'd like to have one of his things for a midwinter show of younger, contemporary men. He listened to this and Emmy heard him trying to make his answers a little disinterested. But when he came back to the table his face was full of secret sudden pleasure and hope.

Emmy thought: My God, who'll look after him now?

Anna coughed again. The sound of that cough made her and Sabina as alike as a length of eyelash or a turn of the mouth. The cough was gentle and resigned, an admission of being of no great account.

What if I'm wrong, Emmy thought. I couldn't stop thinking about these people here, people like Anna. Was it any use, was my pity and my thinking any use? Is Anna really important, understanding only things like love of one's family and how pleasant it is to have health and money and how to bake good bread? Perhaps only in millions could Anna ever count for anything. The young doctor would probably say that like a swarm of bees or an army of ants there would have to be millions of Annas. Perhaps Mark would say so too.

Is Sabina important, is Mark — even as an artist — important? Do we all matter more than the sparrow outside? Because we haven't thought of the right thing yet, is it all useless, all this love for the suffering, the maimed, the inconsequent?

I tried to say at the trial why I'd come here, what made me do what I'd done. They didn't know what I was talking about, there was no communication possible. No precise medium, just as Mark said. But the funny thing is, my action had been entirely clear and precise. They understood that, all right. Too much so.

The smoke blew past, the bird flew away. She began to dream of soup cooking in houses, little packed town houses and lonely farms. And of birds flying over bare brown fields that were stripped and ready for spring. And the love of life rose up slowly through her whole body, so strong it almost choked her.

"Oh, God, let me out of here, let me out!" she cried. But she hadn't really made a sound. Anna still dozed and the footsteps coming down the hall were the creaking boots of Hermann bringing cabbage soup and black bread.

Chapter III

WHEN the train crossed the river Mark half expected to make a definite passage into darkness, but it was like crossing any other river. The town they were leaving was thick on the plain, with a cathedral rising from its core and smoking chimneys on the fringes. Underneath the bridge the water was muddy and full but with no beauty of its powerful name about it. It was only a river in a flat country. On the other side the reddish fields, patched with late snow, were like those he had left. The same bare trees grew in an orderly manner, the houses were alike; even the people waiting, as they drew up to the station, might at first glance have been brothers of those on the other side.

It was about six, and the horizon was dense with a tender, lilac haze deepening into sunset. When the train stopped it was exceedingly quiet. A man passing down the corridor spoke the new language. "Those with trunks in the baggage car," he said, "must go into the station for customs examination." A few passengers got off the train.

Mark opened his window and leaned out. The air was chilly but moist and gentle. In a little yard next to the station two blond children stared at the train. He lit a cigarette and waited.

Presently he saw two men in uniform get aboard. They made their way slowly down the train examining passports. He felt for his in his breast pocket, took it out, then put it back again.

There was only one passenger in his compartment, a middle-aged man, fat, with hair *en brosse* and a big gold watch-chain across his stomach. On one fat finger was a ring with a red stone in it. This man had been asleep and snoring most of the afternoon. Now he was awake. He took out a handkerchief and wiped his face, then a little comb and ran it through his stiff hair. He adjusted his ring several times on his finger and yawned.

The men in uniform stood in the doorway. "Please," they said, bowing, "your passports." They were very courteous. They looked at Mark's, stamped it, and gave it back. His passport was perfectly in order. Why shouldn't it be? To the fat man one of them said, "So you are back again. How's business?"

"Good," the man said ponderously, "very good."

They moved on to the next compartment. Some of the passengers whose trunks had been examined were straggling back to the train. Two women in mink coats, who were obviously Americans, walked past and got into a first class carriage.

Another man in uniform came to the door. He wanted to see their money. That went off all right too. Mark showed what he had and got a receipt for it. And then came another man to open the baggage. Mark had only one bag, holding a few clothes, and a big tin box of oil paints and brushes and some canvas in a roll, wood for a stretcher. These caused no difficulty; he had only brought them for the effect, for "face," and so that was over too.

He put his baggage up on the rack again and sat down by the open window. He lit another cigarette. He looked at the photograph of the Place Stanislaus at Nancy over the fat man's head.

Everything seemed to be settled, but the train didn't start. He got up again and leaned out the window. The platform was clear of passengers. A man in uniform was making signals with his arms. The bell began to ring. The train moved slowly. He closed the window, sat down and took out a handkerchief and wiped his forehead. It was just then that the horror came over him; not the horror of putting himself in a trap but the horror of forcing himself to realize at last, by sight and contact, the existence of what, after all, he had never yet materialized and had therefore believed only in one part of himself. The bell seemed to toll as they moved into the open fields.

The man across from him was staring at him with a heavy, curious stare. He could feel it as he looked out the window trying to see the landscape in the last of the rich sunset haze.

"Your first visit here?" the man asked.

Mark started, and was furious with himself for starting. "Yes," he said carefully, "my first visit."

"But you speak the language," the man said.

"I studied it. And my family came from here."

"Ah, so?" The man looked at him unblinkingly.

"Have a cigarette?" Mark said. He held out his case.

"I don't smoke cigarettes," the man said.

Mark thought, the fellow sees there is something queer about me. He put his case back in his pocket, glanced out the window, but saw nothing now.

"You're an artist?" the man said.

Perhaps it's only that, he thought. "Oh, yes, I paint," he said carelessly.

"I saw your paints," the man said, "then I knew you were an artist."

(Damned bright of you.) He turned and tried to smile heartily at the man. "Lovely country," he said, making a motion toward the window.

"Oh, yes," the man said.

The train had gathered speed. It was hurrying on through a violet twilight. He could begin to see his reflection in the window.

"I am a watch salesman," the man told him. "I cover France, Holland, and Belgium."

"Pretty big territory to cover."

"Yes, it's too much really for one man, especially as we do a lot of business. It's tiring. I'm gone three months. It's good to get back."

"You don't like to travel?"

"No, I don't like it."

"But it's interesting, isn't it? Travel broadens the mind." (Is this too phony? he thought.) "You see how other people live and think. I mean perhaps we aren't so different after all."

"Yes, we are different," the man said. "Different races. The pure races are filled with idealism, honesty, and strength."

"Well, that's just fine, isn't it?"

The man nodded. He fingered his watch chain and moved his hands as though he wanted his ring with the red stone to be noticed.

"The French, for instance, are a mixed race," he said. "What follows? It follows that they are hybrid, with a hybrid intellectuality. The French as a race suffer from schizophrenia. Schizophrenia means a split personality."

"Yes, we use that word, too."

"You see it in their politics. They have nearly fifty political parties in France. Here we have only one."

"Yes, yes, that's right." He looked fixedly at the Place Stanislaus over the man's head. He finished his cigarette and dropped it in the lidded metal container.

The man fingered his watch chain and contemplated Mark in silence.

"You are not interested in politics?" he said finally.

"No, not really. I suppose I don't understand them."

"Ah, so," the man said.

For a while Mark looked at the man's reflection in the glass. This meant acting as though he were looking out the window. But it was dark and he could see nothing. In a moment, he was sure, the man would call his attention to that. "Business good?" he asked.

"Very good," the man said. "We make the best watches and we make them very cheap. But the exchange is not in our favor. That's because the French keep debasing their currency. Still, our watches are the best workmanship and the most artistic, so they sell."

"Naturally." After this he closed his eyes and pretended to sleep. But he needn't have bothered with the man for he got off at the next station, and he probably was, after all, only a salesman.

Two women came in together. After one glance at him they sat and talked in low voices about another woman. They thought the other woman was too extravagant. She spent money as though she had it, as though her husband really made it.

"Of course, I'm not like that," one said. It is always the same mysterious woman, Mark thought, about whom two other women talk. These two never got tired of her. They talked of her for an hour.

He pressed his face to the window and watched the dark earth flow under him. It was still possible to see a little because of the patches of snow, and he had the feeling of being sucked into the heart of the country on a sort of machine belt.

The names of the towns, which seemed to him strangely close together, were all familiar to him. It was curious to see these names, names he had heard all his life, embedded like rich nuggets in the family talk, big black letters now on railway stations in the dark.

The snow grew deeper and the fields had become forests. Sometimes in the lights at crossings or at little stations he saw straight narrow roads cutting into great forests of stiff black trees. Around all the lights hung an aureole of cold mist. The compartment was getting chilly.

He glanced every now and then at people in the corridor as they passed. They were mostly men. Many were in uniform, some of them had thick, shaven necks that broke in painful-looking ridges over their stiff collars.

At one station he opened the window to look out and saw directly below him a man in a black uniform looking up at him. The man had a pale face with dry, chapped-looking lips and his eyes were fiery blue and intent. It seemed almost that the man recognized him, had come there on purpose to see him and to ask him something. Mark looked up and down the platform, nervously feeling the fiery blue eyes, and finally he signaled to a man with a little pushcart and bought a package of Murattis from him. When the train pulled out he felt he had had a narrow escape, and when he sat down he had another moment of strangeness and fear and even the language was thick and mysterious about him.

After that, dinner was called and he got up and walked through several cars to the diner. The maître d'hôtel put him at a table with the two American women. He recognized them by their mink coats, which they had put on the backs of their chairs. It was hard to tell which was mother and which daughter, except when they spoke to each other, for they were both painted and plucked and coiffed to perfection. They had the mannequin, puppet charm of the smart American woman. Their voices were high and a little nasal but sweet, like clarinets. They were not at all self-conscious though no one else in the car had anything like their prosperous air, and no one looked at them admiringly. Only once were they abashed. The meal was very meager and of poor quality, a soup thickened with a gluey substance, a meat stew, black bread, sour and rich-tasting cheese. Only the light beer was excellent. They criticized it freely in English. The waiter, an old man with a face like a skull and a macabre dignity, watched them. They took out cigarettes.

"Waiter, what's this little box for?" the girl said in a clear voice. "For ashes?"

"For our poor," said the waiter, his voice like the echo that comes back from a well.

The girl looked at her mother and hastily got out some money and dropped it in the box.

"How too, too awful!" she murmured, smiling, and she looked across at Mark so innocently, as though to say Wouldn't I just put my foot in it?, that he smiled back. It was for the first time in his life a comfort to see this familiar air of the expensive pet, entirely safe, of whom nothing was to be expected. It was like running across the Pekinese one had never cared for but that had been in a house where one felt at least secure.

When he got back to his compartment it was empty. No one came in and the train hurried on, its eerie whistle giving an occasional cry in the night. He could see nothing outside and he was tired. He hadn't slept more than a few hours each night, not for weeks. The beer dimmed his thought a little.

I'll just take a cat nap. He leaned back on his seat.

Suddenly he woke, all taut at once, seeing all the lights of a big town going past. He jerked out his watch. Ten thirty. They were here. He began to lift his bags off the rack, he put on his overcoat and waited. The train drew into a big station.

He got out holding his bags. A porter took them from him and put them on a baggage truck, saying he would meet him at the side door where the taxis were.

The platform was crowded with skiers coming in from the mountains. They were young and weathered and hoarse from shouting in the cold, they smelled of snow and cold and their boots made a heavy tramping sound. He was swallowed up by them, he had to elbow and push his way.

Ahead of him were the mink coats. He saw their trunks and bags, all alike and striped like zebras, being trundled beside them on a truck. They were the sort who don't like to let their luggage out of their sight, and they had managed to get the most efficient-looking of the porters.

Mark walked just behind them through the gate and then, giving in his ticket, he almost bumped into them. They had been met by a tall woman in a sealskin jacket who was speaking to their porter. Her back was turned to him but he could see the coat was shabby and brownish at the seams, and yet with an air of distinction that he recognized. A knot of too heavy, ash-blond hair was pressed untidily between the collar and a sealskin cap.

As he was trying to decide what made this charming the woman turned and he thought at once, Why, I know her! But she looked at him and her face didn't change and then he thought, No, I must be thinking of someone else. . . . But still he felt sure he'd seen her somewhere. He couldn't have seen two people like her. Her face was given strangeness by the eyes, which were unusually long and seemed dark, though they might be green or blue, and turned up at the ends under dark brows that also turned. Her nose was a little concave, with sensitive, wide, flaring nostrils, her lips full and beautiful. The eyes and her long neck showing through the open collar made him think of a swan and he knew he'd thought of that before too. She turned at once with the mink coats and walked away and he stood frowning, trying to remember.

Absent-mindedly he walked to the front door of the station, where no porters and no taxis were. He stood there breathing in the cold, humid air, full of the special odor of the city, and looked into a large, dimly-lighted square with one or two people crossing it hurriedly. And still thinking of that woman the square looked unreal to him, the houses with their nineteenth-century grandeur of public squares, especially those that are before a railroad station, were false and dreamlike. Almost forgetting for a moment what he was here for, he would have liked to walk alone, receptive, uncritical and romantic, through the strange city. But his porter came around the corner of the station and called to him and he walked over to the side entrance where the lights were and got into the last of the taxis.

"Where do we go?" the driver said.

He hadn't thought of a hotel, hadn't asked anyone's advice or looked one up in the travel folder. Suddenly the name of the place that he'd heard someone speak of, — that had pleased him, making him think of garlanded baroque houses, — came to his mind.

"The Four Seasons Hotel," he said.

The Four Seasons Hotel wasn't baroque but, like the square before the station, it had a look of the Nineteenth Century, when to travel meant something. He was received with an air of importance, almost of conspiracy. He turned in his passport and was shown to a room with long red curtains at the windows, an immense bed, a bath glittering with nickel. He locked the door behind him, opened his bag and took out his toothbrush, soap and bathrobe. He was going to have a bath. But first he sat down to smoke a cigarette.

He felt in his inner pocket where his passport had been and took out an envelope addressed to himself in a spidery foreign hand. He didn't take the letter out; he'd already taken it out so many times that the blue paper lining of the cheap envelope was torn and hung out in a long shred. He stared at the envelope in despair, not at the writing but at the postmark, rubbed and nearly obliterated. The postmark was impossible to read. He had puzzled over it under a magnifying glass, shown it to various people who might know. No one could tell him. When he got his visa at the consulate the indifferent clerk had been unwilling or unable to tell him. For hours he had sat trying to conjure up, out of all the names he had ever heard her speak, one that would match this one. It was no use.

In the letter itself there was no clue. Then once more he took it out, a piece of paper such as is used to wrap small objects, a bottle perhaps, written on in pencil in a hand different from that on the envelope: —

Darling — You were right about not trying to sell that place but I was foolish and did so anyway. The money did you get it it's to be deposited in the Park Bank in your name I'm in some trouble here but don't try to do anything about it they'd only make it worse for me Doctor Miller is the one for Sabina don't forget Doctor Miller he's the best perhaps it will turn out all right . . .

And here something scratched out and no more.

He knew it by heart. He knew every stroke of the pencil, written in terrible haste. He had felt sinking into his blood the anxiety and fear that had reduced these words to a childish babble. He felt, even after all these readings, the

[37]

ever-fresh anguish of fright and disorder and worst of all, the haste, as though she had only time to whisper in his ear as she flew past, as though she had indeed gone and there was no catching her ever again.

He put the letter away and dropped his head in his hands. In his bag were other letters, a little bundle of them, of which he had tried to think with some hope. Letters written by a judge, the president of a society for bettering international relations, a well-known painter, the director of a theater; cautious or indignant letters, asking that he be given what help was possible, deploring that a woman whose art had once made a friendly link between two countries should be treated with a severity perhaps exaggerated. And so on, but all futile because the writers of them knew they were.

He got up and walked up and down the room. Then he decided to go down and find a bar, to have a drink and hear people talk.

Yes, there was an "American Bar." It was an afterthought in the hotel, very modern in its appointments and very small. He sat on a high chromium stool and ordered brandy. In a moment some people came in from the cold street outside and crowded around a table behind him. They were in evening clothes and he thought they were English and Americans, and they astonished him by being like the mink coats, just the sort of people who always travel and come to bars after the theater. What were *they* doing in this country?

They had been to hear *"Rosenkavalier."*

One of the women said, "Ursuliac was divine. She's a better Marschallin than Lehmann."

"Nonsense," a man said, "Lehmann has tenderness. Ursuliac is a marionette."

"But you don't understand, darling," the woman said.

"It's a terribly perverse thing really. All those women making love. That's what's simply heaven. That's what gives it such an unearthly tensity and languor. And then there's a definite tang of madness about it. They recognize that so well here. Of course they're like marionettes. They should be. Lehmann is wholesome as a cabbage."

Mark saw a man behind him in the glass, a man who wasn't either English or American. He was an officer in uniform, with the stiff color of his tunic holding up a strikingly handsome head, a head that made one think at once of Roman emperors. He wasn't young, his hair brushed flat back from his forehead was thin, his sculptured face, with straight nose and fine cheekbones, was a little sagging below the full lips. His pale blue eyes had a heavy, dreamy, fixed look as though he had lived through extraordinary disciplines, or had just taken a drug.

He said to the woman, "And shouldn't one be wholesome?" As he spoke he put a monocle in his eye and turned to look at her.

"Oh, Kurt, you're too divine!" she told him. "You ought to write for the health magazines. Really you ought."

She had a little, dark, agate face and her gestures were those of a sick child, huddled, trivial, and melancholy. She was drinking a glass of milk.

"You talk like Bernarr MacFadden," she said.

"Who is that?" he asked.

"You know, Kurt, you ought to be wearing a clerical collar. I can see you being terrible to the congregation, and then making ghastly, little, naughty jokes to show you're human. What a beastly lover you must make, Kurt. Simply beastly. I've often thought so."

Mark paid for his brandy and got up to go. As he left the bar he heard her say, "Now Kurt's mad. He's leaving. Why do you suppose Kurt's mad?"

At the door he bumped into the officer and each drew aside. The officer looked at him with a blind, sleepwalker's eye. "After you," he said. Mark walked out ahead of him.

The people in there had turned his stomach, and he hated this man whose heavy, contemptuous feet he heard behind him. He's a dope, he said to himself. Positively no opium smoking allowed in the elevators.

Then suddenly one of those lifts came to him, an instinct for hope and for action. A certainty of knowing just what to do.

He stopped at the desk and took out his letter and handed it to the night concierge. "See if you can read where that came from," he said.

The concierge took the letter and held it under a little bulb. He pursed his lips so that his walrus mustaches brushed his nose. "I think it's a town very near here," he said.

"Near here? How near?"

"About two hours by train. In the mountains. It has very good skiing."

"Will you write it down for me?"

"Certainly, sir." The concierge took pencil and paper and wrote it down.

"I want to go there," Mark said. "Will you get me a ticket?"

"Tomorrow?"

"No, not tomorrow. What day is today, Wednesday?"

"Wednesday, sir."

"Then get me a ticket for Friday. I have things to attend to here first."

"Yes, you ought to see the city first, sir."

"That's what I thought. Better make it Friday."

"Very good, sir."

He went giddily upstairs to his room. It was, after all,

as easy as that. Because he had seen the name written at last, and with such assurance everything looked different. Now perhaps he knew exactly where she was, or at least where Fritz was, since the envelope was in Fritz's writing and he must have mailed it for her.

And to get hold of Fritz was all important. It was years since they had seen Fritz. Every Christmas he sent them a postcard and Emmy sent him a present. He moved from town to town at different jobs, each one a little humbler than the one before. It was Emmy who kept track of him and only she knew where he was now. Mark had looked through her desk but found no trace of Fritz's address.

But now it was all going to be settled after all. Difficult perhaps, but when you begin to see the first step . . .

In the long glass between the windows he saw another man, vigorous and efficient. Now I'll do this, he said, and maybe that will happen, and at the very worst . . . Why, I can handle this.

He stepped back and knocked his paint box over. He was too tired to pick it up. He pushed it under the table with his foot. He fell out of his clothes, had a hot bath, got into bed and was asleep as soon as he touched the pillow.

Chapter IV

IN NEW YORK, when he sat in that first blind fear, he had kept saying to himself: Nothing is really hopeless so long as I keep my head. I must cut out all the emotion, go about it as though it were someone else's affair, and as though I'd never heard about those people or anything that happened there.

Hardly knowing what he did, he had taken his sheaf of lithographs and torn them up and thrown them in the wastebasket. . . . He would have to become a new man, unburdened, stronger and more innocent.

The first thing to do, he said, is to keep the worst of it from Sabina. If I talk it over with her we'll both go to pieces. And I can't worry about her knowing it and waiting here. I have to be able to think of Sabina as all right, which means I have to be able not to think of her at all.

The next thing is to get letters from people. I can't get many because it would take too long. And probably they'd be no use anyway. Then of course I must find out the name of a good lawyer, one who would handle a case like this and not be afraid. That's what anyone would insist on first. People always have lawyers.

He spent a day questioning those people with whom Emmy had been working to distribute information and to help refugees. They told him of a lawyer named Henning. He lived in the city where she had sold her home. He was very clever and he had defended So-and-so, and So-and-so. There was no question but that he was the man.

Then on the street he ran into a man he knew rather well. He had been in the embassy in Washington and was a collector of modern painting. He had resigned from the diplomatic service to marry a rich American widow and live in New York. He was greatly interested in Mark's work and had bought two of his pictures. Mark told him where he was going.

"When?" the man asked.

"Day after tomorrow."

"Have a drink with me," the man said.

They stepped into a bar and the man asked him a few questions about his trip, where he would go and whom he would see.

"Poor, dear old town!" he said. "You'll just miss the carnival, won't you? How I'd like to see it all again!"

Mark said nothing, and suddenly the man leaned forward. "In any trouble?" he asked.

"Yes, a little," Mark admitted.

The man didn't ask him any more but as they got up to leave he said: "Wait a minute. I'm going to give you a card to a friend of mine. It may not do you the least bit of good, but you never know."

He took out a large visiting card. "This fellow has a very nasty job," he said apologetically as he wrote a note on it, "but he's powerful, and perhaps that's what you want. I don't know of course. Anyway, he's rather nasty himself, but also a bit of an exquisite. Loves pictures and collects bibelots and goes to the theater a lot. Wrote a play once, in verse. In those days the police wouldn't let it be given. Nasty and exquisite, but rather charming, and right on the top of the heap now."

He handed Mark the card and suddenly his face changed.

He looked uneasy and as though he'd like to take the card back again. But Mark thanked him and put it quickly in his pocket.

"I'm very grateful to you," he said.

"Well, don't use it unless you have to," the other man said. "I mean, it's a far chance. So long and good luck."

When he got home Mark saw the card was addressed to the Commissioner of Secret Police and began in a friendly way, "Dear Rudi . . ."

The morning after he arrived at the Four Seasons he got up early, had his coffee, and looked up Henning in the hotel telephone directory. When he called the house a maid said, "Mr. Henning has been very ill. He has just come back from the hospital yesterday. He sees no one."

"Tell him it's a client from America," he said. "Very urgent."

"Mr. Henning is taking no clients," she said brusquely. "He can see no one," and she hung up.

He sat down and wrote Henning a letter. In it he put a note from a man in New York and sent it by a messenger. Then he went into the bar to wait. He took the telephone book with him and ruffled it through and through, looking at the names, hoping for one that would strike him as familiar, some old friend, some unexpected ally. He said to himself that it was only a matter of doing the right thing, carefully, step by step. Now that he had begun to act he was already more alert, he was sharpening his instinct, uncoiling every fine filament of perception, so as to be ready to seize, when perhaps it came along, some hidden, minute change, some diversion, some tiny tentacle, that would lead him from failure to success.

All he recognized in the telephone book was the consulate of the United States of America, but he distrusted the consulate. If the lawyer, if the influential friend, the letters, the protests, failed, then he'd have to cut himself loose and burrow into obscurity, and the less they knew of him the better.

The answer came saying Mr. Henning would see him at once. He'd half expected a refusal; but the law after all was best, provided it could be made to help him. In his heart he was doubtful of it. It seemed to him to share the perverse and obstinate quality of medicine: when you really need it, it offers only dogma, like an outworn religion. He felt an irritated fear of its mysteries. Even as he snatched his hat and went for a taxi he said to himself that he mustn't hope for too much from Henning, but that after all there are still powerful forces and more living mysteries to fall back on.

Henning lived in an apartment house off Leopold Street, a new building with flower-boxes giving an expensive look to the windows. The elevator was a handsome, bronze, rococo cage. As soon as he stepped into the apartment he knew Henning was a prosperous man who loved his possessions and his family. The drawing room was modern and excellently furnished, pale voile hung at the windows, glass of pure design held sprays of flowering plum, a bronze portrait head he guessed to be by the sculptor Kolbe stood on a low lacquer table. It was also, he saw as he crossed it, a woman's room; the pale colors, the many taffeta cushions, the care of the flower arrangements, the photographs of children on the table, told him that; and the little maid, blond and weazened, prematurely old, in an immaculate uniform, was somehow unmistakably a woman's maid.

She took him into a study lined with books where Henning sat in a chair by the window, a fur coat over his knees. His first impression was that Henning was indeed a very sick man. His sickness, which Mark had taken for an excuse, was so obvious and had such a hold on him, that it was the most important thing about him. His face was waxy, between a stiff brush of grayish hair and a grayish pointed beard. His eyes showed his sickness most. They were small and clever but they had a surprised and exhausted look, as though all his attention were being forced now into the twirling of one fine, fragile thread.

"I must apologize," said Mark, "for insisting on this interview; but I'll try not to take up too much of your time."

"Sit down," said Henning. His voice was weak and he breathed with some trouble. He pointed to a chair and Mark sat down.

"My note," he said, "explained who sent me."

Henning nodded.

"And of course I'm in trouble or I shouldn't have been so urgent."

"I'm used to people in trouble," Henning said. His purplish lips parted, either in a smile or a little gasp for breath.

"Shall I go right to the point?" Mark asked.

Henning nodded.

"I came because of my mother, Madame Emmy Ritter."

"I knew her slightly," said Henning, "many years ago."

"You perhaps know then that she's been living in America for a long time. My father died in America. She came back some months ago to see about a house she had here and she made a bad mistake. She sold it and had the money from the sale deposited in America."

Henning's breathing, he saw, was difficult. The gray tufts of hair on his chin and neck went up and down with little palpitating motions like feathers on a trembling bird.

"Oh," said Henning. "And she has been arrested?"

"I'm afraid so."

"Is your mother an American citizen?"

"No, sir. I am, and my sister also. My mother did, however, take out first citizenship papers before she left America. She had a re-entry card but she was afraid she might lose it. She has a habit of losing things. And the first citizenship papers would help her to get back in any case. Besides, she has wanted for a long time to change her citizenship. She's put it off in the way one does."

"But she is still a citizen of this country and so subject to its laws."

"Yes."

"She realized, I suppose, the danger of violating the exchange laws?"

"I suppose so. It's hard to be sure how much a woman realizes that kind of danger."

"Yes." Henning didn't smile over the light-heartedness of women. "But you're not sure she's been arrested?"

"I suppose I am sure. I had a queer, broken sort of note from her. A month ago. I've heard nothing at all since."

"How did you know about the sale?"

"I knew she came abroad to sell the house. She went first to Belgium because of an advertisement in one of our papers, put there it seems by a broker in Brussels who made a business of exchanging property. She wrote to him first but the answers were slow in coming and not satisfactory. She finally went herself. She wrote me from Brussels that when she got there the office was closed but that they told her it had been moved here. They told her it was now quite safe to come here and negotiate it. As soon as I got the letter I cabled her not to, but unfortunately she'd already left. A little later I had a letter written from here saying she had seen the broker and distrusted him at sight. But she also told me that she'd met a friend of ours from New York who would buy the house. I couldn't cable then because she's so terribly careless she didn't give me her address. She evidently went into a hotel to write her letter and used their paper. She was boarding she said, with the niece of an old servant of ours. I haven't even the servant's address. Then, as I said, came this brief, troubled note, and no more."

"But she did tell you that the sale was made?"

"Yes."

"And that the money was to be deposited in America?"

"Yes. And later I received a short note from our friend and a notification from the bank that the money was deposited."

Henning said, "So I'm to understand that your mother sold her house here (the famous Ritter house no doubt), and had the money deposited in America. I don't think either she or your friend would have dared negotiate such a thing openly. She must have taken a small, token sum for it here. In fact, it couldn't be done any other way. That in itself, if it were discovered, would be enough to warrant her arrest and even a trial for treason, but from the circumstances of the arrest, I mean the apparent secrecy, I think there must be more to it than you are telling me. Was there to your knowledge any other reason why Madame Ritter might have been arrested?"

Mark took a deep breath.

"I don't know what to say. There — there might have been, but her note — the last one — only spoke of the house. I feel sure that's the only thing involved."

"And you have heard nothing from Madame Ritter since that note? Do you know where the note came from?"

"I am very much afraid it came from prison. There is also a possibility — no, I don't know what to think. It was scrawled hastily on a scrap of paper. But the envelope was

[48]

in the handwriting of our old servant. So at first I thought she might have been hiding. But if that were true I would certainly have heard from her again, or even from the servant. But apparently he was badly frightened. No, she must be in prison."

"I think it's extremely likely," said Henning drily. "Tell me, have you made any efforts in America to help Madame Ritter?"

"No. As I told you, she isn't an American citizen."

"And here? What have you tried to do?"

"I've just come. I don't know where to begin. I haven't the servant's address. He's an obscure old man who moves around from job to job as he can get it. All Mother's friends are dead or scattered. She left here twenty-four years ago. I know that except for the man who bought the house, whom she ran into almost by accident and who is now back in New York, she saw no one she knew. But I'm sure that if she was arrested she was given some sort of trial. And she must be in some prison. A lawyer, I thought, is the man to get her out."

Henning looked at him curiously. His questions had been brisk, and Mark could see that, left intact, he was an energetic man who looked at trouble with the bright, precise eye of pleasure. How I am going to clean this up! he would say. But now he was already tired and his breath was coming heavily. Hidden things, that Mark couldn't guess, were dimming his clarity. His spontaneous impetus was lacking. It was almost sad to see the natural talent of the man surrendering to caution.

In a lower voice Henning said: "Of course, I see you don't choose to tell me the whole of what's involved in this story of Madame Ritter. That alone makes it impossible for me to help you. But I have heard a few rumors of it myself, and these, with what you have told me, are enough to show that Madame Ritter was tried, probably before the People's Court, for treason."

His emphasis on the last word made Mark repeat vaguely, "Treason . . ."

"I see," said Henning, "the word doesn't mean much to you."

"Perhaps not. It should, I know." Mark repeated it to himself. Treason . . . In the bookish atmosphere of Henning's room it had something oratorical and false. "I don't believe I have ever used it," he said, "except in a history class."

"That's unfortunate," Henning said. "It's very real here. It can carry the death penalty."

"*What?*" Of course he'd thought of that. But *that* he truly could not believe. A woman is not executed. Not a woman who had laughed with him over private jokes, not a woman who was so full of life that she couldn't fry bacon or take a shower without singing at the top of her lungs, who had a heavy knot of still-black hair, each hair of which he knew, whose hands he knew and the shape of the nails and all the gestures. Something so known, so intricate, so loved, is not destroyed because a house somewhere, that he had never seen, changes hands and money finds its way to a New York bank.

"I can't believe that," he said.

Henning saw he couldn't. "The sentence isn't necessarily death," he said; "and if it is, it isn't necessarily carried out. There may be extenuating circumstances. I don't know. On the other hand, there might be circumstances that would make it worse for her." He looked again questioningly at Mark.

"I think not," Mark said; "nothing they would be likely to know."

"Don't be too sure of that. And don't be too sure, because you come here feeling in your heart very superior to all this, that the authorities here also take a negligent and lofty view."

"Oh, I know that. Don't think, please, I've come here to waste time on questions of superiority. I want to recognize all the facts. Indeed, I want to know exactly what the facts are, so they can be dealt with. And then I want to do whatever can be done. I came here to ask you, as a lawyer, what you can do for me."

It was asthma, among other things, that Henning suffered from. He reached for a little Chinese box and took from it a blackish cigarette. Mark lighted it for him and Henning inhaled it, blowing out a cloud of acrid yellow smoke.

"I'm a sick man," he said, and his clever eyes suddenly looked so helpless that Mark, sitting down again, turned his away. Through the window he watched, for a moment, pigeons walking on a gray roof. He was beginning to get a cramp in his stomach. He took out a cigarette himself. "Do you mind?" he said. Henning shook his head. He lighted it, noticing that his hand shook. As he smoked he leaned his head back, ran his hand across his smooth hair, waiting for Henning to get breath, bracing himself for what he'd have to hear. Yes, or no, good or bad — which will it be?

Henning picked up his card. "MR. MARK PREYSING . . ." he read. "I see you don't use your mother's name." He put the card down. "I'm very sorry, Mr. Preysing, but there's nothing I can do for you."

Mark put down his cigarette. "But Mr. Henning — " he began.

"There's nothing to say," said Henning sharply, "except this: the best thing for you to do is to go back to America."

"You can't expect me to do that!" Mark cried. "The

[51]

more serious it is, the more I must do something about it."

Henning held the yellow smoke in this throat and blew it out slowly through his nostrils. He looked at Mark with a flicker of compassion, the hasty, unwilling pity of a man who has looked on too many accidents and only wants to hurry past.

"Yes, I suppose so," he said. "But in the end you'll have to give it up. As you tell it to me it amounts to this: Madame Ritter, a citizen of this country, has committed the crime of treason against the State."

"But a good lawyer — " Mark began.

Henning said sharply: "Mr. Preysing, this is not the United States."

"But the case of Samson . . ." Mark persisted. "He violated the exchange laws on a larger scale, and I understood you got him off with a heavy fine."

"And how long do you think I can afford to handle such cases?" said Henning. The air, suddenly clear of smoke around him, showed his accusing face. "How long do you suppose I'd be allowed to go on living here if I continued to handle such cases? Samson was a close friend of mine. As it is, that case cost me a great deal, more than you can know. It cost me my health, among other things. I have a family, Mr. Preysing. You don't imagine I would sacrifice them, do you?"

"Perhaps you could tell me of another lawyer."

"That case, Mr. Preysing, is closed."

"You mean it couldn't be appealed?"

"It's not a civil case. There is no court of appeal for a political offense."

"Are you actually telling me there is nothing I can do in a legal way?"

"Nothing whatsoever."

"But you spoke as though you might be able to do something if you were willing to take the risk."

"No, I only meant that I am surprised you would come here expecting me to take such a risk. There appears to be, Mr. Preysing, a strong strain of irresponsibility in your family."

Mark set his teeth and got up. "I'm sorry to have troubled you," he said. "I heard you were an exceptionally courageous man."

Henning looked at him with his clever eyes full of anger; then, as though in spite of himself, a clearer light came back into them. "Sit down a minute," he said.

Mark sat down. Henning took another cigarette but Mark let him light this for himself.

"Mr. Preysing," he said, "I do understand how you feel. Yes, I think exactly. Your feeling now, as I said, is partly one of exasperation at having to put up, even for a time, with the incomprehensible restrictions of a backward country. But you're also frightened, since it is your mother who is involved, so you're sure that with a certain amount of intelligence used, yours or someone else's, a little pressure here or there, a little influence in the right places, even a little money perhaps, the difficulty can be overcome. Isn't that so?"

"I suppose it is."

"Well, let me tell you then that I am fully able to sympathize with you. It is, if I may say so, almost the typical view of the layman toward the law. You, on the other hand, probably don't in the least understand us here. You don't even understand my position."

He looked around his study at the books as though they held suddenly his whole life enclosed in the four walls.

"It wouldn't make any difference if you did," he said. "As for me, I'm a sick man, as I think you can see. I've had a complete breakdown, heart and other things. But still, I'll do all I can for you. Which is so little," he said gravely, "that it won't even put a strain on my courage. I'll tell you those facts you came for. Madame Ritter, if what you say is exact, is in a dangerous position, and there are only two things you can do for her now: you can make an appeal for clemency, and you can get together every possible atom of influence that's available to you. I don't think there is the slightest hope of any change in Madame Ritter's condition resulting from these, but I've lived long enough to know that just as the perfect case is sometimes not so perfect so the hopeless case is sometimes not hopeless."

"An appeal for clemency? You mean I must make one out in a certain form?"

"That I will do for you," said Henning.

"But influence," Mark began — and thought: How many things I know nothing about! Influence, for instance. What of it, and how does anyone get it? Is it a matter of un-heard-of energies, or is it like beauty and talent, just a gift of the gods? "I suppose you mean letters," he said. "I have some letters and a card to an official, an important fellow I think."

He turned them out of his pocket and handed them to Henning.

Henning took his pince-nez carefully from the pocket of his dressing gown and fitted them on his nose. Mark could see by his face that he was not impressed by the letters. He looked them over slowly, however. Then he held the card up.

"Do you know this man?"

"A friend of his gave me the card to him."

"You know who he is?"

"He has something to do with the Secret Police."

"Exactly. He's the local commissioner."

"Does that mean he has a lot of influence?"

Suddenly Mark had in his mind a picture of an Irish police lieutenant, sitting bored behind a high desk.

Henning gathered the letters together and handed them back.

"See him if you can," he said. "That's your only chance." And he looked at Mark with a scrutinizing look, sharp as a needle. Then his eyes, as Mark looked into them, grew dim with fatigue and perhaps like a mirror gave back a certain disgust.

"I'll make out your petition," he said, "but don't expect much from that."

"There's one more thing," said Mark, getting up. "I'd like to be able to communicate with my mother. I don't even know where she is. Do you think they'd let me do that?"

"I don't know. Ask him." He pointed to the card.

Mark said, "I must find out what the sentence is. There might have been a few other things brought up, as you suggested. Perhaps not serious, but on the other hand they might count for a lot here. The sentence might be — it might be — anything. I must find out about that first."

Henning's head had relaxed on the back of his chair, his bearded throat was palpitating in its helpless, birdlike way.

"These trials in almost all cases are secret. I don't know anything really about Madame Ritter's case nor her sentence."

He looked for the first time stupid and Mark thought: It's because he's lying. He's keeping something back from me. But then, I have to keep a great deal back from him too.

Henning reached for a bell and the little weazened blond maid appeared in her starched dress.

"Good-by, Mr. Preysing," Henning said, "I'll let you

know what comes of the petition. You might let me know of any developments."

"Thank you," said Mark.

He crossed the pale, feminine drawing room as fast as he could. He had a fear of meeting Henning's wife. The perfume of the plum blossom accused him, and the photographs of the children on the table. When he reached the front door the little maid looked at him with dislike, and banged it after him.

But as he stood in the street he thought, there's a man who would *like* to help me. He's decent and he's clever. He'd like to use his cleverness and his decency too. But he doesn't dare. What then can I expect from the rest of them? Certainly nothing from the Commissioner. And perhaps not even from Fritz, when I find him.

Chapter V

AT THE outer door stood a guard, a giant well over six feet tall. His long black overcoat hung at an awkward length below his knees, he stood with one foot a little before the other, his rifle butt grounded, the barrel clasped in his outstretched hands. The blue eyes in the handsome, empty, young face were fixed on a spot on the floor. He looked as though he had been frozen in the moment of advancing, or as though a ball had just struck him and he had swayed forward but not yet fallen.

In the room where Mark sat were a clerk, sitting behind a desk, and a man waiting. The man didn't look at him and he didn't look at the man; they seemed to feel an equal despondency and shame at being there. Mark sat with his chair tilted back, leaning his head against the wall.

He had to wait a long time. He would have liked to smoke but saw a sign saying that smoking was forbidden. He wished he had brought a book or a newspaper to read. He hadn't yet learned how to put in an hour of such waiting. He wanted to set his mind loose and to suspend it in emptiness so as to gather strength and freshness for what was coming. But he could think of nothing but what he would say to the Commissioner and what the Commissioner might say to him.

To choose something equal in urgency he began to think about Sabina. On his last day in New York she had managed to get a few hours off. From the third-class rail he had looked down at her face, unpainted and rather plain, emptied of feeling so as to ease his going. Her coat was cheap and too thin for the whistling wind. She held it close around her neck. As the ship pulled into the stream he saw her hold a handkerchief to her mouth but presently she waved it with the rest until she became a blur in the crowd, not leaving, he knew, till the ship had turned in the stream.

He followed her back to the street, to a bus, to the shop again, and finally to their flat. As she opened the door, he knew she felt his absence like cold. He heard the gas sputter under the saucepan of milk and smelled the sudden richness of chocolate. He heard the voice of the old woman, the wife of the doctor. Together they sat by a table in the light of a reading lamp, and the long evening passed over them both. The little boy got out his violin and played in the next room. On the wall behind Sabina a portrait he had done of her three years ago bloomed in the shadow. As he watched, it grew more vivid while below she faded as though it drew life from her. The droop of her lonely wrist on the chair-arm became more than he could bear.

It was a long journey back to the room where he now waited, and he found that one bitterness had refreshed him for the other. The waiting man had disappeared. He came back presently through an inner door. Mark glanced at him as he passed. He was a man with a beard and a fussy walk. He bustled across the room rubbing his fingers together and stopped to speak with an important air to the clerk sitting behind the desk. It was obvious he had succeeded in what he'd come for and was surprised at his success. Mark sat up straighter, bringing his chair down with a sharp click to the floor.

"Mr. Preysing," someone said. He got up and was shown to the inner room.

The first thing he saw was the huge photograph on the

[58]

wall and the draped flag. The face on the wall, the flag, the desk, were so huge that the man caught between them looked small and harmless.

"Sit down."

The voice fell on Mark's nerves as smooth as milk. He sat down and looked at the Commissioner, trying to see everything about him at once. The Commissioner looked at him. Mark saw he was a youngish man, perhaps no more than ten years older than himself, and he, seeing Mark's surprise, smiled, a deprecatory smile. Their common youth made a slight leveling between them. He had a pleasing face, fair-skinned but not unhealthy, with auburn hair and eyes, his mouth so sensitive his full lips twitched sometimes at the corners. He was inclined to fat, but his belt was cinched in very tight and smart over a small, protruding stomach.

"Mr. Preysing," he said, "you come from a very old friend of mine. I'm glad to see you. How is Carl?"

"Very well," said Mark. "He's married. Probably you know that?"

"Successfully I hope?"

"I think very much so."

"An American?"

"Yes, an American."

"Oh, these American women!" the Commissioner said playfully. "She's made him desert us."

"I don't know his wife well," Mark said. He answered mechanically. These were not the questions and answers he had imagined. With Henning there had been a sharp atmosphere of haste. Everything was clear-cut and summary. Here there was a suggestion of amenities, of dawdling away a slack time. He almost expected to be offered a cup of tea. Because it wasn't what he'd anticipated, it didn't seem quite real.

[59]

"Carl always was a lover of the arts," the Commissioner said. "He still is, I suppose?"

"Yes, he's become quite a collector. That's why I know him."

"You're a painter, I believe?"

"Yes, sir."

The Commissioner leaned back in his chair. "You should manage to do some painting here," he said. "The country in the spring is lovely and to my thinking it's never been done, unless you want to admit that Breughel passed here on his way from Italy."

On the desk before him was a neat pile of papers. They were typewritten and along the edge were symmetrical holes as though they had been taken from a file. They looked neat and unused. There was also a little porcelain vase full of purple and yellow crocus. "The first spring flowers," he said, touching them with a plump, white finger.

Mark thought, What was I afraid of? He guessed at a gentleness or a softness, something that seemed vulnerable, and also the recognized and easily pampered vanity of the amateur. Mightn't this man be already delivered into his hands? His imagination leaped to a picture suddenly complete and a complement to the one he had last made: His mother leaning over the rail of a ship, shouting above a din of whistles to Sabina's upturned face. Then, with nothing changed, he felt a recoil: Don't go too fast.

"A family of artists," the Commissioner was saying. "Richard Ritter had a great name here."

"Yes, I think at one time he was well-known. And my mother also." He watched this word as it passed between them. There was no change in the Commissioner's face.

"Ah, Madame Ritter," he said. "Yes, she was one of the promising young actresses of her day. I never saw her

[60]

myself. She was before my time. But I'm passionately fond of the theater."

"I don't go very often," Mark said. He remembered the play the Commissioner had written. The one the police had closed.

"Probably you're absorbed in your own work," the Commissioner said. "But as an artist you should. You see unforgettable beauty in the theater. I always say there's no plastic beauty like that of the human body used to express a truly great emotion. Its charm over sculpture is that it dissolves at once and re-forms again, always follows the exact line of life."

His face became embarrassingly sensitive. It seemed to Mark that he might have become fat as a sort of protection.

"Oh, yes," Mark agreed rather vaguely, "the theater — " A doubt crossed his mind as to whether the Commissioner knew what he was here for. But there were the papers on the desk. A dossier of some sort, by their looks. Before the Commissioner spoke he was uneasy again. It was too unexpected to be true and it was also too good to be true. Henning's face rose in his mind, bitter with sickness and fear. But was Henning perhaps just a hysterical fool? Was he a little touched by his sickness?

The face of the Commissioner was the face of a man looking at a play. In its sensitiveness nothing seemed to be working from within, no indictment, no anger, his face showed only receptive eagerness. He said, "I understand Madame Ritter was a success in America."

"She was at first," Mark said. "She brought her European reputation with her. But the theater there has gone through a lot of phases, as it has here, too, I suppose. Her style of acting was the grand style. Even in comedy she always gave a rather artificial and stylized performance.

That doesn't go over now in America. I suppose the movies there are responsible, but anyway a sort of deadly naturalness takes the place of acting."

"Still, she preferred to live in America even when she wasn't successful there?"

He spoke gently, but Mark knew at once from his tone that he knew all about Madame Ritter. He was glad they were getting down to it. The sooner the better.

"Yes, she preferred to live there," he said; "or perhaps it gradually became a habit with her."

"I see. And her children — she has, I believe, one besides yourself?"

"My sister and myself."

"You are both American subjects?"

"Yes, sir."

"When did you become an American subject?"

"I was born in America."

"You are now what age?"

"Twenty-three."

"And you have never visited your parent's country before?"

"No, sir."

"Still, you speak the language remarkably well."

"We always used it in the family."

He didn't say what the language was to him: its extravagant, endearing diminutives, its rough music, had always been the medium of their close-knit life. It was so dear to him that he had never been able, when thinking in that language, to believe what he must believe. The words, by their association, wove a constant refutation; they were the words of his private happiness.

"She never let us forget it," he said.

"Then you come here for the first time now?"

"Yes."

"But you have friends here surely, someone you are staying with? You must have letters to someone."

"Only to you," said Mark. He thought of Henning and of old Fritz, wherever he might be. You don't imagine, he said silently, that I'd be such a fool as to name anyone.

"I have other letters," he said, "from people at home." He felt in his pockets and got out his packet. "You might be good enough to look at them. I haven't known really just who to show them to."

The Commissioner reached for the packet, spread them on the desk and picked up one to look at. He looked through it quickly and chose another. This he only glanced at, and each one as he opened it got no more than a glance. He didn't seem impatient or hurried, but the letters didn't interest him.

Mark pushed his chair back from the desk, crossed his leg and watched the swinging of his own foot. Presently the slight rustle of the paper stopped and, looking up, he saw the warm, auburn eyes of the Commissioner fixed on him. He braced himself against their dreamy look, expecting some question that would be embarrassing and intimate and would have nothing to do with Madame Ritter. But the eyes suddenly evaded him and that question wasn't asked.

The Commissioner bent over his file and lifted a page or two and peered under with a kind of coyness. "I understand," he said, "that you are a member of the Communist Party."

Mark answered, trying to keep at ease: "I was at one time. At present I am a member of no party."

"Ah, so? Why did you withdraw?"

"I don't see why — " Then he caught himself sharply, said in a honeyed, confidential voice, "I found I couldn't give it much time any more, and also I have to confess I couldn't even pay the dues. But also — I think a man can be excused for being in a perpetual unsettlement of mind these days. The party was taking a new trend. I wanted to think it over more fully."

Forget everything, he told himself, but that glow of friendliness, nourish it as though it were the last warmth on earth.

"My interest in politics," he said, smiling, "has a bad habit of waxing and waning."

A faint smile answered him.

"Still, your sympathies are probably not entirely alienated from the party. Even without a political mind one has one's sympathies."

Mark thought, Now is my chance. He heard the words not spoken yet: *I believe after all I'm becoming a convert to your way of thinking. The sight of this country, prosperous, happy, everyone at work, all of one mind and enthusiasm, has begun to have its effect on me. I'm even considering going back to tell people at home something of what I've seen here.*

Why couldn't he? It didn't really matter to him and it wouldn't be too crass. It was impossible to exaggerate the naïveté of these "political minds." Their thirst for converts was so strong they'd swallow anything, even the worst, the most obvious self-interest.

He said, "In the United States, you've got to realize that the Communist Party occupies no different status, legally and constitutionally, from the Democratic, the Republican, the Farm Labor, or any other party. I may add, it's becoming there more and more what you would call 'respectable,' and that in spite of investigating committees and newspaper agitation."

He smiled again, but there was no answer to that. The Commissioner's face was graver.

[64]

"You see," Mark went on, "the party has had to shift its policy a number of times. It has gone through some shattering disillusionments."

"I should think it might. I should think that the grim spectacle of Russia, of Jewish internationalism —"

"It isn't that so much." And his tongue said in spite of him, "It's that many Communists realize now what a sudden collapse of bourgeois democracy may lead to."

"You mean it may lead to Totalitarianism?"

Mark said, "Well, yes."

"So in America the Communist Party doesn't at present advocate world revolution?"

"I'm not competent to speak for the Communist Party in America. I think, though, that they're content to postpone world revolution indefinitely."

"Then I'm to understand that when the party became what you call 'respectable,' you weren't able to see eye to eye with it any more?"

"Americans, generally speaking, don't concern themselves with political theory," Mark said. "Like most countries, I think we have too much government; but so far the yoke lies on us lightly. Between elections we think of other things. Most of us would like to be liberals, but it is beginning to dawn on us that the liberal has no adequate machinery."

Now he could not read the face at all. It was still bland, it was not unfriendly, but it was blank. The big, sparse room, the photograph, the flag, the desk with papers, and the prying insistence, the slow uncovering of damaging facts, these began to remind him of something. It was of the Headmaster calling him into the office. Mr. Roberts also used to be very pleasant, he joked a little and spoke first of the football scores and a question on the Punic Wars, and presently Mark would be in a sweat of repressed fury and fear. He began to feel very young and helpless.

The Commissioner consulted his papers. "Did you, at one time, do a series of cartoons for a news organ called, I believe, the *Daily Worker?*"

Mark answered slowly: "Why, no. The only time I ever did anything that might be called cartoons was a series of six drawings. They were given to the World Peace Organization. They appeared in their monthly magazine."

"Their subject was the bombing of civilians in wartime, many mutilated women and children and so on?"

"Yes. They weren't very good. I'd like to have done better by them. But I was still imitating other people — Rouault — Picasso — "

"You believe in revolution, Mr. Preysing, but you don't believe in a war in which your theories are getting the worst of it." He handled the papers as though they'd taken on a moral quality. "You have a dangerous lack of logic."

Mark said carefully: "Any talk of this kind between us seems to me a little unfair. You have all the cards and you can make me appear to say anything. Besides, I believe it's my mother who is the one in question. She is not and never has been a member of any party. She has the mind of a woman, I mean an almost conventional woman. Her world has simply been the theater and her family. As an artist she naturally makes no boundaries and sees people as a general humanity, not as separate races. There is no hate in her. She can't even hate those who cheat and abuse her. If you knew her you would recognize this. She's done no harm in her whole life, and she has done more good than most of us. Her art, which you appreciate so much, has given exquisite pleasure. Surely some consideration should be shown her now."

He knew he spoke vaguely, without real direction in the

almost set form of petitions, but what else could he say? He had told Henning that he believed his mother was arrested for selling a house and having the money paid to her outside the country. But he knew well that she might have been arrested for something much more serious. The Commissioner was purposely keeping him from the point. He did this perhaps from mere social embarrassment at dealing with a man sent him by a friend, or vanity that wanted to suggest gentle breeding, perhaps even as protection for a sensitiveness that was genuine, a little thin vein of sensitiveness that ran vertically to some curious, hidden source. In dealing with him Mark knew he would have to blot out whole sections from consideration, but if there was anything about him to take hold on it was somewhere in this sensibility. The man didn't seem to want him to lay hold on it. And yet, perhaps — he did seem to be expecting something.

The Commissioner had been referring again to his file. "I have here," he said, "the full report on Madame Ritter, and here are the main facts of her case. For some time she carried on a correspondence with a man who was one of the most persistent enemies of our State. This man was a so-called intellectual, a physicist. At one time he lectured as an exchange professor in American Universities. He should have stayed there. When he came back he became the head of a society of criminals. They secretly printed pamphlets which were distributed here and abroad. Those distributed here purported to tell us 'the true condition of affairs' in the outside world, the others told the 'true conditions of affairs' in this country and were sent abroad. The pamphlets were supposedly tourist literature, scientific tracts, and so on. In the center somewhere was always a page or even a paragraph of secret information. During the late crisis he got one out saying the army was not willing or able to fight. Madame Ritter was his agent in America. The man is now dead."

So, they knew all about it. No use hoping any longer that it was only the matter of the house. No wonder he had got nowhere with Henning. Henning, he felt sure, had heard a strong rumor of what it really was. The pamphlets hadn't been coming in for months. That was because he was dead. And perhaps his associates were dead, too, or in prison. And for months the police had been waiting with patience to land her — like a not too important fish in their net. And they had landed her. What were they doing to her?

He felt deathly sick and closed his eyes. When he opened them the Commissioner was looking at him with the corners of his mouth twitching.

Mark said, "If the man who sent the pamphlets is dead, what was the sentence on my mother?"

The Commissioner took up a pencil and began to twirl it in his fingers. "To tell the truth," he said, "I'm not sure."

"What!" Mark exclaimed. "But you know all about her. Each detail."

"It was my business to know all that," the Commissioner said. "That's what I'm here for. Once this department's work on a case is done we aren't too interested in what follows. We have, as you can imagine, a great number. We don't follow them beyond a certain point."

"I can hardly believe that," Mark said. "You know exactly what happened to the man who sent the pamphlets."

"Oh, that man? He was very important to us. He was not a mere tool, as I am afraid Madame Ritter was. He was, as I said, one of our most influential and persistent enemies. But the others, the minor criminals who are paid to do minor

[68]

jobs — we find out whatever is necessary to bring them to justice. We turn them over to the court and then lose interest. We don't follow them through all the camps and prisons in the country."

"I still don't believe you," Mark said. "If a death sentence was pronounced on my mother you would know of it."

"Oh, I think that's unlikely," the Commissioner said negligently. "I think Madame Ritter was probably given a long-term sentence, probably at hard labor. Since you're here, and such a friend of Carl's, I'll make an exception in your case. I'll try to find out for you. If it is a long term, you can consider she's been very lucky and that we've been very lenient."

"I'm afraid I won't appreciate that very much. For a number of reasons. Hard labor for a woman of her age is only a slow death sentence. Besides, as the trial was conducted in haste and great secrecy I can't believe it was a fair one. Why, I'd never even have known of her being in any trouble here but for an accident."

The Commissioner's eyes were very distrait. "May I ask what the accident was?"

Mark didn't answer.

The Commissioner said vaguely, "Friends, I suppose. People she was working with. Well, we probably have them in our files. It couldn't have been Rieger," he said suddenly. "Rieger, so far as we know, made an innocent purchase. Or the servant — what's his name? He seemed an obstinate, stupid fellow, much too officious to be clever. Certainly nothing on him."

Mark said shortly: "Neither of them, of course. You know that as well as I. You'll have to let me keep it to myself, but it's obvious that I, that no one, was meant to know. That doesn't argue for the fairness with which the case was conducted. How do I know what counsel she had, or if she had any? In other words, how do I know she had a fair trial?"

The Commissioner twirled his pencil. "You'll have to assume that the law of this country allowed her that."

"But this isn't an ordinary case. It's a political one, that is to say, it's necessarily involved in all sorts of hates and prejudices. It's more important than ever that every chance be given the defendant."

"She was given every chance."

"How can I believe that? How can I believe it when I haven't even seen her or been able to communicate with her? I demand it as a right — to see her, or to communicate with her at least by letter."

"I'm afraid that's not allowed." The Commissioner's lips were set. He put down the pencil and his fingers began to tap out boredom on the edge of the desk.

"Well then, tell me to what authority I can turn? You surely didn't let me come here just to tell me that there is nothing you or anyone else could do for me?"

"I let you come," the Commissioner said, "and believe me I see very few people, because of my friendliness for Carl. And because I thought the sooner you knew that there was nothing for you to do the better. Also, I was a little surprised to learn you were here. These trials we keep secret exactly in order to avoid the sort of outside interference you're prepared to bring, and I was interested to know who had given you your information. You don't choose to tell me. In the most friendly way therefore I advise you to go home again. In your own country you can go on enjoying the peculiar kind of freedom you value so highly — freedom in this case, I believe, to sink to abject poverty and crime."

"Without seeing my mother, without making any effort to save her?"

"You've already made that effort."

"I wonder," said Mark, "if you have any realization here of the effect that will be produced abroad by such a story as I'll have to tell?"

The Commissioner shrugged.

"Do you really want the world to go on piling up evidence against you?" said Mark. "I believe you all suffer, among other things, from a feeling that the world misjudges you. Do you think cases like this help them to admire and respect you?"

"The world will continue to misjudge us, my dear fellow, no matter what we do or do not do in the case of Madame Ritter. And I am afraid, since the events of the last year, that we don't care as much as we did what the outside world thinks of us. It has been proven that the opinion of the outside world doesn't matter. We are stronger than ever. You disapprove of us, but that's mostly bluff. Your papers put up a big hullabaloo for the benefit of the sentimentalists, while all the time you and your fellow democrats give us all, and sometimes even more, than we ask. And you buy our goods, you listen to us and do very quickly what we want. It isn't necessary to be approved of. It's only necessary to be strong."

He spread his pale, plump hand on the papers before him and bent his head as though to look at a suddenly noticed defect in it.

"And now, my dear fellow," he said, "as this isn't getting us anywhere I must really ask you to go. I'm a very busy man."

Mark started to get up. It was time to go, and he wanted to go. Everything in him pressed toward flight. Even his lungs couldn't take in enough air. But he hesitated: with Emmy Ritter locked in absolute silence he couldn't let a chance go by, not the smallest, humblest chance. And

the Commissioner was bored, but still there was something not quite final in his voice. And his eyes had even
now under a film of abstraction a faint spark of warmth
and interest. Mark leaned forward on the desk and clasped
his hands tightly before him.

"Perhaps all I can ask for is clemency," he said. His voice
shook. "Perhaps I can only urge you to be as lenient as
you can. My mother isn't a criminal. It wasn't a sordid
love of money nor a desire to betray her country that
led her into this. Her only daughter has tuberculosis. Only
rest and country air and nourishing food can possibly save
her, but she's obliged to work all day in a shop. My mother,
who adores her, has become gradually distracted at being
unable to help her. Perhaps her mind became a little
clouded from the strain. You know how women are in such
cases."

He knew that his face was not as pleading as his voice,
but sweat had come on his forehead and lips, and something in his anguished desire to plead had caught again
the entire interest of the man before him.

The Commissioner leaned forward, the tight belt forcing out his small, round stomach, and again he was the spec-
tator, almost breathless with attention. He waited for Mark
to go on, his auburn eyes questioning and softening and
that look almost of affection coming into them.

Mark took out his handkerchief to wipe his forehead
and to cover momentarily his face. It occurred to him that
the Commissioner was waiting to see him cry and that he
was disappointed. He didn't look up but sat slumped,
holding his crumpled handkerchief in his hand.

The Commissioner, after a moment, began to talk in a
bantering voice. "Yes," he said, "we also have our dramas
in which the woman sells herself for the sake of the little
sister who has tuberculosis and must be sent to a warm country. Why always tuberculosis? Are there no other dis-

eases? Do people actually think tuberculosis is more esthetic than liver trouble? And she always has blond braids and blue eyes too. But in this case, judging from yourself, I suppose she is dark. With a few changes you might make a pretty girl yourself."

Mark didn't look up. Through other feelings he was able to recognize the tone and the assurance of the man whom people called charming, "a little nasty perhaps, but charming." He was vain and he would rather be considered witty, and even nasty, than solely as the powerful Commissioner of Secret Police. Still, he was that too, and it took other qualities to hold his job. But it wasn't necessary to look and act like the executioner. Executioners have much simpler tasks, and even they are said to be fond of their families, and sometimes to make stamp collections.

The Commissioner waited for an answer and when none came said petulantly, "It's always women, women, in your country. Don't you ever get sick of them? You live in a degenerate matriarchy, you're workers in a great society of bees."

He shot his arm across the desk and waggled a plump finger under Mark's nose. "Read Schopenhauer!" he said. "Read what he has to say on the effect of women in society. Why, I hate even to see them in the theater. Juliet and Antigone were written for men, weren't they? Let them into politics if you must but for God's sake keep them out of the arts. They bring a musky contamination of sex and patronage into everything they touch."

He waited again. "Oh, well," he said, "I see you aren't interested."

Mark, knowing he had lost, reached over and gathered up his packet of letters. He knew he had served only as a momentary irritant, a focus for obscure, shallow dreaming, and that he was now ebbing out. As he looked up the warm, auburn eyes were losing their eagerness. Another man in the Commissioner of Secret Police was going to take charge, was already doing so.

"I'd like to see you again," Mark said, "when you have found out what my mother's sentence was and where she is. I'd like to know if I may see her, or at least write her."

The Commissioner didn't answer. He settled back in his chair and fell into a reverie. His plump face had a childish look. His little stomach bulged despondently and his mouth twitched slightly at the edges. Then he sat up briskly and tore a leaf off the desk calendar.

"Mr. Preysing," he said, "come and see me again sometime. I'm afraid I shall have to ask you to go now."

"You mean," said Mark, "you will tell me more later?"

"Yes. I'll have to make the necessary inquiries."

"When?" Mark asked dully.

The Commissioner ruffled the calendar. "Today's Thursday. Come, say, next Wednesday."

"You can't tell me anything in the meantime? That's a long time to wait."

"I'm afraid not. Come next Wednesday. Good-by, Mr. Preysing. I'm glad to have met you." He held out his hand and Mark took it. The palm was wet.

"Good day," he said.

"Good day, Mr. Preysing."

When he reached the door the Commissioner called out gaily in English, "My regards to Carl."

It was in the outer office that shame began to come up in him again like a sudden desire to vomit. The clerk looked at him. Two more men who had come in looked eagerly to see how he had fared.

At the door the guard in uniform stood like a mute Apollo caught and bound and mocked by a grotesque black uniform. Mark glanced up at his immovable face as he went out.

[74]

Chapter VI

AFTER lunch the Countess dozed a moment. It was a short doze, really a thick bloom of silence falling for a moment, then one of the girls rattled a coffee cup and she woke. It was the newest girl, the one who had just come, direct from St. Joseph, Missouri.

"Well, personally," the girl said, "I don't care if I never learn the darned language. That day Mama and I spent in town we just started boldly out, not knowing a word, and when we got back we found we'd cashed a check, ordered a lunch, bought a ski outfit, seen a museum, had tea, bought a bunch of mimosa and been to a pay toilet. Now you can't tell me we'd have gotten on any better speaking the language."

The tall English girl said, "How horribly resourceful." She was the one the other girls were a bit in awe of. She was the one they considered the most sophisticated. She was Lady Ursula Cannon, but those who knew her well enough called her "Sully" with some pride; and the newcomers, especially the Americans who weren't sure what to call her, said "you," looking right at her.

The Countess thought, that's the second time today I've dozed off. I'm much too young for that. It's because I'm so run down. She poured herself a second cup of coffee, adding lots of whipped cream, and remembered Aunt Medora sitting in a rocking chair on the porch at Newport and herself sitting on the steps reading aloud a novel

[75]

of Robert W. Chambers: she was letting her voice trail lower and lower, and suddenly Aunt Medora raised her head with a jerk and said, "I wasn't asleep, I heard every word." The smell of iodine and seaweed and a white cotton, summer dress she remembered made her feel very American again.

She turned to the girl from St. Joseph and said kindly, "We have tickets for the opera tomorrow night. Do you enjoy music?"

"Oh, I'd rather stay here," the girl said. "Do we have to go back to town?"

The plump, little, bespectacled Marie said, "What opera? Oh, don't say 'Carmen.'"

"I'm afraid so. Why don't you like it?"

Marie looked at her tragically and all the girls listened, for Marie was the "card," the wit. "The times I've sat," she said, "watching the guard change, hoping for a *thin* Don José. But it's always the fattest one. Oh, Countess, can't we just see a *fat* opera?"

When a new batch of girls came, the Countess always looked first for the one who was going to be the wit: it was important to know if she intended to be a collaborator. Marie was a collaborator. Then there would be the difficult girl, and in this case perhaps it was Suzanne, the daughter of a great French dressmaker. Why she should be difficult, and even if she were, she didn't quite know yet. Suzanne was much older than the others, who were all just out of school. Suzanne was thirty. She wrote sometimes for newspapers and magazines, and Madame de Blocqueville had sent her here with a letter. She had been ill and needed rest and mountain air. She was ugly and very smart, intelligent but also reserved and taciturn. Somehow the Countess regretted having let her come. I don't care for girls actually, she thought, I don't care for girls at all. I don't think they care for me. How on earth did I ever get into this?

To come back, of course. To live once more in the beloved country. That was the reason. But each time she thought of her return the same dark shudder of pain came over her as she remembered her arrival in the station in the morning. All night she had been awake from excitement and joy and then there it was, a railroad station, like another, full of pale, early light and a smell of smoke and coffee boiling in the station restaurant and people thinning away and finally an empty station, and he hadn't come. She remembered walking up and down distractedly in it, and the very old porter saying "But, gracious lady, what shall I do with the bags?" And she had gone to the man in the ticket window and said, "I want the next train back. Any train." "Not for an hour," he had said disapprovingly, "a very slow train, a local really. You could change at So-and-so." So she left her baggage and went to walk, away from the empty station, to get a cup of coffee perhaps at a coffee house she knew across the square. She started out blindly, her head bent, and was nearly run down by the big black car. The scream of brakes, before she saw what it was, filled her with intolerable relief and tears began to stream down her face as the door swung open and he pulled her into the car. Yes, that was why she had come back. . . .

"How many are going skiing?" she asked.

"I am" — "I am" — Were they all going? That would be too good to be true. An afternoon alone. She counted their faces. Yes, all of them. "Be back in time for tea," she said gaily, "and you'd better be starting. You," she said to the new girl, "go with Suzanne. She's in the beginners' class. You have to walk about two miles first, you know."

"Oh, that's swell."

"Run along now," she said, "run along all of you."

They got up and clattered out in their stumpy boots. She went with them to the ski room where their skis were stacked, all numbered, along the walls. Then, when the door banged, she went back and sat in the low, comfortable chair watching them pass as shadows before the frosted window.

The silence was so beautiful it could be tasted. On the tables and shelves all her little porcelain figures of shepherds and shepherdesses, of huzzars, goddesses and masked comedians, poised in their perpetually arrested attitudes. The Countess fell suddenly asleep.

In the hall a little musical clock that was held to the wall by a golden hand played its tune, which was the first four bars of "*Voi che sapete,*" and struck three notes. She woke with little agonies of fatigue running through her bones and that first terror: What's wrong, what's hanging over me? Nothing is wrong. Everything is all right. And he'll be here, surely, tonight. But what have I got to do first? Oh, yes. The cloud passed and all she had to do was order a good dinner, a dinner that would do no violence to his regime.

She stumbled out across the hall, through the pantry and into the big clean kitchen, yawning, pressing her fingers to the corners of her eyes. Kathe sat at the table peeling crisp radishes, the size of overstuffed pincushions, piling them in a plate to go on ice. She stood up when the Countess came in and they discussed the meal: soup, and a good ragoût of beef; salad; and a sweet made of whipped cream and chestnuts, say a Viennese *nussroulade;* then cheese and radishes.

"The General," she said, "will be coming this evening. We must be sure to have no garlic in the salad."

[78]

faces, all alike and immaculately fresh like red and white cut strawberries against the snow.

Feeling better now she turned at the track of the little mountain railway and walked along a rough, humpy path into the forest. The snow here was deeper and the boughs weighed down with it. Her lungs labored as she climbed, filled with cold, damp air. Looking up through snowy, living boughs she saw the peaks disappearing with a great leap into the mist and suddenly she was all right, as she had known she would be. The pleasure of the place filled her, driving out all dread, and by the time she reached the lake she was happy.

She didn't want to go as far as the hotel, so she sat on a rustic bench where she could see the lake through the trees. It was a small lake fed by warm springs and it never froze. It was transparently clear; even without sunlight it was vivid, streaky green, and on it two swans floated.

Oh, what pleasure, she thought, and why can't I be like this all the time! What is the matter with me, what am I afraid of? He is right, I must manage to have more courage with life.

As she sat there a man came quickly up the snowy path behind her, and seeing her there stopped a moment. She turned her head at the slight noise and he saw her profile; then with a slower, hesitating step he came and sat at the other end of the bench.

She wanted to get up and go away, quickly before the pleasure faded, but she waited a moment so as not to seem too conscious of him. She fixed her eyes on the swans, but she knew that the man was staring at her and she caught the flash of dark fingers against the snow as he took out a cigarette and lighted it. A wreath of bluish smoke curled past.

"Do you mind the smoke?" he asked.

"Not at all," she said. Then realizing they had spoken her own language, she turned to look at him. She saw a tall, young man, thin and dark, leaning one elbow on the back of the bench. His grace was the first thing she noticed, though it seemed to come partly from indolence or exhaustion; and then she noticed an air of poverty — because he was not correctly dressed for this country but wore a rough, dark red shirt and a too thin, townish overcoat; and lastly his eyes, pale gray in the snow light, intent and unhappy. They were trying to be less unhappy, to look reassuringly at her. He held out a cigarette case.

"Oh, no, thank you," she said hurriedly and started to get up.

"Please don't go," he said, "I didn't mean to annoy you. Please."

"I was just going anyway."

"But it's obvious you weren't. I'll know I've driven you away."

"Well, then — " she sat back helplessly, thinking that she really couldn't be too severe with a young man who looked ill and was probably one of the endless seekers for health who came to these mountains. And while he shouldn't have offered her a cigarette, his voice and accent were gentle and had that international, almost foreign flavor that, in America, usually belongs to those who have had English governesses and been abroad to school. And now he said quite easily: "It's remarkable that that lake doesn't freeze. Are there springs in it?"

"Yes, there are."

She thought, watching a small boat put out from the landing by the hotel, As soon as the boat reaches the nymph I'll get up and go. There was no pleasure for her now in this place. A stranger always had the power to spoil everything. One of her phobias now was the stranger. Except for her girls, she never made a new acquaintance if she could help it. Even if they said nothing, asked no new difficult thing of her, forced her into only the most minute decisions, still she imagined always criticism and sometimes horror in them, and always questioning. When they get to the nymph, she thought, I'll get up and go.

The boat reached the center of the lake and the two men rested their oars and leaned over the side, and one of them pointed down to the water.

"There's actually a nymph in there," she said. "That's what they are looking at."

"What sort of a nymph, a lorelei?"

"I don't know, but a bronze nymph with long hair, very lifelike — if one can say that of a nymph. I can't imagine who put her there."

"Can't you? In this country? I can."

"You think it's too fanciful?"

"I don't think it's fanciful enough."

Oh, she thought with anger, he's that kind of a fellow.

"I find all the minor arts here have a great deal of charm," she said.

"I find all the arts here have the great charm of being minor or second rate."

"Why do you say that?"

"I mean it's always someone else's hard original effort. They make it soft and lovable and easy to take."

"Soft and lovable," she repeated. "Yes, that is true. That's why I like it."

An artist, she thought, without doubt an artist. She glanced at his hands, bony and delicate and broad at the finger-tips, and his eyes too observant for comfort. They had an intent, tired, used look; and already, she imagined, they'd seen her as a formula of some sort, one of those dreadful formulas of the "modern" artist.

[83]

"Are you an artist?" she asked.

"I paint," he said, and she knew he disliked her use of the word or what it obviously meant to her.

"I think you're wrong about the fantasy," she said. "Have you seen the famous blue and silver room?"

"Oh, yes," he said, "by a Frenchman, wasn't it?"

"Why," she said, "I'd forgotten. He was a Frenchman. Still, he worked here, under the influence of this country."

"It shows how far a Frenchman can go when he gets away from the tough, parsimonious atmosphere of France, from such ideas as *le mieux est l'ennemi du bien.*"

"There is nothing in France like it," she insisted. "It's pure fairy tale."

"The French aren't too good at fairy tales," he said. "But there's very little true fantasy in most fairy tales. Read the brothers Grimm."

She gathered her sheepskin collar around her neck.

"Don't go," he said. How too quickly he seemed to gain assurance! "At least not till you remember me. We have met before, you know."

"What!" she exclaimed. Then she knew, looking at him again, that there had been something recognized about him. That was really why she hadn't run away at once.

"Where was it?" she said.

"In Paula Godey's house. We talked for half an hour or so one evening."

"That big studio upstairs? Why, so we did." She saw the room, layered with blue smoke and herself on a big divan, her feet curled up uncomfortably and a cocktail in her hand she didn't want. "New York," she murmured with an involuntary shudder. Now she knew the world he belonged to. Now she knew the exact feel and smell of it. He was what she called vaguely "the New York type." That meant a dangerously flexible creature, mixed in every sense, as to blood and as to experience, with the assurance that came from having no rigid social law, a thrusting curiosity and a blank arrogance; a combination of sewer rat, full of the agility of the streets, and of prince, master of fabulous mechanisms and machine-turned elegances. Still, he wasn't, now, a stranger. "There were some terrible, abstractionist pictures pinned to the walls," she said, "people Paula admired. Was it Chagall and Kandinsky? I can't think how I remember their names, when I can't remember yours."

"Preysing," he said, "Mark Preysing."

"Everyone was talking at once," she said, "I probably never heard it."

Everyone *was* talking at once. She remembered that, and how little she had understood or wanted to understand of what they said. Through it all a woman played the piano and sang in a husky voice *"Parlez-moi d'autre chose."* And a man kept saying "Take a card and don't let me see it." He was drunk and everyone thought he was funny. Later he gave them an imitation of a political speech and the whole room was shattered by laughter. At the wrong moment, it seemed to her, since someone she couldn't remember had just said something very intelligent that she also could not quite recall, about government. Yes, at the wrong moment these people were always making a puerile shift of scale, producing a leveling process, in which indeed all men were equal. She felt breathless now even remembering it, the grotesque and trivial and anarchic excitement of New York. But she felt American again, just the same.

"Remember me now?" he asked.

"Yes. Paula said to me 'You must talk to So-and-so, he's a comer, one of the best.'"

"Paula's always hopeful that a genius will hatch under her wing."

"So we met there. How very strange! And it's even stranger perhaps to meet here by accident."

"I didn't know you had come back," he said; "but curiously enough, I saw you two days ago in the railroad station just as I got in. But I didn't really recognize you then."

"The railroad station? Oh, yes, I'd gone to meet a new girl. I take girls to board with me, Americans, English and French. They're all just out of fashionable schools and they terrify me. But I'm very poor now, you know. In the inflation I lost everything but my house here."

"Why do you live here?"

No European would have asked her that. But Americans always ask questions. Even in New York they remember how they used to meet in lonely places: *Well, stranger, where are you from?*

She smiled. "I live here," she said reasonably, "because I was married here many years ago and in a way it's my country. When my husband died I went back to America, but all my relatives were dead or scattered and my friends and I had grown apart. So I came back. You see I really love it very much."

As she said this she thought of her house in the north, the house she had lost, and the smell of the great beech forests in autumn and her beloved porcelain stoves, and the music in the evenings, and even the dull card games with moths around the lamps, and of the first time Kurt came for the shooting and then of her house here under the white peaks, and of Kurt as he would be this evening when he came for dinner. These things wiped out all other remembrances and she didn't feel American at all.

"What a lot of things you have to see and do here,"

she said, "I envy you almost, seeing them all for the first time. It *is* the first time, isn't it?"

"Yes."

"I think I remember asking you in New York if you'd been here. You said no. But didn't you tell me, or did I imagine it, that you had some connection here? What was it? Have you relatives living here?"

"Yes." He threw his cigarette away and watched it make a hole in the snow from which rose a tiny coil of smoke. "It's my mother's country," he said, "and my father's too."

"So you're visiting them?"

"Not exactly. My father has been dead for years. I hardly knew him. Only my mother is here now, but I'm not visiting her at present. I'm just drifting around on my own." He clasped his hands on the back of the bench and added abruptly, "I wonder if you ever knew my mother — She was Emmy Ritter."

"Of course I've heard her name."

But she was so sensitive to what might bring her discomfort that she thought obscurely, He oughtn't to have said that. He spoke her name in a different voice, and her instinct was to become vague and impersonal again.

"I saw her once too. In New York many years ago. In 'A Doll's House.' She was splendid. But didn't she play mostly in comedy?"

"Yes, she did. Schnitzler wrote one of his best for her."

"Oh, yes." She felt sure now that he wasn't sick after all. Not physically sick. She thought again of Kurt. There was something about them that was alike. For a long time she had known Kurt to be a man who suffered because his natural virtue, virtue in the old Latin sense, was diverted cruelly into another channel, and this man was like that. Only whatever had dried up in him, it seemed a temporary thing and his talent was sharper and more immediate than Kurt's. What hurt him had something to do with his mother. Probably she thwarted him in some special, deadening way.

"How nice," she said pleasantly, "that she has come back here to live."

She thought he hadn't heard her, he let such a long pause come, then suddenly he gave a short laugh, an ugly sound with a tinge of fury in it.

"Yes, it is nice," he said. "It's nice she should have come back to live. Or perhaps to die. Because," he said, "we must all die, mustn't we?"

"Of course," she murmured. She thought his mother might be very old. She thought probably she was the ill one and had come, as he said, to die. If she could only get up and go now. "It's getting awfully chilly," she said, "I ought to be going on." But she added gently, "I hope your mother will live a long time. Perhaps coming back to her home will help her. She too must have loved this country very much to have wanted to come back. After those years abroad. I can understand that. Perhaps her love will help her to recover."

When she turned to look kindly at him and to say good-by and that he must come for tea sometime and talk about New York, she was startled by the hatred in his eyes and the tears shining in them. He said nothing, but she knew then that he too was one of those who were insensitive to all that her people, as she called them, had suffered, who would never try to understand. It was because of him and those like him that she had become almost a recluse, fearing even to walk alone through a friendly village or down a little mountain path.

"I see you don't understand a certain kind of loyalty," she said bitterly; "I see that."

"Oh, I think I do," he said.

"I suppose it must be a deep, human instinct, that one either has or one has not. Some people are born blind."

"Yes, it's a deep, human instinct," he said, "and there's no inherent virtue in it any more than in eyesight. The trouble with loyalty is that you can make a man loyal to anything. You can especially make him loyal to his own interest."

"I think it's rather vulgar to bring interest in, don't you? The loyalty I feel for the country I was most happy in, isn't, for instance, interest?"

"Why not? I wasn't thinking of gain, you know, not gain in the money sense. Why should you imagine I was? I was thinking just that: that it's easy to make a man loyal to what seems to have made him most happy."

"I don't think you should be scornful of what you don't feel yourself. Why shouldn't one be loyal to one's happiness?" But if he's never known happiness, she thought, or not what I mean by happiness, that's a cruel thing to say. "There are many things in human nature that are so universal, so entirely natural to us," she said, "they must surely be for our ultimate good. Like the hope of a future life or like the love of one's children."

He said slowly and mockingly, "Like the desire for knowledge and the passion for ignorance. Like greed and like generosity, like cowardice and like the wildest altruism. Oh, human nature!" he mocked. "Oh, the deep, human instincts! Jesus Christ and Doctor Crippen were both entirely 'natural' men."

She was shocked. "Then how do you suppose we get along," she said, "if the bad is always right there, as deep in us as the good?"

"We get along," he said, "if we get along at all,

through bloody contradictions and out of continuous transformations of your human nature."

"It must be dreadful to believe that," she said. "I can't bear to acknowledge so much evil. It makes me physically ill." She put her hand to her forehead.

"Yes," he agreed somberly; and he added almost indifferently: "You've got to try and be on the right side."

This was what she dreaded most, the choice, the decision. One side that was right and one that was wrong. You picked one side and were sure of it, your whole life poured into it. But then people wouldn't leave you alone. They tugged at your skirts and drew you back, this way and that. They said things that threw little, awful flashes of illumination, in which the dear and the familiar and the chosen were suddenly full of terror.

With a nervous movement of her foot she pushed aside a crust of snow and saw under it a little, dry cluster of stems. She bent over suddenly and picked it up, holding it cupped in her hand.

"What's that?" he asked.

"It's hepatica," she said. She shielded it from him, as though it were too tender for his sight. She looked at the tiny, brownish buds and wished passionately she were alone with it, in the pure empty cold of the forest.

"It blooms under the snow," she said. "And the ice heather comes, too, long before the snow is gone."

She tried to keep her voice calm but it was ridiculously trembling.

"May I see it?"

He took it from her and studied it closely for a moment; his brown fingers, separating the stems, had such sureness and delicacy of touch they were beautiful to watch. For a moment his virtue came back in him and she saw him as altogether another man; and a little twinge of fear, that was quite different from her other fear, stirred in her.

"Very pretty," he said stolidly, handing it back.

She got up and he stood too, holding his hat in his hand and looking at her with blank eyes.

"You must come and have tea with me," she said, "I've got to hear more about New York, about Paula and all of them. Come tomorrow, can you?"

"Thank you," he said, as though he weren't listening.

"Anyone at the hotel can show you my house. By the way, they treat you well there, I hope?"

"Like a relic of the true cross," he said.

"Good," she said smiling. "You'll find everyone here very friendly. Well, I'll expect you then tomorrow."

She held out her hand.

"Good-by."

As she walked away he stood looking after her. Then she said to herself that she was going to town tomorrow with the girls, to see "Carmen," and that she'd known all along she was going. That was why her invitation had lacked conviction, and he'd felt that. She must write him. She began to compose a note to send to his hotel as soon as she got home.

Out of his sight she walked more quickly. Her knees felt weak; and looking up at the now dead mountain splinters through the dead weight of the boughs, she thought: I've just abandoned a man in torment.

I must hurry, she thought, walking faster and faster, I must hurry home and have my tea.

Chapter VII

AFTER the Countess left, Mark walked down the little path back to the hotel by the lake. In the lounge, tables were set for tea and one or two hardy couples were even having their tea on the terrace. Mark sat by the window in the lounge and ordered coffee. He drank it slowly, ordering a second pot; for he had been chilled to the bone, sitting on the bench by the lake in his light overcoat. As he grew warmer he began to look around him. This was the first time he had had a chance to see the sort of people who came to this hotel. He had arrived at about noon and except for a red-faced old man and his wife and a middle-aged English couple, everyone seemed to be off in the mountains. Now the skiers had come back and they were crowding the tables around him, making the room ring with their accounts of what had happened and their jokes and their horseplay.

What gaiety, what spirits, what health! They were crimson-faced, hard-muscled, and life came up out of their skins like steam. There were millions like them, millions more packed hard and close in the rich country. It looked as though they had everything: health, good humor, singleness, ferocity, and a funny, endearing little childishness. He was fascinated by the glow of their flesh in the gray snow light of the room. He thought of a great canvas in which all these bodies would make a sort of Miltonic chute of falling forms, with exactly that flesh, reddish, glistening, damp, iridescent, vulgar, lovely. Only toward the bottom it would change, turn into scale and feather, into stone and corruption. Perhaps I couldn't do it he thought, and besides, Rubens has already done it. Where? Why right here. Right in the town I've left. I must go and see it, if I have time.

He was trying not to think about the Countess. She had managed like the others, like Henning and the Commissioner, to give him a feeling of humiliation. She had managed even more mysteriously, for she couldn't possibly be of any use to him, to add her refusal to theirs. Yes, he couldn't help the feeling that she had broken a secret thread that was essential to him. He knew this was sheer nonsense. She was, in the most literal sense, a woman outside his world. She was also outside the world of the young, roisterous skiers who surrounded him, and of the world of mountains and lakes and towns and people. Strong as he had seen her nostalgia to be, she didn't belong here any more than he did. She didn't belong anywhere. She was hopelessly and completely drugged. As he remembered some of the things she had said he hated her as much as he had ever hated anyone.

The happy skiers at near-by tables, noticing the dark, somber foreigner sitting alone, were made even more happy. See our happiness, they seemed to say, we're like children. Can anyone doubt we're also gentle and good? So why not love us? Please, dark stranger whom we detest, please love us.

He called the waiter over to him and said, "Do you happen to know of anyone around here named Fritz, Fritz Keller I think it is?"

"Fritz Keller," the waiter repeated. "In the hotel do you mean?"

"In the hotel or in the village. Have you ever heard that name?"

"No, sir. I can ask the head waiter if you like."

The head waiter came and stood by the table with the correct mixture of readiness and aloofness. "Fritz Keller," he said, "he's a servant in this hotel?"

"I don't know. He used to be a servant of a man I knew in America. The man was fond of him and asked me to look him up. He wondered what had happened to him."

"He is not in this hotel."

"He might be living in the village. I thought you might know."

"I don't know the village, sir, I don't come from this part of the country. Most of the waiters come here only for the season."

"Well, never mind then."

"There is another hotel though, a smaller, less expensive one about two kilometers down the main road. And there is another big one by the other lake. You might inquire there."

"Yes, I'll do that. Thanks."

He gave them both something and got up. At the desk he stopped to ask when the next train went back to town. The clerk was horrified: "At eight this evening, sir. But you've taken a room for the night, and I'll have to charge you for it anyway. Is anything wrong, sir? Aren't you satisfied?"

"Oh, yes, everything's all right, and I may stay. I'm a painter and if I find something to paint I'll stay."

"But, sir, the country is very beautiful."

"Yes, but I want something out of the ordinary. I want to look around first. I'm going out now to try to find some unusual angle. I suppose I can go anywhere I want?"

"Why, certainly, sir."

"I mean, I can walk anywhere? It's so close to the border I thought there might be some prohibited areas, military zones, something like that."

"No, sir. There's nothing prohibited here."

"I suppose it's too near the border for a prison, say, or a concentration camp?"

The clerk gave him a sharp look, then he pursed his lips and turned to take a note handed him by a bellboy. His eyebrows were raised in an offended stiffness. "You shouldn't believe all the nonsense you hear, sir," he said.

Mark left. He didn't turn off at the forest path but took the main one that led to the broad, valley road. He walked along with his collar turned up and his hands in his pockets. It was about five, and while it was still cloudy the snow and the trees were sharper, as though they felt the sunset behind the clouds. It was like walking on a dazzling white page thick with black print.

When he reached the main road a few cars passed him and he had to step aside to keep from being splashed. Peasants went by on foot, giving him the friendly, devout greeting of the country. He looked closely at each one, in a wild hope of seeing Fritz's face. Until he somehow found Fritz he could never find Emmy. If she was in this place only Fritz would know of it. Wherever she was, Fritz would be the one to know.

The first thing I'll do, he thought, is to go into a tobacconist's or a postcard shop and inquire there. And if they don't know, then the chances are he's not in the village. So, the next thing will be to try the church. Fritz was a good Catholic as I remember. If he's left the priest will probably know where he has gone.

But he knew it would be a bad thing to have to ask too many questions. He didn't want the whole village to know that a man from America was inquiring for Fritz

Keller. Already he had met with suspicion at the hotel. There were the other hotels, too, to be looked into later. Perhaps it would be best to wander around a bit first on the chance of running into him.

Then he wondered if he would even know Fritz if he saw him. It had been ten years since Fritz left them. Ten years since they could afford him. And he must have come back here five years ago. He might be very changed, especially in different clothes and in a different setting and without the subservience of a good servant in all his gestures. Fritz laying out the silver for dinner and Fritz buying tobacco in a shop would be two different men. He remembered once when he was a child having gone into Fritz's room one night to ask him something. He found Fritz sitting by a window with his chair tilted back and his feet on the sill. He had taken off his coat and wore only his waistcoat. It was warm and his shirt-sleeves were rolled up. He was smoking a long pipe. Mark was both shocked and pleased to see how different he looked. It was like a fairy story where the frog turned into a man at night.

About a kilometer from the village he began to hear a lovely sound, very faint and small, a trembling of bells. It was so lovely and so icy clear it absorbed all other sounds in the valley, as the white of the snow absorbed occasional colors. He stood still to listen. It came gradually nearer, growing lovelier as it came, until around a bend of the road a heavy sledge appeared, drawn by oxen and of the sort used to haul logs down the mountains. Two men were perched on it. As it came near Mark drew aside to let it pass.

He saw the two men high over him. One was a brown fellow with a stolid face and a great beard, wearing the coat of the country and the hat with a brush in it. He held a pipe in his mouth and in his hands the long, leather reins. The other also wore the country coat, but his hat, low over his ears, was an ancient Homburg, with a strangely city look about it, and under it his face was long and unhealthily pale. As they passed slowly, in a tremor of bells, the man's pinkish, hare's eyes looked down at Mark and then he looked quickly away again.

Mark stood still, uncertain and even unbelieving; then he turned and ran after the sledge. "Hey, wait a minute!" he called. "Wait, I want to speak to you."

The sledge stopped and with it the music of the bells, leaving a sudden quiet.

The driver drew on his pipe, letting the smoke curl from the thicket of his beard. He looked at Mark with brown eyes, stolid as stones. The other man looked at him too, his wild, hare's eyes pink at the edges and empty of intelligence. He sat still but with a stillness of suppressed agility, as though at a touch or a word he would leap off and scamper away. His whole body, soft and soft-boned as a hare's, was quivering with eagerness to be gone. But he held himself with such an effort under Mark's scrutiny that he might have been trying to make himself invisible.

"Don't you know me?" Mark said.

The man turned to his companion with an exaggerated look of inquiry as though to say, Well, what do you make of this?

"Don't pretend you don't know me," Mark said. Then he began to speak hurriedly in English: "Tell me where she is. I got the letter. You addressed it and it came from here. Is she near here? Is there a prison here, a camp?"

The man lifted a big, pale, supple hand and scratched his ear. He shook his head and smiled in a foolish, yokel embarrassment, or an imitation of a yokel embarrassment.

"Cut it out, Fritz," Mark said sharply, "I know you. You

know me. What are you trying to do? You can't let her down, you know. Where is she? Tell me quickly. That's all I want to know. I'll see you won't get in any trouble."

The man nudged his companion with his elbow and smiled, but the other man was not amused. He drew on his pipe and looked at Mark as his oxen might look at him. He gave a little impatient jerk of his hand and the oxen tossed their heads, letting loose little shivers of bells.

Mark said: "You're not going to make me remind you of all you owe her, are you? The time Minna was sick and she got you the best doctor in New York. A hundred other things, too. You couldn't forget if you wanted."

A car passed so close it splashed wet snow on his legs. The man had stopped smiling his yokel smile but his eyes were lighted up with jeering amusement.

"Then what did you send me the letter for," Mark said, "if you're that scared? Why didn't you keep out of it? You must want to help her."

The man leaned over and shouted at him in his own language, "I don't understand you. I don't know what you want."

His voice was shockingly shrill and loud.

"Why, God damn you," Mark said.

But suddenly another look came in the man's eyes, a sharp, cunning look.

"The railroad station is over there," he said, pointing with his pale, supple hand. "Over there!" he shouted, as one shouts at a foreigner.

"O.K." Mark said. He stared at him but the look was gone. "I'm going back to town," he said, still in English, "if that's what you mean. If you mean she's in town and not here, just tell me she's not here."

The man shook his head violently.

"Not here? Well — I'll be at the Four Seasons Hotel, if you want to see me."

The driver gave the exclamation of a man whose patience has given out and the sledge moved on. It went slowly up the snowy road leaving Mark standing there. There was no use following it. If Fritz were too scared he could easily make trouble for him and spoil his two remaining resources, freedom and obscurity.

Fritz had let him down too, that was all there was to it. He'd been a fool to count on Fritz. He wasn't what he'd remembered him to be. People build up romantic feelings toward their servants that the servants never have toward them. For Fritz to send the letter at all was more than he had a right to expect of him. How had they ever come to look on Fritz as a sort of family savior? Still, he thought, he may look me up at the Four Seasons. In any case, there's no use staying here.

He watched the sledge to a curve in the road and listened to the bells making the air of the valley lovely, long after it had passed from sight.

Then when he could bear them no more he started back to the hotel. His feet would hardly take him. He was drowned in disappointment and despair. Now that he knew she was not here, the country became blank and dark and he felt foolish too for having expected that she would be found so easily. And what was there to do now? Fritz would never look him up.

At eight o'clock that night he took the little mountain train down to the main line station several kilometers away. Wedged in among the skiers he sat with his head down, his hands over his eyes. Some way down the black valley he opened them, looked out and saw the smothered, soft lights of a house, a large house, a manor house, perhaps. The lights went slowly by like a minor constellation in the night.

He thought suddenly, it might be the Countess' house. The train whistled at an unseen crossing and he thought of her out there in the dark. Quite lost she was. Quite lost. He saw her clearly again and her beauty was more potent in memory than when he had seen it, mixed with his anger and disgust. But she was beautiful, sadly and poignantly so, a pale, hollow shell of beauty. He thought of her as though she were already dead.

Chapter VIII

THE girls ate all the black plum jam for tea. From the corner of the room the radio purred out waltzes from Vienna and the windows were squares of violet white in the rosy, dusky room.

The girl from St. Joseph said, "The ski instructor is divine. I've never seen such a figure! And such a funny, popping voice. I can't understand a word but he talks like a little engine, missing fire all the time."

"When we come back from town," said the Countess, "I'll have some of the young officers over from the garrison. I know one or two nice ones. We'll have a little party Monday night, if we get back in time."

"How simply divine! I simply adore them," Marie said. "They're so beautiful and so naïve."

"Couldn't we get Leo Mannheim?" Suzanne asked.

A look of pain came over the Countess' face. She didn't answer immediately and the girls, seeing her distress, assumed vacant expressions until she should recover. Only Suzanne continued to look gravely questioning. Finally the Countess said, "I don't know. I'm afraid he's gone away somewhere. I — that is — I'm sure he's gone."

"Oh," Suzanne said.

Only a week ago Leo Mannheim had come down for the day with his father. When Leo wrote to say they were coming she had been disturbed and felt a grievous sense of

[101]

guilt. For years they had been friends. When her husband was alive they never came south without dining with the Mannheims. The elder Mannheim came often to their place for the shooting and Leo she could remember as a child in a fantastic sailor suit, rolling a hoop in the English garden. But for well over a year she had hardly seen them. It was not to be unkind, not to join in any way in the ring of hate that was surrounding them, not even entirely from cowardice, but from neglect, lassitude, and the growing dread of people.

They used to make the long trip to and from town in their big, luxurious car. This time they came by train, third class. She had one of the best lunches for them and got out her best Riesling and was as kind and natural as she could be. But it was hard to conceal her shock at the change in the elder Mannheim. He had been a suave and worldly man, a little over-elegant in his clothes, a little over-flowery in his speeches. He looked now incredibly old, his coat was shabby, and two long stains ran from his eyes down his cheeks to his beard. He spoke so little she thought he was perhaps slipping into senility, his hands trembled as he ate and as he sat at her table his air of humility and persecution and a sort of innocence produced a hush even among the girls. Even Leo, who was so handsome in his soft, exaggerated way, so gay and talkative, made them silent — and only Suzanne could speak naturally to him. Leo and Suzanne seemed to enjoy each other. After lunch, when the girls had gone skiing and while old Mannheim appeared to doze for a while, he and Suzanne sat on a couch in the library and talked.

As they left, the Countess had drawn Leo aside. Juli was helping the old man on with his coat. "What are you going to do, Leo?" she said. "Are you going to stay here? Can't you get away somewhere?" She felt that they must have some plan. Some plan to find money, to shelter themselves, to go somewhere, to do something that would mitigate their intolerable fate. Everyone, no matter how hard-pressed, has some secret refuge. If they had one and she could know it for a fact, she would be free of them. She wanted terribly to be free of them. "What about your medicine?" she persisted. "In America or England or even France you could go on practising it. You mustn't lose your skill. Think of all you meant to do with it. You can be of value to humanity, Leo. You should try to forget these other sad things that have happened and fix your mind on that end." Leo only laughed. "Do you know what Spinoza said? He said no man tries to preserve his being for the sake of any end." That had seemed to her bookish and pretentious. She had no time to say any more.

Two days later Kurt told her, "Oh, by the way, your friend the young Mannheim shot himself this morning." She had thought she was going to faint. "He was a fool," Kurt said. He spoke with a frosty impatience. "No one who behaves himself need fear anything."

She did not know what she would find to say to the elder Mannheim. She forced herself to go to the funeral but when she met him there, she saw he did not realize at all what had happened.

Sully was saying graciously, "Some of them are very clean and well-groomed, almost like Englishmen."

To the girl from St. Joseph, Marie whispered: "Wait till you see what's coming tonight. You'll simply pass out. He's divine."

The Countess got up and went into the library to write a note to Mr. Mark Preysing. When she had finished it she moved restlessly around the bookshelves looking for a book to distract her. She pulled many in and out. Suddenly she came on one, behind some larger ones, in the "art book" section. What a curious coincidence! she thought; and she took it upstairs with her.

Lying down to rest before dressing for dinner she looked at it. It had been published nearly forty years ago by a famous publishing house, and it was called *The House of Richard Ritter*. It was a record with engravings and photographs of the house built by the painter Ritter for his wife, shortly after he had married her, when he was the most fashionable portrait painter in the country. He had built this house entirely to his own taste, designing and decorating every room himself, in a style that was half Pompeian and half what was then considered "new art." It housed a collection of antique vases and small bronzes, a few genuine Roman, some reproductions, and Ritter's own pictures, done in a half mystic, half classical manner, a little in the style of Gustave Moreau. Looked at even now, some of the rooms still seemed beautiful and had the curious charm of a very personal period piece, like Strawberry Hill or Whistler's Peacock Room. At the time it was built it had been taken very seriously, seriously enough to write a learned book about. The introduction, she saw with some surprise, had been written by the Grand Duke, who was Kurt's father-in-law. She read it and saw that the Grand Duke had been a warm admirer of Ritter and had managed to keep any condescension out of his praise. Then she remembered that she had heard someone say that the Grand Duke had later been a warm admirer of Ritter's daughter. But a woman like Emmy Ritter must have had many admirers and a grand duke was to her almost a staple, like flour or beans, just as such a woman in her turn was almost a staple for a grand duke. She smiled faintly at the thought of the young man she had just met, painting portraits of grand dukes, receiving gratefully their dedications and building himself a Pompeian house.

[104]

She left the book on her chaise longue to dress for dinner.

Knowing that the General would come, Juli had put out the dirndl of silvery gray brocade he liked to see her wear, and the Countess wound her ash-colored braids around her head in a coronet, in the fashion he preferred; but thinking the whole effect needed accent she put on her lips a few strokes of lipstick, rubbing it in so he would think it was natural. He worshiped health but he also insisted on naturalness, and when one was underweight and anemic and had nervous headaches this was hard to live up to.

She waited till she heard his car outside and then went downstairs to the library. He was standing in the midst of the girls, immensely tall and solid and handsome. He wore a uniform and his monocle gleamed in one eye, his thinning hair was brushed back like satin and he held himself very erect so that he would not sag below the waist. Everything about him had that military dandyism so endearing to women because it is so masculine. Sully and Marie were talking to him and the other girls looked on with pleasure, almost with fright. In this short moment he had cast a spell over them, the spell of the great, handsome, male animal, experienced but secret, and each one wanted to shine for him.

He kissed the Countess' hand and said what he had never failed to say for the last fifteen years: "My dear Ruby, how beautiful you look." Then she presented him to the girl from St. Joseph, who knew at once that this room, in this rosy light, these people grouped in exactly this way, were what she had left St. Joseph to see.

At the long table the General sat at the Countess' right with Sully at his other side and the girls in diminishing degrees of importance down the table. When they were seated the Countess noticed a vacant chair. It was for Suzanne.

She wondered if she had fallen asleep in her room or become absorbed in a book. She sent one of the maids to fetch her.

The soup was very good. A warm atmosphere of admiration filled the room, and the girls caught the contagion from each other; and even the maids, their heads tied in silk handkerchiefs, handling dishes just outside the circle of candlelight, moved like the humble followers of a ritual of worship.

The General was affable and talkative. He behaved as though this were his house, and indeed he had managed to make this house seem to be his own. He could never live at ease in anything but his own territory. It must be his, or become his, spiritually, physically if possible. This protected his capacity for being hurt. It also made him more unfailingly the center, since neglect hurt him worse than anything else. He had a hundred ways of protecting himself. Even Loisel the dog, when she was alive, had served him. If a question became difficult, if attention went too far toward a point where he couldn't follow it, "Look at Loisel," he would say, "how fat she is getting." He adored animals.

Now he talked to the girls about skiing and spoke well of their instructor and said the snow had been rather poor this year. To put the new girl at her ease he asked about the snow in America and listened while she told him of a place in New Hampshire where her cousin had been to ski and of Sun Valley in Idaho. The General said he'd like to go to America sometime, and he added jokingly, "when the world becomes a little easier to get around in."

The Countess heard the hoot of a train outside in the dark. It was the little mountain train going down the valley to the main line. It had a sad, harried sound and she had to remind herself that it was actually full of happy skiers going home after a day in the snow.

Suzanne came in and murmured an apology in her ear. Her face was pale and tired. She had taken a nap and overslept, she said, and not heard the bell. It occurred to the Countess that Suzanne had been very much taken with young Mannheim and had perhaps guessed something of his final tragedy. Yes, she must have been very taken by him, even in so short a time, the rather dour and self-sufficient Suzanne. She will forget him, the Countess thought, and so must I. She turned her attention resolutely to the General.

He was talking to the intent young faces turned toward him like sunflowers. It was of an experience of his during the war. The Countess had heard it before. It must have started from talk about the snow, because he was describing now a Polish forest deep in snow, so deep his horse could barely flounder through it. He was in a lancer regiment he said, that was when he was on the eastern front, and he had become lost. "It does not matter why," he said smiling gently, fixing his monocle more firmly in his eye, "but I was lost, — very lost, — and had been for a long time. Finally at night I saw lights and they were the first sign of life I had come on for a whole day. They were from the windows of a low, wooden house, a hunting lodge I imagine, but before I reached it I saw the snow was trampled and I could smell horses. It was so cold the horses had been stabled in a sort of outbuilding which was locked, so I had no way of telling if they belonged to friends or enemies. But as I prowled around I began to smell something better than the smell of horses. It was the smell of food, and I heard voices and laughter from inside the house. I leave you to imagine how hungry and exhausted I was, since I was willing to take any chance that these voices and this laughter would be friendly. There was no guard at the door of the lodge, no sentry. The place was so remote, whoever were there must have imagined themselves to be as safe as on the moon. So I opened the outside door of the lighted room."

He paused and looked around with pleasure at their expectant faces. "There I saw a long table covered with food and wine, and with about twenty officers sitting around it. As I opened the door there was dead silence and a servant who held a great tray of bottles stood right by me and never moved. But I saw that the officers were my enemies. I said, '*Oh, pardon*' and shut the door very quickly. I heard the tray of bottles all crashing to the floor."

"You got away?"

"Yes, I got away. They must have thought I had a regiment outside or else they were hungry and exhausted too. But as I rode off I kept laughing to myself at their faces, so surprised, as though the devil himself had appeared, and thinking of how politely I had said '*Pardon.*'"

The girls laughed tremulously, even now alarmed at his danger, and the General repeated, smiling, "'*Pardon!*' What a thing to say!"

The Countess met Suzanne's eye and saw that this anecdote had made her feel neither admiration nor vicarious alarm. And suddenly she knew by a slight movement of the General's jaw that he also had caught Suzanne's critical look and was hurt by it. He disliked Suzanne. "That girl," he had said to the Countess once, "has a mind like a piece of fake jewelry from the Rue de Rivoli. And she is very ugly." But still he could be hurt by her. It was so difficult to be certain of what was going to hurt him. Once or twice she herself had tried to hurt him. She had used all her knowledge of him, all her skill and whatever cruelty she could summon. But he remained impervious. And then again a slight no sharper than a blade of grass would be enough to make him wince.

"I was saying," the General said to her, "that after dinner you must sing to us."

He had passed from war, she realized, to art and was telling them about his love of music.

"Certainly," she said. "Whatever you like, if Suzanne will play my accompaniment."

The General readjusted his monocle and looked down the table at her. "And does Mademoiselle Suzanne play?"

"I can play Madame's accompaniment," said Suzanne. She spoke with the calm of being the only one who did not find him attractive, but even one who did not find him attractive was enough to spoil the charm, to make a flaw in his little reign over them. Such a reign must be unanimous. For the rest of the meal the General was silent, and the girls felt the enjoyment had gone out of things.

They took their coffee in the music room and presently Suzanne sat down at the piano. The Countess asked the General what he'd like to hear. "Sing *'Du bist die ruh,'*" he said. She leaned on the back of the piano and sang. Her voice had a lovely dark quality and was fairly well trained, though now rather husky and worn. She looked as beautiful and serene as the song, standing there in her antique dress, and the girls applauded her. The General, his arms crossed on his chest, stared at her and said nothing, and a heavy vein that was in one temple pulsed visibly. Suzanne at the piano bowed her head and seemed to be in a momentary submission to the music and to them. "It's heaven," said Sully, and the girl from St. Joseph thought vaguely that it was a pity people couldn't all get together like this all the time, in this sort of union over something nice instead of hating each other the way they did, and having thought this she felt a pleasing glow, as though she had made a contribution to the peace of the world.

After this they played bridge at two tables and the General played with them. The atmosphere of admiration was restored. Suzanne, who didn't play bridge, took a book into a corner and no one noticed her. The General was gay again. He made little jokes. They weren't allowed of course to play for stakes, and he played very badly, overbidding wildly and sometimes even mistaking the suit. "Please be kind to my jack," he would say as he tried a finesse with it. "He's an orphan. I picked him up on the street." Then he'd make an absurd face as it was taken. "You're a scream," the girl from St. Joseph said. He overbid so outrageously that every time he laid down his hand they rocked with laughter. They were all astonished when the little musical clock played the first bars of *"Voi che sapete."* As it struck the hour they counted the strokes. Eleven. It couldn't be believed. The Countess put down her cards. "Off to bed, all of you," she said. "It's very late." The General pleaded for them to be allowed to stay up longer, like an older, privileged child pleading for those younger. The girls watched him delightedly. "No, no," the Countess said, smiling, "they'll be too tired tomorrow."

The girls got up and said good night. Then they went off down the gallery to the other wing of the house where they had their rooms.

The Countess began to gather up the cards and put them back in their cases.

"Would you like something to drink?" she said, and without waiting for an answer she rang for Juli. When the tray of cherry wine and schnapps came the General said to Juli, "Tell my chauffeur to bring the car to the front door." "And then go to bed, Juli," the Countess added. She poured his schnapps and her cherry wine and they sat in silence.

The General took a cigarette from a gold case with a long silk cord hanging from it, put it in a holder and lighted it. He blew the smoke slowly out, looking vaguely at the ceiling. The Countess leaned her elbows on the card table and watched him. The atmosphere of the room had become domestic.

Suddenly she said, "Kurt, you and I never argue, do we?"

"No," he said, "why should we?"

"But we quarrel, don't we?"

"That is different. People of the same mind may quarrel, but they have nothing to argue about."

"Are you entirely sure we're of the same mind?"

"Aren't you?" he said, looking at her.

"How can I be? I don't really know most of the time what's in your mind. How are you so sure you know what's in mine?"

He made a gesture of impatience and closed his eyes. "I'm very tired tonight," he said.

"If you thought for a moment we weren't," she insisted, "would you hate me for it? I think you would. I think you'd hate the tiniest thought that wasn't your thought, even if it lay in such a secret place that you were the only one in the world to know about it. I also think you'd hate me, my skin and my eyes and my hair and all of me. Isn't that so?"

The General got up suddenly and without looking up at him she knew he was angry. "Ruby," he said, "you are ridiculous. You may think exactly what you like, about the cherry wine, about music, about God. It is a sickness that comes on us every now and then to imagine that every little abortion of thought should be respected."

He walked out of the room, across the hall to the vestibule and opened the front door. In a misty, white halo from the outside lamp his car waited. The chauffeur got out and stood before him on the crackling, salty snow. "Drive into the village," the General told him in a low voice, "and stay at the inn as usual. At five in the morning come and wait for me at the foot of the hill, the same place."

The chauffeur saluted, got in the car and drove off.

The General closed the door gently after him and turned off the outside light. Seeing a girl's coat fallen from a hook he picked it up and carefully replaced it. Then he sat down on the bench in the vestibule to smoke another cigarette.

Upstairs the girls heard the car go down the driveway. "There he goes," said Marie, who was sitting on the edge of Sully's bed. "They're too wonderful, — aren't they? — like something in a book. I hear they've been in love for years and years."

"She went to America," said Sully, "when her husband died, and then came back. The music teacher told me all about it, the one who was here last year. She couldn't stand it away from him, he said."

"Why don't they marry?"

"Oh, didn't you know? He's got a wife somewhere, ages older than he and a frightful swell, royal and all that sort of thing."

"Oh, really. I didn't know that. Anyway, I suppose that would spoil it."

Suzanne was talking to the girl from St. Joseph.

"I admit she has a certain quality," she said, "and even he, yes, in his way even he has."

"I think they're sweet," the American said.

"You think they are sweet! What a curious word. I think they are pathetic perhaps, but also a little dangerous, and they are old, old."

The Countess went to her room and undressed, putting on a soft white woolen gown, gathered at the throat and wrists and tied with a red cord around the waist. Its thick folds covered the thinness of her lovely bones. Then she let down her heavy, ash-blond braids. In her room was a yellow porcelain stove, like a great tulip, but it was too old and burned-out to use and the room was very cold. She lay on her chaise longue and pulled a white fur coverlet over her knees. Juli had left a pot of hot peppermint tea on the table by her under a lamp, and seeing the book about Ritter's house on the chaise longue she had placed it there too. The Countess took the book on her lap but didn't look at it.

She was wondering if Kurt had gone away in his car without even saying good-by. That was just the kind of thing he often did. He would go away and sometimes she wouldn't hear from him for weeks. At first she used to write him notes or try to telephone him. When the notes were unanswered and she was told over the telephone that he was not at home she would humiliate herself further. She would walk down windy streets where he might pass, or stand in a crowded drawing room, her head turned from the door, listening for each new voice: if he didn't come she'd be the last to leave, and even if he did come they would perhaps only greet each other coldly and the waiting would begin again. But at least she would have seen him, and there was always the chance that in the midst of all those people he would manage to give her a sudden, tender look of forgiveness. Even to think of these things now made her grow hot with weariness and shame. She had learned to leave him alone. He would always come back when he himself couldn't stand it any longer.

She sat quite still, listening for some sound of him in the house and hearing her own heart beating quickly. And she reproached herself for having angered him. It was not now only a question of their peace but of his health. He was no longer a young man. Like the porcelain stove, he was almost burned-out.

She didn't hear him coming up the stairs but when the door opened her palms broke into a cold sweat of relief.

He said nothing as he came across the room. He sat down on the foot of her chaise longue without kissing her and he looked neither angry nor ardent. His face had its heavy, dreamy look.

"Reading?" he asked, turning over the book on her knees so he could see the title.

"Yes," she said, "I found this in the library after tea. It's about Ritter's house."

"Yes, I see that," he said. "Why are you interested in Ritter's house?"

"I just found it, that's all."

He was going to go on being difficult. Not forever, not all night, but still for a while. She sighed and said, "I think the house is still charming. Look at the library." She made a move to show him but he closed the book and said, "I know that house well."

"Yes, I suppose you do. Ritter was a friend of the Grand Duke, wasn't he? Didn't he once paint your wife?"

"Yes, he painted Ernestine," he said, "as a very young girl. He painted everyone then. He was very fashionable. The Grand Duke made him the fashion."

She remembered what she knew about the Grand Duke's little court and the charm of its modest, intellectual gaiety. She thought of the Princess Ernestine, Kurt's wife, and the few occasions when she had seen her. The Princess Ernestine was already an old maid when she married. It was after the war, and she had long since refused a Scandinavian prince and a Russian grand duke. She was an ugly woman but with a vigorous, eccentric character. When she married Kurt she said it was time someone broke away from these incestuous royal marriages. She said all they ever bred were qualities of courage, idiocy, and love of family life, and her family had enough of these already. Her marriage with Kurt, however, bred nothing at all, least of all a love of family life. Like many brave and honest gestures it led only to another convention and seemed in the end hardly worth the effort.

"I went to the opera the other night with some friends of Ernestine's," he said. "People from New York."

"Were they nice?"

"I don't like them. They are the ones we knew in Paris that time and on Elverton's yacht. Ernestine picked them up. She sometimes has extraordinary tastes."

"It's difficult to judge people of another country," she said.

"Ernestine thinks all Americans entertaining," he said. "You probably know these people — they are from New York."

"You are like the Princess," she said, smiling. "Every time I saw her she said to me, 'I've just met some delightful people from New York. You must know them. Their name is Rosenstein.'"

"Yes, Ernestine has strange tastes," he repeated, smiling. "She belongs in an age where one could afford to have them." His good humor seemed to have come back. He yawned and loosened the collar of his tunic. "Drink your tea," he said, "if you really want it." He leaned across her, took off the quilted cosy and poured her a steaming cup. "Why do you drink this dreadful stuff?" he asked agreeably.

"It makes me sleep," she said.

"I'll make you sleep," he said, but she put her arms around his neck, holding him back teasingly, not to give in too easily and too soon, to make him feel at least a little preliminary uncertainty, since he had made her feel so much.

"I must drink my tea," she said. She released one arm and took her cup up, held it to her lips and blew on it gently. "Whatever became of Ritter's daughter?" she asked. "That actress, Emmy Ritter?"

He got up and crossed the room, took off his tunic and hung it on the back of a chair. His face was turned from her as he said, "She went to America, I believe."

He smoothed the tunic carefully from the shoulders down before turning around. As he came toward her again his face was cold and thoughtful. "Why do you ask that?" he said.

She felt a little prick of fear at once. Perhaps he'd seen young Preysing. He's jealous, she thought. But he couldn't have seen him, or heard of him. Then why should he be angry? "The book made me think of her," she said.

"Did you ever know Emmy Ritter?" he asked. "She lived in New York too."

"No," she said, "you're as bad as the Princess. Why should I know her? I saw her play once. In 'A Doll's House,' I think. Years ago."

"But now you are interested in her," he said. He sat down again on the foot of the chaise longue. "All at once," he said, "I find you interested in this Emmy Ritter. Why?"

The heavy vein in his temple began to pulse visibly and she could see the fine veins in his eyes. She forgot Emmy Ritter in her anxiety for him. The doctor had told him he must avoid excitement. Kurt had admitted this to her once and had even given her, with some embarrassment, a list of the things he must eat and not eat. He had high blood pressure, he said. But then he quickly got over this fear and scorned all the doctor had said and returned to his cult of robust health through an active, virile life. But she hadn't forgotten, even though she hadn't dared speak of it. She kept his regime in her desk drawer and always referred to it. She tried to avoid what would make him angry and even in the midst of love she listened anxiously for his quickening pulse.

"Kurt," she said earnestly, "try not to be angry again. You know how terrible it is for both of us. It has always been my great fear, that anger of yours. It's like a dark hinterland somewhere around us. Have you never thought that we are too old now to be still skirting these borders? Some day you'll drag me in and we'll be lost in it."

"Nonsense," he said, "I ask you why you are interested all of a sudden in this Emmy Ritter, and you don't want to answer me. Doesn't it seem strange to you that you should suddenly pick a forgotten book about her house out of your library, one you've never shown me before, and that you insist on questioning me and will not be put off?"

"No. Why should it seem strange to me?"

"I'll tell you why. But first tell me, have you been reading anything about her in your papers, in your American papers, I mean?"

"I don't know what you're talking about. I hardly ever see an American paper. But I've read nothing about her in any papers. What is all this? It seems to me you are the one who is really concerned about her."

"Well, I'll tell you," he said. "In a few days Emmy Ritter is going to be executed for treason."

"What!" She dropped back and put one hand across her face. Her first feeling was pain. She remembered the eyes of the young man by the lake, the look of anguish in them. Then fright, that was always in her bone marrows, welled up and took charge of her, and she only felt that she must hide anything she knew. There must be no link between the young man and Kurt and herself. She rubbed her forehead and said in a bewildered voice: —

"That's dreadful. A woman I've seen, to be executed."

"Her crime was treason," he said.

"But what does that mean? What did she do?"

"It's a very sordid story," he said, "but since you're so concerned I'll tell you." He reached over and snapped his fingers against the book. "This pretty little house," he said, "that you admire so much — she sold it."

"Sold it? Is that treason?"

"It could be. But as it happens, the house in this case was only a trap. You know how many people here have been going to all sorts of lengths to get their money out of the country. Most of those we can catch. But people who live elsewhere and still work against us sometimes have property here too, or relatives with property. These we keep a careful check on, and it occurred to someone that we should have an agency to encourage exchanges of property, and in that way we might get our hands on criminals we couldn't otherwise touch. We'd take full advantage of their greed and treachery."

He tells it to me just as he told me about Leo Mannheim, she thought. Coldly and impatiently, determined to show no apology.

"So she came to sell her house," she said.

"Yes. But in this case there was bungling. She wasn't meant really to sell her house, but she did after all. Not through our agent but to a friend of hers. He was a man who had never got in trouble and no one suspected him or thought of him. He paid her, it seems, a fantastically small sum. It wasn't worth much of course. But there is a possibility, since he went to America directly after, that he put another, larger sum to her account there. If he did it's of no use to her now."

"What did they want her for? Why did they want to trap her like that?"

"Oh, it's all a sordid story, as I said. But you want to hear it. For years she has lived in America, but for at least a year before she came back the Secret Police had had an eye on her. Rudi told me all this just last night at dinner. It seems she was the American agent for a very dangerous traitor — that's a case you know nothing about as his trial was very secret. This man used to enclose secret information in pamphlets for her to distribute in America. But they couldn't do anything about her. She persisted in staying there and she had no relatives left here through whom she might be reached."

He got up from the chaise longue and began to walk up and down the room, his hands stuck through his belt.

"Ritter died years ago, and so did her mother. I remember them though, when I was a very young man. Her mother had a sort of salon, *à la française*. All the loose-thinking intellectuals and all the morbid poets and decadent painters, of whom no one has ever heard since, used to foregather there. I went there once or twice myself as a young man, with the same curiosity with which I first went to a brothel. I saw this Emmy Ritter there, when she was a girl, a big staring-eyed girl, very thin and sallow. Some people actually thought her beautiful. Those who hadn't been able to become the mother's lovers tried to become hers. Oh, I know the atmosphere she was brought up in."

"But she married, didn't she? I — I think," her voice sank, "I seem to have heard she has children."

"Yes, she married an actor of some sort. I can't even remember his name. They went to America together and he died there. They say she got along very well without him. Oh, yes, she did as she pleased in America. She was safe as long as she stayed in America."

As he paced up and down his voice rose, and a choked, passionate note came in it. His face had turned a dull red. "But she began to need money badly," he said. "She was no

[119]

longer a success and she was used to living luxuriously. Yes," he said, standing before her and looking down at her with a cunning, superior look, "Rudi tells me they had had their eye on this house for some time. They thought if anything would bring her back this would."

"So they're going to kill her!"

"Not to kill her. To execute her. There's a difference."

"And only because of those pamphlets. But what could have been in those pamphlets?"

"Stop these silly questions!" he cried. "I should never try to explain anything to you. What's in the pamphlets? I believe, if you could, you'd save her, from sheer sentimentality. In America, I'm told, criminals are always loved by hordes of degenerate women. Pull yourself together, my dear," he said angrily. "Don't try to meddle in judgments of people who know what they're doing. If I say that woman is guilty, believe me she's guilty. I tell you she's so guilty, if I were to see her here now, I'd shoot her down like a dog."

He made a vulgar gesture of bravado and arrogance.

"Don't!" she said. And she meant, don't go on showing yourself to me like this. I know you half enjoy it. It's a perverse kind of intimacy. It's like some of those things we never talk about. You must love me anyway, you say. You must love me whether you want to or not.

He stood over her aggressively, but wanting already, now that he'd had his say, to change the direction, only not knowing how to do it. She saw this, too, but he was still ugly to her.

"So Rudi told you all this," she said. "How clever of Rudi to catch that woman in one of his traps!"

Suddenly she wanted to cry. "I hate your friend Rudi," she said. "He's vile. Everyone knows just what he is."

"Rudi — " he began, and words failed him. For a moment

he looked frightened himself. Then his voice suddenly became angry again, twice as angry because he had been ready to change.

"Rudi isn't my friend. And don't you suppose I know what he is, as well as you do? I've known him since he was a boy, but I don't like him either. I have to see him occasionally, that's all."

He shouted at her as though he were trying to make a foreigner or an idiot understand him.

"Rudi has nothing to do with it!"

She said, "You're giving me such a fearful headache. I wish I hadn't spoken of her."

"I wish you hadn't either," he shouted, "but since you have, there is your story."

He turned away from her and walked up and down again. His fury showed in his walk, which was too deliberately steady, as though he'd been drinking.

He'll be sick, she thought. This is dangerous for him. But presently he controlled himself. He came back and said more calmly, "And another thing. I must ask you not to mention any of this to anyone. The less said of these things the better. We are acting entirely within our rights but no one on the outside is ever willing to understand, and Rudi tells me that already in some way he hasn't been able to trace, news of this has leaked out. Just yesterday he received a visit from the woman's son. Yes, her son had somehow heard of it and come here to see what he could do."

She put her hands over her eyes and traced the lines of her eyebrows back and forth.

"And can he do anything?" she asked. She was afraid that even through her closed eyes he would see an image of the dark, tormented young man and pluck him out and hold him to the light.

"No, he can't do anything," he said, "except perhaps get in trouble himself, if he isn't careful."

"In trouble?" I was cruel to him, she thought, as ugly to him as Kurt is to me. I wish I could see him again and make it up to him.

Suddenly she cried out hysterically, "Why do you have to execute a woman for that? I think it's beastly. It's stupid. She shouldn't have more than a prison sentence. And you shouldn't defend them for it. You're getting just like them, and sometimes I hate you for it. Sometimes I can't stand even to look at you. I live in a continuous fear for you and for me. You're making us both like that, and I can't stand it, I tell you. I can't stand it."

She dropped her head into her hands and gave a sob, half of fear, half of exhaustion.

They were both exhausted. He looked at her gloomily, feeling like herself suddenly slack and wasted. His anger was all gone.

"Ruby," he said, "control yourself. You'll wake up the house."

He sat down beside her.

"Control yourself," he repeated. "These things have nothing to do with you. I shouldn't have told you if I'd known you'd take it like this. Now forget it at once. And be calm."

She pushed the book to the floor with her knee. It lay there in the fold of the fur rug. She wanted to forget it, to wail it all out in one orgy of pity — pity for him and for herself.

"Oh, don't let's talk about it any more," she said. "Leo's suicide has upset me terribly. I haven't felt well ever since. I can't forget it. I wish I'd never known of it. There is no use my knowing all these things. I wish neither of us knew. I wish we could go away somewhere for a while. I feel so ill and nervous here all the time. It's not like it used to be."

He took her hands gently down from her face and held them in his.

"Poor little Ruby," he said, "poor little goose. How hard it is for you to understand. This is justice, Ruby, and women never understand justice. It's a natural law, as exact as the laws that govern the symmetry of crystals. Don't bother your pretty head about it. Let me attend to it."

She looked at him dully. She hadn't been able even to cry. She felt only cold and sad and full of confusion. It would be better not to think, and then to go to sleep.

With one hand he took her belt and twisted it, tightening it around her thin waist.

"You're such a little goose," he said, his voice tired and heavy, "but I'll explain to you once more. In crystals the law has no consciousness, but the human creature's consciousness breeds forces destructive to himself and his law. His little knowledge, his little thinking machine, his soft, sentimental heart, these distort and interfere with the law. Justice is the re-discovery of that law. Do you see?"

In spite of his words, he was breathing heavily as a man in love.

"Yes, yes," she murmured, "I see what you mean."

The red cord bit into her thin bones, then suddenly he released it and took her shoulders and put his face against her neck.

"Oh, Ruby," he whispered, "don't try to think at all. Let me think for us both. Don't you see what you're trying to do? You're spoiling our hope."

She turned her face away from him but he flung himself beside her and put his arms around her, and all through him she felt the dangerous, quick pounding of his blood.

"These things *are* terrible," he said. "Don't you think I know that? But we've lived through much worse, you and I. Oh, you must remember how much worse it all was. And

[123]

now there's hope for us. Everything is coming out all right. We're back in the rightful place that God gave us. People wanted to drag us down, but we didn't let them."

His voice shook. "God! What we've lived through! Don't spoil our hope, Ruby, yours and mine. Don't spoil it even in your secret heart."

She didn't answer, thinking only of darkness and of silence, trying to hurry them on, to draw them over like a cover.

He said nothing more. After a moment she reached up and put out the light. Gradually his blood grew slower and he lay quite still and she would have thought he was asleep but for the slow drain of tears that ran down her neck and lay in the hollow of her shoulder.

Chapter IX

AT six in the evening when Hermann brought her
Emmy said, "What day is it today?"

"It's Friday."

"Do you know what day it's to be?" Emmy asked.

Hermann answered importantly, "I heard him say ne:
Wednesday. We have to have you up and walking by nex
Wednesday."

All night she lay thinking, So it's Wednesday — Wednesday — If it's Friday now, I have four days.

Now Friday must be gone. Now it must be Saturday, and
that makes only three days. What will I do with three days?
If they let me go out and do what I wanted, what would I
do with three days?

Before daybreak rain began to fall outside and she heard
the bugles, muffled by the sound of it, and presently the
roll call from somewhere inside the barracks, sharp name
and answer.

"Emmy Ritter — Here. Emmy Ritter — Here," she said to
herself at each call.

Now it's really Saturday. What'll I do today? I won't lie
here all day and wait. I'll get up and walk. I'll talk to people.

When her thin coffee and bread came she could barely
choke them down. She couldn't talk to Anna, who seemed
to feel a little better today and would have liked to talk to

her. She lay listening to the cars coming and going. To the rain.

She tried to spend the time left her in thinking of what had been most real, her children, her work on the stage, her people for whom she had sacrificed so much. These, she wanted to say, are my life, and because of them and the flesh and blood and energy and hope I've put into them my life is a continuous thing.

But all her consolations broke and became distorted and monstrous. What had been her work on the stage but a trivial, ephemeral gloss, a mimicry of life, falsified always by the restraints of comedy? And these people here? Weren't they only a sort of group image, made up of idealized memories and associations? Under the image was an entirely different reality, gross, cowardly, unthinking and neurotically vain. As for Mark and Sabina, how real were their brightness and beauty and promise? Her agony at leaving them alone was itself a revelation of how much they were a creation of her love.

Oh, to have things simple and unchangeable just this once! To be released from this pitiful struggle to reconcile and to give form and value. To be released from the effort to preserve that which was never meant for anything but a vast, ever-mounting refuse heap, the great, invisible midden of the race of man.

Truly it was better to die and be over with it. She forced herself into premonitory lapses of consciousness that seemed long, but when she opened her eyes again a drop of rain on the window pane had not even moved.

At mid-morning she said suddenly, "I'm going to get up."

"You'd better wait," Anna said, "till Hermann comes, or the doctor."

"Nonsense," Emmy said, "I'll do better alone." She turned over and put her long legs down to the floor.

[126]

Anna watched her. Her feet were very beautiful, with an arch between the heel and ball and the toes perfectly shaped and curved. Emmy looked at them a moment and a faint look of vanity passed over her face. Her feet at least hadn't changed. Strange, too, since they had been given little rest in her life.

She stood up on them. The floor was icy and she felt sickening tingles spreading from the soles up through her body. She had to sit down again at once.

"How do you feel?" Anna asked.

She hadn't even strength to answer. She sat holding her head. Then the faintness passed a little and she tried again. Without waiting to stand she made a few lurching steps across to Anna's bed and sat on it.

For the first time her face and Anna's were close. They looked at each other and Anna reached out and took her hand. It was the first time they had ever touched each other. Emmy's hands were cold and Anna's dry and hot. Everything about Anna was smaller than she had realized, but her colorless eyelashes were longer. There were one or two freckles left under her eyes. Anna had been exposed to the sun and wind and rain and to the voices of people and had tried on hats before a glass and been made love to. Only the freckles remained to tell of it.

"You have a very fair skin," Emmy said.

"And you have nice feet," Anna answered politely.

She herself was a little afraid of Emmy, seeing her so close, afraid because she seemed so much more alive and at the same time so much more haggard and ravaged by life. Her eyes were large and their look was very strong and her skin was coarse, the hair at the nape of her neck and her eyelashes sprang out like wires, and under her deeply curving, bluish mouth Anna could see the modeling of her teeth and jaws. But she didn't see how anyone had ever

[127]

thought Emmy really beautiful, except perhaps at a distance.

"It's our day for vanity," Emmy said. She was breathing hard after her effort. "They don't exactly encourage us in it, do they?"

She looked at Anna's nightgown. Her own was like it but it was the first time she had noticed them. They were of gray flannel-like material with a number on the collar. Anna's number was thirty-five, Emmy's was eighty-six. They had been boiled out so many times that they had a peculiar smell and the nap was worn to a thread. Down the front of Anna's gown ran a long tear, and the gown was too big for her. Emmy's was too small.

Anna put her finger in the tear. "I ought to mend it," she said. "If I had needle and thread I would. This gown is humiliating. It's because it's torn."

"No, it's because it doesn't fit," Emmy said. "Because when they put it on they took no account of different sizes and so of different selves. That's what is humiliating."

"Still, I'd like a needle and thread."

"You're a neat woman, Anna. Do you sew well? Can you make clothes?"

"No, not clothes, but I can sew all right. Back of our shop was our sitting room, and it was full of doilies and covers for chair backs and tables. I embroidered every one of them."

Emmy made a little sound of admiration. "They must have been pretty," she said.

Anna said dreamily, "I always wanted silk curtains for the sitting room. You know — I mean with ruffles and tied back, like that."

"Yes, I know. Still, muslin curtains are nice. They can be laundered and they always look fresh."

"But silk looks more expensive. I got some silk, finally. I

made it up into curtains myself, and even made valences for the top. But the day I was going to hang them — " Her mouth trembled suddenly. "Oh, I wish everything could have been different!" she said.

Emmy said nothing but gave her hand a little squeeze. Your curtains, she thought; yes, you'd like to have them unchanging too. Immortal silk curtains, hanging in a parlor where no Secret Police could come.

"If Hermann finds you here," Anna said, "she'll be furious. There's no use making her furious."

Emmy nodded. She didn't see how she'd ever be able to get back to her own bed. She was so much weaker than she'd thought she'd be. And presently the doctor and Hermann would come. It would be better to get back and pretend to be asleep before they came. Because something was loose in her today, some distorted, ugly, despairing thing and she'd never be able to stand the sight of them.

Especially of him, with his medical questions and probings and only his wrists to show any sensibility. He was like some ridiculous marine creature, with all of its life in one unfamiliar organ.

She got up slowly and held onto the wall and took a few steps. She forced herself to walk. She reached her bed and walked all the way around it and got in on the other side. She lay there without strength to pull the cover up, her feet dangling over the edge, trembling with cold and fear.

"Here they come," Anna said in a frightened voice.

They heard the young doctor and Hermann coming down the hall for the morning visit.

When they reached the door Hermann saw at once something was wrong. "What does this mean?" she cried. She came and pulled the cover over Emmy. "Do you want to get pneumonia?" she asked.

Emmy laughed derisively. "Why not? I've been walking.

I walked all around the room. I nearly walked through the door and out."

"Who gave you permission to walk?" Hermann said.

"I'm rehearsing."

The doctor stood just inside the door holding his black bag. He looked at Emmy with his piercing, blue eyes and shook his head disapprovingly.

"You don't like to hear me say that," Emmy said, looking over at him. "Why not? I'm rehearsing — I have to know what kind of a spectacle I'll make."

"Stop talking," Hermann said. She seized Emmy's wrists and held them tight.

"Will the spectators cry, or will they only yawn and say, 'By God, the day we beat the rabbi to death was more fun'?"

"I'll have to give you a hypodermic," the doctor said. "You're exciting yourself, you'll bring your temperature up."

Emmy twisted in Hermann's grip.

"Make her get out," she said. "I don't like her. And get out yourself. I don't like you either."

Hermann gave her a sharp blow on the side of her face. Emmy fell back. The doctor came and stood by the bed and looked across at Hermann.

"You'd better go now. I can handle her."

Hermann let go of Emmy and straightened up. She pulled her skirt into place and stared at him, her face red and indignant.

"I didn't hear you, doctor," she said.

"I said you can go."

Hermann clicked her tongue twice. She walked over to Anna and jerked the covers straight on her bed; Anna lay as still as a mouse. Then she stumped out and they heard her muttering to herself as she went down the hall.

The doctor looked speculatively at Emmy.

"Thanks," she said slowly.

"Doctor," Anna called, "I still have that bad pain here."

He took out his stethoscope and went to Anna's bed, leaned over and listened perfunctorily to her breathing, tapped her here and there. Then he came back and stood looking down at Emmy again.

"Do you feel more quiet?"

She was still breathing excitedly.

"I don't need any hypodermics, if that's what you mean."

"You must try not to give way like that," he said. "You see, if you let yourself give way, when I'm not here, you'll be hurt needlessly. There is nothing you can accomplish by this sort of thing. And you will surely want to be brave."

She stared at him, trying to bring her breathing and pulse to normal.

"Brave?" she repeated ironically.

He leaned toward her and said in a low voice, "I'll make it easy for you. But you must help yourself."

"I'll be as brave as I can," she said slowly. He has a right to tell me to be brave, she thought. Whatever brought him here, it wasn't fear. That's more than I can say for most of them.

She heard Anna coughing nervously, muffling her mouth with her hand, her preliminary cough which would presently grow much worse. In a moment she would be fumbling helplessly for her little carton. The doctor would go away, though it almost seemed that he wanted to say something positive that would quiet and silence her for good. But it was a foolish risk. Talking to prisoners was forbidden. And he had defended her too. Hermann would tell on him to curry favor for herself. She'd accuse him of sympathy with prisoners. Just because he was a gentleman and his uncle was an important person, he was too good for the likes of Hermann. He was well-born and proud and stiff-necked and he liked to show it.

Oh, I know his type, too, Emmy thought. I've seen others like him, his face, his bearing, his accent. That petty nobility of the north, she thought, with its mixture of boorishness and a sort of animal breeding, and what is called solid worth. How we used to laugh at them down here in the urban south, in mother's drawing room, for instance.

"Why don't you go?" she said bitterly. "You're only going to get into trouble. You can't talk to me, you know. And don't try to defend me. I have no rights and I don't think you have many yourself."

He sat down on the edge of the bed. "It used to be believed," he said solemnly, "that rights were an indisputable attribute of the individual. But that was in a much simpler day."

Emmy stared at him. This was the tone of a conversation beginning, of a prelude, and it struck her as fantastically comic. She began to smile.

"Wasn't it a better day?" she said.

"I'm not sure. It was a day certainly when we followed a line spontaneous to our genius."

"Oh, our genius," she repeated, struggling with a hysterical desire to laugh. "Our racial genius! What a pity we couldn't keep it pure always."

"To keep it pure would be to keep it immature, and that in the end is idiocy, or a form of corruption," he said. "Yes, I regret it, but that's what it became in the end."

Emmy laughed and her laugh had a hysterical lilt. But she stopped it by a great effort, holding a bit of her sheet across her mouth. Now she didn't want him to go. She wanted to cling to him, because he had suddenly provided a distraction, pungently unexpected. And he had no intention of going. He expected to stay until he had said what he wanted to say. He didn't know, however, how to get around to it.

He said, "And things went from bad to worse. Our history has been one long degeneration. Up to today."

He looked at her tentatively, expecting her to lead him to the point he wanted.

"So we're one long degeneration from our tribal purity, or our feudal purity — Is that it?"

He nodded.

"And you are saving us? How?"

"By restoring the rights that are above and beyond those of the individual. The rights of the State."

"And does the State have an existence apart from the individual?"

"Certainly."

"It seems silly to me. I've always thought the State, in that sense, was just a thing we created in our imaginations and gave an arbitrary meaning to — like, say, the equator." He shook his head, as much as to say, It's useless to talk of these things with a woman.

"It's quite customary, you know," she said, "to dislike what your parents made for you. They ought to have done better by you, and our parents ought to have done better by us, and so ought Frederick and Charlemagne and the Council of Nicaea and the man who invented the wheel, and so on and so on."

She turned on her side and put her hand under her cheek.

"Just imagine a time when all the young men will say, 'Thank you for the world you've made for us. Thank you.' Now the buildings rise forty, fifty stories, and to the very top of them water comes from a lake a hundred miles away. And I can turn a button and hear a voice in San Francisco. They're making a telescope that will bring the

[133]

moon within twenty-five miles of our eyes. We know now all the best ways of disposing of human excrement. Suppose you were telling all that to the Neanderthals! But still, these aren't all our rights, and when I say all this I'm only talking like Jehovah: to Job's perfectly justifiable questions he replied, 'Can you make the whirlwind, can you make even a good whale?' "

A reluctant smile touched the doctor's lips, which were full but because of their severity seemed always to be thin.

"I never imagined you would be as you are," he said.

"What's that?" She looked at him surprised.

"Oh, yes. I had an image of you, like the equator. But mine was a tangible one — a photograph."

"A photograph!"

She thought: One of those dreadful postcards they used to sell. That's slender rations. She looked at him curiously. It occurred to her that he had lived all his life on slender rations. He had, she thought suddenly, a solitary face. Its edges were sharp, as though they hadn't been worn down by the constant pushing and rubbing of other personalities. But what was he about to tell her? She shrank away from it.

"I want to tell you about something," he said. "It's been on my mind for a long time. And I've never tried to speak of it to anyone else." He thought for a moment and went on. "You were really the only person to whom I could ever speak of it."

"I think I'd rather not hear," she said abruptly.

She was partly afraid that she would discover some good in him, and to discover some good in him would be worse than to discover none at all. If there was one spark of good in him he should be somewhere else. That was why his wrists, with their shape of kindness, disturbed her so. But to deny him the human right to talk to her would be cruel, and Emmy could never be cruel.

"Well, what is it?" she said.

"Long before you came here," he said, "I knew all about you. That's why it was a great shock to me to find you here. That's why when you were so sick I persuaded my uncle, who is an important person, to let me operate."

"That was for the practice," she said. "It was because I was an interesting case."

"It was partly that," he said.

"I heard you say so," she insisted. "You said you were rotting with idleness. You enjoyed every moment of it, didn't you? I remember the tone of your voice, talking about saline washes and draining wounds and clear soup. Oh, you enjoyed it all right."

"Perhaps I did. But just the same, it was a shock to me to see your name there on a card over your bed, and to know that it was Emmy Ritter whom I was about to save, and still not save at all."

"Then why did you do it?"

"I'm trying to tell you that," he said, "I'm trying to tell you that I knew of you first when I was a small boy, and that for a long time I kept a photograph of you. And that photograph meant a very curious thing to me."

"Ah, so? Well, I can imagine it."

"I lived in the country," he said, "as a child, until sometime after the war. I never saw a theater or went anywhere. But my father, when he was younger, used to go up to town a great deal, and he was very devoted to the theater. He was the kind of man who saved photographs and newspaper clippings and old programs, I suppose to remind him of the gay times he'd had. He had several photographs of you. I believe he admired you very much. One of them I took one day and kept."

"That's not as curious as you think," she said. She felt a small disappointment. A good deal of courage to say, in the end, so little. . . . "Many young boys have been in love with me," she said. "And many old boys, too."

"But I wasn't in love with you." He spoke quickly and earnestly. "It wasn't nearly as simple as that. If it had been only that, you could laugh at me for telling it."

"Perhaps I'll laugh anyway."

"Laugh if you want," he said; "but still I'm going to tell you. About the photograph and why I kept it."

Again his face had a sharp, lonely look and she saw he persisted in a brazen innocence of what his listener would be thinking of him.

"In this photograph," he said, "you were dressed as a queen, as Elisabeth of Hungary, carrying in a basket the loaves of bread that turned into roses."

"Oh!" she said, "I remember that. It was for a charity, the famous one the Grand Duke gave. I had a wonderful dress. Worth made it for me."

"I used to keep the photograph in a bureau drawer," he said, "along with some other things I valued."

"I'm sure you did. Along with a prize won for jumping and two dirty French novels."

Anna thought, Why does she go on saying the wrong thing? He is being very kind. It's so very kind, so gracious of him to talk to her at all. She's sneering at him. That's wrong, especially, Anna thought acutely, as she is moved by this. In her nervousness at such female ineptitude she let her cough ring out spasmodically. They waited till it passed.

Then Emmy said, "And you want to tell me that as a little boy you thought I was a queen, but now you find I am a disreputable woman who had a gangrenous appendix and committed treason for the sake of a few dollars."

"I am speaking still of the photograph," he said. "You yourself say you were a woman with whom young men and old men fell in love, but what you really were, or still less what you are today, has nothing to do with it. I am speaking now of Elisabeth of Hungary, the queen who lived in my bureau drawer, and of myself as I was then, not as I am now. You raise your eyebrows. But you're not going to question that a boy may think extravagant things, and romantic things?"

Emmy said, "I don't doubt it at all. I have a son, you know. I don't even doubt that the doctor of a political prison was once tender and malleable and romantic. What I wonder at is that he entirely stopped being so. What happened to him? How did he get here?"

The doctor sat with his arms folded on his chest, his small, blue eyes steady and fixed on her. She could see in the sharp bones of his face, his high bony shoulders, his delicate wrists, the unchanging structure of the urchin who had shyly but solemnly hidden the photograph.

And suddenly there flared up in her, without warning, a wild hope. What if he hadn't changed? What if he had built about her a dream strong enough to live a lifetime? What if he was here against his will? A prisoner, as she was. If he wanted to help her. . . . These things blazed in her as one flame. *Perhaps he'll get me out.*

She was afraid he would see it in her too mobile face. She shifted and lay on her other side, her head turned half toward him, looking at the ceiling.

"Well," she said in a stilted voice, "what did the queen do for you, little boy? Did she bring you bread or roses?"

"I'm going to tell you," he said. "I was the youngest of our family. The other boys had gone away. My mother was dead and I was alone with my father. I had very few playmates there in the country."

Yes, she thought, I guessed that.

"And I used to use my imagination a great deal, certainly more than was healthy. But I used it, instinctively, to make myself a conception of what the world — when I got into it — would be like. I can't tell you how the photograph became a focus, but a lot of things too diffuse to talk about led me to it. I used to lie each night and imagine myself to be one of the poor, in some great city of the poor and miserable. This was a natural picture to make at that time. All was starvation and wretchedness around me. And in this world, half dream and half real, I used to lie and think: She will come today. She did come, and then everything was changed, the suffering, the starvation, vanished, the poor were fed, the unhappy received roses. But then I'd think: What if she doesn't come, what if she forgets or goes by another way, or even something she can't help prevents her? What then? What can we do then? Must we endure this misery, with no hope but her caprice, or even her goodness which isn't, maybe, strong enough?"

"But it wasn't I who brought you a knowledge of human misery," Emmy said.

"Yes," he answered, "you did, because misery to children is never really misery at all. And the reasons for that are that the young don't remember from day to day, and also that they carry in them a certainty that misery is temporary. And even more than that, they carry a certainty that the ultimate structure of life is good, and that they're irrevocably included in its goodness. In this goodness there may be temporary annoyances but there must be no accidents.

"Well, partly because I was beginning to see that this wasn't so, partly because the allegory of the queen helped me to see it, it happened you became my first, awful knowledge of the uncertainty of life. Through you I saw that the heavenly grace was all a chance. I might have bread or roses, or I might be left blind and empty."

"You put me in the place of God," said Emmy, "though I never asked you to do it. And because of that I represent all your disappointments. But you'd have had them anyway, because one way or another you expected too much."

"It's true it was a silly allegory," he said, "but just the same, in a way you're responsible for it. In a way it's your legacy to us. It's part of that long degeneration where the idea of the value of the individual ran riot, bloomed into a sort of decay. The heavenly grace will come, you said to us. You're a man, aren't you? Wait for it. Or snatch it, if necessary. And if it comes to you, let the rest starve. The value of the individual usually means in the end the value only of your precious self. So the queen was a criminal in a criminal world."

It was impossible for her to answer. She was humbled now, because, as women are so apt to do, she had let a purely romantic possibility carry her away. It was shameful how quickly she had seized on the picture of the doctor as a shy, adoring child who had never grown up. If she hadn't wanted to believe good of him, a man in this degraded position, it was perhaps partly because she was always prone to believe too easily and too much. And it was always easier to believe in all goodness than in a spark of it hidden in an incongruous place. For a moment it had been sweet to see him, not just as the man with gentle wrists, but as a young archangel come to set her free. Queen and archangel, she thought. We're both alike. We're both meant to be perpetually duped. Like all our race, we can live a whole life in a violent rhythm of energy and dreaming and never a time for thought.

"Why was she a criminal?" she said sadly. "Only because after all she was impotent? And you hadn't the power to make her otherwise? But I don't care how many pictures of actresses you kept in a bureau drawer, because you are simply a young man who has to keep a picture in a bureau drawer. You've got one there right now, as a matter of fact, a new one, I'm sure of it. A new savior of the world, a new bringer of the heavenly grace. If I say it myself, it's a less plausible one and a damned sight less engaging. But still it's the picture of your day. And mine, as you said, was the picture of my day."

"You're right," he said. "Power is necessary. Rights imply power to enforce them. And the State now has power to do that. Instead of gracious and irresponsible ladies with their baskets, we have a machine turning out so many loaves a day, so many for so many, always enough. That's our daily bread."

"You make me cry with pity for you," Emmy said angrily. "First you drug yourself with one kind of mysticism — queens and roses — then you grasp at another. And every day you go on maiming yourself further for that State of yours. Do you know what you remind me of? Of the priests of Attis, or of the boys who were emasculated in order to sing soprano in the Pope's choir."

"Oh, Emmy," whispered Anna, "don't say such things." She lay on her side looking at them. I can see, she thought, how Emmy got here.

The doctor sat with his hands slipping between his knees, his eyes fixed on Emmy in a deep, penetrating thoughtfulness.

"In another age," the doctor said to Emmy, "you might have had your rights inherent in yourself, in your personal qualities, which I know are extraordinary. I want you to know I recognize that. But I don't think, in the world we're making, you have any."

"Neither did the judges," said Emmy. "So that seems to be settled."

She closed her eyes, exhausted. A vague, intimate bitterness and disappointment washed back and forth between them. He went on looking at her as though he expected her to say more, and she felt it and wanted to say more. But no words came.

Anna thought she recognized their silence. It was the hopeless, prison lag that came so often between her and Emmy, the uselessness of talking, when talking is all you can do, and action isn't even to be thought of.

The doctor had forgotten that Anna was there. As though he were alone in the room, he looked at Emmy's closed eyes. His attention changed and became a rigid, painful contradiction of impulse. Anna watched his face, astonished.

Suddenly he got up and went to the door, where he had left his little bag on the floor. He opened it and looked in.

Then he changed his mind again. He closed his bag, turned around, and his face was as usual. He stood feeling in his pockets, feeling for something.

"I have been wondering," he said, in a dry voice, "if you would like to send some communication to your family, your son for instance. You spoke just now of a son. Perhaps you'd like to write him."

Emmy's eyes opened. They were questioning but suddenly they softened. She could hardly believe she had heard the words.

"What do you mean?"

"I mean you might like to write a note."

"But it's forbidden."

"Certainly it's forbidden. Still, I'm asking you if you'd like to write a note. I would see that it's delivered."

He stood by the door, feeling in his pockets, his eyes fixed on the wall.

"Of course," he said, "I would only send this note afterward."

"Naturally." She searched his face to be sure he meant it. "But of course I want to," she said.

"I have paper and pencil," he said.

He brought out a small pad and a pencil. He came and handed them to her and propped her up in bed against the small hard pillow. He saw that at first she did not know what to say and her face was distracted with anguish. Then she began and while she wrote he went over to the window and looked out. The rain had stopped. He put his hands in his pockets and whistled almost soundlessly. The scraping of the pencil sounded very loud in the room. It took her a long time to write the note.

"Here it is," she said. She folded it like an envelope and wrote Mark's name and address.

He came over and took the paper from her and put it in his pocket. Then he took the pencil and pad and put them in too. He handled them deliberately and slowly with his clean, bony fingers. Then with a little nod he went over to the door. He turned there to say something else.

He saw Emmy still sitting with her knees hunched up, her elbows resting on them and her face in her hands. There were heavy tears streaming down through her fingers.

He didn't say what he intended but went hurriedly out.

Chapter X

Mark went back to the Four Seasons and spent the night. The next morning was Saturday. He had his coffee upstairs and when the maid came with it he asked her if she knew of a cheaper place to live. He had begun to be frightened by the spending of so much money. At first twenty thousand dollars had seemed a fortune, a great, solid, massive, unchanging thing. Money, just acquired, always seems like that, as he knew. But the first check drawn on it demonstrates its mutability, and far from being solid it is so fragile you scarcely dare breathe on it. There is an ugly, puckish magic about it. How well he remembered those times when suddenly, in the midst of security, there was no more money and no one could tell how or where it had vanished.

The maid said she had a friend whose sister-in-law kept a pension in a flat over a watch store in Theater Street. But looking at the young man standing by the window, at his shining, black hair and brownish pallor, his worn silk pajamas and the cigarette in his fingers, something about him made her add that it was a very small pension, not elegant in any way, and not patronized by foreigners. Perhaps it wasn't good enough for him. Mark got the address from her and wrote it down.

After breakfast he left, but just as he left he thought of something else. The concierge asked him if he wished to leave a forwarding address, and he suddenly thought that

Henning might wish to get in touch with him. Or even that other fellow. Though there had been at the time such finality about each of these interviews, they didn't seem, two days later, quite so final, and in any case he couldn't afford to leave a possible bolted door behind him. And besides, though he pretended he had given up hope of Fritz, because Fritz after all was a coward, an old man, nursing perhaps a long grudge against them, still, there was Fritz, and he remained an unknown quantity. He wrote out the address of the pension and left it, together with a good-sized tip, with the concierge.

He found the flat on Theater Street. The entrance was on a side street through a dark hall where he took an automatic lift to the floor above. To use the lift cost the equivalent of five cents. The sister-in-law of the friend of the maid was a woman with an immense bust and a reddish wig. She was very taciturn. She took his passport in silence and showed him into a room with red wall paper and a trellis of black poppies. The bed was as usual immense, it was "modern art," with great satin quilts, and an unshaded bulb hanging directly over it. On the table in the center of the room was a white china group representing a warrior in bearskin and horned helmet taking leave of a woman. On the wall hung a calendar showing the head of a young man in a military cap between the cringing, horrible faces of a Jew and a Jesuit. The Jew was clutching a bag of money, the Jesuit had undoubtedly just said the words: "The end justifies the means." As to the young man, there was no doubt about him either. He was at once so stern and so pure that one would imagine any onlooker's first impulse would be to kick him in the backside. The artist, perhaps anticipating this, had cut him off at the waist.

Mark gazed around at these objects of art and culture

while the landlady stood just inside the door watching him. Then he went to the window, which he saw opened onto the bustle of Theater Street. A light rain which had fallen all morning was clearing up.

He said the room would do and told her that he would only be wanting his breakfast here. She replied that he would have to pay for at least two meals a day in the pension. He agreed to that. He felt extraordinarily tired.

It was nearly noon and he knew that any place he might wish to go would be closed on Saturday afternoon. But where could he wish to go? Not so soon again to Henning's, not to a museum or a palace or a movie. He lay down on the bed and fell into a half-sleep of exhaustion and discouragement. He didn't leave the pension all day.

On Sunday morning he woke feeling so lifeless and oppressed that he couldn't make up his mind to get up. A few people moved about in the hall outside, but Theater Street, below his windows, being a street of shops, had become suddenly quiet. Another day when he could accomplish nothing. . . . He rang for his coffee, and when it came it was excellent; but it didn't put any life into him. He could not face even opening the door of his room. He knew, from the day he had passed here, that every time he opened his door a door across from him opened, and the landlady with the immense bust and the reddish wig came out and stared at him across the dim hall. And there were always people waiting to get into the one bathroom and toilet.

If he were to get as far as the street, what then? He might go to Henning's, or he might try to find another lawyer, or even, the thought suddenly struck him, he might take the train back to the country to have tea with the Countess. She had asked him to come and she might easily know people who would be able to help him.

But the Countess had not really been cordial and she wouldn't want to see him. If for no other reason because he would be the petitioner, the man who, even if he left the words unspoken, was still saying incessantly within himself, "I've come to save her. I've come to save Emmy Ritter. You must do something for me." These words, spoken or unspoken, would create at once an isolation. Any single purpose bores people, but the petitioner's single purpose worst of all. They at once take on a protective indifference, like a squid sending out ink. So long as he was forced to be persistent, so long would the peculiar loneliness surround him.

But so also he had no choice. He had to get up. He looked at his watch. Ten o'clock on a Sunday morning. I'll enjoy the bed one minute more, he thought, then I'll get up.

What a great, northern bed it was, deep with feathers, with a huge feather quilt with the sheet buttoned to it and pillows with starched ruffles round the edges. His mother was addicted to these great quilts and carried them everywhere with her.

The bed induced slackness and dreaming. Did anyone ever dream on a hard Mediterranean bed? But its real charm was that in it he was anonymous. He was not only safe but he was not dangerous, his individual self was muted in the general limbo of the half-awake. He was a man in bed; any man in any bed. To become Mark Preysing required a direct, personal test, even such a slight one as leaving a warm bed.

He took his bathrobe, towel and soap. In a widening of the hall outside his door the landlady with the big bust and the wig sat in a wicker chair, knitting a sweater. She looked up as he went by and stared at him as though to say, "You're late, and that's queer too." "*Bonjour, Madame Defarge,*" he said. She stared after him. The bath was occupied. He pounded on the door and presently an indignant fat man came out. He went in, washed out the grease ring from the tub, opened the window to let out the smell of eau de cologne, bathed and shaved.

When he went out he found it was a spring day. Here in town the snow had been gone for some time. The sun shone thinly but warmly from a milky blue sky. The streets had an empty, Sunday look. He walked along and came to the arch where the bookshops were, hundreds of clean, neat books, most of them on art, beautifully printed, and got out. He passed into Salvator, that gay little street of rococo houses, and at the end of it saw over rooftops the ugly domed towers of the Lady Church. He walked toward it. When he got to the square he heard a sound of dying organ music inside. There were a hundred or so people around the door. He joined them, wondering idly for whom they could be waiting. He could tell by the confused murmur that the cathedral was packed, and this surprised him because of what he knew of the persecution of the church. Could they actually be waiting for some priest?

He found out almost at once. A big, shining, black limousine drew up to the door, and at the same time the organ inside broke into a clamorous sound and a great wave of voices joined it. The cardinal accompanied by his priests and a press of people, some of them carrying dry palm branches, came to the door in a sudden burst of red. He was all in crimson, hat, shoes, gloves, his train behind him of burning red *moiré*, ready it seemed to burst into blue flame. His face had an ancient, peeled look, all the veins marbled in it like an *écorché*, his nose was high, his eyebrows like black wings. Very quickly he gave his blessing, touching children's heads, holding his amethyst ring to a woman who flung herself forward to kiss it. The clamor around him broke into a great, hoarse shout. The

[147]

cardinal did not smile, he looked directly at no one. His eyes were fierce, intelligent, icy, and remote.

As he got in the car hands stretched out and the crowd swayed and bent toward him and even Mark caught a shudder from the emotion around him. A man next to him suddenly shouted, "It's a disgrace! It's a shame! He ought to be made to keep his dirty mouth shut." A woman caught at his arm. "Hush, oh hush!" she said. But he went on, though he was obviously embarrassed and not particularly fluent: "Who does he think he is, criticizing our Leader? I can't do it, you can't do it. Why does he think he can? Well, the Leader won't stand it much longer, I tell you. He'll know what to do about it. He'll know how to shut his dirty mouth." The people near him looked at him dully and said nothing. The limousine of the cardinal vanished with an air of elegance and haste down the narrow street.

Mark stood to one side to watch the crowd come out. He heard a sparrow-like chirp of English and suddenly he saw the Mink Coat. She was with a flock of girls and he looked around for the Countess. She couldn't be far away. She's in town too, he thought with chagrin, remembering her invitation for tea in the country. Presently he saw her, elbowed along in the crowd, talking to a woman beside her. She wore the worn sealskin coat and the little sealskin cap on her ash-blond hair. Her long, dark eyes had their swan look. The damned bird woman, he thought, how I hate her. He drew back so she wouldn't see him. Outside, her group of girls were waiting for her and she walked off with them down the little street, without sidewalks, where the cardinal had vanished. Mark, from idleness and some curiosity, followed them at a slight distance. The smartly dressed girls, with their stiff thin legs, twitched from side to side of the street, looking in the shop windows and criticizing their contents. Suddenly the Mink Coat turned around and looked at him and said something to another girl. He turned off abruptly and went down more narrow ways till he came again to Theater Street. Here he walked along as far as the Palace garden, where he decided to sit down at one of the tables in the sun and have a beer.

He had no sooner ordered than he heard the sparrow voices again and the Countess and her girls came walking across the crunching gravel and sat at two tables near by. They ordered coffee.

The air was warm from the sun but with an underlying chill. In the black, velvety ground crocus bloomed, and there were little clusters of snowdrops, immaculate greenish white with minute green spots. It was very pleasant here. He had no intention of running away because of the Countess.

She was much occupied anyway. A man and woman had stopped to speak to her, a handsome couple, well dressed and very blond. Even in side glances he saw they had the beauty of superlative things to eat, such beauty in fact, of such perfect succulence, that they had a sort of fleshly, rosy mystery about them. The man he instantly disliked. He was talking to the Countess with a gay, knowing air, as though he knew a good story about her or even as though he had something on her. Mark suddenly got the idea that she might have a lover and this man knew about it. Perhaps everyone knew about it. Perhaps she was even a Famous Case. Perhaps even his landlady would know, the concierge in the hotel. He had never lived in a close-knit city, or in any city but New York. He was accustomed to standing outside and guessing at things.

As he watched them the Countess suddenly looked across and their eyes met. A painful flicker, almost a look of horror, passed over her face. He was shocked that she should look like that on seeing him. Her dazzling friends noticed it and some of the girls, who began to whisper among themselves. The Countess smiled at once, a conventional smile, and murmured something, and Mark lifted himself a little from his chair and gravely raised his hat to her. He was furious that she had put on such a show. Now the blond young man was teasing her with a sly, gay, amorous smile, calling her, Mark could hear it, "Dear, lovely Ruby." He looked, Mark thought, half Nordic Don Juan, half suckling pig. He turned around in his chair so as not to face them and stolidly drank his beer.

He heard the beautiful couple leave with many endearments. "It is a pity, darling," the woman said, "that you can't come. It would be wonderful." Mark didn't turn and he refused to be forced away. The sun was gradually warming him and the gardens gave out a rich, cool smell. Along the yellow walls of the Residence the formal lines of trees receded in a sunny haze. Everything, even to the trees, was in order, and to one fresh from New York soothingly horizontal. If New York had grown in a series of irregular, volcanic impulses out of the immediate rock, this place had certainly been planned slowly, from the grass roots up, by men sitting at leisure around a table.

He was paying for his beer when he heard them scraping their little iron chairs back on the gravel. Their shadows moved across him, each girl looking as she passed, and lastly the Countess' shadow fell on him.

"Mr. Preysing," she said.

He stood up and saw she was looking at him apologetically. Her voice was uncertain and there was timidity in the way she held out her hand to him. "Isn't it a lovely morning?" she said.

"Lovely," he agreed without smiling.

In the sunlight the Countess' skin looked very white and transparent, he could see blue veins laced along her temple and a blue vein made a faint shadow under one eye. While she certainly did not look young, neither did she look faded or worn. She looked as if, rather than growing older, she had been growing more and more fragile, till she was like a piece of Venetian glass where the fascination is in the tenuous, almost momentary form that holds the space.

"You came back to town sooner than you expected," she said.

"So did you," he reminded her.

"Oh, that was a mistake," she said. "When I asked you for tea I had forgotten I was coming back yesterday."

He bowed his head slightly to show her that he accepted her explanation through indifference. She looked down at the ground and opened her lips to say something but gave it up with a little embarrassed smile. "Shall we walk a little?" she said.

He moved beside her and they dropped behind the girls, who did not like to be left and who themselves lagged as much as they could.

Suddenly he said, "Why did you look at me with such horror just now?"

"Horror? Oh, surely you're mistaken."

"But I'm not. Even your handsome friends noticed it."

"They notice everything," she said, "even what isn't really there. I may have felt a little faint or ill for a moment, that's all. I am glad to see you again. It was just feather-headedness that made me forget I wouldn't be in the country yesterday. You, too, didn't tell me you were coming back. Let's both forgive each other, shall we?"

"If you wish."

She spoke with such real kindness he felt stiff and foolish.

"I really wanted very much to talk to you again," she said. "I'm terribly shy, you know, and sometimes it makes me say the wrong things. Sometimes I only say what I really mean afterward and to myself. Isn't that stupid of me?"

Mark was bewildered. He hadn't really expected ever to see her again. Suddenly here he was walking beside her. And she seemed quite different, no longer the image that retreated and dissolved but gracious and lovely, and if not actually familiar, certainly tangible.

"So I want you to come and see me this afternoon," she said, "will you? Then I'll know you've forgiven me."

"Of course I'll come. You're very kind to ask me. After all," he said, "perhaps you are taking a chance." He couldn't quite forget that first look. "You don't really know anything about me."

"And you don't know anything about me," she said. "We may both be secret criminals." She smiled and the whole character of her face changed. If he hadn't believed it to be impossible, he would have thought she looked at him anxiously and tenderly.

The girls couldn't stand it any longer. The Mink Coat and another girl fell into step with them.

"What's this about criminals?" said the Mink Coat. "You aren't an escaped criminal, are you? What fun!"

"There's no crime allowed in this country," said the other round-faced spectacled one, "didn't you know that? It's all too wonderful."

"We thought you looked like Ronald Colman, only younger," the Mink Coat said, "Mama and I, on the train. Don't you remember?"

"Now really, girls," the Countess murmured. "This is Mr. Preysing," she said to them, and to him, "Miss Barton and Miss Legendre." He thought she was obviously an-

noyed at the interruption and his spirits, which
crushed so long, went suddenly a little upward.

The girls, who evidently looked on the appeara
man from "home" as a minor miracle, were not g
be easily shoved off again. The four of them walked
together, the girls doing most of the talking an
Countess saying scarcely anything. Mark saw an abstr
irritated smile on her face. Presently she stopped
pointed at the sunny, misty reaches of the English gar

"I live just a few streets further on," she said, "Num
twenty, opposite Ohm Street, but on the garden side. Y
can't miss it, it's a big white house." She held out her har
to him. "Then at five o'clock shall we say? You shall sit i
a Biedermeier chair and drink from my best Nymphenbur
cup." He felt the girls' eyes break into a hungry sparkle.

"I wish you'd have tea with me," he said.

She looked startled and the girls drew back in disappointment.

"With you?" she said. "You mean in town?"

"Yes. Why not? Let me have the pleasure of giving
you tea."

She considered this as though it were very important.
"Why, I don't think I should," she said slowly.

A shabby old woman carrying a basket of fresh violets
came and stood by them looking from one to the other
sadly. They both turned and looked down at the basket.
The violets were dark, almost black, against their pale
leaves and sent out a cold perfume. He reached in and
carefully picked out the largest bunch, handed the old
woman a coin and held the bunch to the Countess. As
she took it her fair skin flushed. "How kind of you," she
said.

"Surely," he said teasingly, "you see they were made
for you."

She held them up to her nose. "Delicious," she said.

"Then you'll have tea with me? Tell me a good place to go."

This too, she thought over anxiously. "The Carlton," she said; "do you know where it is?"

"I can find out. At five say?"

"Yes, at five."

She went off with her girls and he turned into the English garden.

He walked about for a while, not sure of where he went. Then he sat down on a bench, beside a loving couple, and looked at the little, clear river running under the willows. Something that was extraordinarily pleasant had broken his grim preoccupation and even the fair day full of little, soft winds and scents was part of it. He wouldn't after all have to spend this day in lonely waiting. If the Countess had sensed in him the persistent demand for help she hadn't been repelled by it. He was so grateful to her for her kindness that he forgot how at first he had disliked her and had thought her stupid and vague. Even then of course her looks and her air of living under a spell had given her a tang of strangeness and had pricked his imagination, but now she was beginning to take on other, shimmering qualities. He thought her very touching in her simplicity and in her combination of timidity and graciousness. He thought her more beautiful than he had realized. And he wanted to know much more about her, how she lived, what she felt, and above all, whom she loved. It was certain that she must love someone. He wanted to know about her, whatever would make her more real, though part of her charm was still just that, that she was not like anyone he'd known and that their meeting in the forest, under the snowy trees, seemed still like a meeting in a somber fairy tale. The couple at the end of the bench were

holding hands and the girl's head fell on the man's shoulder. He looked at them with tolerance.

But at lunchtime, feeling hungry, he went back to the pension to eat the meal he must pay for; and the darkness, the suspicious landlady, at once brought back his former state. He had only allowed himself a moment's escape. He put it baldly to himself that he had been flattered by the interest which a beautiful countess unexpectedly chose to take in him. Whatever happened this afternoon would be bound to have a sting of remorse to it. He wished suddenly he could tell her to go to the devil. He even went to the point of looking her up in the telephone book to ring up and say he couldn't come. Nevertheless, at five o'clock promptly he was at the Carlton, and had engaged the best table he could find.

She was late of course and he had time to look about him. The Carlton was white and gold, with mirrors and thick carpets. It was crowded and the air was full of cigarette smoke and the steam from tea and coffee and the smell of rich cake. He saw some English people, with their stark, bony elegance, sitting near by, and many officers, raw-red but handsome, and a few women who had a style new to him, except that it was like the Countess', a fluid, unpainted and romantic style. When he had about given her up, she appeared. He piloted her to the table in the back room and they ordered tea and cakes with chocolate and whipped cream. She looked excited, her face was flushed from the cold walk and the overheated room, and her long, dark swan's eyes were shining. When she opened the sealskin jacket he saw the violets tucked into the neck of a dark green dress.

"I love this place," she said, settling back on the cushiony chair. Her eyes glanced from side to side, as though on the lookout for people she might speak to. "It has that indescribable murk, that thick mould of relaxation and comfort that the English think of when they say 'I'll just have a cup of tea.'"

"I haven't been in such luxury for a long time," he said smiling, "but I can see that like the violets it was made for you. How adaptable you American women are! You always make the best countesses."

"I've been one such a long time," she said.

"How long?"

"You're much too direct, but I'll tell you," she said. "I was married in nineteen twelve, and I was seventeen years old. You see that means I've lived here longer than anywhere, even with that time in New York."

"And you're more at home here?"

"Yes, I am. Oh, I don't mean in all this, but in the country, in the lovely, simple country, so unspoiled, and in the deep-rooted family life, and even in the little town that was the town of my husband's people and was even on our property."

"Down there in the mountains, is that where you mean?"

"No, we lived in the north. I've only been here since I came back. I have — friends here. Americans and foreigners like to come here, and of course I have to make my living now."

"Your girls are pretty lively," he said. "They must be fun."

"Yes, they're quite fun," she said vaguely and she glanced again at two women coming in. She bowed to them and they waved to her with surprised looks, as though it was unexpected to see her here. He wished she wouldn't look around so much. But of course she must know any number of people. In a small city like this he supposed everyone more or less knew everyone else. Then he thought suddenly of the way the blond young man had looked at her and it crossed his mind again that she might have a lover and was nervous for fear he might come in and see her tête-à-tête with a strange man. He remembered again her first terrified and unexplained look in the English garden. There are all kinds of terror he thought, and without allowing himself time to analyze just what he meant he began to feel a complacency stealing over him. He's probably a jealous devil, he thought agreeably, a big blond pig like that one in the garden.

She went on to tell him about her early life in this country and what it had meant to her, a dreamy, unformed schoolgirl, to come into a world that was so soon to be wiped out, but of which she had nearly two golden years. She saw that time now as a nostalgic picture, flat and perfect, but still she had loved just as much what remained after the splendor and security were gone; simple things, she said, too small almost to speak of: the smallest branches in their great forest, red, green and yellow, covered with the first frost, and a small boy with blue eyes, the youngest child of a neighboring family, whom she had loved. She had no children of her own.

He listened intently to all she said. The hollowness and emptiness he had first seen in her were being more and more filled. He saw they had been an illusion, due solely to his inability to imagine her life. She spoke a little of the war and the even more terrible afteryears, and the death of her husband, and how little by little she had lost the beloved estate, and the last of it sold finally for a song to a rich Jewish banker. Only this place in the mountains remained, and now she had to live in town in a rented house. She spoke of how she had gone to New York to sell her jewels. "I sold them all," she said, spreading out her hands, bare of all but a plain gold wedding ring, "but they

[157]

were mostly old-fashioned pieces, the diamonds of old-fashioned cut. I got very little."

She told him about her love of music and how she thought she might become a singer. "But by that time I was too old."

Then she spoke again of the northern country and her words were still simple and limited. "Oh, it was so lovely, so lovely," she would say. Or, "I loved it so much." But in spite of this she made a real world of it for him. He almost smelled the fresh odor of ferns and mushrooms and wild strawberries, almost saw the rooms with their porcelain stoves and the cleanliness and order and responsibility of the life she lived in them. In the evening she sang at an old rosewood piano, and her friends drove up the long avenue. These things, in spite of her inability to use telling words, she managed to make known to him and he even began to feel something of the special northern poetry which saturated this life, a poetry growing out of the immaculacy of linen and polished wood and butter fresh out of the crock, out of the warmth of crackling fires in the twilight of winter afternoons, a poetry made of the provocative vagueness of beech forests, where along the great roots one came on little cups of cool moss, and finally of the temperate measure of the seasons circling around them, giving never too much and never too little. Of course obviously this life also had in it other things than poetry: there were dirt and jealousy and greed and sickness, just as there are anywhere in the world at any time. Still, that was the distillation that had come out of it for her, as legitimate surely in its homely and personal way as, say, the great classical tradition so dear to the English, which had been their distillation from a world containing, among other things, the ferocious treachery and violence and sodomy of the Greeks. The Countess' dreamy picture of her own past had good precedent and at least it was her own. She had lived it.

He saw how difficult it was for her to live in the world today. She must be, he calculated quickly, forty-four, and she had resisted sorrow and change by retreating into a narrower and narrower circle. He couldn't entirely blame her for not thinking about the right things, those things he had urged on her the other day. There was such a weight of known things to blind her to them. And as he went on thinking like this he smiled to himself, because he knew that when all was said it was principally because she was a lovely woman that he was able to be so tolerant.

Yes, she had made herself come alive for him, but yet two mysteries remained. One was this possible lover whose image had suddenly been evoked out of the gesture and expression of the man in the Palace garden. No one had spoken of him, least of all the Countess, but while she talked his image seemed to grow. When she spoke of the charm the country had for her there were definite moments when he felt sure she spoke of something that had been passionately enjoyed with another. And when she told him of the irresistible urge that had driven her back, even to what was then a ruined country, to one where she didn't know whether she could find money to live, he knew that it had been most of all because she could not stand being separated from him. But finally, he felt sure of it because she had the quality of a woman emotionally, sexually, complete — richly filled. And this being so, the second mystery was all the greater, the mystery of the fear that was always so obvious in her, yes, even now. But what was her unknown fear? And why now was she here alone with him, talking as though to kill time in preparation for something?

He began to think of her so intently that he scarcely

[159]

heard what she said. "But you're not listening," she said suddenly.

"I am," he said, "I'm listening."

"I asked you if you'd like to go."

"Anywhere you say."

"I'm speaking of a concert tonight. Someone has given me two tickets. When we were talking the other day about the arts of the country I forgot to speak of music. Now I'll show you. It's Palm Sunday, you know. They are singing the Matthew's Passion. Would you like to come?"

"I'd like nothing better. Shall we dine together first?"

"There's not time. It will begin at seven. We can have a cocktail here, a sandwich if you like. Afterwards, if it doesn't last too long, we'll have supper somewhere." She took out a little watch from her bag. "It's after six," she said.

He ordered the cocktails and a waiter brought a tray of sandwiches to choose from.

She went on talking. She talked more about music and various musicians she had known. She never said a word directly to him. He thought she talked in order to keep him from talking about himself. But at the concert she would have to be silent and he could absorb himself in her more fully and build up a real determination toward her, and afterwards — well, let what would happen, happen. Something would happen he felt sure. Something not important perhaps. How could it be, with each of them filled with love for another thing? But still, it might be.

"We'd better go now," she said as he paid the bill. "It's just around the corner, at the Odeon. We can walk."

He got up quickly to follow her. She went out looking anxiously to right and left, seeing one or two familiar faces. In the street it was late twilight and they had to bend against a cold wind blowing a few scattered drops. The lovely spring day was over. It was a troubled evening which would bring rain perhaps, which might bring anything. They didn't speak but he took her arm and they began unconsciously to walk faster. It seemed to him that they hurried toward the night and what it might bring, knowing how little time they would have for it.

Chapter XI

THE Odeon was a large chilly hall under a staring light. They sat on hard wooden chairs, the kind that are found in America in the old "opera houses" of small towns. The hall was so crowded that a great many people stood along the walls, and as he looked around he saw it was an audience neither snob nor intellectual. A very few people were well dressed but the greater number whether shabby, dowdy, or downright poor, were plain people come to enjoy themselves. There were a number of soldiers, especially among the standees, and some old bearded men and quite small children. He saw an eager little boy in a starched collar with an open score on his lap, beside him was an old peasant woman with a face like a brown potato. Just in front of Mark sat a girl of the sort he didn't know existed any more. She had a great knot of hair like the Countess' but untidy, with silvery blond wisps spraying from it, her evening dress with big sleeves had an old-fashioned real lace collar, and she wore a topaz cross on a chain tight around her full, slightly goiterous throat. She had drenched herself with the innocent seduction of eau de cologne. When the young man who sat next to her bent every now and then to whisper to her, her ears and cheek blushed a sudden lovely red.

In this audience there seemed to be no one the Countess knew, or at any rate she was determined apparently to enjoy the music and forget them. She sat down and took up her program, studying it with complete absorption, and her attitude was like that of everyone else in the hall, child-like and tense with anticipation of a pleasure to which she expected to give herself fully.

The chorus filed in looking dull in their black clothes, scraping back their chairs and clearing their throats. It seemed impossible that anything of interest would come out of them. There was some delay and the principals whispered to each other and then looked self-consciously around at the lights, the ceiling, the busts of the musicians set in the walls, everywhere but at the audience who presumably, until the moment when they sang at them, weren't supposed to exist. The Evangel walked over and had a consultation with one of the violinists. Finally the conductor appeared, was greeted by the audience, and the music began.

If Mark had been able to choose he would certainly have taken for this occasion an aphrodisiac music, suave and perhaps melancholy, and he had expected at any rate to use this time for an intense meditation of the sort that leads with the least trouble into action. But the music was not what he wanted. He recognized at once that if he allowed himself to listen he would be carried out of his present feeling and perhaps wouldn't be able to come back. So he tried not to listen. But everyone else was listening and especially the Countess, and his resistance had to be both to the music and to the crowd-feeling around her and to her susceptibility to them. He turned in his chair slightly so he could look at her and she noticed this and frowned a little, but then he saw that she forgot him again.

He began to hear the music in spite of himself. He recognized that not only was it creating a world where no pleasant little lusts could possibly survive but it was also a world he recognized. He wasn't a musician, that is, he had never studied music, but he had heard a great deal and he knew there are as many ways of listening to it as there are of looking at a painting. There would only be one way for him to listen to this music and it would not be with a passive giving up of himself but with the activity of every power. It created not only the purest and most tender beauty but it required of him the most active co-operation. The people around him he saw were certainly not all capable of such a co-operation. Certainly he couldn't feel that even the Countess was capable. Though something of a musician she was, he imagined, dreaming a dream: of the love of Christ perhaps, since that was what the music sang of, at any rate of the comfort of divine concern and care, and these translucent lines and curves, these thick, clustered harmonies, made for her a sort of solution, a bath in which she could stretch herself as in a medicated spring and enjoy the delicious, passive heightening of her religious sense. That would be very pleasant too, no doubt; but because he was a painter, a creator himself, he had to recognize the Process. It couldn't remain with him a vague vehicle of mystery, he was obliged to consciously follow it, or stay outside. Yes, he knew this world well. The most difficult, after all, in which one could choose to live . . . He knew each step of it and the uncertainty and the anguish of urging power beyond its power; and finally, he knew the consummation, which if it is attained at all, transcends the Process and is a miracle, a miracle as dangerous as it is perfect. For if all the forces arrive at the same moment and in full flood, if the ecstasy is accomplished, there is then no place to go but back. That was why when looking at a picture he took refuge almost at once in a stolid retreat to Process. "Swell piece of work, well organized. Notice how he balances that red." No, let the music go on creating, by means he was half aware of, heavenly equilibriums, but he shut his ears. He would not enter that world now though Bach himself invited him.

During the intermission they talked a little but the music was still clinging to her. He would have liked to suggest they go now but he didn't dare. She so obviously wanted to stay. He watched her intently, still wondering how in the end this evening of music would make her feel toward him. There wouldn't be any of the sympathy of sharing it. But at least his concentration had finally kept her from a complete abandonment to it. She had become more and more conscious of him. He knew by little tightenings of the mouth or drawing of the eyebrows. Her praise of it now had reproach for him in it. "Did you really like it? Did you really listen?" And when her eyes turned around to the faces of those near them it was not to see anyone else but only to escape his gaze.

Somewhere in the middle of the second half his attention was caught by a man who was staring at him. He was among those standing against the wall, a tall young man, as far as he could see, shabby, or at any rate very unfashionable, in a coat with queer narrow shoulders and sleeves a little too short. His face had a Gothic look, everything in it pointed upward, the flaring nostrils, the lips, the cheekbones. His eyes, even at a distance, showed piercingly blue; and his skin was reddened as though it had never known anything but extreme cold. His appearance was almost grotesque, but as Mark looked at him with some curiosity, he saw there was also something powerful and sensitive about the modeling of his face. He wondered why the fellow had looked at him with such intentness and for a moment he thought it might be someone following him. The young man had turned his eyes away as Mark looked at him but he did not seem self-conscious. He stood for a considerable time without apparently moving a muscle or flicking an eyelash. He seemed to have perfect control of his muscles. Then he turned his eyes again in Mark's direction and gave suddenly an eager smile and bobbed his head several times, managing even in the crowd to execute a stiff bow and heel clicking. Mark saw that he had saluted the Countess. He thought, with annoyance, So she knows him too; and when he glanced up again and saw that the young man still looked at her with an open look of admiration it flashed on him that this might be the lover. He at once rejected the possibility. Not only because the man was so awkward, so homely and so obviously unworldly, but because this was not the sort of man from whom he wished to take her.

As the hall grew warmer from the crowd the smell of her violets came up to him. He hardly took his eyes from her and by the set look of her mouth, the blank, conscious stare of her eyes, he knew she felt it and that whatever he had done he had at last made her fully conscious of him. Finally he began to feel that she silently contended against him and that satisfied him. It was enough for the time. What was that Emmy used to read aloud? "And whilst our souls negotiate there, we like sepulchral statues lay, all day the same our postures were, and we said nothing all the day."

When the music stopped she didn't wait for the hand-clapping to be over but got up hurriedly and pulled her coat together and drew on her gloves. Her program she crumpled into a ball and dropped. They started out, but as they had been close to the stage they were caught in the crowd just the same. He moved behind her holding both her elbows, but she shook her arms and said sharply, "It's not necessary, thanks. I can get along." He held her more lightly but didn't let her go. As they came to the more spacious lobby he freed her and she turned with an exclamation: "It's raining. How maddening." So it was. The sidewalks were glistening and rain hung like a sheet of cellophane between them and the street lights. People who had brought umbrellas were struggling to put them up against the wind.

"We'll have to get a taxi," he said.

"But there's such a crowd. We'll never get one!" Then she looked at him and was startled by his face. Let her be, he thought. She's seen such faces before. He took her arm and drew her over to the wall. "We'll wait till the crowd thins," he said.

She let herself be drawn and stood beside him looking down.

"I think," she said in a low voice, "that I won't want any supper. I think I'll just go home. If you'll call me a taxi I'd better leave you here."

"Certainly I'll call one," he said, "but I'll go with you. I can't let you go alone."

"I think it's better I go alone," she said firmly.

"Then why did you come?" he said. He couldn't believe she meant it. But that was the usual stupid question. He wished he hadn't asked it. She looked up at him not angrily but gently. "I wanted to be friendly and to be kind," she said, her voice still low, "because I know why you're here."

At first he didn't know what she meant. Was "here" the concert? In a confused way he thought she was accusing him of coming back to town and deliberately putting himself in her path. He said nothing. She clasped her gloved hands so tightly the seams strained.

"The trouble is," she said hurriedly, "that others also know, and it's very dangerous for you."

[167]

He looked at her stupefied and she laid her hand on his arm.

"Oh, I know," she said, "how sad and how terrible it is, but you can't do anything, not anything. You must go home," she said. "Go back home at once. Promise me you will."

He couldn't speak but she went on, her voice shaking with sympathy.

"Please believe me that there is nothing you can possibly do, and you'll only get into fearful trouble yourself. You must go. Will you promise me you'll go?"

"I'd like to kill you," he said.

And suddenly here before them were the blond young couple of the Palace garden. Here they came, waving their hands, their faces lighted with surprise and malice. "Why darling!" the woman cried, "but you said you couldn't come. And you changed your mind. How exciting!"

"Wasn't it wonderful!" the man said, "I saw you all through the concert. I could see how you enjoyed it."

Mark didn't even hear their names. He heard the Countess stammer as she made the presentations. Her face was all anxiety, anyone could see it even through her smile.

"I was wondering if you'd give me a lift home," she said to them. "It will save Mr. Preysing from coming so far out of his way."

"Naturally, naturally," they cried together.

Mark wanted to say, "Good night and thank you," but she had turned from him before he could take her hand or speak, and there was another interruption. The young man who had stood with the standees and had greeted her so eagerly, he too had found them. He was making again his stiff formal bow and kissing her hand, and the Countess, still a little distracted, said, "Why Berthold! How nice to see you! This is Doctor Ditten," she said, and she said kindly and as though privately, "You must come and have tea with me." (Oh, these invitations to tea!) "I haven't seen you for so long."

"Our car is waiting, Ruby," the blond young man said, his gleaming, amused look now fixed on the doctor, "though I hate to take you away from so many admirers."

The doctor did not find this amusing and he looked blankly at the young man. Mark said good night and left them. He walked to the entrance and stood in the thinning crowd. It was still pouring. Almost immediately the Countess and her friends got into a car and drove away. In the lobby behind him the lights were being economically dimmed preparatory to turning them off. There were not enough taxis and when one came he seemed unable to move and let someone else get it ahead of him. The Countess, he was saying to himself, he would think of afterward. Maybe not at all. He wasn't sentimental, thank God, whatever he was, and he'd known all along she was of no importance and that he didn't really like her very much. She had been a momentary release for him. He couldn't go on thinking of the other thing at that tension without cracking up and becoming useless. Now she'd thrown him back on it, a little sooner than he'd expected, that was all. He turned his collar up stoically, deciding to walk. Perhaps he'd meet a taxi farther down the street.

Someone touched him on the arm. "Excuse me, sir, but I have an umbrella. May I share it with you?"

Mark looked around into bright enquiring eyes and saw also a large black cotton umbrella. He'd forgotten the doctor already, and his face seen without highlights in the shadow seemed different. But then he knew him. Yes, it was that queer duck.

"Thanks," he said, "which way are you going?"

"I will go in your direction," the doctor said politely.

[169]

"That's very decent of you. I don't believe I have far to go." He gave the number on Theater Street.

They started off together. "These spring rains," the doctor said, "are very bad. It is dangerous to get wet and then not to dry out properly. So one catches severe and sometimes fatal colds."

"Yes, I suppose so," Mark agreed. It is certainly curious, he thought suddenly, that she should know about me. Who would tell her? Would it be Henning, would it be that other fellow? Are they all discussing this thing among themselves?

"Did you enjoy the concert?"

"Oh, yes," Mark said, "very much. Magnificent music."

"Magnificent music indeed," the doctor agreed, "but not very good voices. Except for the Evangel."

"Yes, they weren't good, as a matter of fact."

"Many of our best singers go abroad. Of course they get paid a lot more there. It's natural they should."

"I expect they do." What did she mean about it being dangerous for me to be here? She exaggerates, of course. But still, I'll have to be careful. I certainly can't accomplish anything in jail.

"You are getting damp," the doctor said. "The umbrella isn't big enough. You must be sure to take a strong drink when you get home." He stopped suddenly and took hold of Mark's arm. "Wouldn't it be a good idea to have a drink now?" he said. "Very near us is a famous beer hall. Would you allow me to offer you a glass of beer?"

"I think it's an excellent idea," Mark agreed absently.

Chapter XII

THE beer hall was full of smoke and the slightly sour smell of malt. It was crowded, mostly with men but a few women were scattered among them. As they came in people at tables near the door gave them the party salute and the doctor returned it absently. Mark did not return it and while the doctor stood looking about for a free table he waited, stiffly conscious of their unfriendly stares. Finally a waitress in peasant dress beckoned them to a corner, where there was a small table. Here the doctor stood his umbrella against the wall to drain, wiped the raindrops off his sleeves with his handkerchief, advised Mark to do the same, and finally sat down, ordering from the waitress two large glasses of Salvator, together with cheese and bread.

The chairs they sat on were not comfortable, they had great wooden hearts for backs. Mark wished at once he hadn't accepted so quickly. He didn't like at all the atmosphere of the place, and the fellow would be boring. He would go into one of those earnest conversations in which he would conscientiously try to inform himself about the foreigner and his customs; or worse still, he would try to inform the foreigner about himself and his customs.

While they waited for the beer the doctor took out a pipe and filled it carefully from an oilskin bag. His fingers were very scrubbed and bony but they were shapely. Mark lighted a cigarette. When the beer came the doctor

[171]

held up his long glass: "Good health," he said. "Good health," Mark echoed. The beer was the color of dark Chinese amber and the flavor was deep, nutty, smooth, full of body, and just faintly musky.

"It's excellent," Mark said.

"Yes, we make good beer," the doctor agreed.

At the other end of the hall a man began to sing to an accordion accompaniment. For a little longer I'll forget again, Mark thought. Just for a little longer.

"Beer and music," he said; "all we need now is women."

"There will be no women," the doctor said seriously.

"Then we ought to have brought the Countess."

"She would not come, perhaps, to a beer hall."

"Haven't you ever asked her?"

"Never."

"Try it sometime. I wouldn't be surprised if she took a maternal interest in you."

The doctor studied Mark's face to see if he meant what he said. For some reason, probably loneliness, it appeared he wanted to like him. "I think perhaps she does take such an interest in me," he said. "I have known her always and she is many years older than I. She couldn't take any other kind of interest."

"Ah, so?" said Mark and suddenly he was trying not to be amused. Yes, he need not perhaps think of sorrow for a little longer.

"We come from the same place," the doctor said. "In the north. Our families were friends. Every Sunday afternoon in my childhood my father called on the Countess. Sometimes I went along."

"You come from the north?"

"Yes. Formerly ours was a large family there but in my youth it had already shrunk, and now there is only my uncle and myself. We are very well born," he said simply,

[172]

"but I dropped the prefix. It means nothing today. I came here because of work. I was sent here, in fact. But you, have you known the Countess long?"

"No. I met her in New York once, then again here. That's all. She's an American, of course. That gives us one thing in common."

"A great deal, I should think," the doctor said.

"Oh, I don't know," Mark said, "I was only thinking of the language. There are so many kinds of Americans. But the Countess we can be proud of. She's a very beautiful woman."

The doctor considered this, puffing slowly on his pipe. "I should call her attractive," he said. "She is much too thin to be beautiful. She has a very serious anemic condition, as you could guess to look at her. I have treated her for it from time to time this last year. No, I shouldn't call her beautiful, but I should certainly call her extremely attractive."

"You're looking at her professionally," Mark said. "From my point of view I should say she'd be fun to paint. But we shouldn't let our professional interest play too strong a part in our lives. We'd miss a lot."

"Perhaps so."

"I mean, I don't want to love only the women I'd like to paint, and you'd certainly be limited if you always had to have complete soundness of wind and limb."

The doctor looked at him with slightly startled blue eyes and drew vigorously on his pipe. It was obvious he thought Mark meant he loved the Countess.

Mark said, "I believe there's a convention against talking about women in beer halls, or bars, or clubs, or anywhere in fact where one would be most likely to talk about them. Are you shocked at my mentioning the Countess?"

"But not at all," the doctor said.

"I don't know why I did. I've just met her really. I don't know much about her. But I was, frankly, extremely attracted. That's all I meant to say."

"I can understand that," the doctor said, "I'm extremely attracted to her myself. Even having known her so long ago. Of course I hardly ever see her now. Except to give her liver extract. It's not a romantic moment one might say. And then," he laid down his pipe and looked earnestly at Mark, "since we're speaking frankly, I have to admit that emotionally I'm terribly inhibited."

Mark bent over his beer a moment, then he couldn't resist it. He threw his head back and laughed. The doctor after an instant's surprise joined him.

"I suppose she'd be amused," he said finally, "if she could hear us."

"She certainly would," Mark said. "Now we can't do less than drink to her."

They held up their glasses. When they put them down they were empty. The doctor held up his hand to signal the waitress.

"This is on me," Mark said.

"No, no," the doctor insisted genially, "in my country I buy the beer." He ordered two more.

Mark suddenly found he was hungry. He began to eat the bread and cheese.

"You spoke just now of painting the Countess," the doctor said; "are you a painter by profession?"

"Yes. But it's difficult to be a painter today. Is it difficult to be a doctor?"

"I think it is difficult," the doctor said, "and perhaps what we both mean is that it's difficult to be a man. But that's always the case, isn't it? At any time and any place."

"Harder here now I should think," Mark said, "if

[174]

you mean a man of complete human wholeness."

"I do," the doctor said. "But I also question whether just now it's so important to be a man in that sense."

"What else is important? Isn't that what we all want? Don't you yourself want it in the end?"

"In the end, yes. But at the moment other things must come first. What's important here and now isn't necessarily important tomorrow, just as it wasn't important yesterday. In the flow of time most values are relative to the ones directly preceding and following. But there's one underlying value that at all times is constant, that is almost in the nature of time itself, and that one is survival. Do you agree?"

"Survival? As what? Surely as the creature with his human wholeness intact."

"Perhaps not intact. You may come out of battle with a leg off. You may have to lose an eye, but the important thing is you survive. Come now, admit that if you don't survive there's nothing left to talk about."

"Well, no one wants to extinguish you."

"You say that, but they wanted to put us into a state where we wouldn't have lost one leg but two, not one eye but two. Do you call that survival? It's a state that in your great, rich country you'd consider no better than extinction."

"You had a constitution and a republican government," Mark said.

"Yes, and even if I admit that they were desirable, who was willing to support us in them? No one. That brings me to the value of the moment, the one related to what has just gone and is just coming. Our value here and now is union." He held up his hand. "You're about to tell me of the abuses that exist, the bureaucracy, the death of the trade unions, the race persecutions, the unhealthy lack of an opposition, and so on. Nevertheless, union is still our chance of survival. And eventually, out of our union, will come that human wholeness you spoke of."

"It's impossible to believe that it'll ever come through blind reaction, through cruelty, a calculated destruction of every human decency."

He said fiercely to himself: Shut up. Don't argue in this fake, academic detachment. People have said this over and over till they're black in the face. They've said it politely till their veins burst from restraint. What we want to say is: We loathe your bloody country and everything in it. And you want to say the same to us. We're on two sides of a wall. We can't even meet to have a glass of beer together. We should have known it.

But the doctor apparently was more capable of detachment than he. He looked meditatively at him, thinking slowly.

"Machiavelli," he said, "says that unity is the goal of every political community. That's impossible when there is a continuous formation of parties. But if all parties can be united into one party under good laws, then the highest goal of mankind will follow — civil liberty."

"History isn't limited to politics," Mark said, impatiently. "Anyway, the proof of this pudding is the eating. You're united now, aren't you? Where's your civil liberty?"

"Oh," the doctor said, "that'll come. Or I believe so. If I didn't believe it would come . . ."

He stopped. For a moment he looked down at his pipe. It had gone out. He lighted it again, and in the flare of the match his teeth set on the stem gave his face a stern, melancholy look.

"What I sometimes fear is that we're going contrary to our racial genius," he said. "Of course, necessity drives

[176]

us. Our genius had led us into degeneracy. But still, it's dangerous. What," he said suddenly, "has our social and political genius always been?"

"Nothing, I should say. You've never been Romanized. Perhaps that was your first misfortune."

"But was it a misfortune?" The doctor leaned forward and said earnestly: "Perhaps not to be Romanized was our genius. With the Roman the State had rights, the individual had rights only as part of the State. When he wasn't a citizen, he had no rights. With us, in our tribal, in our feudal State, right was an attribute of the individual. Such a right could scarcely be taken from him. Only yesterday," he said, and his voice grew more somber, "only yesterday I had a discussion on rights. It was very disturbing."

He's unhappy, Mark thought. Devilish unhappy. As unhappy as I am. To come suddenly on unhappiness in a stranger is like stumbling on a deep well. The sensible thing is to draw back from it.

The doctor gave a little shake to his high, thin shoulders. "But I was saying," he said, "that it's just possible we've made a mistake in invoking the Roman idea now. What have we to do with Romanisms?" he said contemptuously.

Suddenly Mark was sure that he wasn't meant to take part in this discussion, that the doctor had begun to argue with himself — or with someone who wasn't there.

"Romanisms," he repeated, casting the word from him.

He put his pipe down and folded his hands, looking off into distance. His lips moved once without saying anything aloud. Then he drew his eyes back to Mark, and gave a shake of his head as though giving a vehement answer.

"It would be impossible for our present society to pro-

[177]

duce such a person," he said. "I mean such as I was talking to yesterday." He ended in confusion.

"No doubt," said Mark vaguely.

The doctor looked at him and said: "Of course there's no variety of product. Saint Francis, Spinoza, Beethoven — all of them would be executed. But we don't need them. That's the point."

Before Mark could answer he suddenly leaned his head in his hand. His eyes closed and he seemed to be reliving a painful experience. Mark would have liked to get up and go but he couldn't leave a man so unconscious of him. He looked at him, embarrassed and indifferent. The doctor's cuffs, he saw, were worn and showed signs of having been clipped smooth with scissors.

Serves him right, Mark thought. Serves him right. He had no interest in the doctor's unhappiness, but it seemed obscurely a sort of retribution for his own. Morosely he stared down at the table. The singer with the accordion began another song.

"How about another beer?" the doctor said briskly. He had recovered himself and his face had its fixed, bright look.

"Perhaps you're tired," Mark said. "Perhaps we'd better go."

"No, no. I'm not tired. I must apologize for letting myself be depressed for a moment. I won't bother you with it. It's one of the things I must learn to get over."

"Yes," Mark said.

They looked at each other questioningly. One word and the doctor would tell him what was on his mind, and the loneliness in Mark, more than any real interest, was willing to let him listen. Some case of his, he thought, or some love affair, that will turn out to be entirely average.

But I wouldn't dare tell him anything about me. He

was about to say something when the waitress came up.

"Two beers," the doctor said.

The waitress looked at them very hard and went off sullenly.

"She's not feeling hospitable," Mark suggested.

"I should have worn my uniform," the doctor said.

"Oh, you have a uniform too?"

"Yes, so many people do here. Without one you feel like a cock who's lost his tail feathers. I hate mine," he said.

"Army?" Mark asked.

"No, no."

They listened to the singer, waiting for the beer to come. It wasn't as easy to talk now. Mark couldn't tell why. He felt a slight inclination, a vague liking for the doctor. He didn't know why he liked him. Perhaps because in spite of what he gave as his opinions there was such deep dissatisfaction in him, or because of something else, honesty perhaps. And he had what has to be called "character." He had his own distinct quality. What he did one would usually expect, but if one didn't expect it, once done it would be instantly stamped with his own quality.

When the beer came the doctor made another effort to liven things up.

"When will you go back to America?" he asked.

"I don't know," Mark said. "It depends on some people here."

"I wish I could go with you."

"Yes? You think you'd like it?"

"I'm not sure. But it attracts me terribly."

"What especially?"

"Lots of things. Some of them professional. I'd like to

[179]

examine, for instance, one of your iron lungs. And then there's a man doing very interesting research on pellagra. I'd like to see him. Oh, a number of things. Tall buildings, of course." He moved his pipe up and down, then sketched a curve. "Pretty girls," he said, with no real gusto. "But mostly I want to see what it's like to breathe the air of anarchy."

"Anarchy? Well, yes, I suppose it is anarchy, compared with this anyway. You say the word as though it were a vice."

"Oh, I don't think it's always a vice. In a new country, no. It can be a virtue. Wherever there's a big enough margin for error. In such places, in such times, it's the highest value. Spain in her colonies didn't realize that. She was always trying for order, so she failed. Order had no value then. Anarchy has no value to us here and now."

"You certainly stick to your guns, don't you? Within a very slight measure I agree with you. I mean, I've lived in this golden state of anarchy for a while and I see that the margin of error, as you say, is thinning down considerably. I've seen how men can suffer in it, what the underdog's life can be. I might even agree that it would be a good thing to bury a few of our beloved little personal freedoms for a while until some more general good could be arrived at. That's even been done, and perhaps will have to be done even more. But it's dangerous. It's dangerous to give up anarchy. It's dangerous to put your head under the yoke and say: I'm only doing this for a moment, I can get right out when I want. You take the risk of coming to what you've come to here. You took it, and look at you!"

Perhaps this was going too far, considering that he was drinking the doctor's beer. But the doctor apparently didn't think so. Indeed, he listened so carefully always that

Mark wished he himself might be more exact and less emotional.

The doctor looked at him sadly, then he sighed.

"Couldn't you conceive of living here?" he asked.

"Not for an instant," Mark said promptly. Then he added evasively, "I imagine it would be worse for me than for you. A man can't paint a single stroke without freedom of choice. But I suppose a man's belly is always a man's belly."

The doctor took a drink of beer and set his glass down with a precise ring.

"I don't think it's possible," he said, "for anyone to be more unhappy than I am."

Mark could hardly reconcile his sharp, bright voice with his words. But he wasn't really surprised. It was the doctor himself who seemed startled. He turned away hastily and beckoned to the waitress. When she came he felt in his pockets, found some coins and paid her, and when she was gone said, "This isn't really a very good place to talk. But I would like very much to talk some more."

"Yes, yes, it would be fine," Mark said. But he told himself that he didn't want to see the doctor again. He didn't want to get entangled with anyone here. In a way it was almost too easy to feel friendliness for the doctor. He was naïve and earnest and pedantic and pompous and stiff and he was disarming. Perhaps he had other qualities. You could even guess them, though nothing had called them to view. They would almost necessarily be the expected complements of those Mark had seen. The doctor, he thought, would never have real surprises for him.

A group of men at the table nearest them were watching them and listening.

"No, it's not a good place to talk," the doctor said

again in a louder voice. "It's a great bore the way everyone listens all the time. But let's finish our beer anyway. How long will you be in town?"

"I don't know," Mark said. He was vaguely uncomfortable because of the notice they had attracted. No one could actually have caught more than an occasional word spoken more loudly for emphasis, but he began to feel that he must go.

"I want to see you again," the doctor repeated. "I have unfortunately a very hard job. Hard in all ways, a dirty job. Among other things I must get up early. And so I must also go to bed early. But I have a little flat here, very tiny indeed, and one servant who cooks my meals. Will you do me the favor to dine with me tomorrow night?"

"I'd like to very much," Mark said. Well, that was done. He was never quick at saving himself. And after all he knew that when he'd lived through another day here he'd even be glad to dine with the doctor.

"You know what I miss most in all this," the doctor said, "is the freedom to talk. I like discussions. In my student days we discussed everything. Yes, everything. It's hard to remember it. Well, we'll have more talk tomorrow night. I'll write you down the address of my flat."

He felt in his pocket and brought out a small pad and pencil. He put them on the table before him and looked at them for a moment.

The paper showed the pressure of a pencil.

His face stiffened. "You're a lucky devil," he said. Then he wrote his name and address and tore off the sheet and gave it to Mark. Mark looked at it and put it in his pocket.

"Shall we go now?" the doctor said. He reached into the corner for his umbrella. Suddenly he said with a little smile, "But do you know that all this time I don't know your name? That's funny, isn't it? The Countess must have said it indistinctly. I noticed at the time she was upset about something."

"My name's Mark Preysing," he said. Then he stood up and added, "I haven't any card with me. I'm sorry."

"Preysing," the doctor repeated slowly as he got to his feet. His smile faded and his face became troubled. He said, "That's very queer."

"Is it?" Mark said.

He pushed his chair back. The doctor put his hands on the table and leaned forward, looking piercingly at him.

"Mark Preysing?" he asked urgently.

"What's the matter?"

"Sit down a moment," the doctor said.

Well, he knows it too, Mark thought. This is beginning to be a nightmare. He sat down and they looked at each other across the table in silence. The doctor felt in his pockets again. This time he brought out a little folded note. He looked at it and a blur of sadness and shock dimmed the sharp blue of his eyes.

"Are you Madame Emmy Ritter's son?"

"Yes," Mark said.

"Then this is for you." He handed him the note across the table.

Mark took it and saw at once that the handwriting was hers. He looked at it stunned; then he opened it and read the note.

It was a note of farewell. Every word of it was a leave-taking, every word was too clearly and simply the last. He read it through twice before he finally grasped its finality. Then he leaned his elbows on the table and buried his head in his hands. If he had been alone perhaps he would have collapsed altogether. But the hum of the beer hall hung dimly around him; at the table with him was the doctor. He knew he'd have to pull himself together, some-how. Long enough to get away.

Then he realized that all along some part of him had known with certainty that it couldn't be less than death. Everything had told him so, the first note, then the silence, then Henning. The Commissioner, Fritz, and the Countess. Each in his own way had told him, had confirmed what he already knew, and like a spoiled child continuously rejected.

He remembered as though it had happened hours ago the first words the doctor spoke to him in the theater. They ought to have rung with the tolling of a bell. But he had only been thinking about the Countess. He'd been in a dream, seeing nothing he should have seen, hearing nothing he should have heard, living in fact as one always lived, in the midst of an illusion. It is a terrible thing to support even momentarily the rending of that illusion, to see the whole lack of knowledge, and to look on the bare plan and armature of the design.

He looked up at the doctor, who sat slumped back in his chair, his hands in his pockets, staring at the table. Near them the men who had watched them were still watching them.

"Did she give it to you?" Mark asked.

"Yes."

"When?"

"Yesterday."

"Then she's still alive?"

"Yes, she's still alive."

One of the men at the table near by said in a loud voice, "They must be drunk."

Mark took out a cigarette and lighted it unsteadily. He inhaled it for a moment.

"Who are you?" he asked.

The doctor answered him, not looking at him. "I'm a doctor. Actually I am in the Department of Health and Sanitation. But the prisons are very full, they need doctors, and for three months I've been attached to the political police. I met Madame Ritter in prison, the prison for the worst criminals of all sorts, civil and political, all those who are condemned to die."

"Is that where she is?"

"No. At present she's in a concentration camp outside the city. That I was able to do."

"Why is she there?"

"She became sick. I found her suffering from an acute inflammation of the appendix. I wanted to operate on her so I persuaded my uncle to ask them to let me do it. He has a good deal of influence."

He looked up and met Mark's eyes. He said hastily, "I'm really a surgeon, but it's hard to live. I had to take what job I could."

"So you operated," Mark said.

"Yes, they let me do it. I had her moved to the concentration camp because there are facilities, of a sort, for operations. The conditions in the prison itself were very bad — she'd have died there. And of course they wouldn't let me put her in a hospital. Now she is in a room with another woman, tubercular, but she has a clean bed and fairly decent treatment."

"She's quite recovered?"

"She walked a little yesterday."

"How much time has she?"

"Not much."

"How much?"

The doctor didn't answer. Mark said angrily, "Tell me. I have to hear."

"Till Wednesday. Early in the morning."

"Wednesday! Of this week? But it's Sunday now."

He snatched his watch from his pocket and held it up to look at. Quarter past twelve. It wasn't Sunday. It was Monday. Day after tomorrow. He put it back in his pocket.

"What can I do?" he said.

"There's nothing you can do," the doctor said in a voice like lead. "If there was anything you could do I'd tell you."

"Are you sure there's nothing?"

"Yes, I'm sure." He leaned forward and said in a voice that barely could be heard, "I would like to save Madame Ritter myself if it could be done. But it can't."

"You're sure?" Mark repeated.

"Yes."

"I don't suppose money would help?"

"No, no. Impossible."

"There must be something."

"There's nothing. You must put out of your head all romantic thoughts of escape from prison."

"People have done it."

"Not here."

"But she's in the camp now."

"Yes, but she has also been very sick. She can barely walk. I tell you it's impossible. Don't torture yourself with thinking about it."

"You said you'd like to save her. Why?"

The doctor said slowly, "It's hard to tell you why. It would be contrary to every one of my principles. I'm honest when I tell you that I believe just now we're doing the only thing possible to do."

He took the edge of the table in his hands and pressed it as though he wanted to push it and Mark away from him. His knuckles turned white in his red, strong hands.

"I think Madame Ritter, because she's one of us," he

[186]

said harshly, "and because she didn't understand, deserves to die. But when I say this I say it in one compartment only. And only in that compartment is it true. When I bring it out, it's no longer true. When I see Madame Ritter, — I see her nearly every day you know, — when I talk to her, it's not true."

"You say you don't want her to die," Mark said, "and you don't really know her. If you did you'd think of something to do."

"Yes, I know her," the doctor said. "I didn't want to. For a long time I would hardly talk to her, because I was afraid of knowing her. I thought, she's chosen to act single-handed: let her go on single-handed. But all the time I was knowing her anyway."

"She can't help going single-handed," Mark said. "She's had to support other people, always, and with very little help. Life has forced her to go single-handed. She's had more burdens than any one woman should. Her husband wasn't much use to her. Her daughter's been always sick. I haven't been what I should. We've all asked too much. So she's become that sort of person. You know how tramps will put a mark on a house to show that you can always count on a handout there, that it's a place where you won't be turned away. Well, everyone who sees her puts that mark on her."

"She could be Saint Elisabeth," the doctor said.

"Who?"

"Nothing. I was thinking of something else."

The singer with the accordion began again, a rollicking song. It had a chorus and several groups joined in banging their steins and stamping their feet.

"Isn't there anything I can do," Mark said, "no matter how crazy, how hard, how dangerous, that could get her out?"

"No. You mustn't think of it."

"Just the same, there must be something. If I knew the country better I'd find it. I tell you, there's nothing I wouldn't try. Would you tell me what to do if you knew?"

"Yes. Now that I've seen you it's worse for me."

"Why?"

"Because I see you're a man like myself. I see her in you and I see you in her. I know what you are to each other. Your coming here shows me that."

"What can I do then?"

"You can't do anything."

"God damn you and your country!" He dropped his cigarette and stamped on it.

"Wait a minute," the doctor said. "After all, it's better she should be in my care."

"Yes," Mark agreed. He sank back and closed his eyes. He felt deathly tired. "Yes, yes, of course it's better. I'm glad. You can make things easier for her. Will you tell her you've seen me?"

"Do you want me to?"

"I don't know. It might make it worse for her to know I'm here. Running futilely about, trying to help her. She'd worry about my getting into trouble. Perhaps it's better not. Still, I want to write her. Will you take her a letter for me?"

"Yes, of course. Will you come tomorrow night to my flat?"

"I don't know. I don't know what I can do. I don't know how I'm going to live till tomorrow night."

He opened his eyes and they looked at each other.

"Will you have another drink with me?" the doctor asked.

"Oh, no," Mark said, so quickly that they both looked

away, overcome with embarrassment worse than anger.

"Then we'd better go," the doctor said.

They got up and the doctor picked up his umbrella. Mark followed him through the tables to the door. The waitress who stood near the door looked at them sullenly. The doctor gave her a coin as he passed, which she took without thanks.

It was still raining.

"You know your way?" the doctor asked.

"Yes."

"Until tomorrow then."

They started off in opposite directions.

Chapter XIII

WHEN Mark began to walk alone he realized completely what had happened. Now Emmy's fate wasn't a matter of possibility, it wasn't just a picture in the back of his mind, a sort of dreadful spur to energy. No, it was a certainty. Certain even as to the exact day: Wednesday, early in the morning. He walked almost at a run, and if his way hadn't led directly he'd have been lost.

Theater Street was empty and all the shops had their iron shutters down so that it looked like a street of blank iron walls. All the lamps were blurred and a cat mewed forlornly in a doorway. The knob of his own door was slippery and large and hard to turn. He let himself in with the key they had given him and found the entrance in total blackness. He felt around the wall for the switch, reached it and turned it on. A paper was fastened to the lift: "Out of order," it said.

He began to climb the stairs slowly, breathless from his headlong walk, but before he could reach the door of the flat the lights gave a click and went off. They had been timed apparently to about what it would take to get up in the lift.

He stood still, feeling an old, childish, nocturnal panic, a fear of strange cities and strange hallways at night. Always they had made him feel a fugitive and lost. He could hear the rain at the top of the shaft. Yes, he was running for cover. Really hunted, really lost, drowned in strangeness.

Then he slowly groped his way up and reached the door of the flat. He lit his *briquet* to read the number and find the lock, but if he had been in any doubt as to the door the smell as soon as he opened it would have told him. It was the special smell of the place, already familiar, gas and filtered coffee and cabbage and stale upholstery and some sort of floor polish. And here too were the wicker chairs, with that peculiar waiting look of inanimate used things in an empty place. He kept his light burning, shading it with his hand, and moved carefully toward his door. He saw things he hadn't noticed in the daylight, a vase of paper flowers on the wicker table and a Chinese jar for umbrellas, a hatrack of imitation stag-horns on the wall. He went on tiptoe so as not to disturb the landlady. As he saw her door across from his own, he had a vision of her coming out to stare at him and to ask him where he had been and why he was so late getting in.

Suddenly he stopped. He was before his own door. He remembered perfectly its number and the location of it, but there was a faint crack of light coming from under it. He hadn't left his light on this afternoon. If he had, or if anyone else had gone into his room since, the light would certainly have been discovered and turned off. The economy that prevailed here would see to that.

Then someone was in his room now. He slipped his watch out. It was a quarter to one. At quarter to one, someone sat in his room waiting for him to come home. He remembered what the Countess had said to him, and he felt a feeling of relief that anxiety should come now to drive away his intolerable sorrow.

Without doubt it was someone from the Secret Police.

Then since he hadn't been heard yet the thing for him to do was to slip away and go somewhere else. He put out his light and stood still, trying to think.

If it was the police, why hadn't they waited in the hall so that just this thing wouldn't happen? And if it was and he got away now, what good would it do? There was no place he could go in the end without turning in his passport. He couldn't even draw his money each day without complete identification. Rather than run it would be better to see them. He had done nothing illegal yet. He was an American subject. Better to take the chance. He felt alert and tingling, his grief momentarily gone.

He opened his door. The bright unshaded bulb over his bed had been turned on, the curtains at the window were drawn and these and the walls latticed with black poppies gave the room a murky, vicious look. On a chair in the center of the room sat a man who looked up at the noise of the door without surprise. He was an elderly man with a long, pale, soft-skinned face, big ears, and long, pale, hare's eyes. His gray hair was stiffly *en brosse* and his high collar holding his flabby chin looked like Humpty Dumpty's collar. As Mark came in he stood up wearily as though he'd been waiting a long time.

"Well, I'll be damned," Mark said. "So you're here."

"Yes, sir."

Mark looked him over again from head to foot. Then he began to feel suddenly cold and trembling. His coat was wet. He began to take it off and Fritz came and helped him, took the coat from him and went over to the wardrobe, found a hanger and hung it up on the open wardrobe door to dry.

Yes, here was Fritz again. And Mark slipped back and stood for a moment in that compartment of time when Fritz always came just as things got too bad. Old Fritz —

always insolent over the telephone, always saying he couldn't come, and not answering the telegram but turning up just the same. And Mark remembered how he and Sabina had hated Fritz, and how even Emmy treated him roughly, as though she were suspicious of the only person who never tried to get something out of her: Fritz, icily self-sufficient and quarrelsome and efficient, who took what satisfaction they could only guess out of being the perpetual last resort.

Mark sat down weakly. He took out a cigarette and lighted it.

"So it's you," he said again.

Fritz stood by his chair. "May I sit down, Mr. Mark?" he asked.

"Sure. Sit down."

Fritz sat down opposite him and clasped his hands loosely between his knees. They were still the long, supple hands Mark remembered, the hands of the good valet. Always his hands remained entirely respectful. He looked very tired but not at all abashed.

"Well," said Mark, "what have you got to say for yourself?"

"You got the note, sir?"

"Of course I got it. I told you I'd got it when I saw you the other day."

"Then you know all about Madame Ritter?"

"Yes, I know."

"You haven't seen her?"

"No, but I know where she is. All that's happened to her. And I know that she's to be executed next Wednesday."

Fritz shook his head and clasped his hands together between his knees in a gesture of outrage and despair. He said nothing. This enormity was too much for him. It was clear he knew her sentence already and it was something he had thought of no remedy for, so there was nothing to say about it.

"Poor Madame," he muttered finally. "Poor Madame." Then he roused himself and said more briskly, "About the other afternoon — I wasn't able to talk to you. I should have thought you might have realized that." His large, pale eyes focused on Mark reproachfully. "I was with my brother," he said.

"That was your brother?"

"Yes, and I thought it was best that he should know nothing about you. Already he wasn't too pleased to have me with him." Fritz turned almost eagerly from the hopelessness of Madame Ritter. "If he thought I was up to anything he'd hand me over just like *that!*" He clicked his supple fingers. They made a loud snap. "And then where would you be?" he added, "knowing no more than you do?"

Mark said, "I'm sorry, Fritz. You're right. Did you go to the Four Seasons?"

"Yes, I did. The concierge there is an acquaintance of mine. He gave me your address. I came just as soon as I dared. I've been here waiting for you since seven o'clock. And the landlady didn't think too much of me either. She's careful about her electricity."

"Yes, I saw that. But what are you worried about, what if your brother does see you talking to me? What have you done? You weren't involved in any way, were you?"

Fritz said in a dry, aggrieved voice, "I did enough to get myself a week in the jug, to lose a good job and to be under surveillance ever since. Yes, I had a good job when Madame Ritter turned up here. I nearly lost it, first, by running errands and doing things for her. After the trial and after I'd spent a week in jail, I lost it altogether."

"I'm sorry," Mark said.

"Then down there in the country," Fritz went on, "my brother is a terribly suspicious man. He makes only a bare living himself now. His butter, milk, and cheese all taken from him at a forced minimum price, practically none for his own use, and everything he has to buy sky-high. And then, it's contributions, contributions, all the time. If he hadn't a little piece of forest land with some wood to sell I don't know what he'd have done last winter, with five children to keep. It's been a hard winter here," he said.

"It's been a hard winter everywhere."

"The room that he usually rents to a skier or an artist," Fritz said, "I've been in for the last month. No, he doesn't think much of me. Living abroad as much as I have hasn't impressed him at all. It isn't as though I'd made a success of service in foreign countries."

"I know, I know," said Mark impatiently, "I'm sorry."

But it was obvious Mark didn't really care and Fritz sat still and looked at him reproachfully. "I've been under constant surveillance," he said with a sort of gloomy satisfaction. "Everywhere I go I'm watched. My brother knows that. I tell you if he thought there was any funny business he'd turn me over like that."

He got up and walked over to the window and lifted back the curtain an inch and peered down into the street. Mark heard the rain against the pane. Fritz came back and sat down again. He pointed his long, pale finger at Mark. "Now if she'd listened to me," he said, "done as I told her to, none of this need have happened. But she wouldn't listen."

Yes, here was old Fritz again. Nothing changed . . . Always complaining that the plumbing in this place was unsanitary and would be the death of them all; that Madame Ritter oughtn't to entertain as much as she did, with prohibition liquor costing so much and her guests all reckless drinkers and no money coming in and he himself not having received a cent in wages for a year now. And Mark was an insolent young pup and had gone to the trouble of putting wet newspapers in his bed and he wouldn't stand it.

But still, as he always liked to say, he was a free man with a tongue in his head, bold enough to use it on anyone. His tongue was his freedom. And besides, who did they turn to the minute they got in trouble? Who repaired things and repaired them perfectly? Who else was at a given place at the exact moment required, who summoned up unlooked-for knowledge? That they didn't love him made no difference to him at all. All he wished to be was in his small scale omnipotent.

"Yes," he said, "I said to Madame Ritter at the time (it was the day before the arrest), I said, 'Madame, you've got your money: if I was you I'd take the night train, go, as they say in America, while the going's good.' She said, 'Very well, Fritz, you get the tickets. I'll go tomorrow night.' But it was too late then."

Mark said wearily, "How did she happen to run into Rieger?" (For what did all that really matter now?)

"I ran into Mr. Rieger. He was just going into the Regina Palace. He knew me right away. We talked for a moment and I said, 'Mr. Rieger, Madame Ritter's here.' 'Is she?' he said. He seemed very much surprised. 'I'd like to see her,' he said. So he came and they talked about the house. Then later they went and looked at it and I went with them. It's in bad condition, I must say. It was rented out to studios, and the agent scarcely turning a penny of it over to Madame. Still, it's got a big garden and every room painted and decorated and all the bronze doors and mouldings and some of the statues even left. Mr. Rieger was very enthusiastic. I suppose, by the way Mr. Mark, that he deposited the money?"

"Oh, yes, he deposited it. Very smart of him to think of that trick, wasn't it? Or did you think of it?"

"We both did," Fritz said calmly. "I told Madame Ritter she couldn't hope to get the money in America any other way. Of course, there's a small sum in the bank here too, the nominal sale price. I don't know what's customary to do with money in a case like this. Now that Madame Ritter is . . . Well, you might make a claim for it and get it."

"I don't want it. What day was she arrested, Fritz?"

"The twentieth of January."

"And how soon after that was the trial?"

"I don't know when it began. Two weeks after her arrest I was taken by the Secret Police out of the house where I was working. They spent all one night asking questions about Madame. I hadn't a moment's sleep for twenty-four hours. Sort of a third degree you might say. They gave me a black eye and beat me till I could hardly stand."

Fritz spoke with a cold jocularity, but his eyes gleamed with hatred.

"All the questions they asked me about Madame! About her life in America, who she knew, what letters she got, what she did with her money and how much she appeared to have and where it came from."

"What did you tell them?"

"I said I had gone to America with the family over twenty years ago and worked for them steadily as long as there was money to pay me. I said I got paid less and less. And finally I left Madame Ritter's service in disgust and went into business for myself."

He screwed up one eye and looked cunningly at Mark.

"But I was really too clever for them," he said, "and I'll tell you why. I knew they wanted me to testify against Madame and were really sounding me out to see what I'd be likely to say. Very wily, these fellows are. But then, I wasn't born yesterday myself. I gave them the impression that I had been very put-upon by Madame and had left her dissatisfied with her treatment and the wages received and even ready to get even with her if I got the chance."

Mark had never heard Fritz talk so much before, not even in his most garrulous moments. What an opportunity this was! Everything was here, bad news, reproach, the stupidity of others, and his own superior cleverness. His eyes gleamed with a frosty animation and slyly he laid his finger against his nose.

"You see, Mr. Mark, I only wanted the chance to testify. I knew once I got in court I could give her a clear bill of health if anyone could."

"Did they let you?"

"Well, yes, they did." The glow diminished in him a little. It was clear that while the idea had been a good one it hadn't worked. "I said all I could but it was no use. You know how these things are," he said darkly. "They were determined to have it their way."

"It was a secret trial?"

"Yes. I was only there one day, in the forenoon. I got the idea the trial had been going on for several days. Well, I said my say, and a few days later they sent for me again. Of course I was still in jail, and they told me I was free to go if I'd leave the city and keep my mouth shut. I said I'd like very much to leave the country. My sister Minna, you know, is in service in England and I thought I'd go and stay with her for a while. But they said I wasn't to leave the country under any circumstances, so I said then I'd go down to my brother's. Then they said to me, 'Madame Ritter has been found guilty and condemned to death, and if you don't want to get into similar trouble you'll keep your mouth shut.'"

"But the note?" Mark said.

"Well, at the noon recess as I was leaving I stepped into the little room where Madame Ritter was waiting. She had said she wanted to speak to me, and she said, in a rather theatric voice she has sometimes, quite loud so it could be heard, 'Thank you, Fritz. You were always good, Fritz,' she said. Then she took my hand in both of hers and slipped the note up my cuff. I had an awful time keeping it there. I managed to get it wedged up under my flannel undershirt. Luckily they never searched me before I left."

"Why didn't you write me yourself?"

"I didn't dare do that. Not even before they told me not to. And still less afterward. But I thought, if they got hold of her note they might think it had got out by means of someone else."

Looking at Fritz, at his face growing each moment more familiar, Mark found it hard to realize he had been with Emmy, had seen and taken actual part in these terrible moments. Fritz had a gift of reducing all things to a common triviality.

"How did she seem, Fritz?" he asked. "Was she worried, did she seem frightened?"

Fritz shook his head. "She looked pretty bad," he said, "very pale. Yellowish, you know. I should say she felt sick. She had a pain, I believe, and asked for some aspirin, and someone went out and got it for her. She wrote the note on the aspirin paper."

"She was sick. She nearly died in prison. They operated on her. But they took her out to the camp to do it. I talked to the doctor who did it."

"Oh," said Fritz. He showed no surprise. Perhaps nothing could surprise him any more. But he also disliked to have it appear that he was not completely informed. He liked to explain but he hated to be told.

"She's still there," Mark said. "Did you know that?"

"No. But I knew she was sick. She wasn't downed certainly. You know her, sir. When things get bad, she's always very excited and gay and what you'd call humorous, and she always says things in an unrestrained sort of way. In fact, she said a lot of things at the trial I think she'd much better not have said. You can imagine her."

Mark smiled wanly. He could imagine her.

Then Fritz said, "But of course that's why she's still alive. I was wondering about that."

"What do you mean?"

Fritz said soberly, "I thought about it a good deal, and I decided there was no one in the world to do anything for Madame Ritter but me. It isn't as though she'd kept all her powerful friends like those she used to have over here, or even those she had in America when we first went there. Madame Ritter doesn't seem to be able to keep important friends. It isn't even as though you, Mr. Mark, had become a successful person either. And poor Miss Sabina, what could she do? No, I said to myself, it's all over and there's only one thing I can do. So when the police told me about the death sentence I asked if I could claim the body. That's allowed sometimes, you know, even with criminals. I went from one bureau to another and I signed all the papers necessary and got it settled. Of course they were to notify me. When they didn't I began to wonder. Whatever their faults, they're usually very exact and methodical about such things. So I thought perhaps she was very sick, or even that they'd decided to commute the sentence."

"They haven't," Mark said.

Fritz said slowly, "Well, anyway, Madame Ritter won't be thrown into any prison lime pit. You can rest assured of that much."

Then quite suddenly he gave a queer cracked sob, almost without changing his expression, staring straight ahead of him. Mark could hardly believe he'd heard it. Then Fritz took out a large handkerchief and blew his nose.

"There's no doubt they'll give me the body," he said. His eyes were suddenly inflamed without a tear having come from them.

"What'll you do then?" Mark said.

"I'll take it to the country. I'll give it decent burial on my brother's place if they'll allow that. I'd have to have a permit for that. If not, in the cemetery. I can get a permit for one or the other. This takes a lot of papers. You can't even get buried now without a lot of papers."

"But what will your brother do? Will he let you use his place?"

"He'll do that for money. He needs it, as I said. I haven't any. But now that you're here, perhaps you've got some."

"I have," said Mark; "I've got what was deposited in America. Enough to do whatever's necessary. Count on me for the money."

There was no more for them to say and suddenly Mark yawned nervously. He was shocked by his yawn and smothered it. It seemed too natural a thing to do.

"The trouble with money," he said, "is getting enough at a time. I'm living on very little but I can only draw out so much a day. If we need any large sum at once we'll have to take it at the regular rate of exchange."

"It won't be much," Fritz said. "We're all very poor here. A little goes a long way."

They listened to the rain for a moment in silence. Fritz sat dejectedly, his pale eyes on the floor, his flabby chin pressing into his Humpty Dumpty collar.

"Yes," he said finally, "they'll call me up sometime between now and Wednesday. Or send me a notification. I gave them the address of a friend of mine in town, Ebers, who married a niece of mine. He has a cleaning and dyeing establishment. I'll arrange to have a truck. The coffin of course they'll supply. If you like I can order a better one, with bronze handles say. And I'll take it down on the train. Then I'll use my brother's sledge to haul it to the farm."

"Don't talk about it now," Mark said. "I can't stand hearing any more now. Come back here tomorrow. No, tonight, I mean. It's Monday already. I'll have the money for you then. I'll go down with you, of course."

"Of course," Fritz said, "when it's all over they oughtn't to deny you that. But it might be better if no one knew who you were. They don't want any of these things known. I don't know what they could do but they might do something."

"The police already know I'm here and who I am."

"Do they?" Fritz shifted uneasily in his chair. "Do they know how you found out?"

"No, of course not."

"I suppose you went straight to the police when you got here."

"Yes."

"They'll guess it was me."

"I didn't tell them. Why should they guess? They may think she has other connections they don't know about."

Fritz got up again and walked over to the window and held back the curtain a crack.

"So you went straight to the police," he said. "They were surprised, I imagine. Did they hold out any hope?"

"None at all. I saw a lawyer, too."

"Waste of time," Fritz said.

Mark, looking at his back, said suddenly, "You can't think of anything else?"

"What else, sir?"

"Anything. Some way to get her out now, while she's still alive."

Fritz turned around, surprised, and dropped the curtain. "Do you mean you and me to try and get her out?"

"Yes. Who else? There's no one but us, as you say. But you said everyone's poor. Perhaps money would do something."

"That's quite impossible," Fritz said. He didn't even think it over, spoke at once in a flat, final voice, and he looked at Mark with a certain contempt for having thought only of the childish thing.

"Why?" Mark said. "You can always do everything, Fritz. You're the one who always helped us out. Don't you remember you could always do what no one else could? Think of some way to get her out, Fritz."

Fritz was disturbed. This flattery coming from Mark upset his natural calculations.

"I don't know what you mean, Mr. Mark."

"Think of something," Mark urged. "It hasn't occurred to you before, all alone and with no money. But I'm here now to help. And we've got money, plenty of money. We can't sit back here like this and plan to carry her out dead in a box. With bronze handles. We've got to carry her out alive, Fritz."

Fritz looked at him with startled eyes. He was wondering if the strain had been too much for him. Then he crossed the room and picked up his shabby overcoat, so old that it had belonged to Mark's father.

"I'm going now, Mr. Mark. It's very late. I'll have a lot to do tomorrow."

"All right," Mark said dully. He watched Fritz put his stiff arms into the coat as though his joints ached.

"I'll come tomorrow night — tonight," he corrected himself.

"All right. Come about eleven. I may be out."

Fritz hesitated. Perhaps he wanted to say a consoling

word. He stood looking awkwardly, feeling in his pockets for something, a key, or a handkerchief, perhaps. But consolation wasn't in his line.

"I'll come tonight at eleven," he repeated, and he went and got his hat, the old Homburg, off the bed.

"Good night," Mark said.

Fritz went over to the door and Mark followed him. At the door they shook hands. Fritz's hands were cold and dry and old. Mark held the door open so he could see his way among the wicker chairs and tables of the hall. The door across from him remained closed. At the other door Fritz felt around for the switch. The outside hall and the lift cage sprang into view. He heard Fritz hurrying downstairs. Presently the light clicked off. He closed his door.

He went over to the window and looked down into the rainy, empty street, full of puddles. Fritz appeared, his overcoat collar turned up, his hands in his pockets. He scurried head down at an angle across the street. Mark could see his pale ears flaring below the brim of his hat. He looked like a harried old rabbit making for his hole.

Mark turned back to his lighted room. But mysteriously he felt consoled. Old Fritz was here. Old Fritz, the insolent and the complaining and the garrulous. It's hard to live down a reputation for omnipotence.

Chapter XIV

The Countess dreamed a short dream just before she woke up. She was on the lawn at Newport, with the thick fog coming in. She heard the fog horn from the Brenton Reef lightship bellowing like a disconsolate sea monster. The great cedar tree was a flat shape in the mist, the grass was vivid and the soles of her slippers, the edges of her long white skirts, were damp. She smelled the wetness of everything. They can't see me from the Wentworths', she thought; how nice to have it so foggy. She sat down in a creaking wicker chair. Of course I can't stay here long, she thought.

Then there was a man moving around in the mist, looking for something. She couldn't see who he was but he was coming nearer, looking always from side to side and on the grass, as though he'd lost something. A dream fear came over her suddenly. She watched him circle around the cedar tree. The letter box, she thought. He is looking for the letter box.

She and Carol Wentworth long ago, ten years old both of them, left love notes in the little hollowed hole by the third bough. Why did I say love notes? We were only children. You had to climb the tree to reach it. He came toward her and she saw it was a dark young man.

It was Leo Mannheim walking toward her. Then it was all right. It was Leo and yet it was not quite Leo. He had a peaceful look on his face and when he saw her he smiled in a friendly way.

Oh, Leo, she cried, you did come after all. I'm so glad, I'm so glad. Leo didn't answer. He only nodded, still smiling, and pointed to something in her lap. It was a bunch of violets. Oh, of course, she said, you want the violets, and she stood up and pressed them into his outstretched hands, bunches and bunches of violets. There were more and more. She pressed them closer and closer, leaning into his arms.

Juli came with her coffee and she smiled up at her; so happy, she hadn't wakened like this for years. She sat up and Juli put the tray on her knees. She thought even to move might destroy it, but the happiness stayed with her. When Juli spoke to her she answered with an absent nod. She tried to keep remembering the dream but presently it dimmed away.

She got up, bathed and dressed. She began to think what she'd have to do today. The girls' studies left her free of them during the morning. But there was the food to be planned, letters to be answered, and a telephone call about the language lessons for the new girl. After lunch she would take them to the Historical Museum.

Toward noon she went downstairs. Her drawing room was filled with pale light from high windows, and the old needlepoint chairs bloomed in it, frail coral and green and yellow. On the old white and gold consoles the light struck two faience artichokes of turquoise color. Juli had filled the vases with freesias and narcissus and huge sprays of forsythia, and these were reflected in the long, dim mirrors. Oh, what a charming room! The gray Persian got up from a chair and came to rub against her ankles. She moved about, readjusting the flowers, pulling some forward, changing the positions of the vases.

At the window she stopped to look out, and the shapes of trees in the sunny mists of the English garden brought a little shock of pleasure. Leaning against the window she remembered the dream again, not the sequence of it but only the poignant, floating sense of happiness it had left. What could it possibly have been about? She couldn't remember at all but the memory of the happiness was so strong that she experienced it once more, only a little less strongly than the first time.

A bell rang somewhere in the house. She drew back uneasily. She could never accustom herself to the sound made by a hand as yet unknown. How servants must dislike bells, she thought. But of course it would be nothing, a package for one of the girls, the postman. Juli came to say it was the General.

He never came in the morning. He assumed that no one knew or could know anything about them. No one treated her in public with greater respect and he was very proud of never doing anything, not the slightest thing, that might suggest intimacy with her. So, something must have happened. Something must be wrong.

He came in, however, quite radiant with good humor, freshly shaven and in a sort of ruddy overglow of apparent health. The whole room danced for a moment on the glass of his monocle and only the swollen vein beside it showed her that his health, if not his good humor, was an illusion.

"My dear," he said, kissing her hand, "I thought I'd surprise you. Are you very busy? Have you time to see me?"

"Of course. Sit down. But you never come in the morning. It *is* something of a surprise."

"A pleasant one, I hope."

"But naturally."

He was in uniform and she remembered that this morning he had had to take the visiting Marshal to the airport.

All day yesterday he had accompanied him on his inspection.

Then today he had got away earlier than he expected. He had told her to look for him no sooner than teatime. She guessed that he had made a success with the Marshal and that was the reason for his good humor. He was writing a book on war, a further application, he told her, of the principles of Clausewitz to the late war. Probably he had managed to bring up the subject with the Marshal and had succeeded in interesting him. If he had it wouldn't be long before he'd find an excuse to tell her.

They sat down and he said, "How nice your room smells. Flowers, I see. So many of them. May I smoke?"

"Of course."

He lit a cigarette and leaned his head back against the chair. He looked like a great cat who has found exactly the right tension for each muscle. He looked across at her under his lowered eyelids. "You are flowerlike yourself," he said. "I've not seen you so blooming in a long time."

"I slept well."

"But you're not being very hospitable. Aren't you going to offer me a glass of schnapps?"

She reached out for the bell but Juli, who had anticipated this, appeared just then with the tray and set it down beside him. He looked at Juli with approval. When she had left he said, "An excellent servant, Juli, excellent."

"You seem very pleased with life this morning," she said.

"Why shouldn't I be? I'm here with you, and a lot of trouble I had to get here too. I got up an hour earlier than usual so as to be quite free after he left. I saw him off at ten. Very tiring it's been, too."

"I'm sure it has."

"All day yesterday making this inspection! He's a devil

for detail. And then the official dinner last night. Not a free moment. I hadn't even a chance to telephone you. But you didn't expect it probably. You knew I'd be busy all day."

"I supposed you would be. How was he? Was he boring?"

"He's a remarkable man. Remarkable," he said emphatically. "It's the first chance I've had to talk to him really since the war. Yes, he's got a great character and great power."

He waited a moment, listening for her approval. Nothing came, and he said with a modesty she knew he didn't feel, "We talked a little about the book. I had the opportunity to get some of his ideas and they were most interesting."

Still she said nothing.

The General tapped out his cigarette impatiently. "You don't like him, I suppose?"

She said, "He's too fat."

"What a frightfully silly thing to say! Of course he's fat. No one can deny that. That has nothing at all to do with what I've just been saying, which is that he's a powerful and original fellow with a keen mind and a great personality."

"Is he?"

"What's the matter with you, Ruby? Anyone would think you wanted to irritate me. You must remember that the Marshal suffered terribly during the war."

"Didn't everyone? And don't people ever suffer between wars?"

The General looked at her with a rebuking gravity.

"Then there was his wife, you remember," he said. "He adored her. He couldn't forget her."

"Not even with the second?"

"It's not for us to say about that. I think, though, that he's suffered more than most."

"Is that why he takes drugs?"

"He no longer takes drugs."

She saw him make an effort to control his irritation. He took a deep breath and smiled, showing all his fine strong white teeth. Then he said, "I mean, he's always been a peculiarly sensitive patriot. Some men have a special sensibility as patriots, just as others have as lovers. Those suffer more."

"That makes me quite sick," she said.

She herself couldn't understand what made her talk like this. She was feeling actually exceptionally well, so free from the down-dragging dread that was always worst in the mornings. No, she didn't feel any irritation at all. Certainly not with him. She was swimming along in a pleasant light-headedness, not thinking at all of what she said, speaking quite naturally for once. Her naturalness was so unfamiliar it made her a little giddy.

It was he who held back this time and watched himself. He shut his lips tight; and, looking around for something to handle, saw the gray cat curled up beside his chair. He reached down and rubbed it expertly behind the ears. The cat half-closed its eyes and purred. With his other hand he took a long swallow of schnapps, put down the glass carefully, and as though on purpose turned his head to the best angle, so that the light brought out the Roman emperor modeling of his nose and forehead and lips. He relaxed into beauty, he and the cat together, both of them looking at her with heavy, dreamy eyes.

"Well," he said, "and what did you do? Were you bored yesterday?"

It was just as though the bell rang again in the house and her well-being was gone in one startled leap of the heart.

Nervous and alert, she thought: I oughtn't to have put him in a bad humor.

"No, as a matter of fact," she said, "I wasn't."

"So? How did you manage to amuse yourself?"

"Well, in the morning I took the girls to church. The Cardinal was there."

"The old fool! Did he say anything?"

"Not much. We came back by the garden and had a coffee, and there I met Bob and Lotte, who had tickets for the concert."

She knew him so well that though not a muscle flickered and his eyes didn't change, she saw exactly what was in his mind. Why he'd come, and what he was going to say. How stupid, and how dangerous, for both of them, that she hadn't taken the trouble to see it before. Of course Bob and Lotte had been talking to him. But when had they had a chance to see him? At the airport, of course. Bob was leaving for the north. When they brought her home last night he said he hadn't decided whether to fly or go by train. But probably he'd flown. And at the airport, seeing Kurt there, especially seeing him with the great man, he and Lotte would certainly find an excuse to join him. But then, perhaps Bob went by train after all, and Kurt knew nothing. No, it was wasting time to pretend that. She'd much better concentrate on how to smooth it all out, make it seem unimportant and even wearisome and banal.

"Did they offer to take you?"

"Where?"

"Why, to the concert of course. You seem to be still half asleep, my dear."

"Yes, they did. But I don't care terribly for them. I thought they'd spoil the music for me."

"You didn't go then?"

"Yes, I went. I went with an American friend of mine who turned up rather unexpectedly."

"How very nice! And did the American friend not spoil the music?"

"No. But he wasn't as much of a musician as I'd thought. It's a mistake to go to a concert with anyone who doesn't care for music. This was simply a young man I met once in New York. Probably Bob and Lotte told you. We all met outside afterward and Bob and Lotte brought me home."

"The young man is visiting here?"

"I suppose so. I ran into him quite by accident and he asked me to tea and then we went to the concert. I don't expect to see him again. I rather hope I don't."

"That would be too bad. You don't often see your American friends. Why not see him again?"

What if he should ask his name? Should she make up one for him? What name? And wasn't it really just an odious habit, all this dread and timid scampering about?

"I don't really think there would be any point in seeing him again," she said. "He's leaving anyway."

"Too bad," he said. "I see the fellow would have done better to be a musician. You used to be always picking up musicians. I'll never forget the long-haired viola player you found who was going to write the great symphony." He laughed amiably. "What a bore he turned out to be!"

"Yes, didn't he?" She smiled and dropped her eyes and sat silent.

He shifted around in his chair and laughed again, presumably still thinking of the viola player. Then he took a drink of schnapps.

"Well," he said teasingly, "we won't talk any more of your American. I didn't come to talk about him anyway. As a matter of fact, I came to suggest something. I want

[212]

to get away for a while. I had the most fearful headache all day yesterday. Aspirin wouldn't touch it. Even today I've got some of it. It's nothing serious, just that I've been working too hard. I thought I'd take a week's leave."

Gone for a week. She looked up, trying to show quick anxiety and regret. "That's too bad!" she exclaimed. "Are you following your regime? I suppose with official dinners you couldn't. Do be careful, Kurt."

She labored her voice into a show of concern but her heart was lightening again, rising like a balloon. She shot a sidelong look to the window. A lovely day, and what was that other thing that had made her so happy?

"I thought I'd go to Kitzbühel for a week," he said. "You remember that little Golden Goose Inn where we had such a wonderful day once?"

"Of course I remember it," she said tenderly, thinking only in a skimming, hurried way of the day he spoke of. It *had* been a wonderful day, but she was going to be released from such days for a week and for a whole week would be free and empty and light of heart. "Of course I remember it," she repeated.

He leaned forward, resting his elbows on the chair arms. He adjusted his monocle so as to see her more clearly.

"As I came here," he said, "a brilliant idea struck me. I said to myself, I must get away all right. That's obvious. But why go alone? Why can't Ruby come with me?"

Never before had he suggested such a thing. Always it had been he who was careful, who reminded her of how easily they might be compromised and what the consequences of that would be.

"Why, you must be mad!" she exclaimed. "You and I can't go away anywhere together."

"Why not? No one need see us. You could go by train, I by car. You stay at the Golden Goose, I stay somewhere else. We had a day there once more or less by accident. Why not have seven?"

"I can't leave the girls," she said.

"Get someone to stay with them."

"Who?"

"Anyone. There must be a dozen people you could get."

"Only Bertha would do it."

"Get Bertha then."

"But when are you leaving?"

"Tomorrow. Tuesday."

"I can't possibly get Bertha by then."

"You sound, my dear, like a wild little hen being chased from corner to corner of the barnyard. Come, it's not so serious. Telegraph to Bertha."

"She couldn't get here for three days. You know how Bertha is. She'll never leave home unless all the bureau drawers are in order. And maybe she won't come at all! If you weren't going so soon! If you could wait a while — "

"I can't wait." He got up and came over and stood behind her chair. He put his hands around her neck and drew her head back against him.

Aunt Medora had said once, "Pick a man for character, my dear, and for mutual compatibility. Physical love doesn't last." What did Aunt Medora know about it? And what is physical love anyway? Her husband she had picked for compatibility and because of admiration and respect. But Kurt and she had picked each other almost altogether for what Aunt Medora called "physical love," and it had outlasted everything. After fifteen years it was all that remained. Long ago their minds had begun to distrust each other, each had turned insensitive and finally blind to nearly everything that flourished in the other. In their dislike they used all they remembered of each other only to inflict pain, but still their love went on. Like the cycle of the seasons it continually renewed itself, whether the year had been good or bad or drought or pestilence had come. It was for both of them a yoke and a perpetual renewal. And since they knew now by experience how vital it was they took every chance with it, treating it roughly and without concern. Wasn't it imperishable? So imperishable, she though, that it does no harm to hate him for a while, or to be indifferent to him for a whole week and to be alone and not to think of him. But that was to be impossible this time.

"Let's go up to the country then," he said. He dropped the monocle from his eye, leaned over and pressed his cheek against her knot of hair. "Let's go up to the country house. Take your precious girls with you. I'll stay at the Inn. I'll ski all day. It'll do me good. Let's leave at once."

"You mean tonight?"

"Tonight or tomorrow. I'd better leave tomorrow and you tonight. You'll do that?"

"Why, yes," she said slowly, "I can manage that. I'll tell the girls it's the last of the skiing. It will be, too."

"You promise?" He said it in her ear. "You promise?"

"Of course."

He kissed her ear and then straightened up.

"I'd better go," he said. "It's nearly lunchtime."

"Will you stay for lunch?"

"I'd better not, especially if I am to appear up in the country. You're not worried about that, are you? They need hardly see me up there."

"I think we ought to be very careful," she said sharply. "After all, they're my living."

"We'll be careful. But you do want this week, don't you?"

"Of course I do."

She stood up too. As they walked to the door he stopped her in the middle of the room, and, first looking toward the door, put his arms around her and kissed her. The kiss, smelling a little of schnapps, had to her who knew him so well a tension and reserve. He shouldn't have kissed her if he wished to hide these. But it didn't matter. She would go to the country with him and they would have what was as necessary to their lives as bread and air and water. But they wouldn't be happy. She couldn't remember when they had stopped knowing happiness. Perhaps happiness was too delicate and it demanded a sort of purification that could only be had now on the edge of sleep.

In the hall Juli waited, holding out his overcoat. As he put his arms in the sleeves he said calmly, "Oh, by the way, your American friend couldn't be that young Ritter boy by any chance?"

She stared at him and couldn't say a word. Juli stepped back to open the door and held his cap in her hand waiting. He took his gloves from his pocket and put them on slowly.

"What does he call himself? Not the mother's name. The father's I suppose, but I can't remember it. But of course, it couldn't be he. I don't imagine you'd know anyone like that."

He took his cap from Juli and said, "An awfully funny story about that young man. I was talking to Rudi about him. You know he came to see Rudi about his mother but of course Rudi wouldn't tell him a word about what was to happen. And by the way, if he is your young man you'd better not tell him either. Well, anyway, as I was saying, this Madame Ritter as I remember her looked to me like a rather handsome boy. That's one reason I didn't like her. And now, Rudi tells me the son looks like a rather handsome girl, rather silky and sensitive — you know —

Well, it seems he made advances to Rudi." Kurt laughed. "Yes, actually. Rudi told me so himself. And the joke is — *Rudi repulsed him.*" He took her icy hand and kissed it. "Until tomorrow then."

He went down the steps to his waiting car and Juli closed the door after him.

She walked slowly back to the drawing room. She went over to the desk and stood looking down at the papers on it. There would be a lot to do if she was to get off tonight. She must telephone ahead to have the house warmed, order food, and remember to speak of drying the sheets thoroughly. And the language teacher would have to be called up again. And as she was dining with Margaret tomorrow she'd have to call her too. And there would be very little time to think of much else.

The old sickness and fear were making her tremble again. Her head ached. And this time it was much worse, the room as she looked around it seemed to change, it was darkened by something that flowed out from herself and the things in the room were hurtful and alive, more alive than she or than Kurt.

Only one thing in it made a refuge. The desk was blond, satiny wood and in the center of it was a little circular space with ebony columns and mirrors. It looked like a tiny baroque hall of reception with inlaid floors. By pressing a button the recess turned and another recess came to light. She loved it because it was like the tiny places in fairy tales. Looking at it she wanted now to become tiny, to look into the mirrors, to pirouette once, to press the button, to turn behind the ebony columns, and to vanish.

Chapter XV

THE day after the doctor had talked to Emmy was Sunday. He didn't come that day. After all, she thought, it's
Sunday, a man must have some rest. And besides, she
thought, I'm so much better. There's nothing he can do
for me.

But Monday morning he didn't come either. All morning she kept turning her eyes toward the door. At each
sound in the hall she was quite still so as to listen, but no
one came in.

It was a fair, slightly misty, spring day after the rain
that had fallen all the night before. The sky through the
window was pale blue. It was a day for strolling along the
streets, looking in shop windows and taking a glass of
beer in the Palace garden, or for a drive somewhere in
the country, smelling the new sap and picking a bunch of
snowdrops to put in the hat.

"It's a lovely day, Anna," she said. "Can you see what
a lovely day it is?"

But Anna was much worse. During the night she had
had another hemorrhage, a bad one, and now she lay on
her back, her eyes closed, and only once or twice did she
speak in a faint whisper. She seemed now to be asleep.

"How do you feel, Anna?" Emmy asked her, but she
didn't answer. When their noonday soup came she only
turned away her head. "You'd better eat it," Hermann

said. She stood looking down at Anna, then she shrugged and took it away again.

After noon the sky suddenly clouded over and in the middle of the afternoon it began to rain again. The narrow room grew so dark Emmy could barely see to the other bed. The sheets and blankets were damp and great patches of damp appeared on the walls. She was so cold she couldn't even doze as she usually did in the afternoon. She lay listening to the cold, heavy spring rain. Because of the rain there wasn't the stamp of men's feet exercising in the outside yard, but once an automobile came in a great hurry. Hermann talked to someone for quite a while out in the hall.

Suddenly Emmy said aloud, "Well, he's gone back on me."

Now she had said it, it didn't seem so bad really. There was so short a time before the end that perhaps it didn't matter. She knew now how much he had helped her. He alone of the people who had been with her at the trial and of those in the prison had been willing to let her feel like a human being. Even when they were not physically cruel they were destroying a portion of her humanity. She could stand up to them but, still, they had power to damage her irreparably. Their own descent dragged her too far, no matter how she held herself. But the doctor wasn't like that, and if he wasn't here now he had helped her to keep intact what was necessary for the end.

There was still the end to be gone through. So as to be strong and prepared she began to go over it all in her mind as it would be. I'm asleep, she thought, I'm dozing, and it's very early, before daybreak. And suddenly I hear voices down the hall and I wake up with fear, certainly with dreadful fear, and the first thing I think is: It's here. Someone will come in and say, It's time; but I'll already have said it to myself. It will be very dark and very cold and I'll get up and be dressed. What was I wearing when I came here? The brown suit — so then I put on the brown suit. Hermann helps me put it on and Anna lies there and watches me with frightened and pitying eyes, not saying anything. And then two people take my arms and I walk. Perhaps the doctor is one of them. He holds my arm and I walk. I walk — How far must I walk?

Not to be able to see a detail clearly worried her. She tried to imagine the corridor outside the room, the other rooms. But she had been carried in unconscious. She didn't know what it was like outside this room. Anyway, there'll be a car waiting.

Black leather seats. They'll pull the blinds down. There'll be the damp, musty smell of taxis. No one will speak. The noise of the car starting in the cold and a smell of gasoline. As it goes out Anna will hear it. She'll say, "There she goes, there she goes. Poor Emmy!"

I'll feel a little carsick, so early in the morning and without breakfast. And cold of course, horribly cold. Somewhere at that time Mark and Sabina will be having breakfast. No, not breakfast; what am I thinking of? There's the difference in time. What is the difference in time, five hours, plus one? or two? Make it six hours. It'll be the night before. Or is that right?

But maybe Sabina's already in the West. And maybe Mark went with her. Anyway, at some time, perhaps just now, he's saying, "You know she hates to write."

"But she always does, or she sends cables or telegrams. She's not just silent like this."

"But they probably censor the mails. And sometimes the concierges don't mail them: they steal the stamps."

Do you think anything could have happened?

They'll look at each other and be afraid to say it.

Well, anyway, I'm in the car. I'll know when we reach town because there will be more cars passing. The horn will blow more often and we'll make stops for the lights. Are the lights on that early? It's a good thing there's no seeing out of the windows. I might see a house I knew, one I had a happy time in once, or just one that was very familiar to me, or perhaps Mother's house. I might see the garden with all the trees bare and the window of my room, with the mask carved above it, the mask with soot in the eyes and the corners of the lips — No, I wouldn't want to see that.

No one'll speak to me in the car and I mustn't try to say anything. It would be the wrong thing certainly. Better to sit very quiet, and perhaps I might ask for a cigarette. A cigarette goes with an execution. They always ask for a cigarette. And someone gives it to them — solemnly. . . .

But then here we are. I get out and take a step or two on the wet pavement. It'll still be raining. I hope so. I couldn't bear a lovely spring dawn. No, it must be raining. And so then a door closes — and then what?

Then what? I don't know. But I must — I must make it up. I must live it now and die it now, and have it over with. But I really don't know how I will feel. It's always the thing you can't imagine that happens. Will the doctor stay with me? Will they put a handkerchief over my eyes? Will it take very long? Oh — what was that other thing I was trying to think of?

Late in the afternoon Emmy fell asleep, but even in her sleep she was conscious of horror and of cold in all her body that was a part of the horror.

She opened her eyes and the doctor stood over her. She could hardly see him because of the staring light bulb behind his head. It hung down on a cord into the center of the room and it had no shade. Outside the cold rain was still falling and the window was quite dark. She turned over on her back trying to see his face against the light. "It must be late," she said, "I'm freezing."

He spoke sharply to Hermann, who waited in the door. "You will get a hot-water bottle," he said, "and have it good and hot, too. And an extra blanket. Two extra blankets."

"But doctor — "

"You do as I say," he said. "If this woman dies do you know what I'll do? I'll say you let her die on purpose. To escape execution. I'll tell them how friendly you've always been."

"Friendly!"

"Yes. Always giving her little attentions."

"But doctor, it's you — "

"I heard a phonograph in the canteen as I came by." His voice was high and angry. "Where do you get a thing like that? Who gives you so much money? Is it Madame Ritter? I think you've been accepting bribes."

"Thou dear God!" Hermann exclaimed.

"Two blankets and a hot-water bottle, I said, and keep it hot all night, too."

With a loud groan Hermann went out.

Against the light the doctor's hair was tousled and little drops of water shone on it.

"You've been in the rain," she said. "Did you walk here?"

"Not here. But I've been walking. I suppose in the rain."

"You didn't come this morning, or yesterday either."

"I had other things to do. I have to have some time to myself, don't I?"

"What's the matter today?" she said.

"Why should anything be the matter?"

"Your voice has changed. You sound nervous and excited. You're always so calm."

"No, I'm all right. And how are you? That cretin would let you die of pneumonia."

"I'm all right, too, I suppose. But I'm cold. You try so hard to save me, don't you? You've been good. I was thinking before I went to sleep how good you've been. You *have* saved me in a way, too. You've helped me to die intact."

"Don't let's talk about it," he said. "There isn't any use talking about it now."

He sat down on the edge of the bed. His hands fell rigidly to his sides. She could feel the tension of his body along the bed. It's hard on him too, she thought: a decent fellow, really a romantic fellow.

The white, cruel light fell on his face and all its peaked, flying lines were sharpened.

"Anna's much worse," she said. "She had a hemorrhage last night."

"I know. I looked at her before you woke up."

Emmy looked over at Anna lying with her closed eyes that made bluish hollows in her face.

"I thought she was going to die last night."

"She won't live long," he said.

"How long?"

"Maybe only a few hours."

"Poor Anna!" She looked at her and felt ready to cry. But it didn't matter about Anna either. Everything comes to it in the end. "I want you to know," she said, "that I don't really mind it now. Hardly at all. I feel as though it had already happened, and as though my children already knew about it, and as though the tiny break that I'll make around me is already filling up."

"Would you like to see a priest?" he asked.

"Why should I see a priest? You know I'm not very religious. I can die without one. It's raining very hard, isn't it? I hope it keeps on. No, Bach and Leonardo and Spinoza have all died, haven't they?"

"And so have a host of criminals and idiots."

"Yes, I was going to say that. The consciousness of being Spinoza and the consciousness of being a criminal comes to an end. And the consciousness of being Emmy Ritter will stop too. That's all there is to it."

He watched her intently, as a physician watches but also as the young man who had kept her faded photograph. He leaned closer and took her wrist.

She went on dreamily, "I guess you're right about that separate value we think we have. It doesn't seem to stand up very well at the end. But just the same, I still want to go on being conscious of my separate consciousness, even if it hasn't let me ever learn the rules, even if it has only thickened the mystery."

His whole attention was on her pulse and he seemed to be listening to it as though it spoke for her.

She said, "If I were God and making a creature like myself I'd give him an eternal life. It would be a conscious life of the spirit with a little of the earthly love and joy I've learned here thrown in. And I'd let him find out about it somehow in advance. I might make it hard but I'd let him know. That's why we'd like to make a God who'd do that for us, isn't it?"

"Yes," he said absently, his fingers tightening.

"And so that lets that out I suppose. It's too much what children want. But it's curious that we can bear to live all our lives never really hoping, isn't it? For a long time I've had to live as though that kind of God didn't exist."

"I never think about God," he said.

"No? He's disappointed you too, hasn't he? But it can

all be understood if you take it for once and all as a hopeless battle. Candide asked why the world was made and Martin answered, 'To infuriate us.' But then, that's too easy, too."

"Yes, it's too easy."

"Evil and death are too easy to explain. Even Bach and Leonardo and Spinoza, even the sudden, heightened consciousness. People try to make the kind of God they want, and those men made the kind of consciousness they wanted. But there's still something left to explain. Something small and maybe not important. Why is Anna so gentle and patient and un-hating? Why are you so kind to me here? Those are the things I can't explain. And you can't either."

"Don't always keep trying to explain," he said roughly, letting her wrist fall. "It can't matter to you any more."

"Well," she said with a faint smile, "it matters for about thirty-six hours."

He got up and stood looking down at her and his eyelids lifted with a flickering, indecisive motion. Suddenly he turned and went to his black bag which he left always on the cane-bottomed chair by the door. He bent over it and opened it slowly and stood looking into it. His back was turned to her and for a long time he stood absolutely immobile.

Then she heard him tapping one of the bottles with his finger. Suddenly he made his decision, snatched up his bag and turned around. He came back to her bed and she was startled by the change in him. His eyes were shining with a bald, wild elation.

He said, "Now, Madame Ritter, I've told you that I want to make things as easy for you as I can, and I have something here that'll produce a complete relaxation of nerve tension. I want you to take it."

[225]

She watched him fumble in the bag for what he wanted. "I think *you* need it," she said. "But I'll take it. What is it, a shot in the arm?"

"No, it's taken by mouth. A tablet." He held it up. "I want you to take one now and one every three hours. You have no watch but you can more or less guess at the time." He took out his watch and looked at it. "Six o'clock," he said. Then he lifted her head suddenly and put the tablet between her lips. She swallowed it obediently and lay back.

"One every three hours," he repeated. "Do you understand?" He dropped the remaining tablets into an envelope. "I'll slip this under the mattress," he said, "so Hermann won't see it. She's such a fool."

His eyes, which ordinarily looked so directly, evaded her. He bent his head so she only caught the glisten of them.

"What are you doing?" she asked.

He shrugged his shoulders.

"What are you doing?" she repeated.

"Will you do as I say?"

She watched him, more and more troubled. He didn't seem to be the young man she had known before and on whom she had begun to depend. As he straightened up she saw his eyes and he made her think suddenly of a young man she had seen once who, for a reason she couldn't remember, had gone into a lion's cage, someone connected with a circus perhaps, but he seemed to be an amateur of lions. His eyes, blue like the doctor's, had been shining with an almost drunken look of relief — yes, as though he were making a direct personal test of himself, so headlong that he felt only exquisite relief.

Am I imagining this, she thought as he stood again in his stiff attitude by her bed, what does one really ever see looking at another's face? It's nonsense to suppose one sees

[226]

anything. Another explanation will always do just as well. What do I really know of him?

"I wish I knew why you want me to do this," she said. "Is it a drug to deaden things for me?"

He put his hand up and pressed the skin of his forehead back and forth.

"Can't you leave this to me?" he said. "You've made the sort of life you wanted, broken laws when you thought it was necessary. Now you let me make the sort I want."

"I think you're upset," she said. "You don't seem yourself."

"Well, it doesn't matter now, does it? Will you take those tablets or won't you?"

"I suppose I will."

"I don't believe you."

"Does it mean so much to you?"

"Yes, it does. See here," he said, taking her roughly by the arm. She looked at his fingers pressing into her loose, sunken skin. They were reddened by many scrubbings, strong and lean. His wrist started from his sleeve and the sharp wristbone made her remember Mark's thin young arms when he was a gangling boy. "See here. You've told me to be a man. To think and act for myself. Now I'm doing it. I've been in prison too. This is prison for me as much as it is for you. Now I tell you this: I don't choose to have you die on that scaffold. Is that enough?"

She slackened her arm so he let it go. She looked up into his blue, sparkling eyes. "Are you killing me?" she whispered.

"Shut up," he said. "Here comes Hermann."

She came stumping in with two blankets over her arm and a hot-water bottle. The doctor took the bottle from her and felt it. He put it inside the covers next to Emmy's side and Hermann spread the blanket.

[227]

"It's my own bottle," Hermann said. "There weren't any others."

"You remember what I told you," he said bullyingly. "Warm all night, see? That means you keep awake if necessary, and I don't care how you do that. A fine business it'll be for you if they come here Wednesday morning and you have to say, 'I let her die. She'd rather die here than there, so I let her have her way.'"

He went on scolding her. When Emmy was tucked in he picked up his bag. "Scream for her if you want anything," he said. He pointed his finger at Hermann and Herman turned and scuffled off down the hall.

"Good night, Madame Ritter," he said. He closed his bag with a snap. "I'll be back sometime tomorrow." He gave her a brisk salute, clicked his heels, and went out.

Emmy lay still. The rain poured against the pane and it was quite dark outside, but the room was full of sharp edges in the light of the electric bulb, and she was getting warm again.

So it was to be this way. It was to be this death. Coming slowly. Loosening one by one each tight-drawn band. All alone — No brutal eyes or hands — no crystal-sharp world and its indifference — gently, in a warm bed — Frightened, if that must be, but free to be frightened unashamed — Wrapped only in what was most comforting (Let tears soak down if they must) — Knowing so surely that among these people was at least one friend. One man courageous and clean of all cruelty — God save them for the sake of one just man — Yes, at the last he had given the best of all. Hope. It's all that can be asked. To die hoping.

She felt no effect from the tablet she'd taken. She spent what seemed three hours waiting for it to begin, but noth-

[228]

ing happened. Then she felt under the mattress, got another out and swallowed it.

Hermann had forgotten to turn out the light. She forgot it even when quite late she came in with hot soup. She was in an ugly mood because she had been frightened. She pushed Emmy up in bed and stood with her arms on her hips watching her dip the black bread slowly and tremblingly lift the spoon to her mouth. Emmy was hungry. She felt quite well and hungry.

"Doesn't Anna get any?" she asked.

Anna hadn't stirred.

"No hot food for her," Hermann said. "She'll begin to bleed again."

"She hasn't had any all day."

"You stop trying to run this place," Hermann said in a loud voice. "I'll do what I think's right, see?"

Emmy kept still. She ate her soup and Hermann took away the plate. Contrary to regulations, she left the light on.

Emmy felt no drowsiness or dullness at all. On the contrary she felt better than she had since coming to the prison, almost exhilarated. She wanted to talk to someone; to Anna. "Anna," she whispered, "how do you feel?"

Anna opened her eyes and Emmy saw the whites of them turning in her head. They were glazed and unseeing. She seemed to listen but she couldn't answer.

In a moment Emmy whispered again, "Anna, are you better?" and this time she didn't stir. Her breathing was so faint it was like a feather lifting in a faint draft. It couldn't be heard over the noise of the rain outside. She seemed to be suffering no pain. If she was dying now it was so peacefully that it came also gently to the beholder. And who could doubt that Anna, too, was better off?

As she ebbed there imperceptibly Emmy began even

[229]

against her will to feel more and more alive. Yes, with Anna dying and herself dying too she felt indifferent to their deaths. She felt a mounting energy growing. It seemed irresistible. Her blood began to flow quickly and her breath to come fast and strong. She felt she couldn't stay in bed. A vivid nervousness itched in her. To be moving, to throw off this inactivity, to get up, to go down the hall for instance, or to bend over Anna and see if she was cold —

She lifted her covers to get up but her heart gave a leap and a trembling weakness seized her all over. She fell back hugging the hot-water bottle, stilling the sudden chill that had struck her.

After all, she couldn't move. She was not really strong. But once quiet, the illusion of energy began to rise in her. Shall I think of the end again? She tried to. But no — Her mind wandered from it. As though she had years to live, she began to make plans. What they might do with that money, where they'd go, how they'd live.

Arizona certainly. She remembered a one-night stand in Tucson. Lying here with the cold rain on the window and the damp smell of plaster and whitewash filling the room, she remembered desert air, dry and tinseled with light. She remembered hills, blue and jewel-like against the sky in the mornings and evenings. The desert she'd only seen from a train and over town rooftops, from a hotel window; but now it stretched around her, pale flesh-color, full of little dry plants, precisely shaped, like coral and starfish. The deserts of the Persian miniatures. Was there a gazelle, bent like an arrow, looking at her out of a human eye? No, there were no gazelles in Arizona.

But she was riding on a spotted horse, red and white. And beside her Mark, beautiful under a big gray hat, with his painting kit strapped behind the saddle, rode with her into the pink sand. Sabina in the sun watched them go. To Sabina they would presently return. They were close together again in their own circle, as they had always been and must be. She thought she heard a cock crow, a sudden sound of joy.

Am I going to sleep? Am I a little feverish, a little delirious? Then I'll be entirely practical. One has to live in Arizona. One has to eat. One can't eat gazelle's meat and the red flowers of cactus. But in a state of freedom we can each do what we were made to do, and I, for instance, can act. There will certainly be a theater there. I mean, a theater in a barn or in a tent or in a school auditorium. We'll put on plays. I'll take the young men and girls with arms they can't control and voices they can't hear and I'll stretch them out like taffy and make them flexible and let them listen to their voices. And the plays will be only gay and new and without meanness. Mark can paint the scenes and Sabina shall dress them. Is this practical, or is this a dream? Because I lie here it must be a dream but in another place it would be only the solidest practicality.

All night she lay under the staring bulb, half asleep, half awake, but thinking only of life, never again of death. When she remembered she took a tablet.

Toward morning Hermann came, puffy-eyed, her whole face swollen with sleep. She wore a flannel dressing gown like a man's and she looked, with her short, straight blond hair, like a prize fighter leaving the ring after a bad bout. Emmy burst into a gay, nervous laugh at the sight of her. Hermann had come with a fresh hot-water bottle, and to turn off the light. As she put the bottle against her she looked curiously at her.

"What's funny?" she asked. "Why do you laugh?"

Emmy said nothing. She'd already forgotten Hermann.

[231]

She was rehearsing a play that hadn't yet been written, so it was a little difficult to imagine properly. But it didn't matter because she knew what was supposed to be in it. It was full of a special atmosphere of gaiety and joy. The people in it all, one by one, discovered that a thing they had for a long time wished to be true did really exist. Was it a treasure they had made a legend about, and then was it really found? Or what was it? At the end of the play a cock crowed. But she went to sleep, into deep sleep without any dreams.

She only half-wakened when her coffee came in the morning. She sipped it, lying on her side and drowsing. She heard voices and knew that two people were talking about Anna. Mechanically she slipped the last tablet into her mouth and swallowed it.

Some time after she lay in a half consciousness, not knowing whether it was day or night, and then something began. Outside she thought at first, but no, then it was inside. Deeply inside. A break in the rhythm, a lapse, the breath stopping, then going on again. In the muscles, through the veins, a sudden and awful pause, then the renewal, hurried, breathless with panic.

What's happening to me?

She sat up, and at once she began to vomit violently.

"Hermann!" she screamed. "Hermann!"

She had forgotten her real name, but her cry was hoarse and strong. She leaned over the side of the bed, retching onto the floor.

"Come!" she cried.

She looked across and saw Anna's bed was empty.

Anna's dead.

Blind terror seized her. She caught her temples in her hands, holding back her long black hair. She vomited again and again and her heart leaped up in her with each wrenching. The sweat broke out all over her body.

When she lay back at last on the bed she knew it was here. No use lying very still when the seat of life was actually crumbling. She knew it was here before she heard the man's voice. Not the doctor, not *her* doctor at least. The other one that came sometimes to Anna and gave her only a prying look as he went by. He was quite old, a prisoner himself, with dull, peering eyes. His lower jaw sometimes shook. He held her wrist now and his sharp, senile fingers pinched her flesh.

"Heart block," he said, and Hermann on the other side of the bed, creaking in her starched dress, said in a frightened gust, "Then I must call him. He came and went this morning while she was asleep. He'll be furious but it's not my fault, is it? I've done all I could. You'll tell him it's not my fault, please, doctor."

"You couldn't do anything," the doctor said. "Better call him."

"Oh, but he'll be so angry! Will she die, doctor?" she said reproachfully. "He said her heart was so strong."

The doctor leaned over and Emmy saw his liverish pupils, yellow and stained, and smelled his stale breath. There was no pity in him, no humanity, only a feeble, spiteful curiosity.

"Madame Ritter," he murmured, as though he'd been wanting for some time to confirm an opinion he had of her: "About forty-five years?" he asked.

She nodded.

"I thought so." He took out his stethoscope. "Ditten thought fifty. Had many of these before?"

She was about to shake her head. Of course not: haven't I always been strong and clean? But it was so hard to speak. She didn't move. She looked up at him as he leaned over, putting the ends of the stethoscope in his ears, watching her with that malevolent peering, and she thought of the young doctor who had touched her with thin, reddened hands. She remembered his sharp wrist-bones that reminded her of Mark, and the wild look of elation she had last seen on his face.

She opened her lips and tried to whisper, forcing herself to what was going to be her last act.

To lie, of course, because that was necessary, to be bold and to be even frivolous, to taste the joy of being at the end so completely herself.

She managed to whisper, "Yes. I've had a bad heart always, since a child. Doctors never thought I'd live."

"We're usually right," he said. "You're lucky."

Chapter XVI

WHEN the hour came Mark hadn't yet decided whether or not to go to the doctor's house. He felt only horror at seeing him again. He knew that the Commissioner was one of those directly responsible for her fate, yet the doctor, because he was with her daily, seemed much more closely involved in it. If it hadn't been for his offer to carry a letter to her he certainly would not have thought of going. And even the letter had become a matter for doubt.

All day he had sat in his room with a sheet of paper and a pencil, writing a few words and tearing them up again. He couldn't, as Emmy had done, write a simple farewell. If he said anything at all there was so much more than that to be said. The one who was still to live must cover everything, and she had the right to know that they had got the money she had earned for them and would survive, as she had hoped they would. But this reassurance put into words on paper became horrible. His letters started always with a stilted and practical account, becoming suddenly a cry of despair. None of them would do. He tore them up one after the other.

At noon he had gone out to get some food but instead he went into a bar and drank several brandies.

In the afternoon when he went back to his room it was no better. When the darkness came and the staring light was turned on he still hadn't written anything.

If I could see her, he thought, for just a moment, if the doctor could arrange just a moment of sight and touch. But the doctor had told him flatly last night that it was impossible.

At seven o'clock he was still sitting with his sheet of paper. He tore it up and snatching his hat and overcoat went down to the street.

He would have wandered about aimlessly but the rain drove him indoors again and he found himself, hardly knowing how he got there, in the bar of the Four Seasons. He ordered a double brandy, sitting where he could watch the chromium clock set in the wall. For the last day he had had his watch on the table before him or he sat where he could see a clock. He was conscious of each moment as it passed, and if from exhaustion or some distraction he let a few moments slip by uncounted, the anguish of re-membering again was only doubled.

Still thinking about the letter he called for some hotel paper and tried again to write. He drank another brandy and sat holding his pencil tentatively over the paper, but that had become now only an empty nervous movement.

The place was crowded, as it had been the other night, with Americans and English, all coming in hurriedly out of the driving cold rain outside. It was a bar like any other bar — and why not? Were these people really expected to care because miles away, behind a barricade of electrified barbed wire, Emmy Ritter was waiting execution? Were they to be disturbed because he wanted to write a letter to her and couldn't?

Suppose he were suddenly to tell them, what would they say? "I simply can't believe it." "After all, she shouldn't have done it, should she?" "Perhaps she's a Communist." "It's simply bloody but the world is like that." "Is she as attractive as she used to be?" "Was it Belasco or Frohman who brought her over?" "But after all, he has saved the country, hasn't he?" No use God-damning any of them. . . . The world is sown with graves.

His hand had been unconsciously moving. He looked down and saw marks on the paper. He'd made a strange and bold drawing, a great, sprawling, obscene shape of fear. It was good. It was indeed the only good he had in him. And it was absolutely useless. He crumpled it up and threw it over in the corner, paid for his drinks, and went out.

It was the rain again that drove him off the streets. Such a simple thing as rain and cold and the emptiness of having nothing to do. He didn't know how long he'd walked or how far but suddenly he saw, across a glistening square, a row of taxis waiting and he hailed one and got in.

"Where to, sir?" the driver said.

There was no place in this city where he could go. Except to the doctor's . . . He gave the driver his address.

The doctor lived in a rather shabby suburb in a street of flats all alike with ornate façades, built about fifty years ago when it was thought that this quarter toward the old country palace might be fashionable. His flat was on the top floor of one of the houses and Mark walked up flights of uncarpeted stairs to reach it. When he pressed the button outside the door the sound of the bell ringing inside made him think of empty rooms, but almost immediately the door was opened by a manservant. He was an oldish fellow with stiffly brushed hair and he looked at Mark with pale, clear eyes. He reminded him vaguely of Fritz. Probably because he, too, was obviously an old family relic, but his manner was more simple and benign; after all, he served the high and well born, even if in a flat in an unfashionable suburb. It must always have been hard on

Fritz, Mark thought, as he was helped off with his wet coat, to have given his allegiance to such doubtful persons as the Ritters.

As he handed the servant his hat, a door opened and the doctor came out. He was taller than Mark remembered him, and it was strange to be seeing him again, to think Oh, yes, that's what he looks like.

He shook Mark's hand vigorously: "Come in here," he said. "You'll find it's warmer."

Mark followed him into a rather large room where a fire was burning in an old iron stove. On either side of it were chairs, one covered in old, printed cotton material, the other with a worn cashmere shawl thrown over it to hide its decrepitude. Between them was a little table with a jar of tobacco and a box of cigarettes, two glasses and a bottle of schnapps. In the far corner of the room a table covered with a white cloth was set for two. The bread was already cut, in a wicker basket, and there was a plate of hors d'oeuvres — pink sliced sausage and bright red radish and curls of celery. Two little porcelain figurines of drummer boys stood in the center for ornament. From the door where the servant had just gone came a smell of soup.

Mark was nearly two hours late, but they were still keeping the soup warm. The doctor, he saw, wore a dark red smoking jacket with frogs ornamenting the front. Why had he put that on? Perhaps he always wore it, but it had a slightly festive air as though to show intimacy and friend-liness. Like the supper kept warm, the drinks waiting, the warm fire. How like them, he thought. Always that talent for the misplaced, the grotesque. He sat down uncertainly in one of the chairs.

"A little schnapps?" the doctor asked. He stood by the table, holding the bottle and a glass. "It will warm you up. I think you were very wet when you came in."

"No, thanks," Mark said, "I've had too much to drink already." He took out one of his own cigarettes and lighted it. The doctor put the glass he had just filled and the bottle slowly down.

"Then perhaps as you're very late you'd like to eat at once," he said.

"I've eaten already," Mark said. "I hope you didn't wait for me."

The doctor looked down at him and said nothing. Then he crossed to the door leading to a pantry or kitchen and spoke to his servant. They held a low consultation. Mark looked over at him leaning against the door and saw again the table with the clean white cloth, the radishes cut in great slices, the little porcelain figurines that were probably the most valuable thing he possessed.

People like me, Mark thought, get what's coming to them because they're soft. To hell with him and his supper.

The doctor came back and sat down opposite him. His head made the exact center for a cluster of fencing foils crossed behind him on the wall. He took his pipe from the table and filled it, pressing the tobacco carefully with his bony, flat-tipped fingers.

"You've seen her today?" Mark asked. Suddenly when he heard his voice he felt that he was going the wrong way, allowing himself too headlong a rein. Even his grief, because he was straining it to the last point, took on a faint tinge of falseness.

The doctor, not looking at him, went on filling his pipe. "Yes, I've seen her," he said.

Mark held back his questions, tried to accept the pace the doctor set, for he was right: there need be no impatience about his grief.

"I've seen her," the doctor repeated, striking a match to

his pipe, "and she was very well. I went over her again. Especially the heart."

"Her heart's always been strong," Mark said. "An actress' heart has to be strong. It's a hard life."

"I am counting on it to be very strong indeed." The doctor took a few puffs and put the burnt match carefully in a little tray.

Mark said, "Let's hope so. Though it might be better for her if it failed suddenly."

"Do you feel it would be better if she were to die — from natural causes?"

"Yes." Mark spoke shortly.

The doctor looked at him with close attention and then turned to the stove, stretching his feet out toward it. They sat in silence and Mark smoked out his cigarette, listening to the heavy rain on the window and to a slight noise of cutlery in the kitchen. When he had finished his cigarettes the doctor glanced up and handed him an ash tray but he didn't offer him another cigarette.

There were books lining all one wall of the room. Mark's eyes unconsciously strayed toward them. Suddenly he would have liked to go over and pick out a book and bring it back and doze over it in his chair by the warm fire. In the compass of such a grief as his, it would be possible, as the doctor had known better than he, to do many simple and natural things: to eat a dinner and read a book and talk with a man by the fire.

The doctor said, as though there had been no long silence, "So you feel it would be better if she died first, of natural causes."

"Yes," Mark said. "Why do you keep saying that?"

The doctor turned and looked at him, with his sharp, bright, blue eyes. "Because," he said, "today I did a criminal thing."

[240]

"What!" Mark cried. Then, looking at the doctor's face, he whispered, "She's dead," and in that moment he knew for the first time the difference between any grief that still includes a hope of life, and the complete finality of death. The doctor didn't answer him but went on looking at him and Mark for a moment felt faint. Then a sweat broke out all over him. He pulled out a handkerchief and wiped his face. He leaned his head back against the chair. "You gave her something," he said. He turned his head to avoid the doctor's eyes. "I'm sure you meant well," he said, "yes, I know you meant well." In that moment he felt strangely and trustfully his friend.

"I want to explain to you fully what I meant."

"It doesn't matter," Mark said. "I'd rather not hear. It would be too awful for both of us. But I understand. I might have done it myself. If I'd had the chance."

"You don't quite understand," the doctor went on. His voice was harsh and high. "Or rather, you understand only half of it. You know why I did it, but you don't know yet what I've done. I've taken a chance of saving her."

"Of saving her? Then she won't die from what you did?" His trustfulness took another sharp curve. So sharp he was only bewildered.

"She may die, but she may not," the doctor said.

"What have you done?"

"I'll tell you. But first I advise you, as you've evidently been drinking a good deal, to have a cup of black coffee. I want you to understand very clearly everything I say."

Mark, sitting very still, watched him ring for the man and order two cups of black coffee. "Two large cups," he said.

Then he went on. "What I did I had to do without consulting you, because when the idea occurred to me I had no time for that. Also, I wanted to take the full responsibility myself. For the crime against the State and for the possible crime against Madame Ritter. The crime against the State is my own affair. As to the other — I saw just now that when you thought she was actually dead your first feeling was of relief. Isn't that so? Be honest."

"Yes," Mark said, "it's so."

"You were relieved that her sufferings and therefore your own worst suffering were over. That's natural. Well, maybe they are over. Maybe she'll die. In that case I see you won't blame me. But maybe she has a chance to live."

"But what did you do?"

"I'll tell you. See, here comes the black coffee. Drink it all."

The calm-eyed elderly servant brought a tray with two big cups and a pot of coffee. He put it on the table between them and went out. Mark, bewildered into blankness, drank his in quick gulps, the doctor sipped his, holding it with a steady hand.

"Listen very carefully," he said. "I went out to the camp this morning rather late. And when I got there I was asked to go to the office of the head physician. He is a member of the police, as I am, but I'm only in it temporarily and he's senior to me of course. He knows about my uncle though, he knows I do get special consideration, and he's always very polite to me. He wanted to ask me about Madame Ritter — things I needn't tell you. Then he said rather jokingly, 'I hear you've been interesting yourself in this Anna Hoffman too.' I said, 'Yes, I have.' Naturally I didn't want him to think I was any more interested in one than in the other. You remember, Anna Hoffman is the woman I told you is in the same room with your mother."

"Yes, yes, I remember. Go on."

"Well, what he wanted to say was something about this Anna. The doctor who'd been looking out for her was a

prisoner. A wretched old broken-down, thoroughly discredited physician. Whatever most of them out there are,
he deserves to be there. But it seems he was jealous of my
interference — little as it's been. I haven't done any more
really than listen to her lungs and give her a sedative every
now and then. Last night she had a hemorrhage, and today
she was dying. The head physician said to me, 'This fellow came here this morning, and said, "Ever since your
political police have interfered with that woman she's worse.
Now she's dying. But I suppose I'm not good enough to
take charge of a case like that. I'm not even good enough
to sign a death certificate." ' (Of course these prisoners can't
sign death certificates, you understand.) The head physician then said, 'I'm going off for a week's leave tomorrow,
so I'll ask you to take charge. When she dies see that all
the formalities are correct, will you?' "

"Well?" Mark said.

The doctor got up and poured Mark another cup of
coffee.

"Don't you see what I'm leading up to? If this woman,
Anna, dies, I certify to her death. If Madame Ritter dies
there in prison it is also I who certify to her death. The head
physician won't be there to do it."

"Well, but if she doesn't die?"

"Then I can still certify to it."

Mark caught his head between his hands. "I don't see —
How can that help us — You mean to get her out somehow — How?"

"I'll have to tell you bit by bit," the doctor said. "All
these things came to me at different times and they aren't
important separately. It's only when they're finally put
together that they mean anything. When I first saw Madame Ritter in prison I felt only acute distress. After all,
I didn't really know her. But I decided to operate on her.

[243]

It was a first step and I took it almost unconsciously. When I was making the arrangements to bring her to the camp someone told me at the prison that a man had put in a claim for her body. That's allowed even in the case of criminals, but in telling me the man said he was surprised because no one seemed to think she had any relatives or close friends in the country. When I found out who you were, for a moment I thought you were the man, but I realized right away that you hadn't even been sure of her sentence. But you must know who put in the claim. It's very important."

"An old servant of ours," Mark said. "I saw him last night after I left you and he told me he'd done it. He told me he had signed the papers and it was settled." He spoke automatically, in a dream.

"What was he going to do with the body?"

"He was going to take it down to the country and bury it in a little town where his brother lives, either on his brother's property or in the cemetery if it was allowed."

"To take it by train?"

"I think so."

"Well, we'll speak of that later."

"For God's sake!" Mark said. "Tell me what you've done. Tell me the rest afterward."

"This morning," the doctor said in an unhurried voice, "after I had talked to the doctor, I went into the little pharmacy and prepared some tablets. Then I went to Madame Ritter and examined her heart, which I found to be apparently in good condition. I say apparently because an examination like that isn't conclusive. But I gave her a dose of digitalis in tablet form. I had made a hasty computation of what would be the right amount for a woman of her age and weight and I left her the tablets. I told her to take them faithfully over a period of twenty-four hours.

There should be about one grain to each three kilos. She weighs I should guess about sixty-three or four kilos, and I added two grains to produce complete digitalization."

"I don't understand."

"But I am now explaining. In twenty-four hours these tablets should produce what's known as bradycardia."

"It would kill her?"

"It might, but that's the chance. If it does not, I reasoned that the following will happen: she will begin by such symptoms as a slow pulse, an irregular heart action, accompanied by extreme nervousness and probably vomiting. The prisoner doctor I spoke of will first be called. He'll at once recognize it, or think he recognizes it, as heart block. It would be a natural condition for a woman with a weak heart after a serious operation, especially as she's under such a severe mental strain. He won't be astonished by it. Indeed, he'll be very pleased. He'll think: The damned busybody has lost another patient. Perhaps he'll be pleased that a fellow prisoner is cheating the executioner. As the head physician has gone and the hospital has only other prisoners in charge, they'll send for me. Yes, at some hour tomorrow, if Madame Ritter carries out my instructions, I'll certainly be called. I will of course show concern. Naturally, no doctor likes to lose a patient. I'll insist on staying with her. I'll appear to do my best to save her. The rest of them will certainly leave her to me. They'll either go about their business or, if it's late, they'll go to bed. Only a female prisoner, a nurse of sorts, may possibly stay with me, a horrible cretin, but I can handle her easily. At eight-thirty the camp is dark and the lights out. After that I'll be alone with my patient. At ten or eleven I'll pronounce Madame Ritter dead. I shall then notify by telephone the authorities in town. I shall sign the certificate of death, and I shall have them telephone at once to the man

[245]

who is to claim the body. It will be turned over to him. That's all."

Mark whispered, "It's impossible." He hadn't understood a word but some deep confidence in the doctor had made him try unconsciously to follow him.

He knew that he had given up his whole will to the idea of death and that now the doctor was saying there was a crack, a flaw, in the circle of death if they had the strength to force it.

But he repeated more emphatically, "It's impossible," and something in him began to resist.

"The other night I told you nothing possible would save her," the doctor said irritably, "and so you demanded a miracle." He got up, and with his hands behind his back walked up and down the room. It was easy to believe he was a little mad. As he passed the table he snatched up a radish and crunched it in his strong white teeth.

"I'm a surgeon," he said, "I've taken the cornea from a dead man's eyes and grafted it in the living tissue. Don't talk to me about miracles." He curled up a slice of sausage, laid it on a piece of bread, and began to eat it.

Mark watched him, lying back in his chair. "It's impossible," he repeated. He saw more clearly and his will came fully to life.

The doctor stood by the table munching. "You think it's impossible because it hasn't been done, yet. Actually, that's the sole reason why it *is* possible. No one has thought of it, so it might be done — once."

"You say no one has thought of it. But does anyone know you take a special interest in her, I mean other than as a case?"

"No. I very often experiment on prisoners. Everyone is used to that. My uncle knows I never saw Madame Ritter till she came to the prison." Then he added with a

shade of contempt: "After all, you can accept her death —
I saw you do it — but not her escape. The will to life
isn't as strong as we like to think. I've often found that
out."

Mark said, "Perhaps it's just plain funk — You're braver
than I am. And perhaps too you have less imagination. You
can't see suddenly, as I can now, all the things that'll go
wrong. The horror of placing a living woman in a coffin.
Suppose she suffocates. There'll be the suspicion of someone we haven't thought of suddenly breaking in — all the
appalling difficulties afterward. No, you haven't the imagination to see all that." He felt he was dismissing it, right-
eously, almost in anger.

"That's obviously untrue," the doctor said, "since I
thought of it in the first place. What you can't imagine
is overcoming the difficulties. What you can't imagine is
success."

"But it couldn't be done! There are so many details we
couldn't ever foresee."

"You only mean that, so far as you know, it never has
been done. As for those details, we'll go over them now
one by one. You'd better eat something."

Mark got up and walked over to the table. He made a
sausage sandwich for himself and tried to eat it.

"How long will this digitalization last?" he said aggressively.

"About forty-eight hours."

"Well then, she's helpless all that time?"

"More or less, yes. But during the time she's most helpless she doesn't need to be doing anything. In fact, the
whole point is that she must be inanimate. Afterward you
can treat her. Keep her warm, make her sweat it out of
her system as soon as you can."

"Do you expect her to lie still and play dead convinc-
ingly?"

[247]

"No, I don't think anyone could. I'll give her a morphine injection."

"Who'll see her beside you?"

"I hope no one. It'll be late at night, as I said, and I'm
the doctor in charge. No one need see her, but the men
who put her in the coffin."

"Who'll they be?"

"Prisoners. Half asleep, perhaps, at that hour."

"But the time element — will there be a coffin ready?"

"Many people die out there. There are always pine
boxes on hand."

"Won't she suffocate?"

"I'll tell them not to nail it down too tight. I'll say that
relatives are claiming it, they may want to open it and
look at her. Besides, these plain pine coffins are loosely
made."

Mark gave a convulsive movement of the shoulders. He
dropped his half-eaten sandwich. The doctor, standing
across the table, made himself another one.

"Of course, you must open it," he said, "and get her
out as soon as possible, and there's always this: when you
open it she may actually be dead. It's not certain at all
that she can stand all this."

Mark said, "Don't they embalm them, shoot formalde-
hyde into them, or put them in quicklime — something horrible?"

"No. You don't imagine they'd go to the trouble of
embalming a prisoner, do you? If she were buried in the
prison they'd probably put quicklime in the coffin. But
as the relatives have claimed the body — no."

Mark suddenly felt very hungry. He picked up his sandwich and leaned against the table eating it. The doctor,
still eating his, paced up and down the room.

"Do you begin to understand?" he said. "Do you begin

to see in your famous imagination a possibility of success?"

"I see that, if you could manage it, my mother would be placed alive in a coffin and delivered to me. What in God's name would I do then?"

He went back to his chair and sat down heavily. A sudden feeling of hope, as though everything were done and she was saved, had gone through him for a moment and then passed.

"But it's impossible, it's impossible," he said again, angrily.

"What did you come to this country for?" the doctor asked him. "Wasn't it to do the impossible? The impossible is an entirely relative term. It only exists in certain combinations of time and circumstance. It's not an absolute. But I really can't waste time on your impossible. We've got to see what can be done afterward. To begin with, this servant. What kind of a fellow is he?"

"He's been a very faithful servant."

"Can you count on him?"

Mark drew closer to the warm stove and thought of Fritz, tried to make a complete picture of all he knew of him. Fritz, as a man, he suddenly couldn't see.

"I don't know," he said, "whether he'd be up to this or not."

"Well, you'll have to count on him anyway. You say she was to be buried on his property, or in the local churchyard if it could be arranged?"

"Yes, but not his property. His brother's."

The doctor came back and sat down across from him. He took up his pipe again and holding it absently in his hand tapped the bowl against the other palm.

"Something will have to be buried," he said, as though he were talking to himself, "and better there where it was planned. Because he's undoubtedly made arrangements for that already. His brother, for instance, might suspect something wrong if the arrangements weren't carried out."

"Yes." He was straining his imagination to follow these mad sequences but only to fight them. He couldn't see himself and Fritz and the coffin and his mother. "Yes, yes," he repeated hurriedly. The final denial would come later.

"So, somewhere in the time between leaving prison and arrival at the house of this brother you'll have to get Madame Ritter out and you'll have to put something — say a bundle of clothes wrapped carefully and laid around some small logs — into the coffin. And the coffin can be buried. As to what you'll do with Madame Ritter — I can't think yet."

"No," said Mark in despair, "I can't either."

Suddenly he saw it would be possible to accept the escape from prison. The doctor's assurance that it could be done, the tone of his voice, as though he were telling about a fantastic operation he expected to do but knew that he could do, would in time infect him with a sense of reality. But even if that were so, even if that had somewhere in time and space a reality, it only had it so long as the doctor could be a part of it. From the moment the doctor stepped out the darkness would close over it again.

"What," he said with a last desperate reasonableness, "can a man do with a helpless, hunted woman in the middle of the night in an absolutely strange country?"

"Well," the doctor said briskly, "would you rather not go on with it?"

And there of course was the real answer to this "impossible." Once the thing had been conceived, even in a sort of madness, there was no choice but to go on with it.

Mark didn't even answer.

"You see," the doctor said, "now we've started it, and

we *have* started it, we've got to go on. Now we must think what you'll do afterward."

He supposed, then, he had accepted it. At any rate temporarily, defensively. He said, "I don't know. Perhaps I can think of something later. When the time comes."

"No. No. You must have it all planned beforehand. To begin with, you say you'll have a helpless, hunted woman on your hands in a strange country. Let's begin with the helpless. Madame Ritter, when the morphine wears off, will still be partially helpless. But all the time she'll be becoming less so. After about thirty-six hours she can do within reason whatever's necessary. But for that time you must have a place to put her where she can have rest in a warm bed. Haven't you got any friends here in the country?"

"No."

"What about the Countess?"

"Out of the question," Mark said violently. "She'd never help me, for one thing."

The doctor thought of her for a while. "Yes, we must not involve her," he said. "It's not fair. You have no one else then?"

"No one."

"Then you must find a way to get into a hotel. You must certainly take the coffin in a camion, not on a train. In the camion you can get her out of the coffin almost at once. You must have clothes for her. Dress her, warmly of course. Warmth is terribly important. Aside from the danger of chill the sooner you sweat it out of her, as I told you, the better."

"Should I give her stimulants — brandy, say? Coffee?"

"No, no. Neither of them. Don't you understand? Digitalis is a stimulant. It's self-limiting. Leave her alone, keep her warm."

Mark looked at him with vague envy. How much he knew and how surely his knowledge was a vital part of him! The scholar that's somewhere in all of them served him harmoniously and with full obedience. He looked like a victor. Well, Mark thought, why not? As he says, he's begun it. I've got to go on.

"You might," the doctor said, "arrange what looks like a motor accident. Say you're in the camion and you find a woman lying in the road unconscious, struck by another car. You pick her up and get her into a little country hotel for a while. Then take her on farther, before the police begin to make a thorough investigation. You and your servant must arrange that. Or by then you may have thought of something better."

Mark said, "We'd better not do anything to make the police notice us."

"I don't think that would matter much. For a short time. And it would have to be short in any case. You spoke of her being hunted. Remember, she's not being hunted. The local, rural police will know nothing about her. Here, she is dead — officially dead; no one is hunting for her at all."

"How can I get her out of the country?" But he was ashamed to ask any more. He added quickly: "I'll manage that. Where we're going is very close to the border. I'll think of something to do."

For another moment, just from having said so, he really thought he might be able to think of something.

"It's so terribly strange, all this," he said apologetically, "so unexpected. Give me a little time. I'll try to pull myself together."

"You'll have from now till tomorrow night to figure it all out. Just go at it step by step. First, the servant must be ready to come instantly when telephoned. Then you must get her out. Then you must have a good story to account for finding her on the road at that hour. And so on."

As he talked Mark found his head swimming. He got up again, went to the table, and, fixing a sandwich, he said, "Any more coffee?"

"Yes," the doctor answered. He took the pot himself and went to the pantry, smiling a little because Mark had not only accepted his food but had asked him for it.

When he came back Mark watched him fill the cup. "You realize," Mark said, "if this goes wrong it will be pretty terrible for you?"

"It won't be nice," the doctor admitted. He poured himself a cup.

"But you're willing to do your part of it and count on a man you don't know not to bungle the rest of it."

"I have to count on you. And you have to count on me."

"I'm counting on the better man," Mark said. He meant it. A queer feeling of peace and confidence came over him again.

The doctor was pleased, though he said nothing and shrugged his shoulders, raising his cup to drink rather noisily.

He took it back to his chair and sat down. Mark stood by the table sipping his.

"I still don't know why you are doing it," Mark said.

"Don't worry about that," the doctor said jovially. "No one could ever tell you. To know why I did it you'd have to know my entire life and my parents' lives and the lives of everyone I've ever met. You'd have to know every word ever said to me, every word I've ever said, what I've seen, read, thought about, done, even what kind of food I've eaten. But to put it simply, say that for the moment I'm like a cat who chews green stuff so as to vomit and purge his stomach of poison."

"It may finish you."

[253]

"Oh, yes, it may. There's no one else I have to think of, though."

Again Mark noticed the loneliness of his face, the sharp, bold lines that had never been rubbed down.

"Why don't you come to America?" he asked suddenly. He wanted to make some openly friendly move but he held back because his debt to him, whatever happened, was too overpowering.

The doctor, glancing at him, guessed this. "I'd like to," he said slowly. "I'd like to see you again. But I suppose I won't."

"I want to see you again. We can't let it go at this, you know."

"I'm afraid we have to. Yes, some day I'd like to be your friend, but too many things would always divide us."

"You're a lot more than a friend already."

"You mean I'm a savior." The doctor laughed shortly. "Well, that too would divide us."

Mark couldn't go on. He looked around the room, knowing he'd never be in it again, and tried to see everything in it so vividly that he'd never forget it. He thought of the table where he'd never sit down to eat, the books he'd never read, and the long talks they would certainly never have. But it was true just the same that they were more than friends. A man he didn't know and wouldn't see again had become his brother.

Suddenly he said, "I told Fritz to come tonight. He'll be waiting. If I don't get back soon he'll give up and go home."

"I'll call you a taxi," the doctor said. He got out of his chair slowly, went out into the hall and Mark heard him giving the number.

He looked once more around the room and followed him out. The servant had apparently gone to bed but his coat and hat waited on a chair. They had been taken to the kitchen to dry and were still warm.

"There is a station at the corner," the doctor said. "It will be here at once. I'll go down with you."

He opened the door and together they went downstairs, suddenly running lightly like young men hurrying off on a lark. In the front hall they stood by the door, half opened, looking out to the rainy street.

In a moment the taxi came.

Mark turned and grasped the doctor's hand. "Are you sure there's not more we ought to plan together? Oughtn't we to meet again?"

But the doctor was ruthless to the last. "No, there's nothing more to plan together. I do my part. You do yours. Only be sure the man comes as quickly as he's called."

"I will. You don't think we should meet?"

"It's better not. It's safer for us both."

"You know I'll never forget my debt."

The doctor shook his head smiling. He shook Mark's hand up and down. "My regards to America," he said, "and when you get back remember us. Remember it's easy to lose what you started with."

"I'll remember."

"Good-by." Their word for it was "Till we meet," but they neither of them had any hope of that.

Chapter XVII

As soon as he got into the taxi he knew he'd been made a fool of. He felt savagely angry with the doctor for taking him in and with himself for being the dupe. It shows, he thought, how easy it is to work on a man who has reached a certain stage of despair. The doctor's madness had infected him. The doctor had been breathing madness for the last four years, madness and puerile conceits. He'd even watched them inflate those around him into a fantastic victory. Mark could see him sitting before that stove, putting tobacco into his pipe with his lean surgeon's fingers, thinking of some surgeon's problem perhaps and slowly hearing, from the streets outside, from all over the town, the obedient roar, the slobbering, rhythmic howl of love and hate. And Kant and Hegel and Spinoza mute on the walls . . .

But, oh, if he could only have thought of some possible plan, a plan with even the most meager germ of success, how eagerly, Mark thought, he would have poured his life into it to make it go! But no. The doctor had gone back to reading Dumas: "The burial ground of the Château d'If was the sea." Mark felt sodden with disgust.

And worst of all he had no alternative, no one to turn to, no action to take. Giving up madness left him empty.

But he couldn't quite reject it either. Once it had taken form he couldn't quite give it up. He couldn't forget the deep, strange confidence he had felt. I'll see Fritz, he thought. Fritz, the cold and practical. He can put his finger on the weak spot in anything, because Fritz never listens to anyone, neither to the leaders nor to the followers. Because if anyone was ever a lone wolf it's Fritz, or perhaps just a lone rabbit. But just the same, he's never taken in. No, not he. He keeps his mind on the pipes of the water closet and the electric light wires and the poor quality of the bread. You can't tell him it's the bread of sacrifice and victory. There's no nourishment in it, he says; for two years now I've had pains in the joints. If Fritz were inclined to talk philosophically he'd say, There is no such thing as victory anyway — it's a word. Is it possible, he'd say, to exalt into Godlikeness what is only tripe and spoiled meat? . . . Good old Fritz!

"Driver, I'm in a hurry. Can you go a little faster?"

As they turned into Theater Street he pressed his face to the window to see if there was a light in his room. If there was he couldn't see it through the blurred pane. Maybe the curtains were drawn. Maybe Fritz had got tired and gone home.

He paid the driver and ran across the wet pavement to his door. The hall, as usual, was in darkness. He found the switch, turned it on, and saw again on the lift door the white card, hanging now at a disconsolate angle: OUT OF ORDER. He ran up the stairs two at a time and reached the door of the flat just as the light clicked off. In the dark hall inside he saw the crack of light under his door. So Fritz waited. He moved cautiously among the wicker chairs, avoiding the staghorns and the porcelain jar for umbrellas. He opened his door.

There, under the staring light, sat Fritz. His arms hung loosely from their sockets, his head leaned toward his shoulder. His mouth was a little open and a gentle whistling came from between his lips. He looked very old and threadbare, and faintly disreputable and comic. To be defenseless is always both disreputable and comic. Old Fritz, literally caught napping! But he felt his state at once and opened his eyes. He got up with a look of reproof and drew himself together, pulling his coat inward by the lapels.

"I didn't hear you come," he said. "You're very late. I've been here since ten o'clock. You ought to have told me you were going to be out all evening." He helped Mark off with his coat and hat.

"I saw someone like you tonight," Mark said. "Or rather he reminded me of you. He took my coat and warmed it for me. I think he had a better temper."

"So?" Fritz said. He looked sharply at Mark, surprised at his tone. "I'm glad to know you have acquaintances here. I didn't think you had any."

"Several," Mark said. "Sit down."

They sat down opposite each other.

"I wish I had a drink," Mark said. "I can't get any in this place at this hour. I ought to have brought a bottle in with me. I suppose you could do with something too."

"I never touch anything but beer," Fritz said. "If you like I can go out and try to get something."

"No, don't go. It's too late. I want to talk to you. We have a lot of things to arrange."

"Yes," said Fritz, "we have."

But Mark didn't like to begin and Fritz was puzzled. He saw that Mark was more excited now than sorrowful. He stared disapprovingly first at him and then at the floor. He's like his mother, Fritz thought, never quite in good form.

Finally Mark said, nervously, "Now about tomorrow. Have you done anything more about the burial?"

"I've arranged for the funeral service," Fritz said, severely. "The priest down there is a friend of mine. I've always been a good Catholic. He has no objection and the authorities have no objection."

Mark's eyes were shining and wavering. Fritz went on with emphasis, "There is no law to prevent a criminal from having the burial service read. Madame Ritter was brought up a Catholic, though I must say she hasn't practised her religion for years. But it's all right about that."

Mark nodded. He wasn't thinking about the service now and Fritz knew he wasn't.

"My brother knows you're here," Fritz said. "He's expecting us both some time Wednesday. I might add that he's also expecting a slight bonus for being involved in something that won't bring any credit to him, and I wouldn't be surprised if Father Alois wouldn't accept a little something for the parish."

"That's all right. We'll fix that."

"It needn't be much."

"Oh, that's all right. Now about the burial, where will that be?"

"In my brother's land." He added hurriedly, "There's a nice spot up at the edge of the forest." It was evident he hadn't been able to arrange for the graveyard, which would have been much more suitable. "There was some difficulty," he said evasively, "about the other."

"It doesn't matter," Mark said. He took out a cigarette fumblingly.

"You smoke too much," Fritz told him. "You'll ruin your health. People get cancer of the throat from smoking too much. I knew a man — "

"Yes, yes. I know, Fritz, but there are other things to talk about just now. The country end of it is settled then. Now as to this end. You're absolutely sure that there won't

[259]

be any hitch about your getting the body? They won't refuse to let you have it at the last minute?"

"I don't think so. Of course nothing's absolutely sure. But I've signed all the papers. There's no reason they should change their minds."

"No, I suppose not."

"I wouldn't worry about that," Fritz said almost gently.

Mark closed his eyes. Buried alive, he thought. Buried alive. No. No. Sweat broke out all over his body. Why didn't I think of that too? I should have told that madman. But then he thought: He didn't mean it anyway. It was all madness. Everything he said was in his own mind. In that crazy circle alone the whole thing began and will finish, from the dose of digitalis to the coffin.

He opened his eyes and looked at Fritz. Fritz was looking at him with deep despondency.

"How will you know what time to go?" Mark said.

"I'll know when they telephone me. When I made the request they wouldn't tell me the day or the hour. From what you say I know now it was because she was sick. They couldn't tell me. But I left a telephone number that will reach me. They'll call me up."

"Maybe they won't. Maybe they'll lose your number."

"They never lose anything. It's on file. They're very careful about everything."

He seemed very sure. And everyone knew they were practical, were exact and did things by rule. Perhaps that part was secure enough. But he still saw the number written on a scrap of paper, lost under a great heap of other papers, a living number buried alive under papers like dead leaves.

He took out a handkerchief and wiped his face.

"I think, Mr. Mark, you're going to be sick," Fritz said.

"No, I'm not. Don't be a fool. Now tell me the rest.

[260]

You call at the camp for the coffin. How do you propose to get it down to the country?"

"I thought first of taking it by train. Buying two tickets would be cheaper than hiring a camion. But the camion would be quicker and more convenient, because from the station to the village I'd have to get a sledge or something anyway. And besides, if she's at the camp, as you say, the camion is the only thing."

"Would you hire a driver with the camion?"

"Of course."

"Can you drive yourself?"

"Yes, I can. But then I'd have to put up a deposit for the camion."

"You're sure you can drive?"

"Didn't I use to drive Madame's car when she had one?"

"That was a long time ago. Have you driven since? Have you a driver's license?"

"Yes. For a week or so, the first of the year, I drove for a gentleman here."

"Then you think you can drive it yourself."

"Mr. Mark, if it's the money that's worrying you — "

"Shut up," Mark said. He got up and walked over to the window. He was afraid of everything. And he was afraid of Fritz too, afraid to tell him what he was thinking, afraid to open the door even a chink into that mad world he'd shared. He could see Fritz peering in, incredulous and scornful.

"How long will it take," he said, "to drive to your brother's place?"

"About two hours from town. Most of it will be over the big new auto road. But maybe more, because there'll be snow up there, and off the main road it's not cleared. And half an hour from the camp to town."

"Then we should get there before daylight tomorrow morning?"

"Before daylight! No, we won't get there till mid-morning. If they send for me at daybreak Wednesday morning, we'll get there around noon."

Mark wrenched his collar around free of his neck.

"Fritz," he said, and his voice sounded to himself very feeble and young, "I think you'll be called for around midnight tomorrow night."

"Ah, so," Fritz said. "You've had more news? Is the execution at midnight? I had figured it would be daybreak. If it's at midnight we'll certainly get there before daylight."

"I think there won't be any execution."

He turned around and found Fritz looking at him with his head cocked a little to one side.

"Is she worse?" he asked.

Mark came back and sat down. He faced Fritz with resolution but Fritz said in a low voice, "It would be a blessing." He shook his head several times, clasped his big, pale, flexible hands and sighed. He considered it all over.

"I've got to tell you something, Fritz. I've just come from talking to the doctor of the prison. The one who operated on her. Maybe I mentioned him before. He's a queer fellow. Damned queer. It seems he's not entirely in sympathy with all of this. And he admires my mother a great deal. He used to know her. Or rather, he didn't really know her, but that doesn't matter either. The point is, he wants to save her."

Fritz, watching him first laxly, became suddenly alert. The pupils of his eyes drew to a point and his pinkish, wide nostrils quivered. He said nothing.

"What do you think of that?" Mark said. "Do you see any possibility of success?"

Fritz waited a moment. "How can I say?" he said finally. "I don't know what the doctor had in mind."

"Well, he had this in mind: to produce a state like death in my mother, to sign her death certificate, put her in the coffin, and turn her over to us."

Fritz held himself so tensely not a breath stirred in him, then his breath escaped in a whistling sound.

"That's very dangerous," he said.

"Is it impossible?"

"I have no way of knowing."

"Neither have I. But he says he'll do it. He says he's even begun the treatment to produce a state that'll be taken for death. So perhaps he has. What I want to know is this: if he does his part of it, what can we do?"

Then he turned away from him to fumble again for a cigarette, not because he wanted one but to be doing something, and not to see Fritz's face. Not to look at incredulity, nor fear, nor instant repudiation.

Men are all cowards. Look at them today. They only have the outward semblance of men, their semblance only remains to testify more shamefully to what they once were. He remembered a bull fight he'd seen as a young man in Mexico, when suddenly the bull broke before the steely, mincing advance of the matador and trotted away from him across the arena with an absurd show of hurrying about his own affairs. In his flight all his exposed male force became helpless, ridiculous, and shameful. Mark had felt shamed for the bull and would have liked to cover him up. And lately he had seen much of the world's population in the role of the bull. At first he'd have liked to cover it up. But he now accepted it. He'd accepted it with the rest of them, and quickly. The courage of the doctor he couldn't believe. He thought of it as madness. To make a demand on anyone for courage embarrassed him. Fritz was afraid, of course.

[263]

He himself was afraid, and it was better to trot off than to risk anything, because if you don't risk anything then you can live longer, maybe only a few minutes longer, but still longer.

He lit his cigarette and glanced over at Fritz. He was sitting on the edge of his chair, his knees pressed closely together, one hand enclosing the other hand tightly, and he was staring ahead of him, his eyes focused somewhere beyond the walls of the room. Then his nostrils began to dilate again in their rabbit way and a cold speculative look came into his eyes.

"I suppose we could do something," he said. "Let's think it over."

He didn't speak with any bravado, rather doubtfully, but Mark gave a faint, incredulous laugh.

"You think we really could?"

"Why not? After all, he takes the worse chance. The rest ought to be possible."

"Possible!" Mark wanted to laugh again. He wanted to laugh till it hurt. Old Fritz, the repairer of electric light switches, thought it was possible. He would consider the disposal of a helpless woman under sentence of death in the middle of a hostile country as an achievement worthy of him at last.

"Fritz," he said. "My God — " and he did laugh. But the sound of it warned him. He stopped abruptly.

Fritz began to rub his hands together as though he were washing them. "Well now, let's see," he said. "I get a camion, drive it myself and take it to the camp. Then I bring it back and meet you here. Or better, not here. Better at the camp, or near by. The town there will do. It's a half-hour from camp. You can wait in a restaurant or somewhere I'll think of. The moment we leave you can

[264]

open the coffin and get Madame Ritter out. That's the beginning."

"It's only the beginning though."

"Of course, of course," said Fritz impatiently. He went on rubbing his hands, staring in front of him with sparkling eyes. He became alive with speculation. "*H'm*," he said aloud — "*H'm*" accepting or rejecting a possibility.

"The coffin must go to the country and be buried," he said finally. "That's certain. I must get hold of something to put in the coffin. I'll go to a lumber yard and buy some short and heavy logs. These we'll sew up in an old quilt or something. I must bring a screwdriver, a hammer, and some extra nails. Now as to Madame Ritter — "

"Yes, that's the trouble. The doctor suggested we take her to a hotel. Pretend she's been run down by the camion on the road."

"Won't she be able to walk?"

"No, not for a time."

"That's bad of course. Will she be conscious?"

"When the morphine wears off I suppose she will. But she can't move about for a day at least."

"We certainly need Madame Ritter's co-operation."

He seemed a bit set back by not being able to count on her, meaning of course that he didn't expect to count much on Mark. He scratched his Adam's apple gingerly, looking at him with his head cocked on one side.

"She's a clever woman," he said grudgingly.

"Yes, but at first we've got to get along without her. The doctor suggested we take her to a hotel; tell them we'd run her down on the road." He watched Fritz closely. "What do you think of that?"

Fritz got up and walked up and down the room.

"There would be a few things to account for, there. The

first is, what was she doing on the road in the early morning?"

"I can't think," said Mark. "Unless — How would it be if I got a car? And you ran into it. She and I driving, say. That seems more likely."

"Have you got a driver's license?"

"No."

"Then that's out. You couldn't even hire a car without that."

"You might hire it."

"No, the first thing after an accident would be to ask for your license. No, that's no good."

He paused before Mark, stared down at him for a moment, and went on walking.

Mark thought it must be near daylight. He looked at his watch, but it was only one-thirty. The whole eccentric lag and rush of time added to his instability.

"It's Tuesday," he said dully.

Fritz went on walking.

"There's got to be an accident," Fritz said; "no doubt about that. How else are we going to account for a helpless woman? But the hour's wrong, and the circumstances. Now try this: instead of before daybreak, make it later. The first train up there gets in at eight-thirty. Say you and Madame Ritter come in on the train, get off to enjoy the early morning air, and walk toward the village. It's only five kilometers. On the way I run her down. I pick you both up and take you to the hotel."

"I've been there already."

"There are other hotels."

"They'll think you're damned careless, running down women in broad daylight."

"I have the excuse of being on a sad errand. And the roads are covered with snow. Anyone can skid. Or it could be another car that ran her down and went on. That's even better. That lets me out of too much investigation. I come along and find you bending over her body. You haven't seen the other car's license." Fritz waved his hands dramatically. Mark thought, How he's enjoying this! But suddenly he stopped and his sour look came back to his face. "No, it won't do either," he said. "There are too many weak spots in it."

He snapped his long fingers and began to walk again.

"Once there's been an accident," he said, "a report is made and the police stick their noses in. That hotel idea is bad. Now I've thought of another thing. Right near the village there's an American lady living. She has a big house and lots of people stay with her. She's known as a better patriot than some who are born here. People in very high places are her friends — "

"Wait a minute. You mean the Countess?"

Fritz turned and looked at him in surprise. "You know her?"

"Yes."

"You're sure it's the lady I mean?"

"Of course. And if you think of our going there, that's out too."

"Well," Fritz gave up the idea reluctantly. "You *could* have gone there. We'd have staged the accident at her very door and no one need have reported it for quite a while. But if she knows you already — How on earth did you meet her?"

"I knew her in New York."

Fritz looked at him cunningly. "You don't know her very intimately by any chance?"

"No."

"Oh, well." Fritz gave a heavy disconsolate sigh and sat down again. His hands hung loosely clasped between his knees and he looked at the floor. "Then it's the hotel," he said, "though it might be better to go to a farm. I don't know. I'll think it over. In any case you'd better both be natives of the country, since you speak the language perfectly. And I'd suggest man and wife rather than mother and son —"

They sat in silence for a moment.

"You ought to be able to stay in a farm, or even a hotel, for one day," he said, "or maybe even two. Then you'll have to move on. I don't know what would happen about that. It's uncertain. That afternoon will be the funeral. Right after that I'll come back to town. I'll drive up in the camion and I'll set right about the passport."

"Oh, yes, the passport. Of course she can't leave the country without a passport."

"Certainly not. I know a man who makes a business furnishing fake passports. They're expensive, too. One costs about three hundred dollars. I can't answer as to its getting her back into America though."

"We'll worry about that later. She's got re-entry papers. I suppose the police took those?"

"I don't know. She didn't leave them with me."

"Well, anyway, she took out first citizenship papers. They'll help to identify her. Don't worry about that now. You're sure you can get a passport?"

"Yes. I need a photograph though. Have you got one, one that could be re-photographed if necessary?"

Mark took out his wallet. In it was a small, staring photograph. It was an extra one of those made for her passport. She'd given it to him as a joke, just before she left.

"Good!" Fritz exclaimed. He took it, examined it carefully, and got out his own worn wallet. He tucked it carefully inside, put the wallet back in an inside pocket, and patted it affectionately.

"How had we better leave?" Mark said. "By train, by plane — ?"

"We'll decide that later too. But you'd best leave separately. First Madame Ritter, then you. Clothes!" he exclaimed suddenly, striking his forehead. "Of course she'll need clothes."

"Did she leave any with you?"

"Yes, she did, but I gave them to my niece. I can get them back of course. Only I'd rather my niece didn't know. Perhaps we'd better buy more."

"I imagine they'd bury her in whatever she wore in prison. Some sort of nightgown."

"You'd better let me buy them," Fritz said. "It will look strange for a man of your sort to be shopping for a lady. I know little places to go. I'll buy one bit here and one bit there."

"She'll need a fur coat."

"Then you'd better buy that. It would look strange for *me* to be buying that. She'll need a dress. A sort of suit I should think would do. Say," Fritz raised his pale eyes to the ceiling and made a weaving gesture with his fingers, "say a knitted suit. I know a woman who makes them very cheap. And shoes, stockings, gloves, and some sort of handbag. And underneath, I suppose a corset — what sort of corset do you think Madame likes?"

"We'd better leave the corset out. I couldn't get a corset on her — get petticoats, or slips I think they are. Anyway, ask some saleswoman for a nice set of underwear for a lady. Say it's a gift to someone."

"You can leave it to me," Fritz said confidently; "but you'd better buy the coat."

"The most important thing is to keep her warm."

"Yes, and the next most important thing is for her to look like a nice, inconspicuous, middle-class lady."

"That will be hard," Mark said. He laughed, almost naturally, and Fritz, as their eyes met, allowed himself to smile.

"This certainly puts a more cheerful aspect on things, eh, sir?" he said mildly.

"Fritz," Mark began. He felt weak from momentary relief and excitement. But they couldn't go on like this, he thought, without some inquiry into the framework of what they were doing. "Do you think this doctor chap can be trusted?" he asked. As he spoke he was hurt by his own mistrust. He knew how much he wanted to believe in him.

Fritz pursed his lips and raised his eyebrows. "Oh, as to that — " he said. "Well, if you mean are his intentions honest, I should say they are. It would be a fairly elaborate plan just to trap us with, don't you think?"

"I don't mean that. I know he's honest about that. I mean, do you think he can do what he says?"

"If he wants to try, we'll have to take a chance."

"But you think it could be done?"

Fritz considered. "What you want me to say, Mr. Mark, is that it *can* be done — Well, that I can't say."

"Aren't you worried over what'll happen to you, if it can't?"

"Now see here," Fritz said, "that also isn't for us to consider. But I've lived through a lot of queer experiences here lately. The world isn't what it used to be, Mr. Mark. As to what happens to me — " He stopped and looked gloomily up at the ceiling. "I've had a hard life," he said, biting the words off with a certain relish, "and Madame Ritter was pretty nearly the only good thing in it." Suddenly he snapped his fingers and said in an exasperated voice, "What are we wasting time over this for? Didn't you say the treatment, or whatever it is, has started? It's *tonight* then, that they'll send for me; and I've got a lot to do between now and then. And so have you." He got a pad and pencil out of his pocket. "We'd better write down what we have to do," he said, balancing the pad on his knee.

"I thought of another thing," Mark said. "A hot-water bottle. That's very necessary."

Fritz began to make his list. "We'll memorize them and then burn them," he said.

They talked a while longer. Fritz told him he would spend that night with his nephew and niece. They knew he was waiting to claim Madame Ritter's body, and it was their telephone number he'd left at the prison. When he was in town he slept in a room over their shop. As soon as he got the call he'd get the camion and drive straight to the camp. Perhaps he could borrow their delivery wagon or pay them a little to rent it. In the wagon would be a few heavy logs and some old quilts, a screwdriver, nails and hammer, the clothes he'd buy.

Mark was to go sometime in the evening to a little restaurant in the square of the village near the camp and wait there till the wagon drew up outside. He would bring the fur coat, hot-water bottle, a thermos of hot water, and all the money he could draw up to that time, first tourist money — as much as was due him — and more at the regular rate of exchange, so as to be sure to have enough.

On one slip of paper Fritz wrote: *Wagon — Clothes — Passport if possible* ("as I may find time for that today," he explained), *Logs — Old Quilts — Screwdriver — Hammer — Nails.*

Then very neatly he wrote on another slip: *Money — Luggage* ("You must be sure to bring your bags. You must look like a couple going to the country for a few days. Fortunately, it's near Easter. People go off like that for the holidays.") — *Fur Coat — Hot-water Bottle — Thermos.*

He studied them for a while. They looked like two exceptionally neat shopping lists. "Can you think of anything else?" he asked.

"No."

"Well, here's the telephone number." Fritz added it. "If anything unexpected turns up during the day you can phone me. Here's the address of the shop, too, in case you have to see me. But if you do, please be calm and speak only English. Then here's the name of the restaurant you're to go to. Don't go too early. A bus leaves the Central Station at seven. That's early enough. You don't want to have everyone beginning to wonder who you are."

He laid a list on each knee and scrutinized them again. Then he handed one to Mark. He took out a match, lighted his own, and burned it, holding the paper out in his long, unhealthy-looking fingers.

When it had dropped in charred flakes he got up and took out a large turnip watch. "I've got to be going," he said. "I've got a lot to do."

He took his overcoat from the bed and put it on, took his shabby Homburg and twirled it around his hand.

"Good night, Mr. Mark," he said, "try to get some sleep. You look to me as though you were going to come down with something."

"I'm as well as you are," Mark said. "Then, unless something turns up, we'll meet around midnight tonight. O.K.?"

"O.K., sir."

Mark held out his hand and Fritz shook it in his limp, cold one.

"Good night, Mr. Mark."

"Good night."

Mark followed him to the door. He was reluctant to see Fritz go, but there was no excuse for keeping him. He did have a lot to do. And even Fritz presumably had to sleep and eat and function like other human beings.

He watched Fritz make his way across the hall by the light from the open bedroom and let himself out, carefully closing the hall door behind him.

And now he was alone again, and he felt sick, as Fritz had said. Perhaps it was exhaustion. Perhaps it was intolerable nervous strain. Perhaps it was lack of courage. Fritz would finish his work and go home to sleep. He was a brave man. The doctor, too, was probably asleep. He envied them.

He put his pillow at the footboard and, taking off his coat and shoes, lay down. He didn't expect to sleep, and yet he feared to drop off and sleep heavily. In his hand was still the paper. He lit his *briquet* and held it out to burn. But once more he read: *Money — Luggage — Fur Coat — Hot-water Bottle — Thermos*. He repeated the telephone number and the two addresses. Then he burned the paper. He thought, The light's too bright — I must turn it out.

Then before he could reach for it, he dozed off, accomplishing in his half-consciousness what he still had to do awake. He rescued her under difficulties that loomed and dissolved, not once but many times, because to do it even once seemed never to be enough.

Chapter XVIII

MARK woke up abruptly and looked around the unfamiliar room. Is it over? he thought. Then he remembered. He looked at his watch. It was eight o'clock. He had slept toward morning heavily and it was later than he had planned. He got up and bathed and ordered his coffee. Then he told the maid who brought it that he was leaving that morning and wanted his bill, and he began to pack his few belongings.

The landlady knocked on the door and when he opened it she stood looking at him accusingly.

"You are leaving!"

"Yes, I'm going to join some friends on a trip."

"Ah, so." She stepped into the room and walked around, examining with suspicion the bed, the washstand and the dressing table. She would have liked, undoubtedly, to find some damage to her property. Finding none, she crushed out a cigarette he had left smoking in an ashtray and handed him a large piece of paper.

It surprised him to find that the establishment could afford elaborately printed paper with all the possible items set down, also that it had a name. It was the Pension Eden. He paid the bill without question.

When he left he took his bag and painting kit with him. He went to the railroad station and checked them in the baggage room. Then he began his shopping. He found the hot-water bottle with a flannel bag, and the thermos he bought in a chemist's. Then he went to the American Express and drew out all the money due him at the tourist rate, and got five hundred dollars more at the regular exchange. To the young lady at the mail desk he asked where was the best place to buy a fur coat. She gave him an address and he thought suddenly to ask for mail. She brought him a letter. He saw at once it was from Sabina.

He went outside and sat on a bench under the trees of Maximilian Place. It was a long and strangely cheerful letter. She was feeling very well, the new clothes were fortunately very effective on her, and everyone was talking about a play in which a friend of theirs had got special notice. Bill was having a show this week. At the end she said, "I suppose you and Mama will be back any day now."

As he read it he thought Sabina had her own courage. She was naturally melancholy, the only one of them who could always see in advance what would inevitably go wrong and could accept it. It made a sort of reserve around her in the midst of their exuberant hopes and despairs. She didn't take a Narcissus-like pleasure in her courage, as many people do, but now she wrote cheerfully and as though she believed there was nothing out of the way in this trip of his.

He found himself longing to have her here. Not only longing for her, but suddenly homesick for New York. He was not used to thinking of New York with affection, thinking of it as home. The apartment they had now was the worst they'd ever had, the top floor of an old-fashioned house, a decent one, in the midst of a raddled quarter. On these gray days of March you could smell the harbor. The sidewalks had a coating of foggy damp and grime, you heard the ships' whistles, and sometimes a gull lighted on the iron railing of the stoop. Down Ninth Avenue the "El" rattled like a toy snake.

He'd like to see Bill's pictures. He'd like to be sitting in the first balcony, — on a pass of course, — getting up between acts, with the peculiar headache of theaters, to smoke a cigarette and discuss the second act on the fire escape. He'd like to go with Sabina to Paula Godey's house. (Was Sabina there that night he'd met the Countess?) He wanted to talk again, to say whatever came into his head. He wanted to be free, to be unhunted, to be unafraid. Such a spasm of homesickness came over him he could only close his eyes and set his teeth till it passed. A pigeon with a harsh whirr of wings came and lighted on his bench.

He got up and went to the shop the girl had told him of. A red-faced salesgirl with a hissing voice took him in charge. Yes, they had fur coats. She sat him on a small chair and brought several out on hangers to show him. They all smelled strongly of moth preventive. She told him with hissing enthusiasm that they were very chic. She pronounced the word in a peculiar way and used it a great deal — "wonderful," "chic," she cried as she held each one before him; "the latest ideas of Paris."

He remembered Sabina and doubted that. "It's got to be warm," he said.

"Oh, no," she assured him. "At this time of year, no. It is spring. What the lady will want is chic, not warmth," and she showed him a short bolero jacket of some sort of leopard cat with leg-o'-mutton sleeves.

"You'll permit me to know what the lady wants," he said stiffly, but he felt confused and anxious over even the difficulties of this small transaction. Finally he selected a long coat of what appeared to be shaved sheep, dyed brown. It reminded him of the youngsters coming back from New Haven in frosty, red evenings, and their voices, joyous as pistol shots. It would be warm and he hoped it would be inconspicuous. It was also, he found, rather expensive. He bought it and took it out over his arm. People would think he was an actor perhaps, or a tenor.

And then suddenly he realized he had done all he could do and that it was only eleven o'clock. There were at least twelve hours to wait — or rather, nine or ten hours until he could begin to wait.

In what conceivable way could he fill in twelve hours? These hours had their place in the plan of what had to be gone through. They were important as part of the plan, but their importance was not in a form that was tangible. They were the negative phase, in them it was only necessary that certain things did not happen. That he was not followed by someone from the Secret Police, that he did not become involved in any accident — a motor crash perhaps — or even with someone turning up ("What on earth are you doing here?") — that he break no rule or regulation, attract no attention in any way. Also that he fight off despair and fear and lassitude.

But I've got to do something, he thought. A gallery perhaps . . . I'll go to see those Rubens . . . Or perhaps go out to the Country Palace, look at her famous Blue and Silver Room. No, that's too far. It would take too long. And to hell with them anyway, Blue Rooms and Rubens and galleries of quaint little peasant arts.

It was a warm day, cloudy and gray. He noticed tiny buds on the trees and saw he had walked as far as the English garden. The Countess had said she lived near here. He'd never even seen her house. I'll go and look at it, he thought. I won't go in. Not after the way she ran from me. It might be dangerous to see her. But then he thought, She wouldn't even be dangerous. She wasn't a woman to take any action, either for or against him. She was all an ambiguous but empty kindness. Nothing about her to take hold of. Stupid really. Not interesting in any way. He walked more briskly along the edge of the gardens, walked till he saw a big white house, square and a little Greekish-looking, on the garden side. He couldn't remember if she'd told him the number but here was Ohm Street, just passed on the left.

Yes, it was the only house on the garden side. He walked up close enough to see at the windows the pale linings and edges of yellow brocade curtains, the lyre-back of a chair. In another window a gray cat sat under a spray of forsythia. From an upper window, left open, white flounced curtains stirred in a slight breeze. It was certainly her house. It had her "air."

He went up three steps to the front door and stood between clipped shrubs in painted tubs. He rang the bell.

When no one came he rang again, murmuring indignantly that he'd seen a window open and someone was surely there. He heard footsteps inside and suddenly his blood began to run quickly. Only a door stood between him and her own special world, strongly feminine, muted, and mysterious. In it he knew now exactly what he hoped to find, what he'd come here for, something revealed in the last look she had given him, just as he was already turning from her in the crowded Odeon. He had been too angry and too alarmed, too much already on his way, to see what it was. But still the look had entered his consciousness and settled there. It had denied everything she said and had even denied her flight.

A little maid opened the door. She was in a striped dress with a big apron over it and a white handkerchief tied around her hair. She had a broom in her hand. She looked surprised.

"Is the Countess at home?" he asked, but already he knew she wasn't.

"She is not in town, sir," the maid said. "She left not fifteen minutes ago."

"Oh — Fifteen minutes ago?"

"Fifteen minutes," the maid repeated.

"Do you know when she'll be back?"

"Not for a week anyway. She and the young ladies have gone to the country."

"I see."

"Who shall I say called?"

"It doesn't matter," he said.

He went down the steps and stood blankly on the sidewalk. He cursed himself for a full moment. I imagined it all, he said. Thank God I needn't see her again.

Now it was twelve o'clock. Now by walking all the long way back again he could have lunch somewhere and that might take him up to two o'clock. He walked slowly, holding the heavy coat, back along the garden by the palace and along Theater Street, and finally into one of the business streets running off from the Town Hall. There he found a big, clean restaurant vaguely like a Child's restaurant at home. It was bare of local color. Foreigners didn't come here and no one wanted them. Townspeople, shopkeepers came here, small-business men, women typists and such, to get a cheap meal and not to sit too long over it. The ceiling was high and the floor was tile and the place full of echoing sounds, plates rattling, voices, the stamping feet of the big, sturdy waitresses, and an air of small commerce and industrious effort. He ordered a veal cutlet and a glass of beer. Neither was very good. But he took a long time to eat them. After he had eaten and paid his bill he saw that it was two-thirty.

He walked again, the fur coat heavy on his arm. He looked in shop windows, seeing beautiful radio sets and postcards of the city and porcelains. Some time after three he went into a movie. He saw a few propaganda newsreels and then a long historical film taken against an Italian background of fabulous beauty. It was, he gathered, a story of Giovanni de' Medici; and among the various liberties taken with his career Mark was hardly surprised to find that Giovanni became in the end a Heroic Leader, a Superman, A Redeemer of Wrongs, an Upholder of Race Purity, a Unifier, a Boy Scout. His death was so edifying that the audience yawned. Still, Mark felt safe in the darkness of the little theater. It was like being buried in a deep bed. The reeling of the film acted as a clock ticking, it made him conscious that time did indeed go forward. But when the film began to repeat he couldn't stand it. It had the nightmare quality then of the thing to be done over and over and never accomplished. That he couldn't stand.

He got up and walked down the aisle and when he pushed through the curtain he saw that it was dark outside. Street lights were on and a show window across the way held in its glittering cavern various fancy lamps and crystalline electrical fixtures.

It was cold and damp now, and a chill struck him through his light overcoat. And it was night. The day of waiting, of suspension, was over — the implacable, hazardous night had come.

It was six o'clock. His bus left from the Central Railroad Station at seven o'clock. He had his packages, the coat, the thermos and hot-water bottle tied together, but he had to get his two bags, left checked at the station. He was suddenly afraid he'd miss the bus, the last of the day. He hailed a taxi to take him to the station. It was not actually as dark as he'd thought. Over the roofs he saw a greenish sky, bruise color, and the shapes of a few trees moved against it. In Maximilian Place people were walking home in the lamplight under the trees.

At the station he went to the baggage room and collected his bags. Now he had two bags, a package, and a fur coat. It was three quarters of an hour before the bus would leave. He bought his ticket and as he spoke the name a feeling of dread struck him in the pit of the stomach. What am I doing here — going to this place — is she really there?

When he went back and sat down he said again to himself, But is she really there? Is she really alive? Is it all true? At this moment she's perhaps dead. Or perhaps something is going wrong. Perhaps she is being put in the coffin — And they haven't sent word to Fritz. Perhaps something has happened to Fritz. He also had to live through the day without any accidents. Maybe they've arrested him. Maybe they've lost his telephone number. Maybe they never intended to notify him at all.

He asked if there was a telephone and someone directed him to it. He called the number Fritz had given him and waited to hear his voice over the wire. He had a bad cramp in the bowels. I've eaten something bad, he thought. The cutlet must have been spoiled. He said to the operator, "Please ring again — I know there is someone there."

A voice came, but it wasn't Fritz's voice. It was a young woman's voice he thought. Breathless, as though she'd been running or was frightened. He asked for Fritz Keller.

"He is not here," she said.

"When will he be back?"

"In a few minutes."

"You're sure?"

"What do you say?"

"Are you sure he'll be back in a few minutes?"

"Yes, he'll be back in a few minutes."

Has something gone wrong? Has Fritz run out? Why isn't he there? Suppose they were to call from the camp, now, earlier than he expected. Was this the niece? Why was she out of breath?

"Any message to leave?"

"No message." He hung up.

He went back to wait. Now the bus left in thirty-five minutes.

He knew he couldn't wait. Besides, he might be sick on the bus.

He'd take a taxi, and stop by Fritz's place and find out if he was there, and then drive on to the town. He went out to the side door where the taxis were and got in one, but just as he was about to give Fritz's address he thought, No: it's better I shouldn't turn up there. Fritz has just gone out for a moment. Surely Fritz can go out for a moment. I mustn't lose my head. I'll do what we planned.

He told the driver where he wanted to go and arranged the price. They started off.

As they passed through the streets the lights in the houses gave him a sick feeling of longing. They came to the suburbs of the town and there the pain in his bowels grew worse.

"Driver," he said, "stop a minute."

The driver drew the car to a curb.

"I feel a little sick," Mark said, "I want to stop somewhere where I can get a glass of brandy."

The driver went slowly on and stopped before a little café. He turned around and Mark saw he had a grave face full of seams and folds as though underneath he'd grown too thin for it.

"I'll get it for you, sir, if you'd like."

Mark gave him the money and in a moment he came out with a glass. Mark drained it and felt better. The scorch of it eased the pain and made him a little numb.

"Better?" the driver asked.

"Yes, thanks."

"It's the chill," the driver said.

"Get one for yourself," Mark said.

"Thank you."

The driver took the glass back. Presently he came back and climbed in, turned around and handed Mark his change. He looked at him soberly.

"Better?" he repeated.

"Yes."

They drove on.

Outside the town the driver said, "Are you going to the Brickmakers' Tavern, or have you another inn?"

"Just to the town."

After a while the driver said, "It's a pretty town. At least the country's pretty. There's a fine view of the mountains from the Palace garden."

"Yes, so I hear."

"A museum, too. A museum of the history of civilization."

Mark wondered if he imagined a note of irony in the heavy, grave voice. There were less lights now to look at.

He smoked a cigarette. Then he closed his eyes and leaned his head back. Just before they reached the town he opened his eyes and the name of it flashed out on a roadside sign. Then a little later the driver drew up in a small square.

"Where do you want to go?" he asked.

"Isn't there a little café here on the square?"

"You can get coffee or beer over there." Mark saw the name of the café and it was the one Fritz had given him. The driver turned the car and crossed the square.

Mark got out, holding his coat and parcel. The driver took out his bag and painting box as though he would carry them into the café for him. Then he changed his mind suddenly and set them down on the ground. As Mark paid him the man said nothing, only watching closely his hands count out the change.

Mark saw two men in militia uniforms standing on the edge of the walk. The driver had seen them first. He took the money with a thank you, but without looking at Mark, and got in his taxi and drove off.

The militiamen stared at Mark curiously. He put the coat over his shoulder, the package under his arm, and picked up his bags.

Outside the café were a few iron tables with chairs turned upside-down against them, an awning rolled up for the night and a few plants in tubs. Inside was a big white room which seemed empty at first because there were so many marble-topped tables with no one at them. In the center of each table was a little glass for toothpicks and another of paper napkins.

Two men were sitting at one table. They weren't looking at each other and they didn't speak. Across the room four men were playing cards and one man sat a little back and watched them. One after the other, they leaned far over the table, holding a card poised while considering the play, then slapping it down with a muffled sound.

Mark's shoes as he crossed the room made a loud squeaking and his chair scraped back harshly as he pulled it out to sit down. He put his bags by the table and laid the coat and parcel on a chair beside him. As he settled himself the two men who sat in silence watched him with dull, bored eyes, but the card players only glanced up indifferently. The cards as they were slapped down became the only sound in the room.

Mark felt that someone had wished to make this place into a café but had given up the idea almost as soon as he began. There was the blight on it of a dreary impersonality. It was a queer place for this country. Here in every beer hall and coffee house and eating place the diverse states of mind of the clients — jovial, eccentric, or melancholy — seemed to him to form a slow, rich compost on the walls. But not here. And it was in this place, nearly void of distraction and filled with the chill and weariness of a waiting room, that he must now sit until he heard the sound of a camion outside.

From an inner door a waiter appeared in a white apron, with a napkin under his arm. He was an old man with an ash-colored face that looked numb, as though at one time it had been paralyzed.

"I'd like some coffee," Mark said, "very strong and hot, please."

The waiter nodded and leaned over, wiping the table-top with his napkin, then walked slowly across to the kitchen.

Mark leaned against the table and thought, yes, it's here that I'll have to wait. For hours perhaps. Perhaps most of the night. I'll know this pale, blank room as I'll never know any other place on earth. I'll remember the look of it, the sound of those playing cards as they fall, and the smell of the chilly, damp air, the gray mottled marble of the table and how cool it feels, I'll know all these forever. And he couldn't remember anything else in his whole life. Not New York, not his trip here, not anything that had happened up to now.

The waiter brought him his coffee and a newspaper with a few pages missing. He drank the coffee and felt better. But he was really sick. He had to cross the room several times to the little toilet that opened off a narrow hall lighted by a flickering bulb. Each time he got up the men at the tables glanced after him.

Two men in uniform came in. On their caps were skull and crossbones. They sat down at a table near the door and ordered beer. They talked in such natural voices, loud and unconcerned, that they made Mark think of real men moving in a museum full of wax figures. No one there appeared to notice them. One of the two men who sat without talking got a newspaper from the waiter and began to read, the other picked his teeth slowly and absently. At the other table the slow-motion card game with occasional muffled words went on. The waiter, after he'd brought the newcomer's beer, leaned against the wall, his arms crossed, looking vacantly across the room.

Mark caught his eye and motioned for a second cup. When the waiter brought it he asked him in a low voice, "Who are they?"

The waiter took the white napkin off his arm and leaned over again to wipe off the table. "Political police," he whispered.

Mark looked at them furtively, but his eyes seemed to be dimmed, he couldn't see their faces clearly, only two reddish blurs with the caps set well back, showing their ears. He couldn't even be sure whether they were looking at him.

He began to count the mottlings and cracks in his table top. With his finger he made a design around them.

If they ask me what I'm doing here, what shall I say?

He watched them under his lowered lids, making his design always with one finger. Each time they lifted a glass or turned their heads he felt a sharp fear; but he couldn't be sure yet whether they were conscious of him. Gradually he felt better and he made no more trips to the toilet. He opened the damp newspaper and pretended to read it.

Outside in the night a distant rumble began and came nearer. At first Mark thought it was thunder. Then he thought: No, it's a camion. Perhaps it's Fritz already. If it were Fritz he would stop. This was the appointed place. . . . Mark wanted to get up, to run to the door and look

[286]

out, but he didn't dare move for fear of attracting the attention of the police.

But the two men who weren't playing cards got up and went to the door. And then Mark got up and followed them. The noise of the camion seemed so loud it almost made a cover for him. He saw when he got to the door that it had grown misty outside: a white ground fog was lying along the street and the lights were milky and blurred in it. Two camions drove up. They were filled with men in dark green uniforms. The two militiamen who had been outside got in one of them and the camions rolled off. The two men who had come to the door said good night and separated, going in opposite directions across the square. Mark came back and sat down.

After that at intervals he heard more camions or cars pass, and once the explosive machine-gun sound of a motorcycle. The mist was too thick on the panes now to see and he didn't get up to look again.

When the waiter brought his third cup Mark said, "It seems misty."

"Yes, a mist often comes up at night. It's from the marshes. Unhealthy," he said.

The two political police stayed at their table drinking beer. The card game went on. In this ashen place it seemed he was going to live forever. He was hung, he felt, like a drop of water on a pane. One breath would send him skidding down to dissolution. He was afraid nearly to breathe. If they asked him what he was doing here he still didn't know what to say.

Then suddenly he couldn't stand it. He called the waiter again. "Have you got a pack of cards?"

"Yes, sir."

He brought him a worn pack and set it down before him.

"And more coffee," Mark said. "Make it stronger, will

you, and bring me a glass of brandy to put in it? I don't feel well."

He lit a cigarette and began to lay out a hand of Canfield. His arms ached with weakness as he played. But this helped him a little, made him feel less suspended on a long slide of fear. He took a few deep breaths and went on playing. He heard several cars pass and more camions.

He said to himself, If I win this game we'll succeed. Or if I make thirty points we'll succeed. This one doesn't count. If I make ten points the police won't speak to me. If I make less they will. If I make ten points the next camion will stop here — or the next one will.

Then for a time nothing passed at all. He had no further idea of time. It had broken, like a great machine-belt, and the wheel no longer turned. He simply knew that he wasn't hearing anything more outside. Also the mist was very thick, and what was to happen over there was surely happening. Certain inevitable things already had come to pass.

He had said to himself that he wouldn't keep looking at his watch, and he hadn't once taken it out. But presently the old waiter came up and leaned over him.

"Do you want anything else, sir?"

"No, not now — Why?"

"We're closing in half an hour."

"Closing!" Fritz hadn't thought of that. Where would he go when the place closed?

"What time is it?"

"Half-past eleven."

"You close at midnight?"

"Yes, sir. They're pretty strict here because of — " He nodded over his shoulder. He again absently wiped the table.

"Do you put them out too?" Mark asked.

"Well, no sir. They'll leave around twelve. They know

the regulations. But if they should stay a little longer, we'd stay open a few minutes for them."

He moved off and Mark began to shuffle the cards again. If I were clever, he thought, if I had any guts, I'd think of something to explain why I'm here, and manage to keep the place open longer, and I'd think of a reason for my going with Fritz when he comes.

Now what could that be?

Then for the first time he took out his watch. It was twenty-five minutes to twelve.

Whatever was to be had already begun. Was she alive still? Or was she dead? He said: Certainly she is dead. It couldn't have been done, he thought. She couldn't stand it. The doctor knew that. . . . But he didn't feel the anguish of her death. . . . She's dead, he repeated to himself. He still didn't feel it.

The two men of the police got up and came toward him. Here it is, he thought, and the sharp cramp went through him again. But he put a black five on a black four on the top row of aces and that brought to light a red six he needed.

The two men stood just behind him and watched him over his shoulders.

"What's the game?" one said. He had a loud young voice, not of itself terrifying.

"It's an American game," Mark said.

The men watched him for a moment. He saw the old waiter across the room standing by the wall. He was trying to appear unconcerned, his arms were crossed and his look was scattered. But Mark knew he was intent on what the police were doing. Even the men at the card table were glancing at him furtively. One of the police came around the table and sat down opposite Mark and the other came and stood behind his chair. Their eyes were still on Mark's cards. With a hand that seemed half-paralyzed he lifted another card over and looked at it. He felt he couldn't keep his hand from trembling a moment longer. He put the cards down and felt in his pocket for his cigarette case. He held it out, open.

"Have a cigarette?" he said.

Both men declined with curt nods. Mark took one out and lit his *briquet*. By holding both hands together over it, as though he were in a high wind, he managed to steady it.

"What are you doing here?" one of them said abruptly. It was the seated man. Mark picked up his cards again.

Here it was. And instead of paralyzing him further it set something loose in him. His blood began to flow warmly through him. He looked directly at the men for the first time. They were young and he couldn't tell whether their faces were really brutal or only unformed, insensitive. They had, both of them, straw colored hair, pale eyes. Yes, they had the lumpish, slightly brutal look that some children have.

"What am I doing here?" he repeated. He frowned at them and looked them up and down with insolence. "I don't like your manner. I might ask what you're doing here at my table."

The seated one stared at him with opaque, expressionless eyes. There were fine hair-like blood vessels showing in the whites. "Political police," he said briefly.

Mark shrugged. "Yes, I've heard of you. Well, I'm an American."

"You have your passport?"

"Certainly."

"Let's see it."

Mark tried to look like an innocent foreigner, both puzzled and outraged. He hesitated. "I suppose you have to see it," he said. He took it out and let it skid across the table. The man reached out a hand with extraordinarily stubby fingers and took it. The other leaned over him to examine it with him. The passport was all right — if they hadn't heard the name before and hadn't been told to look out for it. They could examine it till Doomsday. They looked at it a long time. Then they handed it back. Mark took it and put it back in his pocket. With an offended air he took up the cards again.

"What are you doing here?" the man said.

"I'm here to meet a friend," Mark said.

"What friend?"

Mark put his cards down with a bang. The noise they made was sharp in the flat silence of the room. Everyone in the room looked at him.

"I suppose you're required to annoy foreigners," he said sarcastically. "Well, I'll tell you. I have a friend who is also in the political police. A doctor." As he said the words he felt a queer steadying, as though a strong hand reached out to him . . .

"What's his name?"

"His name is Ditten."

"You want to meet him here? Why?'"

"He's attached to the camp."

"Where is he now?"

"I suppose he's at the camp. He phoned me to meet him here."

"How did you come?"

"In a taxi. See here, you have no right to ask all this. Is this a police court?"

"You're required to answer all questions."

It wasn't hard to pretend rage: he was really feeling it. His face began to get hot.

"Why does Doctor Ditten want you to meet him here?"

"He's a friend, I told you. An old friend. We did some work in Vienna together."

"Are you a doctor?"

"Yes. He's doing some special work out there. He thought I'd be interested. I was to meet him and go there with him. I must have just missed him."

"What time did he say to meet him?"

"He said seven-thirty, but I was late. My taxi had some trouble on the road."

"You expect to go on waiting here? All night?"

"I think he gave me up and went on to the camp. I'll wait to see if he stops on his way back."

Everyone in the café was listening, and the police were enjoying this. They made their curt inquiries with a self-satisfied air. They felt very important and very much in the know.

"What did you say his name is?"

"His name is Ditten. Doctor Ditten."

The two men looked at each other. The man in the chair said, "There's no Doctor Ditten at the camp."

The old waiter had been moving closer. Now he stepped up to them. "Excuse me, gentlemen," he said, "but there is a Doctor Ditten. He often stops here for a beer on his way to and from town. He is of the political police. He's handling a special case out there, it seems."

"What do you know about him?"

As the seated man looked up at the waiter his face congested, and Mark felt that if a foreigner hadn't been there he might have struck him. The old, dimmed face of the waiter showed a flicker of distress. He said, more hesitatingly, "Doctor Ditten came here once with another man." He leaned over and whispered the man's name in the ear of the policeman. Then he said apologetically, "Everyone knows him, of course. It's Doctor Ditten's uncle. Then later the commander of the camp came in his car and I heard him speak of Doctor Ditten. They all drove away together. After that I knew who Doctor Ditten was."

The flush died out of the policeman's face but the look of rage grew deeper. The man standing lifted his eyebrows and gave a childish whistle. He wasn't displeased at the discomfiture of the man who had done the questioning. It was obviously an awkward moment for him.

The man got up. "You are Doctor Ditten's friend," he said brusquely.

"I told you that," Mark said, with all his arrogance intact now.

"Then your presence is explained. I'm sorry to have inconvenienced you."

Mark nodded slightly, still keeping his offended expression. The two police clicked their heels, saluted, and walked over to the door. There they stood looking out into the street.

Mark was stunned by the sudden relief. How had that business of meeting Ditten here come to him? Maybe it wasn't a very good story. Maybe, except for the waiter coming in with the arresting name of the uncle, it wouldn't have worked. But it had worked for the time and that was enough. Also, it had shown him that even he must have reservoirs of strength and resource under the envelopment of fear. That fear as he was knowing it now was too new, perhaps, to impair him as much as he thought. All the time he had believed himself paralyzed he was capable of producing that story. He felt a faint flicker of pride in himself, but he also thought, more deeply, I owed that also to the doctor.

That passed quickly away. The two police had not gone. They were still standing in the door. When they left he would feel safer, but then the place would close and he couldn't stand outside to wait for Fritz. Not for long anyway. Someone would question him again.

[293]

Perhaps the place had a room to rent. He looked around for the waiter but he wasn't in the room. Now the card players got up and with good nights and salutes to the police went out.

Five minutes to twelve. The waiter came back and Mark beckoned him again.

"If you have any hot water out there," he said, "fill these two for me, will you? I'm feeling sick and I may need them."

He untied the parcel and gave the water bottle and thermos to the waiter. The waiter looked at them blankly and then took them, one in each hand, to the kitchen.

Presently he came back with them and laid them on the table. Mark opened his bag and put them in. The waiter watched him. Then he laid his bill before him.

Mark took out a good-sized note. "Keep the change," he said. The waiter looked at it, surprised. A mistake, Mark thought. He said casually, "You helped me to get rid of those fellows. Tell me, as it's so late and Doctor Ditten hasn't come, could you put me up here for the night? Any sort of room would do me. I feel too badly to go back to town this late."

The waiter looked at the money in the tray he carried. He seemed thoughtful but his old face showed very little. Then he said, "No, sir, I'm afraid there is no room."

"Then is there a room anywhere in town?"

"Yes, sir. There are several good hotels — the Brickmakers' Tavern, for instance."

Shall I go there? Mark thought. No. This was the place to meet him. If he doesn't come, I must go back to town. Find out if he's turned up there. Or go down to the country. But I must stay here as long as I can.

He looked at the waiter and imagined he saw a warning

in his abstract, waiting look. Perhaps he suspected his story. Perhaps Ditten had come in earlier in the evening, obviously expecting to meet no one, leaving no message for anyone who might come later. Perhaps he hadn't come in at all. The waiter must think Mark had strained his luck far enough.

He took the fur coat from the chair and got up, took his bags and carried them to the door. As he crossed the room Mark saw that his two police had been joined by another man in uniform. This one had been standing just outside the door talking to them. As Mark came up the police who had questioned him touched his cap: "Excuse me, please, this man here says Doctor Ditten left the camp well over an hour ago. He must have gone straight back to town."

"Thanks," Mark said. He turned to the man. "You say he left over an hour ago?"

"Yes, sir."

Mark stepped out on the sidewalk. The whole little town was covered in white mist. Only the near-by street-lamps showed in it. The houses were all wiped out, not a light came from them. Mark listened. There was no sound in the night. God, or somebody, help me, he thought.

"I should think he'd have stopped for me," he grumbled, loud enough to be heard. "Well," he said to the waiter, "I guess there's nothing to do but take a taxi back to town. Where do I get one?"

"I'll phone for one," the waiter said. "There won't be any around town this late. I can't get one before twenty minutes or so."

"All right. Please phone."

The waiter went inside. There was no one on the street. There wasn't a sound on the road.

A small car stood in front of the café. The two police

stepped out and joined their companion on the sidewalk. After a moment's talk they went over and got in the car. At last they were going away.

But they got in and sat there talking. Mark couldn't hear what they said and he was afraid they were talking about him. (Fishy story that fellow told. Suppose we pick him up and take him to headquarters.)

His story had been stupid, and worse than stupid, because it involved the doctor. He had no right to connect himself with him. They might call him up, and he'd say Oh, yes, he's my friend all right. But then, where was Fritz? In the meantime they might have picked up Fritz, and this story of his, if it came out that he was Emmy's son, would take the doctor's last chance away. The doctor would be less able to insist, then, that he'd only made a grave mistake in thinking Madame Ritter dead.

Mark was no longer pleased with himself. He was cold with shame at having told it.

Inside the café the waiter was turning off the lights. Only one he left on. He came to the door and said to Mark, "Would you like to wait inside, sir? I have to clean up. It'll take me a few minutes."

"No thanks. Did you get a taxi?"

"Yes, sir. One'll be here in a little while."

He let down an outside shutter and went inside again. Mark saw him through the glass of the door. He wiped all the tables and then took a broom and began to sweep.

Mark stood helplessly on the sidewalk. The only light now came through the glass door and he was in a white, cold bath of mist. One of the police in their car called out to him, "Good night." They seemed to have got over their awe at the uncle's name, and the other policeman echoed the good night with a mimicking, mocking sound. Then their engine started with a sputter. But it was cold and a series of sharp reports came from the exhaust. The car wouldn't move.

In the noise they made Mark would have liked to shout at them: Get out, for God's sake, get out!

Finally with a jerk they lurched forward and at that moment a halo of light came out of the thick mist. They swerved just in time to avoid something dark that appeared to be steaming up at them. They hadn't heard it coming for the noise they made. "Careful!" they shouted. But they swerved past and on in explosions of exhaust, and were swallowed at once in the fog. A strong smell of gasoline filled the misty air.

With screeching brakes a delivery wagon stopped a little beyond the café. Mark ran to it, and saw in black letters on the side: *Ebers Cleaning and Dyeing. Satisfaction guaranteed.*

He looked up into the pale face of Fritz. The mist threw the headlights back onto his face and long shadows streamed up from his nose and eyes. He looked down like a man who had just been hit and is slightly stunned.

"You were going too fast," Mark said.

"Yes, that was a close shave."

"It was the police."

"Get up," Fritz said.

Mark looked back at the café behind him. He could see the old waiter inside in the light of one bulb, sweeping the floor with a tired, slow motion of his arms. Mark threw his bags and the coat up to Fritz and got up beside him on the driver's seat. Fritz threw in the clutch and they rolled down the slippery street of the town. They could see only the aureoled street-lamps and when those ended they knew they were in the open country.

Fritz drew over to the side of the road and stopped.

Chapter XIX

WITHOUT turning off the engine he turned around and
Mark, seeing his white face with all the flying shadows,
thought: She's dead.

He said, like an echo of himself, "She's dead."

Fritz said, "You'd better get back and see."

"You don't know?"

"I didn't dare wait till I picked you up. It's quite a way
here. I drew off the road, a little after I left the camp, and
I got her out. I was afraid she'd suffocate."

"Was she alive then?"

"I think so. But she was so low you could hardly tell."

Mark thought, It's enough, for now, if she's alive, and
enough that Fritz has already taken the first step and got
her out. Mark could never have faced the horror of that.
Opening the coffin, seeing her face in it. Seeing her dead.
Or even seeing her alive in those narrow boards.

"That's why I'm late," Fritz said. "I had to get the lid
off and then lift her out. She's heavy. I wrapped her in some
old quilts. Just as I got started again the police stopped me.
They looked at my permit and my license. I had to explain
everything. God be thanked, they didn't look inside."

"What'll we do now?"

"We've got a long way to go. You get back and keep her
warm. The clothes are in a paper bundle. I hadn't time to
put them on. I only pushed the coffin lid back. It's not
nailed. Better hammer it down tight. Here's a torch." He

handed him a flashlight. "You'll find everything in there. Hurry now."

Mark took the water bottle and thermos out of his bag. He took the fur coat and flashlight and got out. He went to the back of the wagon, opened the door and climbed in, shut it behind him and crouched on his knees in the dark. Fritz, hearing the door bang, drove on.

Mark turned on the flashlight. It was smaller in there than it looked from outside. The coffin, of rough pine, seemed to take up almost the whole space. It was wedged tightly crosswise, so as not to slide back and forth. He climbed over it, holding his lighted torch before him. Behind it lay a great bundle of quilt and across it a long braid of black hair.

Hardly conscious, he crouched beside her and lifted back the quilt. He turned the light directly on her face. She was lying with closed eyes and slightly parted lips and he had never seen anything so white as her face. The lips were faintly blue and the lids dark. The nostrils were shrunken and he saw no flutter of life around them.

He thought, This must be death. He had hardly been able to believe all that was happening, but now he knew. He saw in her face every pang she had endured, every indignity up to the final one. He saw also at last the courage that had brought her here. But what had happened was so visible it made her strange to him. It was she and it was not she; because of the whole world of suffering and daring and effort that lay between them. Only her icy hands when he took them were still innocent and familiar to him.

"Oh, they've killed her!" he cried aloud and let his torch go out. He put his head beside hers and cried, holding her hands close to him. But he thought also: And he tried to save her.

After a time a tiny thing began to stir in his conscious-

[299]

ness. Her hands that he held so closely were flexible, not stiff. He could hardly believe it. The place where they lay huddled was so small and dark, so tomblike and crowded with the horror of death, but still, her hands were flexible. They were even, while he held them in his, growing faintly warm.

He turned the light to look at her, brought it close to her face again. There was a change in it. The lashes were spiked, separate and glistening, the cheekbones had a glistening line. As he looked two long tears slid from under the lids and ran down her cheeks. He watched them fall, and then her eyes half-opened and he saw the pale vitreous shine of the eyeballs in the torchlight. He didn't know if she saw him or knew him, but suddenly he picked her up, kissing her eyes and whispering in her ear, "It's Mark, it's Mark."

He wrapped the fur coat around her, held the hot-water bottle close to her. He began to stroke her arms, to rub her hands and feet, coaxing the blood to flow again, to take up its work, warming away the deathly chill. He felt even a pulse in her wrist and he labored on gently but with growing power. They have taken life away but we'll be stronger than they, and make it come back.

He had no idea how time went now. He didn't dare to dress her. To move her about that much seemed to him impossible. He covered her closer with the fur coat, wrapped the old quilts around her feet. He thought her lips moved, though he didn't hear a sound.

She's alive. She's going to live.

When he had imagined all this, he and Fritz driving with her through the dark, he had thought, But what'll we do, where can we go or turn?

Now he didn't think of that at all. He looked at the pine coffin, rough and carelessly made, the top not nailed down, and he knew that was the thing he had been seeing and fearing: the symbol of death. But now he looked again at her face, her hands, the strong web of her hair. And he saw her suffering again, but suffering was part of life. And he saw courage. If she'd been dead there would have been only acceptance. No, she was alive. And she was going to live. Now, he thought, we can do something; we can do anything.

From the different quality of the road, the many turns and slowings down, the occasional noises of auto horns, he guessed that they had reached the town. That would be a bad time. Here they might be stopped. Fritz might bang into something. Drive carefully, Fritz. Drive carefully. She's alive.

They got through without accident, and now by the smooth gliding he knew they were on the great auto road, four cars wide, leading toward the south. Now it was going to be easy. Now they'd get away.

Half an hour farther the car slowed and stopped, and his heart leaped when the door opened. But it was only Fritz, come to see what had happened.

"She's alive, Fritz," he said jubilantly; "she's alive."

Fritz, standing in the roadside, said, "God be thanked."

Mark saw past his head a straight wide ribbon vanishing in the dark, and long marches of stiff pine trunks. The night air felt damp and cool, but they had left the mist behind.

"Have you got her as warm as you can? Have you dressed her?"

"No. I'm afraid to. I'll put her stockings and shoes on. The fur coat. That's all I dare do now."

"Well, do that. Make her comfortable as you can on those quilts. With the coffin shifted this way it hides all that end. You'd better nail it down tight. Then you come up front. If we should be stopped by a motorcycle police and he should by any chance want to look in . . . It would be more natural if you were up in front with me. She'll ride comfortably enough. Hurry now. I'll leave you here while I drive on. In ten minutes I'll stop again."

He closed the door and in a moment they started. Mark, by the flashlight, tried to do all he'd said. He opened the neat paper bundle and got out the wool stockings and large sensible shoes. As he put the shoes on her elegant, narrow feet he smiled because her feet were getting warmer. "Forgive me, darling," he whispered, smiling, "these shoes are horrible."

After he had made a comfortable place with one of the quilts and a pillow with the clothes, he tucked the coat around her and wrapped up her feet in the other quilt. He filled the hot-water bottle with hotter water from the thermos and put it under her feet.

"I've got to go outside," he told her, "Fritz insists. You know Fritz. Now you must keep warm, get strong. Don't go back on us, will you? Aside from that you haven't a thing to do."

Her eyes half-opened again and he saw a relaxation of her face that he might imagine was a smile.

Then he wedged the coffin again as nearly crosswise as it would go, wedged it in tight so it wouldn't move. He found Fritz's hammer and violently, with a joyful hatred, hammered down the lid.

When Fritz opened the door again he was ready to get out.

"I'll want to come back every now and then, to see how she's getting on."

"All right," said Fritz. "Do you need more hot water?"

"Later, yes."

"I brought a thermos myself, of nearly boiling water, and some brandy. In case she needs that. It's up in front with me."

They got up in the driver's seat and Fritz drove on.

The road flowed steadily under them. There was a continuous unreeling of stiff, black pines, close as an army. Sometimes they went through a town, one quite large, once they came close to a long glimmering lake. They saw no lights in any house and no one stopped them.

The air seemed full of extraordinary refreshment. Mark felt empty and light headed. He thought of nothing, he was floating on the pleasure of night, and the swift motion, the exaltation of flight.

Every now and then he realized that they were simply going forward, with no real objective, no real plan; but he couldn't gather himself together around that. It was flight, and the intoxication of flight. Even Fritz seemed to be feeling it. He drove faster and faster, his hands making little scarcely perceptible movements of the wheel. He kept his eyes on the road but every now and then he'd shift them a bit to include Mark in a look of intense satisfaction. Even old Fritz thought they were getting somewhere. The pines hurled themselves backward as they passed.

But Fritz wasn't letting himself be carried away. In the little villages he slowed down, even though no one was about. And if he saw the lights of another car ahead he slowed too. He said once, "It's the road patrol I'm worried about. They're out, even this late."

Once a motorcycle passed them, going the other way. "There's one of them," said Fritz.

But it seemed nothing was to stop them. They drove on for an hour. Then the air began to get colder and streaks of snow appeared under the trees. Along the edges of the roofs was a line of snow. In one town a car was left standing before a lighted house. The whole top of the car was hooded in snow.

"They've come from higher up," Fritz said. "It'll be colder up there."

Outside the town he said, "How about a nip of brandy?"

"Good."

He took the bottle out from behind him and handed it to Mark. The cork had been loosened. Mark took it out and swallowed a big gulp of brandy. He handed it to Fritz. Fritz shook his head.

They drove on. Suddenly a cat's luminous eyes flashed at them for a second and disappeared, leaving only a small black streak across the road.

"A black cat," said Fritz, his face suddenly concerned; "that's bad luck."

He drew abruptly into a little side road among the trees, drove along it for a hundred yards and cut off the engine and lights.

"Better see how she is," he said.

Mark took the torch again, climbed down, and got in the wagon. Now he could hear her breathing distinctly and her pulse was like a little irregular twitching of a cord. She opened her eyes fully and in the light the pupils were dilated. He was sure now she saw him. Her lips that were still colorless seemed to make the shape of his name.

For a moment he thought, She's getting on fine. . . . But he saw she still couldn't move at all. She couldn't speak nor could she lift her hand. To dress her seemed too dangerous and delicate a thing to try.

Fritz had crawled in after him. He was looking at her over Mark's shoulder. He said in a low voice, "Madame's very sick."

Mark turned irritably. "Of course she's sick. But it's all artificially produced. She'll be better by the time we get there. How much time have we now?"

"An hour or so till daylight. Then we must kill time till eight o'clock."

"Better stay here a while," Mark said. "It's as good as any

other place, isn't it? It won't be as cold as when we get higher up."

Fritz nodded.

For a long time they both watched her, taking turns rubbing her gently. They refilled the hot-water bottle. Fritz got out and walked to the main road to listen. At long intervals a car passed, a camion, then another car. Fritz was worried about the motorcycle police.

She was conscious now, but she could do nothing. She couldn't speak. The joy of her being alive began to pass and anxiety flowed back again.

When Fritz came back Mark said, "Do you think we can dress her?"

"We've got to."

"Let's wait a bit."

"Is she warm enough?"

"She's as warm as we can make her. Can you think of anything else to do now?"

"No."

"When we get her in a hotel she'll be all right."

"That hotel," said Fritz, "isn't such a good idea."

"Have you got another?"

"Maybe I have. Wait and see how she is."

They left her finally and went back to the driver's seat and drove on.

They went slower as they climbed and the engine labored with a fuming sound. The whole earth became gradually one white world of snow. The houses that flashed in their head lights were the little mountain houses with carved balconies and great overhanging eaves loaded with snow. It was very cold.

At last they reached the big resort town at the foot of the high mountains. Here in one of the hotels lights were on. A climbing party stood in front of it ready to start out

for the great peak. Standing in the snow with a light streaming behind them they looked like cut-out figures. Their
voices were shrill and joyous. For them it wasn't the end
of a long night but the beginning of a day.

"It must be about five o'clock," Mark said. He looked at
his watch. "Five o'clock," he said. "Three hours more to
kill."

They turned onto the smaller single road leading up the
valley. It was packed hard in snow with snow banked up
along the sides. At first there were open snowy fields but
the pine woods grew thicker as they went on. It was much
colder. Mark began to shiver and Fritz had to stop every
now and then to beat his hands. Even the heat of the engine
wasn't enough. Mark wanted to see again if she was warm
enough, but Fritz couldn't turn off the road. There were
no side roads here, and the snow was banked up so that
they couldn't draw to one side.

Finally Mark insisted on getting down anyway. He took
the brandy with him and into the wagon; he closed the
door behind him. When Fritz heard the door close he
started again. Mark climbed over the coffin and turned the
light on her. She had slipped deeper into the fur, but when
he felt her she was cold. Her hands and arms were cold,
her breath was coming in little sharp clips, her eyes were
closed and there was a tiny ring of sweat around them;
her eyelids looked like moist clay pressed deeply around
the eyeballs.

"It's all artificial," he said; "she's quite well, really." But
then terror filled him: *No, she's dying.* It's all going wrong.
This damned wagon — the cold — she ought to be in a warm
bed. What'll we do?

He began to rub her again, using Fritz's brandy to stimu-
late the blood. At the chill of it her eyelids winced a little.
He became terribly conscious of the movement, the jolting,

that had gone on now for hours. This was no ambulance, it was a rough delivery wagon. They had to get her out of here at once.

At this moment he heard outside the sputtering of a motorcycle, then with a sliding scream of brakes the wagon stopped. His heart nearly stopped, too.

What's happened? Fritz is talking to someone. The motorcycle police. I'll be found in here.

He put out his torch, crawled back over the coffin, and sat beside the door, his knees drawn up, listening.

Over the noise of the engine still running he couldn't hear what was being said, but Fritz and another man were talking. The voice of the other man was sharp. Fritz answered slowly. There were intervals between their voices, filled perhaps with hesitation, suspicion, scrutiny. Perhaps he was only showing his papers. Perhaps it was routine and they'd let him pass.

He heard a sharp, high word and some reply from Fritz. The wagon started. Whatever it was, it was over.

A little later the wagon stopped again. Fritz opened the door. "Come up here," he said quickly, "I have to talk to you."

Mark followed him and he saw something was wrong. But Fritz didn't speak till they were back in the driver's seat and going again.

"What's happened?" Mark said.

"That was the highway police. I was afraid of running into one of them, but it was bad luck running into him up here."

"Why? He didn't look in."

"No, but he asked questions. I had to tell him what I was doing. He knows now I'm taking the coffin to the village. I am allowed to do that. I have the papers. But how am I going to explain picking you and Madame Ritter up on the road three hours later, after the first train gets in? Because if I take you to a hotel then they'll notify the police of the accident. This fellow'll remember having seen me at five this morning, about ten minutes from the village. What was I doing in the interval — and still with the coffin? No, the hotel's out now."

Mark saw that the feeling of flight and of escape was nonsense. They hadn't really been getting out of a trap by a direct, swift passage to freedom. They had only been circling around in a slightly larger area, enclosed on all sides and still a trap. Here he saw around him a little funnel of light in which they moved. It showed, now, snow banked up and the lower trunks of pine trees that appeared to change, but in reality hadn't changed because they could get nowhere. The great circle of impossibility still hemmed them in.

He said despairingly, "She's not reacting as she should. It's too cold and she's being jolted around too much. If we don't get her somewhere she'll die."

They came out of the woods to an open stretch and Fritz said, "The village is over there."

"What can we do?" Mark said. "We've got to get her somewhere at once." Fritz drove slower. Finally he said, "Mr. Mark, there's only one chance now and I don't know if that's a good one or not. But it's all I can think of. There's that American lady: her house is a quarter of a mile from here."

"I told you she knows me."

"We can't help it now if she does."

"She'll give us up."

"We'll have to chance that. But I don't think she will."

"You don't know her."

"You could tell her some story — enough to make her keep Madame Ritter there for a day. Even a few hours."

"She knows the whole thing."

"Everything?"

"Yes."

"You'll have to make her help you," Fritz said obstinately. "Unless you want Madame to die in there. Unless you want to take her to a hotel right now, and try to tell *them* some cock-and-bull story."

"Fritz — Good God — "

"Of course," Fritz said, "we might try to hide her in some cowbarn around here. If I could find one far enough from a house and we could get there without anyone seeing us. The barn would be warm. They stink though; the air would be bad for her." He was obviously just talking. He glanced sideways at Mark.

Mark looked in despair at the white circle in the stream of the headlight. Their breaths were making a mist before their faces and the windshield was blurring. Certain words, pictures, slid like ice crystals before his eyes. Snow, forest, cold, daylight, pneumonia, barn, police . . . Now at last I'm up against the decision. It was like being against the blade of a knife.

Fritz said with a voice that suddenly had a note of nagging smugness in it, "You'd be surprised at what ladies will do for young gentlemen like yourself."

"All right, all right," he cried distractedly, "we'll go there."

The possible and the impossible . . . One moment they were free, the next they were caught. One moment she was alive. The next she was dying. So he had to choose, no matter what came of it, the one open way.

Fritz didn't say any more. He drove on slowly, peering out around the dimmed windshield.

A little later a letter-box flashed into the light. It sprang from the snow beside the road, a little painted box on a pole, made like a chalet, with an absurd, painted bird on top.

"It is just about here," Fritz said.

They saw a driveway leading off to the right. As their lights swung slowly into it a large black limousine without lights rose before them. The lights went on at once and the car passed them, turning out of the drive and into the road. They saw a man in uniform at the wheel, and inside a man leaning back on the far side. They couldn't see his face.

Fritz whistled. A few yards up the drive he stopped to be sure the other car had gone on. They watched its beam gliding up the roadway toward the village.

Fritz whistled again. "I was afraid she wasn't at home," he said. "It seems she is." He was grinning with the ugly, cold satisfaction of the peeper.

Mark hated him. "Oh, it's the God-damned lover," he said, and his own voice was coarse and ugly. But he forgot for a moment even Emmy lying behind the coffin and a new, gentle sadness blurred his thoughts again. "Let's get on," he said impatiently.

They drove around a curve up a little hill where a cluster of snow-laden evergreens brushed out into the road. A little farther on they saw the house, on sloping ground with a rise of mountain behind it.

Before the door Fritz stopped. He cut off the engine and the lights and they sat in the midst of silence. Mark didn't speak or look at Fritz but he got slowly down and went up the little walk to the front door. He stopped for a moment to look at the house.

It was two very large chalets, with galleries and immense eaves, joined together by a closed gallery making a sort of court. Every window was dark but the snow all around was lighted with a greenish pallor and the tall pine trees at one side were sharpening against a faintly luminous sky. The cold air smelled of snow and a faint tang of wood-smoke from down the valley where someone was already lighting a fire.

His heart grew more calm as he stood there looking at her house. Not that he hoped for any peace in it, but that it looked safe — and in a way that was strange and her own. Because it was hers, it had something of the fairy tale. And in the fairy tale there is always a certainty, a fatality; everything turns out all right. There a magic ring is enough to teach the language of beasts, and that bird singing like a woman is indeed a woman, whose enchantment will inevitably be broken.

He felt around for the bell but then he changed his mind and rapped softly and urgently on the door.

Chapter XX

THE tiny alarm that she kept by her bed rang with a muffled twirring like a cricket. She sat up suddenly in the dark and looked at the illuminated dial. It was five o'clock.

"Kurt! Kurt!" she whispered. He had overslept again. It was becoming harder and harder now to make him wake out of his heavy sleep. "Kurt!" she whispered sharply. She felt for the white woolen robe and wrapped it around her, set her feet in little fur slippers on the floor.

How cold it was! She went over to the window and shut it, drawing the heavy curtain across, and then leaning over turned on the light of the little table lamp. Beside it was a thermos of coffee. She poured some into a cup for him and looked over to the alcove. He was sitting on the edge of the bed staring heavily at her, his eyes bloodshot and his face sagged and swollen. Sleep gave him a debauched look.

"Are you all right?" she asked.

"Yes, yes," he grumbled. He got up, yawning, and came over to take his coffee. He swallowed it, making sucking sounds and gasping at the hot sting of it on his tongue. In the morning, before he had his coffee, before he put his head under the cold water of the shower and smoothed down his hair and put on his uniform, he was uncouth and disordered, not only physically but in his manner. Half-awake he was gross as a peasant.

"Hurry, Kurt," she said. "It's getting toward daylight."

He answered by a sort of grunt and went into the bath-room. She sat waiting on the edge of the chair, running the red cord through her cold fingers, hearing the shower turned full force.

In ten minutes he'd be gone, but her little room, dimly lit by the yellow table lamp, was still his, his clothes on a chair, his boots beside them, on the table the empty coffee-cup with a ring of coffee stain, in the bed the rumpled pil-low where he'd slept. The room was still his, even the air she breathed — cold and a little stale; and she herself, thin, middle-aged, trembling with cold and a slight feeling of nausea and headache, waiting his good pleasure to leave.

He took longer than usual. When he came out she didn't look at him but sat stiffly, her eyes on the floor, while he dressed. Vaguely to attract her attention he made growling noises as he pulled on his boots. It was hard for him now to lean over; he wore an inner, stiff, boned belt to hold his stomach flat under the uniform. Finally he was dressed. He buttoned his tunic and smoothed his hair before her mirror. Now he was the general again, polished and magnificent.

He turned toward her. "Well, my dear, I must be off."

"But naturally," she said — only she said it to herself. She smiled wistfully as she had always done, and he was satis-fied. He pulled her up to her feet and kissed her.

"Go back to bed," he said, using a sort of baby talk, "go back and get a good sleep. Be fresh and beautiful when I come this evening. Your big man will be out skiing all day."

"Do you think you ought to come this evening?" she said. "The girls will certainly think it's queer."

"Perhaps I'll just drop in for tea today," he said, "and not stay for dinner. Perhaps that's better. Then I'll come back tonight about twelve. Leave the door unbolted."

"Do you think you ought to come for tea?"

"Why did I come up here?" he said. "Your little foreigners are all geese. They'll think nothing."

"All right," she said.

Something about her didn't satisfy him.

"You ought to be going with me," he said. "You never ski any more. You never exercise. But you remember that glorious day at Kitzbühel, what a champion you were? You're letting yourself get slack, Ruby, you're letting yourself get old."

She saw the sun on the snow and the violet arabesques left by the runners, and she saw also a man turning suddenly high in the air, like a hobbled animal in the snow. "Do be careful," she said guiltily.

"I will, I will," he assured her.

The feeling of guilt made her decide to go down with him. She took his arm and they walked softly out and down the carpeted stairs. Her rooms were in the larger house, separated by the gallery from the house where the girls and the servants slept. There was little fear of their being heard but they went like fugitives anyway, because they were accustomed to it.

At the front door she kissed him good-by. It was too cold for her to go into the vestibule. She closed the door and heard him close the outer one. Through a small window she watched him walk down the drive, down a little slope, to where his car should be waiting behind evergreens. In the stillness of the early morning she heard the car starting.

She began to take deep, free breaths. He was off, and she was alone in her own house, dark now and safe behind her.

She waited a moment longer, to be quite sure he'd gone and that the house was truly hers. As she waited she was conscious of its special odor, indescribably reassuring. Though it was perhaps only floor polish, book leather, scented powder, it seemed to be the odor of herself.

Along the distant road she saw the long beam of his car. She gave a great sigh and turned to go upstairs.

But suddenly fright went through her. She stopped by the lower stair, peering around as though in the house itself something had betrayed her.

He was coming back. She heard the car on the driveway and then saw on the wall before her a bright flash from the headlight.

What's happened — What's happened? Her heart beat like a hammer. And while she waited she heard the little gold clock strike the half-hour — one stroke, tinkling and fairylike and sinister.

Something was terribly wrong — Why had he come back? Why was she so frightened that he'd come back?

There was no sound outside. The car had stopped. The headlights were out. She waited. Then she turned and walked to the inner door and opened it. She heard then a soft, urgent knocking on the outer door.

The certainty of disaster locked her where she stood. "Kurt," she whispered, "what's wrong?" But no one answered her. She saw again the man falling, legs up, grotesque in the snow. I've wished evil to him, she thought. He's hurt. Something's wrong. I must let him in. She leaned toward the door and fumbling drew back the lock.

Outside a man was standing, but it wasn't Kurt.

At first she thought it was Leo Mannheim, coming toward her as he had come in her dream. Then she saw who it was. She stared at him and couldn't speak. She heard his low, mumbling voice.

"I've come to you for help," he said. "I'm in fearful trouble. You're the only one in the world who can help me."

His voice sounded unreal and ashamed. "You're the only one in the world I can turn to. The only one."

[315]

Behind him was a dark wagon and a man getting down from the driver's seat.

Like the man in the dream he stood before her. "Do you want us to die," he said, "both of us, here and now? Our blood'll be on your head."

It's a good thing it's still dark, she thought. No one can see. But it wasn't quite dark. Standing in the shadow of her doorway, the snow was greenish pale, the earth was turning toward the sun, she could feel herself very small on its vast roundness.

"Do you want to hide here?" she whispered.

"No, not I. It's her I'm talking of. I've got her here. I have no place to take her."

"You mean your mother?"

"Yes."

"You can't do that," she said.

But the other man was carrying something up the little walk in the snow. Carrying it right to her door, right to her.

"You can't," she repeated.

"I must. I must," he said. He stepped inside the door and drew her aside, holding her suddenly in his arms, flattening her against the wall to make room for the other. For a moment she felt his mouth pressed awkwardly on her cheek, young, ice-cold, and trembling. Then he let her go. He took the great bundle from the man, staggered into the dark hall with it.

"Turn on the light," he said firmly. She followed him, put out her hand and turned on the light. Then she saw the long, black braid dangling from his arm.

She screamed, throwing both hands across her mouth. "Not here! Not here!"

"Where can I put her?" he said. "Quick. I'm afraid she's dying."

The words came out of her automatically. "Upstairs," she said.

He leaned against the newel post of the stairs and the woman he carried sagged out of his arms till her feet rested on the floor. The Countess' eyes followed the drop of her feet, in great, clumsy shoes that struck the floor with a dead sound. Above them she saw thin ankles, turned helplessly but with elegance. Then she looked at him again and she thought he was nearly dead himself. His gray eyes were colorless in dark lashes and darkened lids, but she knew that they looked at her blindly, furiously, begging for help.

The man who had followed him in went and took hold of the woman and together they began to climb the stairs, carrying her between them. The Countess followed after them.

At the top step she said, "Here," and slipped past them, leading the way down a long hall. She turned on the lights as she went. Which room, she thought, which room? Shall it be — this one? No, this one. At the end of the hall she opened a door, turned on the light. There was a great bed. Mark saw it and with his last strength laid Emmy Ritter on it.

Afterward he couldn't remember what they did. Someone took her shoes off and the fur coat, turned back the covers and laid her inside. The hot-water bottle fell out. The Countess picked it up and said, "It's cold." She opened a door into a bathroom where he heard her letting the hot water run. She came back with the bottle and slipped it between the sheets. "The water's always hot," she said. "I'll get mine too." She went out and came back with another bottle. Mark sat on the edge of the bed and she and Fritz both moved about.

The Countess wore a long, white robe with a red cord at the waist; her ash-colored hair, very long, hung down her back. The room had gay prints on the walls, pleasure palaces of Austria and baroque gardens. The pillows were very clean and had ruffles around them. The sheets were fine linen embroidered with crowns. In the house was a nice, spicy smell of floor polish.

He looked everywhere but at his mother. But when the Countess leaned over her he said, "Is she alive?"

"Yes," said Emmy Ritter.

Then Fritz's voice came, full of grudging concern. "You lie down, too. Here on the couch. No need to do any more." He put a pillow under Mark's head.

The Countess stood outside the door with Fritz. She turned the key in the lock and slipped the key out, holding it in her hand.

Fritz said, "There's no need for me to thank the gracious lady. Those two in there, they'll never forget."

She looked at him and saw he was a servant and an old man. He was respectful, soured by life, but still capable.

"What happens now?" she asked. "It's not over by any means."

"No," he admitted gloomily, "not at all. The most delicate part remains."

"What did you do?"

Fritz shrugged. There was no use to tell her. If they were caught it would be easier for her, and perhaps for the doctor too, if she knew nothing. He recognized that they both had secondary rights in this matter.

"Madame Ritter died last night," he said. He watched her closely to see the effect of each word. He saw her face was still full of horror and pity. "She died of heart attack. I'm an old servant of hers and I claimed the body. Mr. Mark naturally was with me. We found, then, that she wasn't really dead. So we got her out and revived her. You can't expect us to turn her over to them again."

"I don't think I believe you," the Countess said.

Fritz lifted his pale eyebrows and spread out his supple hands in a fan movement but he said nothing.

"I suppose it doesn't matter," the Countess said. She clasped her hands tightly to steady herself.

"The gracious lady need fear nothing," he told her. "I've arranged everything satisfactorily so far. I can arrange to get Madame Ritter out of here with no inconvenience to anyone. In a few days."

She didn't answer, but he boldly took her assent for granted. "It was only a difference of political opinion," he said; "but they were going to execute her this morning." He looked at her out of the corner of his eye and saw her turn whiter. "I thought Mr. Mark was going to die of it. Poor young man!"

She began to walk toward the stair and Fritz walked with her. "The young man can't stay here," she said. "That's impossible."

"Naturally," Fritz agreed. "An hour's sleep and a good breakfast will cure him. Then he can get up and come to the Inn. I'll leave his bags in the hall for him. Besides, I want him to come to the funeral this afternoon. It looks better, in case anyone should find out he was here."

"Funeral?"

The old man looked at her with his whole face turned to acrid triumph. In this moment he seemed to feel he had got the best of anyone who in all his life had ever done him in, anyone who had ever thought in his blindness that he was smarter than Fritz Keller.

"Madame Ritter's funeral," he said sardonically. "Oh, yes, we're burying her this afternoon at three. Why, I've got the coffin out there now." He waved a long, supple hand toward the well of the stairs. "I've got to be going, too. It's daylight. Would the gracious lady be kind enough to tell the young man that he's to be at the church in the village at three o'clock?"

"I'll tell him."

She went downstairs and Fritz followed her. He went out to the wagon and brought back Mark's bags. When he came back she seemed much more controlled. She said slowly, "I hope you understand that this whole thing was forced on me. I couldn't leave a dying woman in the snow. I don't want to turn Madame Ritter over to the police. But you'll have to get her out as soon as you can. She can't stay in the house tonight. That's entirely impossible."

She had no idea why she said this. It was only a loose residue of words. Nothing in her planned or meant it. It was like a jangling of bells accidentally touched.

Fritz stood turning his battered hat in his hands. "You don't give me much time," he said.

"Until tonight," she said firmly. "After that I'll have to notify the police."

Fritz after a moment nodded acceptance. "Kiss your hand, gracious lady," he said, and caught her hand and kissed it with an obviously natural servility, as the old-fashioned servants used to do. "There is no danger, gracious lady," he added.

He went out and she watched him get in the wagon and drive off.

She stood again in her hall. All the windows were gray. Not twenty minutes ago she had stood here in the dark, paralyzed with fear. But she wasn't afraid now. She wasn't afraid because the vague and the formless, the terrible choice which had haunted her so long, had come at last. And without knowing it or willing it, as though under an anesthetic, she found she had made it. Or perhaps it had been made outside herself. At any rate, to go to a phone, to ring the police, to say "Madame Ritter is here," was impossible.

She thought of the two of them upstairs locked in one of her rooms. She thought of the opening of the door and the strange, young, despairing face looking at her in the morning twilight, the great heavy burden he carried upstairs, the braid of hair on his arm, and lastly she felt again the sudden kiss, reserved and tremulous but, in all its desperation, never hesitant, never empty and formal. It had been direct and delicate and sure. She put her hand to her cheek.

From the little closet under the stair the phone rang sharply, and then another fear came, a simple, new fear, easily supportable.

That's Kurt, she said. The bell might as well have been his voice. She ran to answer it before it should ring again.

"It's Ruby," she said at once.

"Did I wake you?"

"No."

"As I left, a car turned into your drive. A queer thing like a delivery wagon. What was it?"

"I don't know. I heard it too. It turned around and went out. It must have mistaken the road."

"It didn't stop?"

"No."

"Well, that's all right then. I was a little uneasy. It seemed so queer at that hour."

"No, it's all right."

"What are you doing now?"

"I'm making some coffee for myself. I feel very wakeful."

"Better go back to sleep. I'll be there by four."

"Good."

"Good-by, my dear."

"Good-by."

She shut the door of the closet behind her.

Just time to get some food, she thought. She went to her kitchen and turned on the light. In great haste and trembling with excitement she put coffee on the stove to boil, made toast, and boiled four eggs. She got a big tray and set the breakfast on it. Then she also cut one or two slices of ham and cheese and put the remains of a fruit compote on a plate. What else could she take up now? Perhaps enough coffee to last all day, in a thermos jug, a jug of warm milk. Rolls on a napkin, butter, cookies — these would have to do. More would be missed. She carried the heavy tray upstairs to the room she had chosen for them. It was a room used when her house was full, as it often was in summer. In the winter no one went in it. She set the tray down and unlocked the door, picked it up, and carried it in.

The light was still on, though the daylight was clear outside. Mark, on the couch, did not stir. He lay with his back to her, and the light from the window made bluish his smooth black hair.

From the bed the dark eyes of Emmy Ritter watched her come in. She brought her tray over and set it down on a table by her.

"I have some food for you," she said. "Could you eat a little of it?"

"Some milk I think, yes."

"An egg, too, perhaps."

"If you'll be good enough to help me."

The Countess sat down by the bed, broke the top off an egg and fed her soft spoonfuls. She held a glass of warm milk to her lips. Emmy swallowed slowly. They attended to this seriously, in silence. The Countess watched her as she ate, and saw first the rugged strength of her bones, barely covered by emaciated skin. Her eyes, with their still dilated pupils and wandering look, were magnificent. So was her thick hair. This was the woman Kurt had seen as a girl in her mother's house, young, thin, and with devouring eyes, too robust, too vital, like a handsome boy. Now her illness made her sexless again, in spite of long braids. The collar of the gray prison gown was like that of a man's old-fashioned nightshirt. Even in her dreamy half-consciousness she wore humiliation and weakness as of no consequence. Perhaps even today her head should have been rolling from her body. But that seemed impossible. The Countess saw why people tried to save her: not because she was a woman, but because she seemed indestructible, and they would feel they were conforming to a natural law.

"I can't eat any more," she said.

The Countess took the spoon and the egg-cup into the bathroom and washed them. She brought them back and put them on the tray, covered everything with a napkin.

"I think I've been taking a drug," Emmy said.

"Don't mind that," the Countess said. "It will pass off."

"I don't know where I am," Emmy said. "It's not a hospital, is it?"

"No, it's my house."

"Have I seen you before?"

"No."

Emmy closed her eyes and frowned as though she were trying to think it all out.

"I believe you're being very kind to me," she said finally.

The Countess stood by her bed, looking across it to the couch where Mark lay asleep.

"No, no," she murmured politely, "it's nothing."

Emmy opened her eyes and tried to concentrate. "But I think you are. I won't ask why," she said with difficulty.

[323]

"People have a right to do these things without questions or too much gratitude."

The Countess had no idea what to say to this, but she felt again that she'd made her choice, and that it stretched further than she'd realized, while it was so vaguely and fearfully made.

"Are you warm enough?" she asked.

"Yes, quite warm, thank you." She lifted her head slightly so she could see over the curve of the pillow. "That *is* Mark, isn't it?" she asked.

"Yes," the Countess said.

Emmy's face relaxed suddenly in a helpless, happy smile. The Countess felt, herself, a little shock of happiness. "Oh, yes, it's he," she said.

"I thought so a while ago. But in the wagon I thought I was dead. Is the doctor here?" she asked.

"No, no doctor is here."

Emmy's eyelids closed slowly again. She seemed to go to sleep. Suddenly she said clearly, "I wasn't worth it."

The Countess stood waiting for her to say more. But she had dozed off. Only one more thing was necessary. She leaned over and said close to her ear, "I want you to have a long quiet rest. I'm going to pull the curtain a little and turn out the light. Will you remember to be very quiet? Don't call for anything or ring. I'll come in from time to time to see if there's anything you want."

Emmy nodded.

The Countess turned out the light and drew the curtain. The room was full of twilight again. She was about to go but she thought of something. She took the fur coat that lay on the chair and spread it slowly over Mark. He didn't stir.

Then she went out and locked the door behind her and took the key. She ran downstairs and in the hall she heard her servants in the kitchen. She saw Mark's shabby bag and his painting box standing by the door. She gathered them up noiselessly and put them in the back part of the dark little closet where the phone was. Then she went to the kitchen door and opened it.

Kathe and Juli were fixing breakfast trays. They stared at her.

"Good morning," she said.

"Good morning, gracious lady."

"I couldn't sleep," she said, "I came down early and got some coffee and some fruit for myself. Please bring me another cup to the writing room."

She went to the little room off the stair landing. It was really a small library, with bright blue painted walls over bookshelves, a little, white porcelain stove, a blond Biedermeier desk. One immense French window, hung with crossed loops of white muslin, took up one wall and opened into her own little rock garden.

She sat down at the desk, took a sheet of paper and pencil to write a note. This was to be instructions for Mark when he should wake, how he was to get out of the house without being seen. Or perhaps being seen, but not causing surprise. How could that be? He couldn't possibly take his bags and walk out without someone on the place stopping him as a thief who was just making off with the silver. No, he couldn't chance getting *out* without being noticed. He could only perhaps get *in*. Then to leave again would be easy. She looked out the window to the rock garden; a little path through the snow led to the drive. It will be as though he came up the drive, she thought, and in this door. Only he needn't really come in, so of course no one will see him. He'll come to the hall as we're all at lunch and call out, "Anyone here?" and I'll say, "Why, it's Mr. Preysing. Come on in. But how did you get in?" "I just wandered in by that little side door. I'm on my way from the station. I walked." Each servant will think only he failed to see or hear him. Then he'll lunch and I'll call a car for him from the village. It's very simple. . . . This plan was to be slipped in an envelope under his door.

On the wide desk there was a notebook left open, with a pencil laid across it. She knew whose it was because the girls never came in here. When her pencil-point broke she reached for this one and her eye lingered on the fine, neat, almost womanish script. It was the Book, of course.

She read, "War of today is a return to war of the Middle Ages in that cities, not armies, are the objective, with this obvious difference, that instead of the lingering siege, the clumsy assault, conditions now lend themselves to the light-ning stroke whose purpose is not so much destruction as the instant paralysis of civilian morale. That this can sometimes even be accomplished psychologically, and without the fir-ing of a shot, is proved by the last crisis in which civilian morale broke in anticipation; and the mere fear of such a war paralyzed a whole national policy . . ." The last word had a jerky line showing the contempt amounting to nerv-ous rage with which he had written it. Contempt with him, she had seen it often, became what fear did in those people of whom he wrote: a sort of hysteria.

Yes, he was here, and no farther away than the village. He was here and for an hour she had forgotten him. But now the room filled with him and she couldn't write her note. She sat looking at the page on which she had only written very stiffly, as though it were an invitation to din-ner, "Dear Mr. Preysing."

But the note had to be written. She closed the notebook and stuck it in a pigeonhole of the desk. Then she went on: —

At exactly twelve forty-five will you please come down-stairs and take your bags which are in the closet where the telephone is, under the stair. Please be sure no one sees you come down. You will know we are at lunch by the voices from the dining room at the back of the house and the sound of dishes . . .

As she wrote the sun began to come up. It had not reached over the low notch at the eastern end of the val-ley, but the sky was pink, the snow outside was turning pink. She got up and went to the French window to see it. A whole flock of little golden clouds streamed up from the dark crests. The sky behind them was deep and luminous. Every snowy shrub, every rock in her little garden, cast a delicate image on the rosy snow. She leaned against the cold glass and she felt so flooded with sudden happiness that it seemed only the glass held her from dissolving into the light outside.

A clutch of the old fear told her that perhaps this also was too much, this also was forbidden, but she knew the joy of having gone too far, of having committed herself too deeply, to turn back. She had the hope that such happiness might create slowly another world where fear would be finally impotent. Only her knees and hands trembled, her throat contracted unnoticed.

Chapter XXI

MARK woke and looked over at the bed.

She was really there.

He thought in flurried, acute flashes of what had happened, but he tried not to remember too clearly. Each step taken separately had the pain of failure, but in the end it was success. He couldn't feel at what point it became success, but success was enough. Only failure had to be examined. There she was. The triumph and miracle of her lying there grew and filled him till it was more than he could support.

He got up and stretched out his arms and yawned. The fur coat lay by the couch. It must have been put over him. Fritz must have covered him. He hadn't noticed but it didn't matter. This, he thought, is the way *they* feel all the time, the megalomaniacs, the supermen. He felt a little of a superman himself.

He tiptoed over to look at her. She was asleep. Really asleep this time, naturally and with a look of freshness about her. There was even color in her lips. Her hand when he touched it was warm and moist. He sat down on the edge of the bed to look at her. Seeing her so relaxed and smooth he suddenly remembered her vividly as she had been in the wagon, and he remembered the doctor. He knew it was the first of many hauntings that would come to him, hauntings that would have to be endured and that could be endured so long as he saw her safe. He loved her more now, lying safe, than he had ever loved her before. So much that no matter what happened, this moment, though she was unconscious of him, was the best they would ever have together.

The Countess, it seemed, had given her food. His eyes wandered to the tray covered by the napkin. He felt proud of the Countess, as though she had managed to do him credit with the family. He knew he would presently feel more than that, but he wasn't free to feel it till he had taken the last drop from this.

Already it was diminishing a little. He thought again of the long way ahead to safety. Of course Fritz will get the passport by some time tomorrow, certainly. Then I can put her quietly on the train. She'll have a bad moment of fear at the border and it'll be over. Then all she'll have to do will be to remember. Just now I forget easily, but I'll be remembering more and more, and she'll have to remember too. Her sleep, her air of innocence, will pass. We'll both have to support the remembrance of these things.

For the first time he, who was so young, saw that what makes age is the accumulating weight of memory. That a thing come to pass never quite loses its solidity, never quite vanishes. If we could forget, we'd never grow old.

He saw the white note lying on the floor just inside the door where the Countess had pushed it. He got up and picked it up and saw it held a small, flat key. He read it and felt lighter, triumphant again.

"My dear Mr. Preysing." It covered two pages — delicate, meticulous instructions, written as though all she asked him to do were the most natural thing in the world. What was clear in it was that he was to leave the house and stay away and that she herself would look out for Madame Ritter. But he thought, smiling in spite of himself: I may have to wait here for days. She can't keep me away all that time.

[329]

It doesn't matter what she tries to do. It's clear she isn't one of those who know how to direct her plan, her destiny, or whatever you want to call it. And I'm stronger than she is, I can bring what I want to pass. Actually he saw her as an exquisite, supplementary creature taking her place in his and Emmy's destiny. Her legend was only a part of theirs, dovetailing into it at the exact moment required. She was to be always the passive one, taking what was sent her or forced on her. Her fate was clearly written as in a fairy tale.

Emmy still slept and he decided not to wake her. Her sleep was precious. He washed himself in the bathroom, smoothed his hair. Then he re-read the Countess' instructions and set a match to them. He waited till his watch told him it was twelve-thirty, then he put on his overcoat, took his hat, and unlocked the door gently with the little key. He opened it a crack to listen. He could hear somewhere below the voices of the girls. They were probably not in the dining room yet. The upstairs corridor was thickly carpeted. On a chest by the door stood an old wooden Tyrolean saint. The light was cold, snow light from the window at the end and a skylight overhead. He stepped out, looked around, and saw only closed doors around him, the head of the stair.

Then the voices suddenly grew louder and he knew the girls had come out into the hall and were going across to the dining room. He waited till they had been there for a few minutes, then closed the door of the bedroom, locked it carefully and put the key in his pocket. She had told him there were two keys. He tiptoed down the stairs. On the landing he looked into a little blue writing room with French windows opening onto a rock garden on a ledge of the hill. This was the way he was supposed to come in. He went on down, looking around the lower hall. He didn't remember anything about it. It surprised him by being a hall with no special peculiarity.

No one was in sight. He found the telephone closet under the stairs and got his bags out. Then he came back where he could look into the dining room.

He saw light striking the ash-blond hair of the Countess and the reflected light from the white cloth and glasses illuminating her face. She was in the midst of the girls of course, but with a self-conscious look, as if she was listening for him. He felt a sudden shyness himself at seeing her again under all those acute, watchful eyes.

He set his bags down and stepped inside the door. The girls all turned and a servant with her head tied in a silk handkerchief stood still in surprise. Only the Countess, expecting him, was slow to look up.

"Hello," he said.

"Why, Mr. Preysing!" she exclaimed in a voice of surprise, "What are you doing here?" She held out her hand cordially.

"I just walked in," he said. "I got lost somewhere in your garden."

"Really? Where have you come from?"

"I got in on the noon train. I thought I'd walk to the village."

"Girls," she said, "you remember Mr. Preysing. Juli, bring another chair. You'll have some lunch with us?"

"Thanks. Just coffee, if I may."

"Sit down. Juli, Mr. Preysing will take coffee. Have you any luggage?" she asked.

"I left it in the hall."

"Good. But it's quite a way to town, you know. You'd better let me call you a taxi later. Yes, we actually have taxis here in the country."

She talked gaily and rapidly. He was surprised at the

determination with which she undertook to deceive everybody. But she had a critical audience. The girls remembered him very well. They remembered, also, how he had preferred to see the Countess alone and how she had disappeared at tea-time last Sunday. They were very curious about this Mr. Preysing, but they also remembered he had let them down.

They looked at his face and hands, the way his hair was cut, his tie, his coat, his cigarette case, the cigarette he took out and the way he lighted it. They listened to his voice and accent and what he said. They couldn't make him out. He was intensely interesting to them but he didn't seem to be quite the Countess' cup of tea. Was he an actor perhaps? That would be marvelous. They sat with intense curiosity and cold reserve while the Countess made conversation with him.

After they had eaten he said, "I think I'll call that taxi now if you don't mind."

"Juli will call it," she said. "Have another coffee while you wait. I suppose," she said, "you're here to do some painting. Will you paint this afternoon?"

A painter, they thought. So that's it.

"Yes," he answered. And he added suddenly, "Let me paint you."

"Good heavens! I'm too old," she said. "Besides, I'm afraid of you modern painters. You should paint one of the girls," she said.

He looked slowly around at them and a tremor of excitement passed through them. They were entering into competition, and Marie, who couldn't any longer resist attracting attention, said hypocritically, "Oh, do paint Sully — she's simply divine," and she nodded toward the tall English girl beside her. Then they all began to talk at once but his eyes, moving over them, rested on Suzanne, and the girls were disappointed again. They thought her very chic (why shouldn't she be, with her mother the great dressmaker?), but she was the ugliest of them all. She was also the oldest. Mark looked at her because he thought she looked in a curious way like Emmy. Like a younger sister perhaps of Emmy, with the shape of her eyes and bones somewhat the same and with thick black hair.

But he didn't suggest painting her. He told them the story of Gainsborough — or was it someone else? — who said a portrait was a picture of someone where the nose was too long. They hadn't heard that, but they asked him who was the most beautiful woman he'd ever seen in his life, and what type he liked best, and what famous people he had painted.

Juli came to say the taxi had come. He got up and the Countess said, "I'll come with you."

She stood up and went into the hall with him. They stopped just inside the front door.

"There it is," she said.

She didn't look at him because it was just here that he had held her in his arms last night and kissed her. He thought of it too, saying nothing but watching her.

"Don't worry," she said, still evading his look. "I'll take care of her. But don't come back, please."

"Why not?"

"Surely you see why not. You read what I wrote you about the funeral? He expects you to go to the church. At three o'clock."

"Yes, I'll go."

"Of course, when everything is arranged, when she's better, then you will have to come and take her away. You can telephone me though, if you like. Where no one will hear you of course. And speak English. I'll tell you

[333]

how she is, and you must tell me what you've been able to do about getting her away."

"When shall I telephone?"

"About eight," she said, "or perhaps later. Any time during the evening will do. Don't make it too late."

He wanted to say, Why can't I come back? Because of the lover? Will he be here again tonight?

It was curious of how little account he had become, that shadowy man, leaning back in the car in the early morning. He'd easily forgotten about him. But he wanted to speak of him now, and he would have if they hadn't been standing where they stood the night before. He wondered if she remembered it, or if she had been so frightened she hadn't even realized what he had done. Or if it was of no consequence to her, the clumsy kiss of a boy. He wasn't even sure of what consequence it was to him. He had so little time for her.

She looked up at him and suddenly she smiled unconsciously and eagerly. She looked at him almost blindly and said, "Then you'll telephone of course." Her eyes shone with pure joy.

He was speechless and he caught at her hand awkwardly and kissed it, in the custom of the country. "I'll telephone of course," he stammered, "eight o'clock."

"Yes, eight o'clock."

He dropped her hand, picked up his bags, and went out to the taxi.

He had the driver take him to another, simpler hotel, one Fritz had told him of, in the village itself. There they gave him a bare, little, clean room under the eaves, with furniture made by the local carpenter, a window box inside the window full of geraniums.

After he'd left his things there he got himself some sandwiches and beer in the little restaurant. Then, as it was

[334]

only two o'clock, he went for a walk. He wanted to find the forest path to the lake where he had first met the Countess. But that had been just in front of the other hotel. Now he couldn't find it. He went through the village and on toward a mountain path.

It was a sunny day, full of spring in spite of the snow still covering the ground. On the balconies of the wooden houses, housewives were hanging out all their bedding to dry in the sun. The little town was fluttering as though with banners. The air was so pure and full of sun, smelling at once of snow and pine sap, that he felt drunk from it. He hummed as he went, filling his lungs in the effort of the climb.

A little dark stream rushed along beside him, full of tiny waves, each tipped with light. Farther up it formed a pool and he saw at the bottom brown leaves on a gray rock, the dart of a trout, the gleam of a little tin can.

He saw the little red cable car, sliding up what seemed a tiny thread, to the highest peak on his left. All the peaks were brittle and nearly transparent in the light, and such sharp motion was apparent in their stillness that they looked as though they had been thrown up the instant before.

Farther on, when he'd reached the fringes of forest, he heard singing, so robust and melodious he would have liked to join it, until he recognized it as one of the party songs. A file of young men, healthily colored but gangling in their short breeches, came down the path. They saluted him gaily as they passed.

Farther up he heard a pleasanter song, and a little way off in a clearing he saw woodcutters resting in the sun. They were stripped to the waist and their milk-white backs were stained with the red blood underneath. They too waved at him as he passed, not stopping their song. The mountains seemed to echo with music.

[335]

At last he came to a higher open meadow, sloping steeply upward, and looking at his watch he saw he had no time to go farther. He sat down on a rock to rest before climbing back.

As he sat a skier came out of the woods at the far tip of the meadow. He paused to look around, a small figure not much darker than the snow. Then with a noiseless, incredibly sharp and graceful motion he swung down in the Norwegian manner, coming so swiftly, growing so much bigger as he came, that Mark felt a tingle of awe. In his mind he tried to record the swirl of converging curves that would give on a flat surface, the impression of that amazing beauty of flight. He was staring with interest and admiration as the man stemmed to a stop beside him, a very big man, he saw, blond, with something familiar about his cold, crimson face, in a white sweater rolled up around his ears, white cap and gloves. The man did no more than glance at him and went on down a nearly parallel ski trail through the forest.

I must go back to the funeral, Mark thought. But the mountains held him, and his own happiness held him. I may have to stay for days, he thought. Tomorrow I can come here again. Perhaps I can make her come here with me. The thought of this blurred into a general brightness.

Fortunately it was much quicker going down.

Before he reached the village he heard a bell tolling. In all the sun and song-laden air of the valley the bell made a small darkness each time it sounded. It was for Emmy — for Emmy Ritter, who lay warm and safe in the Countess' bed; or rather it was for death and the certainty of death, which if it doesn't come today comes tomorrow. It frightened him a little to hear it; but he thought, at any rate not today, and tomorrow doesn't exist till it comes.

The church, with a pincushion tower, was on the edge of

the town. The door was open and a small group of peasants were standing around it. The women wore dark shawls and their strange, tilted little hats. The men had their hats in their hands. He saw the brown bearded man who was Fritz's brother, and the sledge with the big horses waiting just outside in the yard. As he came up they all stared at him gravely, with curiosity and a little conventional sadness. No one spoke but Fritz's brother, who came up and took him by the arm and said, "Mr. Preysing?"

"Yes."

"Come in."

He went inside with his heart beating fast. He looked around the little white church with high, pale windows, pink-and-white virgins in niches and ex-votos on the walls, and saw at the end before the altar the wooden coffin that contained, he reminded himself, only some logs and old quilts. On it was a wreath of evergreens and a bunch of florist's roses. Fritz had thought of the roses. A small, old priest stood there and Fritz in a black suit with a collar that reached up to his ears. The few people outside moved in after them and the priest, after a word or two to Fritz, began the service.

He had wondered a little, as he came down the mountain side, whether he could give the right impression at this service. Now he didn't think of it. The church was icy cold. The priest seemed frightened, he scampered through the service in a whispering voice; with his aged hand he shook holy water from the aspergill onto the coffin. The peasants from time to time looked at Fritz or Mark, drawing what satisfaction was their due out of this grief, but at the same time they looked concerned and kindly.

To Mark the gestures of the priest, the solemnity of the peasants, had an air of sacrilege that made him uneasy. It was false and he feared it was punishable. The simple acceptance of these people was being mocked. He glanced at Fritz, who stood, hands clasped on the ancient Homburg, staring somberly at the coffin. Fritz looked as though he really believed it held her. He looked as though truly she lay in there dead. For a moment Mark nearly believed it. In a pause of the priest's voice he heard a bird twitter outside and remembered the high, sunny slopes again, and the rush of the little stream and smell of pine sap and all life in which she was still a part.

Two men, curious as to what was going on, came to the door and looked in and went on again.

He thought the service, short as it was, would never end. Don't let it be a sacrilege, he begged. Death is so certain anyway. It is always here and now and we can truly mourn her death now as well as later, even though she is still living. And it isn't this death which is the illusion, he thought, but all living. All living isn't really a part of time but a part of death. And so let me mourn her honestly now, as I must, and then let me escape once more into life outside and into joy, no matter how much of an illusion they may be.

The priest stopped and turned to Fritz.

It was over, but it was not over. Fritz introduced Mark to the priest, who shook his hand mournfully and hurriedly. Then Fritz made a signal and two stalwart peasants, one the bearded brother, stepped forward.

"You take one end," said Fritz.

They and Fritz and Mark lifted the coffin and carried it out to the yard. It seemed very light. There they put it on the sledge and the brother climbed up and motioned Mark to climb up beside him. All this, he thought, I'm going to try not to be aware of. There were no bells now on the horses, but the church bell began to toll once more. A knot of people by the gate moved aside as they went through. They turned up toward the meadows above the village, going very slowly so that Fritz and the few people with him could follow on foot. Mark sat with eyes down, not looking at what they passed.

Presently they turned through an opening in a wooden fence and stopped before a house. They got down, lifted the coffin again, and carried it up a snowy slope to a newly dug grave in a little cluster of white birch trees. There was a man waiting and ropes for lowering it. This took some time, and the sun reached the top of the mountains and vanished, turning the valley below them into a great, violet bowl of snow, with the sky above still luminous day-color. Mark heard the first earth falling on the coffin, and Fritz took him by the arm.

"We're giving these people a little food," he said. "You probably won't want to join them."

"No," Mark said.

They walked back down the miry slope, the others following at a little distance.

"I have a list of the expenses," Fritz said. He took a folded paper out of his pocket. "Here it is. The truck, the clothes, and so forth, gasoline, priest, gravedigger, food for the mourners, some extras, all enumerated. You'll find it here."

Mark got out his purse and took a roll of paper bills. "Here," he said. "Now what about the passport?"

"I'm taking the wagon back right away. It's a good excuse for leaving at once. I'll start attending to it to-night."

He drew Mark around the corner of the house and they watched the others go past and into the front door. They were talking now naturally and cheerfully, in anticipation of the food and beer.

"How are things down there?" Fritz pointed his thumb

toward the violet valley below, growing rapidly darker so that a few lights shone in it.

"Everything's fine. She's getting along beautifully."

"The lady is making no trouble?"

"None at all."

"Good. Now, Mr. Mark, you stay as quietly at the hotel as you can. Be sad and quiet. Everyone in the village will know by now what you're here for. Better come up tomorrow and visit the grave. Bring flowers. Be sentimental about it and cry a little if you can. People here like that. But don't talk to anyone more than you can help. You might pay a call on the Countess. That way you can keep an eye on Madame Ritter and people will notice it and think you're in good society."

Mark gave a suppressed laugh. Now that he was happy it was a pity there was no one to share Fritz with.

"We'd better go in for a minute," Fritz said. "They'll want to meet you."

The house was the least attractive of its kind that Mark had seen. It was new, of yellow brick but built with the great sloping roof and wooden gallery of the country.

"Besides," Fritz said, "my brother wants you to see his cows."

They went in the front door. In a room to the right some people sat around a green faïence stove, and on a table were plates and bottles. They stopped a moment at the door and one by one the peasants came in silence and shook Mark's hand.

Then Fritz and the brown-bearded brother took him down the long hall. At the end the brother opened the door and led them into the stable. It took up most of the house. As the door opened they were enveloped in the sharp stink. All winter the cows and horses had been stabled here, and there were twenty-four cows and calves, five

[340]

bulls, and five horses. Their condition, Mark thought, would surely make a sanitary inspector faint. As they passed slowly between the stalls he heard them pouring water into the manure piles, already heaped high in their stalls. He had to look at each animal carefully. The brother said nothing but pointed out the finer points. He smoked his pipe, looking at Mark steadily to be sure he was giving all his attention. Fritz had a sad, bored look.

They came out at the door opening onto the back of the yard. There were great piles of manure here, and two sledges for hauling wood down from the mountains, one of them the sledge that had hauled the coffin. He also noticed the delivery wagon, very urban and sleek in the littered yard.

Fritz said, "I'll drive you as far as the hotel."

Mark shook hands with the brother who had never to this moment spoken a word. He held Mark's hand and taking his pipe from his mouth said gravely, "Well, now you've seen my cows."

"Yes," Mark said, "they were magnificent beasts."

He climbed up beside Fritz on the driver's seat. Fritz, after a word with his brother, started the engine. It was quite dark now, stars were out. Fritz turned on the head-lights and then drove out of the yard into the miry road.

As they drove Fritz said, "Well, it's better this way, isn't it?"

"Good God, yes," Mark said.

They were both spent. They had nothing now to say to each other. Once Mark said, "I suppose you'll be getting out yourself shortly."

"Oh, I don't know," Fritz said. "You see how these people live. Pretty bad. But still, it's my own country. And then, everything's getting better now."

"Yes, I suppose so."

"You've got to admit he's done a lot for us," he said. "More than that fellow of yours over there." He spoke with an insolent side look at Mark, and added sourly, "I'm a strictly practical man. As long as I can make money I'll stay anywhere."

Mark laughed again. "Old Fritz!" he cried. "Fixer of water closets! You're a mad romantic. No use trying to fool anyone."

Fritz drove on in disapproving silence. At the hotel he stopped.

Mark said, "You'd better come in so I can give you a check, in case you need more money."

They went into the little office and borrowed a pen from a young, polite clerk at the desk, and Mark signed a check, leaving the amount blank.

"O.K.?" he asked.

"O.K., Mr. Mark, but I don't think I'll need any more." He folded it carefully.

"Well, good luck then," Mark said.

Fritz put the check in an inside pocket. By the way he folded it you would have known he was an honest man. Then he looked at Mark and a desire to be rude again, together with real anxiety, showed in his face.

"Are you sure you can get along by yourself?"

"Without you?" Mark asked mockingly. "Watch me. Just watch me."

"I might be able to get back tomorrow night."

"Don't hurry."

"You're crazy," Fritz said. He shrugged, gave Mark a last disagreeable, anxious, almost affectionate look, and went out.

Mark went up to his room. It was quite dark now. He turned on the light and lay down on his bed. It was after five.

In a few hours, he thought, I'll telephone her. If I can't go myself into that house of hers my voice can, and she will have to listen to it. He was thinking of what he would say. He was still thinking of it when he heard a knock on his door.

"Yes?"

It opened and the young clerk from below stood there with his eyes wide open in an interested surprise.

"A gentleman to see you, sir."

"Who is it?"

The name the clerk gave him was one he had never heard before but it had a very formidable sound. Mark sat up.

"Who? Say that again, please."

The clerk repeated it.

"You're sure he wants to see me?"

"Yes, sir. He asked for Mr. Preysing."

"I'll come down."

But he already heard his visitor's heavy steps on the stair.

Chapter XXII

THE girls would be gathered in the library for tea, but the Countess had not heard the General's car so she went in once more to see how Emmy was getting on.

She was sitting on the edge of the bed; she must have been up because the fur coat was around her shoulders.

"Oh!" the Countess exclaimed, "You're better."

"I'm trying to see how well I am."

Her voice was stronger now, it had the deep flexibility of the actress' voice, and sitting up, more fully awake, she looked entirely different. The Countess searched her face for a resemblance to Mark and saw it only vaguely in the dark coloring. What was alike was a grace of movement, a manner of holding the head and lifting the hands, something bold and silky smooth as though their bones had been chiseled and fitted together by jewelers.

She sat down beside her on the bed and took her hand. "You have no fever?"

"I don't think so. I think I'm pretty well. I've eaten some fruit and drunk some milk. How terribly good it tasted!"

"It's not much. But I didn't dare bring more. You see, I'm the only one in the house who knows you're here. I mean my servants don't know."

"I see — " Emmy looked thoughtfully at her. She wished to ask no prying questions. "I've been thinking that I'm a great danger to you," she said, "and that I ought to go."

"No, no. Not yet. That's impossible." The Countess

spoke earnestly. "Please don't think of it until everything's arranged. It will be very soon. Your — your son," she said haltingly, "will do what has to be done."

Out of her own confusion of motive she wanted instinctively to throw the credit for Emmy's rescue back on Mark. She wasn't willing yet to accept the full implication of what she herself had done. But in Emmy's direct eyes she was beginning to see, for Emmy wasn't a woman to balk at the truth in others, or in herself, even if it meant strange involvements and unexpected gratitude.

Emmy leaned back on the pillow and clasped her hands behind her head. Her dark eyes turned from the Countess to the room, seeing its simple but also worldly elegance, and came back slowly to the face of the woman she'd never seen before today, the woman whose name she still didn't know.

Twenty-four hours ago she'd been lying in the prison bed and the doctor had whispered in her ear, "Whatever happens, try to stay asleep, because it will be all right." He'd done that at the risk of his life. And now this unknown woman also was ready, or so it seemed, to risk as much.

The world had to be learned all over. She said, "Those who come back from the dead have to begin again, don't they? Lazarus never said a word. I always wondered why — I think I know now."

"Do you feel like Lazarus?" the Countess said, smiling.

"I feel as though I were seeing for the first time, and so have to learn all over again. I must learn to live with people who are more generous and more courageous than I ever dared believe. You can't just thank them for that."

The Countess flushed. "You must be sure," she stammered, "that your being here makes me very happy." She felt she spoke conventionally and foolishly. But their eyes searched in each other honestly till the Countess' eyes lowered. She dropped Emmy's hand and stood up again. Through the closed door they heard the little golden clock strike five notes and play its little tune. "Why, it's five o'clock!" the Countess exclaimed.

"Such a lovely clock," Emmy said. "I've heard it all through the day. No one could feel alone with such a clock."

"Yes, I love it," the Countess said. "But it often reminds me to do what I don't want to do. Now I must leave you and have tea with my girls. When they are all in bed I'll come back and bring you some more warm food." She gave a little gentle stroke to Emmy's knee. "I hope you'll be all right," she said.

When she got to the door she realized she hadn't said what she came to say and what Emmy was probably waiting to hear.

"Your son is in the village you know," she said. "We thought it would be better if he weren't seen here."

"Oh, yes," Emmy's eyes grew brighter and she gave a deep, luxurious sigh of contentment. "Thank you," she said.

The Countess went out, locked the door behind her, and took the key to her own room and put it in her desk. Then she went downstairs.

When she got to the library she saw with a disagreeable shock that the General was already there. He was sitting in the midst of the girls, waiting for her to come and pour his tea. He was in skiing clothes, a white sweater was rolled up around his neck, and he had come, he said, on foot, just dropped in really, since he was on his way back to the hotel.

"Have you been here long?" she asked, sitting down at the tea table.

"Just five minutes," he said.

"Juli didn't tell me."

"I told her not to announce me. I knew you'd come down any moment."

His presence here, while she hadn't known of it, startled her. It affected her physically so that her hands shook as she poured her tea.

He didn't notice it. He sat by her, looking around him with satisfaction. "It was a wonderful afternoon," he was telling them. "The snow on the upper slopes was quite firm. But one had to climb like a mountain goat to get there. Tomorrow I'll take the cable car up to the peak and ski down. Who'd like to come up with me? You, Ruby, ought to come. It will be your last chance this year."

"I may," she said absently. She was filling her own cup, thinking how she would be able to tell him that he must not come back tonight, and how to put it in such a way that he really would not come. It would mean a quarrel. It would mean one of his dark, brutal angers, but she didn't feel afraid of that. She even longed for the dark storm-cloud that would keep him away from her. As he went on talking, partly to the girls and partly to her, she thought of these angers and how strange it was that now she longed only to bring one of them on, and her fingers began to get colder, her face flushed with excitement.

The General, drinking hot tea, lounging back in his chair, was enjoying himself in every way. He was enjoying himself because he had been exercising violently; and while he had felt very ill for a while up there on the slopes, that had passed — and now he was only conscious that he had put in a thoroughly manly afternoon. He liked the feel of hot tea and food in his stomach, he liked to be taking it in this chic way *à l'anglaise* and with foreigners. He felt younger and handsomer in his white sweater rolled around his chin than he did in his uniform. But best of all, as he looked at the Countess he was enjoying the secret of what was between them, made always so much more poignant, as at this moment, by these hard but inexperienced young eyes turned on him.

Suddenly, in the midst of these pleasures, he felt a change in the atmosphere. He was not sensitive to atmosphere unless it threatened his satisfaction or his security. But now he was suddenly aware that something here was very subtly not quite right.

He could hardly believe himself that anything was wrong. Still talking, he began to go lightly over the ground, taking one point after another to see what was wrong with it. When he came in the front door everything had been the same; Juli had greeted him as usual. He scrutinized her manner: yes, she was quite as usual. Ruby hadn't greeted him too warmly, but that was her way. That was because of the girls. The girls themselves were hanging on his words. None of them, not even Suzanne, talked among themselves. All of them listened to him.

"Another cup of tea, please," he said, holding his cup out to the Countess.

Then at what moment had the air of the house begun to strike him? "Yes," he said, continuing a story of a bobsled accident, "it's an Olympic run. Only experts should try it." As he talked he became gradually aware that in the fixed attention of the girls there was something light and vigorous and mocking. He looked from one to another as he talked. He felt in the pocket of his ski jacket and got out his monocle and fixed it in his eye. Yes, they listened demurely, but it was that that was off-key. It was their demureness that was too good to be true. They were overdoing it. His eyes rested last on the French girl. She was looking down, turning a big link bracelet on her arm.

Her face, so far as he could make it out, was gravely amused. But not amused by what he was saying, for there was nothing to be amused by in his bobsled accident.

Then they knew something. Something perhaps very trivial, but inimical to him. How disgusting they were! Only a few nights ago they were all uncritical adoration. Now they had decided there was something absurd about him. He felt horribly ill at ease. Finishing abruptly his account of the accident, he let the conversation drop.

Ruby he saw made no gracious attempts to retrieve it. She leaned back in her chair, her head resting on her hand, forgetting even to drink her tea. The girls began to talk back and forth to each other, including him, sometimes asking him a direct question, but they too made no real effort. They were waiting for something to happen.

He began to feel ill again, as he had up on the slopes. He was furious at all of them for bringing this sickness back, because they were certainly responsible. He was getting one of his headaches. He looked at every object in the room with suspicion, the books, the porcelain figures of shepherds and shepherdesses. One of the girls got up to turn on the radio. It was the hour when they heard waltzes from Vienna, but the air was full of static this evening and only buzzes and whining sounds came through.

"Let's not have that," he said peremptorily.

The girl turned it off, surprised at the tone of his voice, and the others at once looked at him in an unfriendly way. Now they were passing judgment on him. Now they didn't like him. And he knew that for that he hated them. He had really always hated them and that fact had made their adoration the sweeter, as now it made their critical attitude the more intolerable. But he had done nothing. What was it? He wanted to get up, to say, I must find out what's wrong here. He felt, almost, that when he got up there would be an absurd sign pinned on his back.

Then the new American girl said in a careless, general voice, "Suzanne and I passed Mr. Preysing in the village this afternoon, but he didn't see us."

"Oh, where was he?" said Marie.

"We were going in the postcard shop. He was walking along at a great rate. I suppose he was going painting, but he didn't have any paints."

The General said, "Mr. Preysing?"

The Countess, without taking her head from her hand, felt a long wave of fright. She had now only an instant's safety, only until he asked her a question.

"Why didn't you bring him back to tea?" Marie said. "I'm sure the Countess wouldn't have minded, would you, Countess?"

The Countess didn't answer but she managed a smile in which the girls instantly detected reproach. At once they were sorry. Perhaps they shouldn't have said anything. And they knew they shouldn't when they heard the General's voice, so elaborately smooth, "And who is Mr. Preysing?"

No one answered and he repeated sharply, "Who is Mr. Preysing?"

Marie said, "He's an artist."

He could see that they had spontaneously started out to tease him and had almost immediately decided to stop. They now looked — each according to her way of expressing ill-ease — sullen, abstracted, or sarcastic. On Suzanne's face only was a quick look of concern. This then was what had been wrong. This he'd begun to feel, even before they gave it away.

"You should certainly have brought Mr. Preysing for tea," the General said. "Tell me, Ruby, is he by any chance that young man we were talking about?"

"What young man?" she said vaguely.

"Surely you remember. The one who took you to the concert. The young painter. The one," he added with emphasis, "who came to settle his mother's estate."

"Yes, he is," she said. No use lying, because a few inquiries in the village would settle that.

He turned to the girls, adjusting his monocle again. "Then you should certainly have brought him. I'm sure the Countess would want to see him. I'd like to see the famous young man myself."

"Oh, is he famous?" said Sully languidly.

"So I hear. Or else he expects to be. I can't remember which."

"He's very attractive," said the new American girl, feeling an irresistible desire to back up her compatriot.

"Is he indeed? Then I'm all the more anxious to meet him. But I don't see, Ruby, why he doesn't come of his own accord. Surely he expects to pay his respects to you. It's the least he could do after all your entertainment of him. Or isn't that an American custom?"

"He did come," the American said bluntly. Suzanne looked at her with an imploring expression. The American looked around at the girls' disapproving faces. "Well — he did," she said.

"He had lunch with us," the Countess said.

"Lunch?" the General cried. "How delightful. But not tea, and not breakfast? Perhaps he's coming for dinner, then."

"No. Why should he come for dinner?"

"Why not? I'm coming for dinner. He might as well come too. The young ladies will certainly enjoy a younger man about. Perhaps you would enjoy a younger man yourself."

"I haven't asked him."

"Then I'll ask him. Where is he staying?"

"I have no idea."

"No idea! Well then, I must find out. That will be easy. There are so few hotels. Come, let's make a gala evening of it. I'll bring him back with me, shall I?"

"Please don't," the Countess said. "I'll invite my own guests."

This was nearly becoming a public quarrel. It gave him a further idea. "Am I to believe you've had a quarrel?" he said. "Why, that won't do at all. We must make that up at once."

"Kurt," she said sharply, "have you forgotten why he is here?"

He shook his head, his monocle fell from his eye and he looked at her with his heavy, persistent raillery. A child could have seen his deep anger underneath it. The girls' distaste for him he could feel now without question. How they wished they had left him alone! And Ruby's fright he also felt, and her fluttering resistance. But he didn't care. He was blind with anger.

"Why, no, I haven't forgotten," he said. "But perhaps he has. Or else he thinks it is better to pass the time with a few distractions—lunches, concerts, lovely ladies, and so on."

She thought, I should never have forgotten for an instant how dangerous he can be. Then a phrase of his struck her, "to pass the time." That meant Kurt had not bothered to find out when the day of execution was and did not know that it was to have been this very morning. He did not know that in the meantime Emmy had officially died in prison. Best of all he did not know yet that Mark had found out anything about it. He thought of him as still making inquiries, as still "passing the time." It would be easy for her to say, You must not ask him here, his mother was

[352]

buried this afternoon. But wouldn't he find it strange then that Mark had come for lunch? If he found out that Madame Ritter's funeral was this afternoon, and that Mark had even been to it, then he would already know the first link of the whole fantastic tale, and he might find other strange points to remember, the delivery wagon coming in the driveway for instance. No, better he should still think that Mark was only fumbling around, ignorant of the true state of his mother. Of course, anyone in the village could tell him of the funeral, but Kurt wasn't one to inquire about village happenings unless his suspicion was aroused. If she let him have his way and bring Mark here he'd not have to ask questions at the hotel about him. Perhaps tomorrow they could get away.

"Write him a note," he said, "I'll take it to him myself."

She thought of writing a warning. Say nothing about your mother's death; he doesn't know. Whatever Kurt would do, she thought he wouldn't be a man to read a letter entrusted to him. But how did she really know if he would or not? It was too dangerous to count on his code as opposed to his jealousy and anger. She could think of no way to conceal a warning in a casual note. If I were only clever, she thought desperately.

"Well, if you insist," she said.

"Or better still, I'll call at his hotel on the way back. Oh, don't worry. I can easily find it. No doubt the first man I ask will know where he is. Such an attractive young man must have already created a sensation in the village."

He went on with his raillery, looking from one to another of the girls, smiling and showing his white teeth, but they were only embarrassed now that he should go on knowing none of their rules. And they were embarrassed too that they had made a mistake and let the Countess in for something more serious than they had expected. She, with a pained look on her face, slowly emptied her cold, untouched cup of tea and poured herself another.

"Will any of you have more tea?" she asked.

They shook their heads.

"Why, we'll take him skiing with us tomorrow," the General went on. "No doubt he's a formidable sportsman too. No doubt he'd show us all how much better it's done in America. Perhaps he's even a champion at this too."

One of the girls excused herself and went upstairs. Others followed her. Only Suzanne and the American stayed. They went over to the bookshelves, took up a book and began to look at it together. They had the feeling that they were protecting the Countess by their presence. The General watched the girls leave, and when he saw the other two intended to stay he knew just why they were doing it. There was nothing he could say here and now to Ruby. Besides, he couldn't think. In his thickened veins the blood was pounding heavily. He felt quite sick.

He got up and said, "Well, Ruby, I must leave you. I'll go and change and get your young man. At eight we'll be back."

She didn't get up to go to the door with him as she always did. He bent over her hand. "Make yourself very beautiful," he said, "tonight will be a gala night."

When he got outside the cold air restored him a little. It was dark as night already, and he had nearly a mile to walk to the village. He hadn't stopped here on his way as he said. He'd been skiing on the slopes high above the village and had gone through the town, left his skis at his hotel, and hurried on here without waiting to change. The snow on the road had melted during the day's sun and he splashed along the slushy edge of the road, standing aside once or twice to let a car pass. It was so clear that the serrated, black edges of the mountains cut sharp into the starry sky. One immense star blazed over the softer sprinkling of lights in the valley. He hated to walk. It wasn't the exertion. He told himself it was because he had the blood of too many horsemen in his veins. Actually it was because it made him feel diminished. Only when he walked down a line of troops standing at attention, with the great red, black, and white banners flapping like terrible great birds overhead, was it different. Though even then he would have felt better on a horse. But the Leader was not a horseman, so they followed him on foot. Now he knew that to walk along a country road at night, to step aside every now and then into a snowbank to avoid a stream of slush, was only one more indignity put on him by Ruby.

For fifteen years, for fifteen years, he thought, she had never given him a moment's jealousy until now. How dared she do it, she with her pliant, gentle bending, that was sometimes a charm and sometimes an irritation. How dared she stiffen into a disloyalty to himself! And it was deeper than that, he felt, priding himself on his penetration. It was disloyalty to his creed, to his country. How she had changed since this man appeared! He didn't seriously consider even now that she was planning to be unfaithful to him. From what Rudi had told him, from what he knew of the fellow, the son of an actress, a poor artist, he was sure she was suffering from a passion entirely of the nerves, a sort of thwarted maternalism. It was a pity she could never have been allowed to have children. Yes, this was a last flare-up, undoubtedly, of her maternal instinct. Women were known to suffer from such things. But how it had changed her! The things she had said! He began to remember them. She who was so easily frightened wasn't now easy to frighten at all. It was she now who did the hurting, not he. For he was hurt; from head to foot he quivered with hurt. But he would stop it, beat it down. With the lightning stroke, as in war, he'd crush it out and this fellow would vanish. He felt suddenly headlong and furious and invincible.

But suddenly he was sorry for himself too. Ruby had been so good for him; he had felt so healthy and balanced in his love for her, with its recurrent rhythms of anger and peace. He had felt so happy that for fifteen years he had been easily faithful and ardent. This love had been in one sense pure and had made him feel pure again, after those darker or even perverse loves that now he never even admitted to himself, or, if he did, thought of hastily as youthful follies. Sometimes he said to her: Ruby, you are my salvation; and he was truly grateful to her. He told himself that he loved her with his soul and that she had no right to disillusion him. Tears of self-pity and rage came in his eyes.

And then under that, the deep uneasiness came again. There was more to it even than this. There was some subterranean current he couldn't detect. Some involvement that remained mysterious and unguessed.

But I'll soon find out, he thought. It won't take me long. Perhaps I'll find out tonight.

He had no trouble locating her young man. The first little hotel he stopped at said Mr. Preysing had come in that afternoon. That afternoon? At what time? About two o'clock. Then he had certainly stopped for lunch on his way from the train. As he climbed the stairs he thought, After all, is a lunch with all those silly girls around really so bad?

He followed the clerk into the little bare room, very clean and smelling of fresh wood and geraniums blooming inside the glass. The floor and walls were bare; it was lighted by an oil lamp. It was perhaps the cheapest room in a moderately priced hotel.

The young man was sitting on the edge of the bed when he came in. The clerk stepped aside respectfully and went downstairs.

"Mr. Preysing?"

"Yes."

"I'm sure you know who I am."

"The clerk told me."

The young man got up with a tired movement that surprised him. In this poverty and insignificance, could anyone in the face of a man like himself be both graceful and assured?

"Will you sit down?"

He took a small cane-bottomed chair too small for him. It creaked under his weight, and the young man, looking about for another and finding none, sat down on the bed without apology.

"The Countess sent me here," said the General. "Will you smoke?" He held out his cigarette case with the colored cord and jeweled crown. Mark took one. As they lighted them they looked at each other.

The General's chest expanded as he drew in a deep breath of smoke. Now at last he saw him. He was very young, and he was poor. He was under a cloud of disgrace. He was exhausted and he was probably afraid. In his shadowed eyes (a woman *might* find his eyes handsome) you could guess all this, even though now they were only wary and cold. He himself was this man's exact opposite. He was at the peak of his success, a tremendous, full-blooded male, a successful lover. Like an aura his distinguished career and his great name hung around him. What kept the other from melting away before him?

Contemptuously he flung his burnt match into the corner of the clean little room.

But then, as the young man didn't speak, didn't hasten to placate him with politeness and protestation, he thought more deeply, No, there is always danger in them, the dark ones, the supple and slippery minds, even the weaker, dark bodies with their insolent grace. Only the strong should dare to possess any beauty.

"We were afraid you might be lonely this evening," he said, "so I suggested she ask you for dinner."

"Oh! That was kind of you."

"Not at all. Not at all. We're having a very quiet evening. No one but the girls (you know the girls), you and I, and the Countess."

Mark looked at his cigarette. He didn't know what this meant but he knew there was nothing good in it for him. And he also knew that here now at last was the lover. This great, handsome male filling the room with himself, this was the lover. He saw the white sweater rolled around his thick neck, his blond hair a little thin on top, his noble nose and chin and a thread of white scar down his cheek, and lastly his very small hands, delicate and unworn, with a big signet ring on one finger. He remembered when for one absurd moment he had thought the doctor was her lover and had at once thought, even before he knew him, that he wouldn't want to take her from such a man. But from this man, he thought in a flood of suffocating jealousy, from this man I *will* take her.

"You'll come?" the General said.

"I'm not sure the Countess wants me. I think I'd better not."

"But she does. She insists. I don't dare to go back without you." The General laughed condescendingly.

Could that be true? What had happened then? Did the General know anything at all about him? Did he know this was the day his mother was supposed to die? Would he insist on his dining with them if he did? Would he of necessity know anything about him? But someone had told the Countess already. That was why she had warned him in the Odeon to go home. Perhaps, indeed certainly, this was the one. It was being kept secret. Only a lover might tell it in confidence. It seemed she might have written a note to warn him again. But she didn't dare. She doesn't want me, he thought. It's his own idea.

"I don't feel much like dining out tonight," he said. That would cover everything, no matter what this man knew.

"Come, come," the General said, "the Countess' invitations aren't to be refused, I can tell you. They are very much sought-after. Perhaps you think because you lunched there today that you shouldn't go again so soon. But that's excessive delicacy, I tell you. You've only whetted their interest. Yes, I speak for the famous maidens as well. They all want to see you again."

Mark smiled dimly as the General urged. He hated him so it seemed to constrict his throat. This was her lover and it was also the oppressor, the arch type of the men who had loosed their neurotic brutalities on so many defenseless creatures, as Emmy Ritter was now defenseless and as he was defenseless. It was better to be meek before him as the defenseless must be, better for Emmy and for him. Emmy, he thought with terror, in that house where this man could come and go at will . . . Yes, better to plead illness and stay away, to lie low in weakness and humbleness, until obscurely they could burrow their way out to freedom.

When he and Emmy were gone only the Countess would be left. And then this man could roam her house at will. Then *she* could be the one to be meek and humble, as she must have been for so long. She didn't deserve saving.

He was about to say, I'm ill, I must stay here, take aspirin and go to bed; but something rose in him: pure hatred too strong to be resisted, and then mere daring, sudden, lightheaded frivolity that had once or twice been Emmy's undoing.

"All right," he said, "I'll come."

The General said, "That's good." He blew out a cloud of smoke and added, "You're here for the skiing?"

"No, I don't ski."

"But you're a painter, I hear."

"Yes."

"You must show me your work sometime. I'm very much interested in painting. My father-in-law was a famous patron of the arts. I believe at one time he actually had his portrait done by your grandfather. That is, if your grandfather was Richard Ritter."

"Yes, he was."

"That's interesting now, isn't it? I must tell the Countess that. Well, I tell you what I'll do. I'll go now and dress and come back for you. Shall I? I'm just a bit down the road. I'll come back in my car."

(What bonhomie!) Mark said aloud: "I've no evening clothes with me. I must go as I am."

"Then I'll just change from these things. I can't very well dine in ski clothes, can I? As soon as I'm changed I'll come back. It will be better to drive in my car than to go on foot, eh?"

(What condescension! What *noblesse oblige!*) He said, "Thanks."

"Settled then." The General stood up, swelled his chest again to look larger, to take up more space in the little room. Mark watched him darkly from the bed. He too got up slowly.

The General's heels clicked. "Till we meet," he said.

"Till we meet."

[360]

Chapter XXIII

THE girls were agreed it would be an exciting evening. They put on their most becoming dresses and came downstairs early so as to miss nothing. The Countess they found already waiting. She wore a pale blue brocade dirndl and old garnet earrings and necklace. She looked to them as though she too had consciously made herself as beautiful as possible. They understood her feeling that in any crisis, no matter how subtle or how trivial, she would influence more surely whatever currents were favorable if she looked her best.

But the Countess looked also very ill-at-ease; her peculiar grace was dimmed and diminished, and it seemed to them for the first time that the style of beauty she had chosen was archaic and without life and a little ridiculous.

They were also disappointed in the two men who came in together, quietly, with no visible signs of antagonism. They found themselves all seated at the long table in the dining room almost before they knew it, and during dinner nothing went wrong at all. On the contrary.

The Countess put the General on her right and Mark she put far down the table between Sully and the American girl whom Mark thought of as Mink Coat. These were generally considered by the other girls the most attractive. The table was long and it divided itself at once into two sections. The General and the Countess talked and for a while the girls near them listened and made an occasional remark, but that was from politeness. They couldn't keep up their interest and began one by one to turn toward the other end of the table. The situation they had helped to build up had apparently flattened out, and they forgot it in the pleasure of having a young man to talk to, a young man who, unlike the General and the occasional young officers who had come here, really knew about the things that they knew.

They had placed him now. He was an artist and lived in New York and knew a lot of "Bohemian" celebrities, and some not so Bohemian. When they got home they'd all say they'd met him. He made them feel that they were being sophisticated. All of them knew, however, that he was a poor chance as far as their vital interests were concerned. When it came down to it, the Countess could have him. She could afford to. But for the time being he was theirs; and they enjoyed the dinner, which had turned out to be, after all, more interesting because they didn't have to be merely spectators. The table was noisier with talk and laughter than it had ever been; even the maids moving around with the big silver platters and dishes smiled every now and then in a startled, apologetic way.

They began to think it was going to be fun, much more fun than just watching two jealous men. They got up and trooped into the music room for coffee, all talking at once. But here something they didn't seem able to help began to happen. Their loose circle of youth was broken up and the General took charge of things, heavily and relentlessly. He sat in the middle of the couch that was the central point of the room and looked around at all of them coldly, screwing his monocle more firmly into his eye. "Sing something for us, Ruby," he said. That brought their conversation to an abrupt end.

She'll sing *Du bist die Ruh*," they thought, because that's

[362]

his favorite, and they all felt a curious mixture of dullness, irritation and apprehension settling down on them. It was exactly what she did sing, and she sang it badly, with a quavering voice. Afterward she sang one or two songs from *"Frauenliebe,"* and whatever the General asked for. The evening swung slowly away from them, and from Mark, too, who sat silently looking at the floor.

Suzanne played the accompaniments. Between songs there were long silences and they could hear the melting snow dripping from the eaves.

Once there was a slight sound like a thump on the floor overhead, and Suzanne, who happened to be looking at the Countess to be sure she was ready to begin, saw her look up at the ceiling and then glance quickly at the General. He was looking at her, and she yawned suddenly, nervously, almost spasmodically.

"Are you tired?" he asked.

"Oh, no, no. Not a bit."

"Then go ahead," he said.

She gave Suzanne a nod to begin the song.

The General, sitting on the couch with his arms folded on his chest, became now the master of the house and everyone in it. The Countess sang for him obediently, in a vague, quavering voice. Mark, who had been such fun at dinner, became a small boy who was bored and distrustful of his elders. The girls knew only that presently they would be sent to bed.

"Your voice is tired," the General said finally. "You'd better stop. Suppose we play bridge."

The bridge tables were set out.

"Do you play bridge, Mr. Preysing?" the General asked.

"No."

The General raised his eyebrows.

"I thought everyone played bridge." He got up from

the couch, went over to one of the tables, and spread a deck out, face down.

"Let's cut for partners."

Mark got up too. "I'll watch," he said. "If anyone wants to make it worth my while I'll signal what's in the hands."

"Sit by me," Marie said, "I'll make it worth your while."

The General and the Countess cut as partners, Marie and the Mink Coat played against them. The others went on to the second table and Suzanne went into the library to read. As she walked past them Mark watched her.

Marie whispered to him, "I think you've got a crush on her. I'm jealous."

"She reminds me of someone."

"How unfair of her."

"Your deal," the General said sharply.

Marie made a faint grimace and took up the cards.

The General did no clowning tonight. He didn't joke about his mistakes or his reckless bidding. He didn't make mistakes or bid recklessly. He could really, when he wanted, play very well. It was the Countess who played badly. She made endless mistakes and the General reproved her for every one of them. The more tyrannically he reproved her the more she tried to please him. "Now do trump this," he said, and to their surprise, because no one thought she had a trump left, she did. They smiled a little at that.

It seemed he would never stop ordering her around. He who was so careful to appear always the old friend of the family, bantering, full of anecdote, dropping in more or less by accident, had not really deceived the girls for a moment as to his true status in this house. They were modern girls who read everything they pleased and heard everything talked about. His assumption of their ignorance was partly based on the further assumption that the truth would shock them. But he knew the truth with all its physical and emotional contents; the truth in its ideal form didn't shock them at all. They had guessed it by the way he watched her sing, by the way he held a chair for her to sit in. They saw only the gleams and the reflections, so while they were not deceived about the fact, at the same time they were deceived by their own inexperience. But now he did not care at all whether they were deceived or not. He was acting recklessly, as the master of the house, and his behavior did shock them. It made them uneasy, and also contemptuous. He was showing off in a way that was inexcusable. He was showing off for Mark.

"Are we to have no wine?" he complained. "My throat is as dry as a bone."

She got up to ring for Juli, and no sooner had the tray of glasses and cherry wine come than he said, "You really should arrange to have a better light in this room. I can't see what's in my hand."

Mark, who had tried to make a few forced jokes with Marie, had grown quickly silent again. He sat a little behind Marie and every time she turned to speak to him she saw his face was paler. When the Countess got up to move a bridge light behind the General's shoulder he started as though he were going to do it for her but changed his mind and sat with his mouth set. The General noticed it and smiled a little. "No, put it here," he said, "or rather, here. It's in everyone's eyes."

The Countess never looked at Mark, nor he at her, but everyone at the table could feel his gradual disgust, which was too sharp and youthful to keep hidden.

The little golden clock struck ten and played its few notes. It was time for them to go to bed, but the Countess apparently had not heard the clock. She said nothing about their going to bed nor did the General either.

For some time no one said anything. Only the General, with a few words and gestures, went on parading his possession against the deep sullenness of the room. "Here, here, trump," he'd say peremptorily, tapping with his small, delicate finger the card on which he expected the Countess to play. And "Never wear blue," he told her suddenly, apropos of nothing but a long look he had given her. "It washes you out entirely. You look like a ghost."

Then his eyes, glancing through the open door, fell on the clock held to the wall by its little golden hand. "It's nearly ten-thirty," he exclaimed. "Surely your charges ought to be in bed. You're not forgetting them, are you, in all the excitement of this delightful evening?"

The Countess laid down her cards. She looked at Marie with a blank humbled look. "Girls, I think it's time you went to bed."

"Oh, no!" Marie cried. She looked around the room as though to urge someone to rebel with her. She saw Mark looking across at the Countess with his gray eyes shining with resentment. "No," Marie repeated, "please let us have a cigarette first. I don't feel at all sleepy."

"Certainly," the General said in his most jocular manner, "certainly. These young ladies are the flower of the earth. They are accustomed to have their slightest whims obeyed. A cigarette, a cigarette, Ruby. Where do you keep your cigarettes?"

The Countess got up and took from another table some ashtrays and an old, carved wooden box. When she opened the box before them a fat spider scuttled out of it.

The girls shrieked. The General caught the spider just as it reached the edge of the table, held it up and lighted a match to it. Its legs curled up and vanished and he let it drop into an ashtray.

No one said anything.

[366]

From the next table Sully called out, "What was it?"

"A spider," the General said. He took out his own case with the colored silk cord and the jeweled crown and offered it to Marie. "Have one of mine. Perhaps you'll like them better anyway."

"No, thanks."

"But it isn't pleasant to smoke from spider-haunted boxes. Better try one."

"No, thanks." Marie took a cigarette from the wooden box. "I'd rather have this," she said.

The General's jaw set as it did when someone had hurt him. His face stiffened into what was meant to be the beginning of a silence. Then he saw at once that his silence would be mistaken for theirs, so he began to talk in a reasonable, informative voice.

"Some spiders are dangerous," he said, "but none of them are as dangerous as people think." He lighted a cigarette for himself and leaned back. "I knew a lady in London once," he said, "who kept a tarantula as a pet."

Mark said suddenly and brightly, "I knew a tarantula once who kept a lady."

Marie gave a little gasp of laughter and looked around. She saw by Mark's eyes that it had finally become too much for him. At the other table the girls put down their cards to listen. The air of the room grew brittle, as though it were about to be broken.

"Is that good taste?" the General asked coldly. "There are well-brought-up young ladies present."

"Oh, we're not that well-brought-up," the Mink Coat exclaimed.

"There are no well-brought-up young ladies any more," said Mark.

"In this country there are. Mr. Preysing should be more careful."

[367]

"You'll have to excuse me," Mark said, "I've never known any."

"I think that's very possible," the General said. "And yet I understand you have female relatives. A sister, isn't that so?"

"Yes, a sister. She works in a sweatshop."

Marie laughed again. "Oh, how marvelous! And do you paint pictures while she works in a sweatshop?"

"Certainly. And she buys my paints. She has no tarantula. There's no one but me for her to keep."

"Very interesting," the General said. He never turned to look at Mark, but tilting his chair back he addressed the table, the suddenly teasing faces of the girls, the unchanged pale face of the Countess. "I see," he said, groping his way through the smoke screen of the ridiculous which they had managed to throw around him, "I see that it is considered humorous for a woman to support her brother."

"Don't women support you?" asked Mark.

"Me? My dear young fellow — "

"Who buys your uniforms, your gold lace, your sabers?" Mark said. "Who pays for your motor car and your driver? Who buys your cigarettes, your gold cases with fancy silk cords? Who, in other words, pay taxes? Don't women pay taxes? Don't they scrimp so men can pay taxes? All over this country women are saving carrot-tops and potato-peelings to keep a general."

The General knew himself to be surrounded by unfriendliness. Even Ruby, yes, even Ruby, for all her air of submission, wasn't really loyal. That was what hurt him in all this. All his baiting of her had been to drag some reassuring, unmistakable gestures of loyalty from her. But her response had been routine only, and also perhaps deception. She remained now blank, as though she hadn't heard.

[368]

"Very ingenious," he said, raising his voice a little. "And I can see this is not the time or place to be serious. If it were, I might remind you why it's necessary for the women of this country to save potato-peelings in order that generals may live. If I were to tell you," he said, "it might be more than these not-too-well-brought-up young ladies could stand to hear."

He spoke of the girls, but he looked at the downcast face of the Countess. And Mark also looked at her.

"What makes you think they couldn't stand it?" Mark said. "They can stand anything you can, and probably more."

"You bet we can," said the Mink Coat enthusiastically. Whatever Mark said, she was ready to support him.

"I don't think you know much about them," Mark went on. "They'll keep tarantulas or artists or generals or whatever they like. They squealed just now at the sight of a spider, but they were quite silent when you burned it. Do you know why?"

"Perhaps they were shocked," said the General. "Perhaps they thought it was our much-advertised cruelty."

"Not a bit of it. They squealed because it was expected of them. But they didn't say anything because they really despise a mediocre exhibition of cruelty. They were bored by it, as the expert is always bored by the clumsiness of the amateur."

The General, turning, saw that Mark was directing his anger at the Countess. He looked from one to the other of them, and for a moment the girls had the pleasure of seeing the rivalry of the two men flare brightly to the surface.

"You don't think very highly of women," the General said. "You accuse them of having no delicacy, no sensitiveness."

"Have they? I thought everyone was agreed by now that their delicacy and sensitiveness are all of the body and the nerves. And that these have been beaten into them through countless generations, by harems, corsets, bound feet, civil and religious codes, anything we could lay our hands to. And still have to be beaten into them. Leaving, of course, their natural toughness entirely unimpaired, as fresh and magnificently resistant as ever. Personally, I find nothing in the world so pitiful as a man, his battle-axe in his hand, shouting at some woman, 'Be sensitive, be delicate, God damn you, because I like you that way!'"

"Wow!" said the Mink Coat, and Marie went into a fit of giggles and choked on her cigarette smoke.

But as is always the case, just as a dull evening gets lively, it's time to go to bed. The Countess suddenly lifted her blank face.

"Really, girls," she said vaguely, "the General's right. It is getting awfully late."

Her words punctured everything. The air of the room wasn't shattered, but returned suddenly to normal.

"Oh, it's so early," Marie grumbled, but without any conviction, and she got up slowly as she spoke. The girls left the other table and came over to say good night. Mark stood up and each one shook his hand. "Good night, Mr. Preysing. See you tomorrow," said Marie.

The Mink Coat was the last to say good night. "Be careful of him!" she whispered in Mark's ear, throwing a half derisive look at the General. "Be careful of that man. He's a killer," she said.

"Maybe I'm a killer," said Mark.

They went off, murmuring and laughing a little among themselves, down the gallery to their own part of the house.

After they had gone no one had anything to say. The Countess rang again and Juli brought schnapps and more cherry wine. "And bring my peppermint tea," the Countess said. "I'll have it here."

The General looked at her sharply. The tea she usually took upstairs in her own room just before going to bed. It was a routine of theirs for him to tease her about it; sometimes, — if he felt in the mood, — to hold the cup for her to sip from. This drinking of the tea now, publicly, was itself almost a dismissal.

Mark went to the radio in the library and turned the dial around, letting the music of all Europe come in shreds and patches. He wanted to get away from them both for a moment, and calm down his anger. He wanted to consider the true position of things so as not to forget himself again. He was aghast at having forgotten, at having been so childishly carried away by jealousy and disgust.

As he turned the dial he saw the General through the door. The light struck brightly on his monocle and his other eye was in the shadow. He looked blind; and suddenly Mark remembered him in the bar of the Four Seasons, the sleepwalker, as he had then seemed, the drugtaker. He felt the peculiar fear one has of the blind, whose dangerousness is made more horrible by blundering.

The radio sent out slow music that suggested old dance-cards with faded tassels and forgotten theater programs. It took a sharp effort to go back and join them, but he left the waltz on and went back and sat down at the table with them. The General drank his schnapps, the Countess stirred the cards around with one finger.

"Have a drink?" the General said.

Mark shook his head.

They all pretended to listen to the music.

What a fool I am, Mark thought, what a bloody fool. Everyone knows I am a fool. Even the Mink Coat, saying with her dreadful, light, innocent perception, Be careful

[371]

of him; he's a killer. Maybe I am a killer, too, I said. But I'm not, and he knows it. The General knows I'm a weakling. And I've got to be a weakling. There's no choice for me. I must sit helplessly and watch. Because somewhere up in the city old Fritz is scurrying around, down a dark passage perhaps, into the back room of a house. He and some man are leaning over a table examining a fake passport. I must be helpless because the doctor is sitting in his room, able perhaps to read Spinoza again, though he listens all the time for the doorbell and for the special sound of the bell, whether it's rung in haste, violently, or in the usual way. And above all, I've got to be helpless because Emmy is upstairs, just above us, in the Countess' bed, with only a thin door to shut her in. The General, the big full-blooded man, could push in that door with one drive of his shoulder.

"That's a nice thing," the General said; "what is it?"

"It's the '*Valse Triste*,'" the Countess said.

The thing to decide on now, Mark thought, is how much he does know. And how much he thinks I know. Is he, in the first place, likely to have inquired about the exact date of the execution? If he has, does he know already that she died suddenly this morning? Surely he's in no position that would require any notification of this. Later he'll hear it — perhaps. Perhaps never. How do I even know he has ever heard of her? Maybe someone else told the Countess. But he spoke of Sabina. That was queer. How did he know of her? I don't think I spoke of her to anyone. Yes, I did. I spoke of her to that Commissioner. Does the Countess know about Sabina? Was Sabina really there that night? Who told him? Fritz said everyone in the village would be talking about the funeral; would anyone speak of it to him? Suppose I said now, My mother was buried this afternoon.

But a man whose mother is being buried doesn't drop in for lunch, make jokes with young girls, go out for dinner and show signs of resentment because the lover of a beautiful woman chooses to be obviously her lover.

On the other hand, a man like the General doesn't so publicly disregard the decencies. He doesn't insist that a man who knows his mother has just died should dine with a group of comparative strangers. So the inference is that either he doesn't know or, if he does, he thinks I don't know.

Perhaps by morning Fritz will be back with the passport. Then we can get out without even seeing him again. Then he'll forget it all. He isn't even yet concerned too deeply with me. He thinks of me perhaps as a nuisance, more than anything. His contempt may blind him long enough for us to get away. Then when we're gone his contempt may triumph. We'll be lost in it and vanish.

Yes, that sounds all right, but still there's tonight to be lived through. Here I am. Upstairs is Emmy. Earlier this evening I heard a slight thump on the ceiling and the Countess couldn't resist looking up, and the General noticed that.

The General said, "Ruby, did you know Mr. Preysing's grandfather was Richard Ritter, the painter?"

"Yes, I did."

"Curious coincidence, isn't it? As I told Mr. Preysing, he once painted my wife."

"Yes."

"He also built that house everyone used to admire so much. Do you admire it, Mr. Preysing?"

"I've never seen it."

"Never seen it! What an extraordinary lack of curiosity. I can hardly believe it."

"I've only been here a few days. It's not ours now, anyway."

"Yes, that's right. It was sold, wasn't it? Not long ago, I believe."

"Yes, it was."

"How long *have* you been here, Mr. Preysing?"

"Let me see — a week — I think; or is it — Yes, a week." He really found it impossible to remember. This week had no dimension in time.

"You've spent a good deal of it down here, haven't you?"

"Only two days. Last Friday, and today."

But he felt a little more at ease. These questions were aimless. They weren't asked by a man with any definite direction. No, the General didn't know. But he was still trying to find out.

The music changed to "The Swan of Tuonela," and the General recognized that. "How that music fits you, Ruby," he said. "You've always made me think of a swan. Doesn't she make you think of a swan, Mr. Preysing?"

"Yes," said Mark absently, and then he was annoyed, even now, because he and the General had thought of the same thing. "A white swan with a brilliant orange beak and narrow, vicious eyes," he said.

The General said, "So young, so carefree, so poetic!" He screwed his monocle in to look him up and down. "As I probably was at your age. You *are* carefree, aren't you, Mr. Preysing?"

"Is anyone?"

"Some men have a gift for throwing off care. Even grave care."

"Perhaps I have."

"You like to be cryptic. To answer a question with a question. It's an easy evasion. But perhaps you're just

[374]

heartless, Mr. Preysing. Perhaps you have a feminine streak in you that makes you heartless — that is, if your interesting ideas about women are true."

Mark shrugged. He thought, He's even a bore. How can she stand him? But don't despise him for that. Don't underestimate him. We move on one level now, and on that he's at a disadvantage, though only temporarily. There are other levels. He's not at a disadvantage on them. He's groping. He wants to find out what's wrong here. He doesn't see yet, but perhaps he has unconsciously begun to see. He is like a hound confused by many smells, too many people, but his muzzle is pointed in the right direction, his snout is to the ground, and at any moment he'll pick up the smell of the hunted. It is only a question of time.

I ought to get out, Mark thought. It's my being here that is wrong. I ought to leave him to her. She can handle him, and I oughtn't to care how she does it. She can lull him into his drug-taking and his sleep. She is his drug and his sleep too.

Yes, I must leave him with her.

He took a long look at her, seeing her with her arms laid across the card table, her deathly, autumnal beauty full of chill and blight. Perhaps I'll never see her again. What will it be like in America? Never seeing her again, never even hoping to see her.

He caught the General's eyes on him in astonishment and knew his face had shown too much.

"I think I'd better be leaving," he said. "Don't bother to drive me. I'd like to walk."

"I think you had both better go," the Countess said. "I have a bad headache tonight." She ran her hand along her forehead.

[375]

"So!" the General said slowly. Mark saw the instant tightening of his face. The vein in his forehead began to pulse. "So! We are dismissed, are we?"

He said no more, but neither he nor Mark moved. He might be inept and heavy but he had power in him, and when he wished could control things by the mere holding of it in leash.

Then he said, "The classic headache, Mr. Preysing. You and I will share the headache. If I must leave, so must you, and vice versa. Well — " He put his hands on the table and got up as though it were an unexpected physical effort. "Or will you have a drink before we leave? It may be cold going back."

The Countess said, "Perhaps you'd like whisky." She got up too.

"Can't he drink what we have?" the General said.

"Americans like whisky," the Countess said.

"Then ring for it."

"No, I'll see to it myself. Juli is in bed."

She turned and went quickly out. The General's face was ugly with anger, and suddenly Mark knew in a flash what it was that had so far been their salvation. It was not the General's contempt. It was true he despised Mark, but still his attention was all focused upon him. Upon him and the Countess. Mark and the Countess together hid the real danger from him. He was concerned entirely with their relation to each other, what was its quality, how far it had gone, whether it endangered his own. He could only concentrate on what would affect himself, even though his instinct might already have told him there was more to it than that. It was his jealousy that was their salvation. As long as he kept to that they were safe, and Emmy might get up and walk out the front door undisturbed.

Mark got up and followed the Countess out of the room.

He walked boldly after her and the General didn't follow him. Across the hall he went and into the white pantry.

The Countess was standing by the table watching the swinging door. As he pushed it open her face changed and he knew she had heard his steps and thought he was the General. When he reached her she put her hand on his shoulder and leaned against him as though to steady herself. Mark put his arm around her waist and bent so that his cheek touched her hair. They stood together for a moment, supporting each other against whatever might come.

"Don't make him too jealous," she whispered.

"I won't. But a little jealousy will save us perhaps."

"Perhaps."

He was afraid to stir, or even to tighten his arm, for fear she would break away.

"How is she?" he whispered.

"She's quite all right. She had some food and sleep. She can walk a little bit."

"I want to see her."

"It's impossible now. Don't think of it. She's quite all right."

He looked over her head at the door, expecting to see it swing inward at any moment.

"When can you get away?" she asked.

"I don't know. It depends on Fritz and the passport. Does *he* know?"

"The General? He knows about the trial. He doesn't know what day it was to have been. I think he doesn't know about the funeral. Not yet. But I'm not sure. I don't dare ask him."

How helpless they seemed, standing there together with no plan, no knowledge, almost no will between them. He let his arm slip from her.

She went over to a cupboard and opened it. "Of course

I have no whisky, really," she said. "It's terribly expensive here."

"Will he be here tonight?" he asked.

She said without turning, "No. He'll go when you do."

"You promise that?"

"Yes, I promise."

She reached up to the shelf and pretended to look. "I'll send you a note tomorrow to tell you when you can come."

"You've got to get rid of him," he said. "I don't mean only tomorrow. I mean forever. He's ruining you. Maybe he'll even kill you in the end. Can't you see that?"

She didn't answer.

"Do you love him?" he asked.

She closed the cupboard door and turned around, leaning against it with her hands behind her.

"You shouldn't have asked me that."

"I have to. Tell me, do you?"

His eyes searched her face, but saw only uncertainty and pain.

"I don't know. I have loved him — for many years."

He felt a shudder go all through him: how can these things be understood or accepted?

"You're not happy!" he cried. Then he added desperately, "But you were happy this morning. I could see it."

"Yes, it's true. I'm not happy. I don't know whether it's because of him. Perhaps it's not all his fault. It's everything here. We're locked up here really. The two of us. I feel dead. Perhaps he does too. There've been things I've wanted to do and couldn't. Just like in a nightmare. This morning when you came, when both of you came in my house, it was suddenly different. I suddenly felt alive."

"Do you love me?" he asked.

"No, it's not that. Or it's not love, as I think you meant it at the concert that night."

"Don't give me any of your spiritual loves," he said fiercely.

"I give what I must." Suddenly her face lightened, the look he had seen in the morning came over it again. "No, that's not true this time. I give what I want."

"I'm asking you what that is. What is it you want?"

"I want you to be free."

How little that would seem in another time, in another place. But not here. Not in this little white pantry with a swinging door between him and the General. And another door just upstairs. But he wanted love too.

"If we only had more time!" he cried.

"We've got to go back."

She went quickly over and pushed open the door. They walked back sedately.

The General was standing by the window with his back to them. He had lifted the curtain and was looking out at the night.

"The snow is melting," he said. "There will be no skiing tomorrow."

He turned around and his face was frozen. The radio was still going and the last notes of the Swan filled the room.

"Shall we go now, Mr. Preysing, or would you prefer to stay and have your whisky?"

"There was no whisky," the Countess said. "No, you must both go now. It's late."

The General walked over and stood between them. "What are our plans for tomorrow?" he asked. "Since there's no skiing, what shall we do — the three of us?"

"Oh, Mr. Preysing's going to be very busy," she said. "He's going to make some sketches of the girls here. Suppose you and I go off for the day. We could make a little excursion. Drive somewhere and have lunch."

She will get him away, Mark thought. Give me a free hand for the day.

But the General was suddenly suspicious. "You and I, my dear?" he said ironically. "Isn't it a bit rude to leave Mr. Preysing?"

"No, he doesn't want to go. I asked him. Some other time, perhaps."

The General looked from one to the other. It was true. He could see it in their faces. They were indeed absorbed in each other. That, he thought, was to put it in its most innocent form. But they didn't want to be together. At any rate not tomorrow. They wanted to be apart tomorrow. Why was that? Again the deep feeling of something very out of key, something illogical and sinister, struck him. Again he felt that the house was strangely part of it.

The music had stopped. He stood so still he heard the whole silence of the house, and in the silence the drip of snow melting and the faint creak of the Countess' skirt as she stirred uneasily.

"Well, I'll come for you at nine," he said.

He kissed her hand and he and Mark said good night. She went with them to the door. She walked quickly and lightly, too obviously relieved at getting them out of the house.

"Good night," she called almost gaily as they stood in the path. Before they had even got in the car they heard her setting the bolt in the door.

They rode back to the village in silence. The General was preoccupied with the strangeness of what he had just seen. The two of them, the young man as well as Ruby, had not seized the opportunity when he offered it to them of being together. Did they meet secretly? It was hardly thinkable. He held to his certainty that Ruby did not love Preysing, except as an older woman may be flattered and touched and put in a sickly glow of rejuvenation by the obvious devotion of a very young man. And yet, it was strange she didn't want him tomorrow. She hadn't really wanted him tonight either. He remembered that too. Nor had the young man shown any eagerness to come. His face had lighted with relief when he heard her say that she would be away all day with her lover. And yet the young man was in love. And Ruby perhaps strongly pitied him. Pity? He tried out that word too. He couldn't find the exact feeling that was in her. Pity — perhaps.

Suddenly the whole thing was clear: She pities him *and so she is trying to help him.*

That's the whole secret. That's the pattern into which everything fits: her disloyalty, not sexual but spiritual, her faint air of guilt, her too obvious submission. It's his reluctance, too. He doesn't dare compromise her.

I oughtn't to have told her about him. I aroused her pity. He'd never perhaps have dared, himself.

Now that this was clear his jealousy suddenly dimmed almost to nothing. But another fear took its place.

But that's terribly dangerous, he thought. Terribly dangerous. Ruby mustn't meddle in these things. She knows nothing at all about them. No, she's as ignorant as it's possible to be. What on earth would be Ruby's idea of help? How would she even start? What would she go on to?

He couldn't imagine.

I must find out all about this, he thought. I must find out about the Ritter woman. Where she is . . . What day she's to be executed. . . .

It's obvious the young man doesn't know. Or is it? He saw Rudi and Rudi told him nothing, but he may have many underground contacts I know nothing about. He may have, through his mother, a whole host of secret contacts. He may already have involved Ruby in the network of a criminal underworld. I mustn't let him put her in a position I couldn't get her out of. If she should go too far . . .

He felt her to be in terrible danger, and he himself along with her. What devil had given the boy such a hold on her? He had become a terrible danger to all of them, not only because of his dirty involvements but because he created some mysterious atmosphere in which Ruby could feel a new and powerful emotion. He could barely guess what it was. (Pity was perhaps too narrow and limited.) Didn't he, Kurt, know them all? In this unknown atmosphere he might even lose what he couldn't live without.

He'd have to get rid of him at once.

Mark glanced every now and then at the General's profile, seen dimly against the window of the car, and he also felt himself to be in deadly danger. Not himself alone, but all of them . . . Emmy, the Countess, Fritz, the doctor . . . All of them were trembling just outside the General's grasp. Contempt wasn't enough now to save them. Jealousy wasn't enough. Ignorance wasn't enough. The clue was almost in the General's hand.

When they got to the little inn the car stopped.

"Well, thanks for the ride," Mark said.

He got out, and the General followed him slowly and heavily.

"Please don't bother to get out."

The General said curtly, "I want to speak to you."

"Will you come up?"

"No, here will do."

They stood facing each other before the inn door. A lantern on a rusty iron hook shed yellow light down on their faces. The dark street of low peaked houses was full of rivulets of melting snow from the mountains.

"I don't think I like you, Mr. Preysing," the General said.

"No? Well, I don't like you either."

He tried to keep his voice calm and bantering. Must I even now, he thought, be so concerned as to retort? Why not shut up altogether?

"Unfortunately for you," the General said, "I'm in a position to enforce my dislikes. I want to tell you that you must manage to leave here very shortly."

"How shortly would you suggest?"

"Tomorrow."

"I must try to do that." He thought, I sound like a ham actor. This is preposterous.

He turned angrily to go, but the General caught his arm and whirled him back. His fingers were like iron. Shall we roll in the mud now, Mark thought. Is it now that he kills me, or that I try to kill him?

He stood quite still.

"You take a great deal from me, Mr. Preysing," the General said. "I can't help wondering why."

"Don't wonder," Mark said. He laughed a little. "You've got all the odds. For one thing, you're a bigger man, and for another, it's your country."

"I don't think I'd stand it, anywhere," the General said.

"Don't you? That's easy to say. Come over sometime and find out."

"I think you're a coward," the General said.

"I think in our own ways we both are."

The General let him go so suddenly he almost fell. Mark wheeled into the door, and he would have liked at least to make a dignified exit, but even that was denied him. The door was locked for the night. He had to ring the bell and stand there waiting while the General, majestic and arrogant, got back in his car and was driven off.

When the door was finally opened he understood a little why some grievances may make you want to kick an innocent man. He'd have liked to kick the meek, obsequious little clerk who stood there in the hall.

Chapter XXIV

AFTER she had bolted the door the Countess went into the kitchen and warmed some milk and some of the soup left from dinner. She put these and some fruit on a tray and carried them upstairs. When she unlocked the door she found Emmy sitting up in bed. The table lamp was on and she had evidently found a book and was reading it.

"I'm so glad you're awake," the Countess said. "I wanted to say good night to you. And here is some warm food."

"How splendid!" Emmy exclaimed. "I'm hungry as a wolf. I never saw food look so good."

She dropped her book and the Countess laid the tray across her knees. She could feed herself now and she began to drink the soup and milk. The Countess sat on the edge of the bed and peeled an apple. Emmy ate with great relish for a few moments, all but smacking her lips. When she had finished the Countess took the tray and put it on the table. She handed her the peeled apple on a plate.

"Thank you," Emmy said. Then she added, "You look very worried this evening. Has anything gone wrong?"

"I don't think anything has gone wrong. I think everything will probably go very well. It was just that my house seemed to frighten me this evening."

Emmy drew her knees up and threw one of her braids back over her shoulder. She began to munch the apple. "Does it frighten you because I'm in it?" she asked.

"No," the Countess said. "Not at all. It was just when my guests left, and for the moment when I felt alone in

it, that I was frightened. Usually I feel so safe in my own house and it's such a pleasure for me to feel alone in it. Especially when people have just left me."

"I read somewhere once," Emmy said, "I think it was in a book by a very clever Englishwoman, that there is no pleasure like the departure of guests."

"Yes, that's usually so." The Countess smiled. "But it wasn't entirely so tonight, and it was only when I came up here and found you that I felt less afraid."

"I heard the guests. They seemed very gay and young."

"Those were my girls. They sleep in another house. It's joined to this, of course. But I had guests, too."

"Was Mark one of them?"

"Yes. He's staying at one of the inns in the village. Didn't I tell you that? He wanted very much to see you tonight. But it didn't seem possible."

"I didn't really expect it. I don't know how things are here. I'm willing to put myself in your hands without question."

But the Countess knew she had stayed awake in the hope of seeing Mark. Now that the drugs had worn off and she was so much stronger, the resemblance between them was clearer. Especially in the movements of her hands, her way of turning the eyes. She looked very much younger, younger even than the Countess.

"Do you want to sleep now?" the Countess asked. "Or may I stay with you for a minute?"

"Do stay, please. I've slept all day."

"I sleep so badly. Sometimes I can't sleep till nearly morning, and then I have to take veronal."

Emmy shook her head sympathetically. But the Countess guessed she was too healthy to know what long, white nights can mean. "I suppose you've never had insomnia," she said.

[386]

"Oh, yes," Emmy said. "Once I didn't sleep well for months. I lay for hours in the dark. Not quite dark; there were street lights shining onto the walls. I was trying to come to a decision about something — whether I should or should not take a part in trying to right something; something that seemed to me wrong. It meant risking a good deal. I couldn't quite make up my mind. Principally because to risk it meant also to throw away a lot of things I'd treasured. But in the end I did throw them all away. Nothing has ever refreshed me so much as that insomnia."

"I can't do that. I mean I can't throw things away. They cling to me. Everything I do seems to cling to me forever."

She spoke with that light, frivolous despair that always seems the most sick of all.

"You're not happy!" Emmy exclaimed.

It was the second time this evening this had been said to her, and in almost the same voice.

"I know it's not important whether I'm happy or not. But I have been happy. I know what it is to be happy. Now it's true I haven't been for a long time. Except just in a few flashes, such short flashes I don't know quite what they mean. They come in the midst of so much else that I know so well and can't get rid of."

Emmy clasped her hands behind her head and looked up at the ceiling. "You're a very beautiful woman," she said. "I suppose you're fairly healthy. I heard you singing a while ago, so you have music and things to enjoy. A great many people must love you, and you're fortunate in many ways. If I were a Martian come to observe the race of man I'd probably decide that the only happy people to be found were a select few with failing eyesight, faithless friends, incurable diseases, and no money. Probably because these are the only ones who are ever willing to throw dead experiences away."

The Countess laughed nervously. This sounded so much like what Mark would say. She lost herself for a moment in the pleasure of their identity.

"You mean they're the only ones capable of making a fresh start."

"I suppose I do. I was reading a play by Sudermann just as you came in. I used to play in it. It's a good play, but reading it now it bored me to death. I was thinking all the time of a play I'd like to have written and how I'd act it and put it on."

"A play not even written?"

"A play not even conceived. But maybe it will be. It makes me happier to think of a good play that may be written than a good play that has been. I suppose I think happiness, like health, is a process of circulation and elimination."

"Then you're happy," the Countess said. She looked at her closely, at her thick hair, the strong, delicate bones of her face, her eyes, as though the true secret would show in them.

"Oh, not quite as easily as that. I'm not an idiot. I'm happy at times and within reason. Enough to keep me living and circulating. I'm not one to insist that everything is for the best in the best of all possible worlds. I don't congratulate myself that it was worth while being raped and disemboweled by the Bulgars, like Cunegonde, in order to sit here eating candied pistache nuts."

She gave a great ringing laugh, but the Countess shuddered. "The world is so horrible now," she said. "It's grown too horrible for anyone to be happy in it. Who could be happy today? No, it's too horrible."

"It's always horrible. History, when you're in the midst of it, is always nearly intolerable to a decent and sensitive man. It's only when a period is over and everything has

[388]

been burned away but a few selected shells — buildings, books, a bit of law or music — that we can stand it. That's because we see the form and direction and at the same time we don't know what it really was like to live in it."

"Then you think we can't ever be happy in the present?"

"At times, certainly. But I should say, only if we are willing to throw a lot of it overboard the very instant it becomes the past. And it becomes the past the very instant after it's lived."

The Countess sighed heavily. "I don't know what's the matter with me," she said, "but I'll tell you one thing: the happiest moment I've known in a long time was just after I had taken you into my house. Then I really did throw a great deal overboard. I don't know that I can go on with it. But I know I need a new life. Entirely different. A new life where I can love new things, in a way I've never known."

Suddenly her face went blank and reticent again. She sat aghast at what she had said. It was as though a cloth had wiped her face, leaving it almost idiotic in its emptiness. Emmy had the sensation of watching the Countess drop away from her like a falling leaf. The good, kind woman, she thought hotly, who had risked so much to help her. But she respected her reticence and said nothing. She looked away from her.

The Countess got up. "I must let you sleep," she said. "I shouldn't have talked so long. But I'm a little uneasy tonight."

Emmy asked again, "Has anything gone wrong?"

"I don't really know. I can't tell. There is something out there," she said, "that's like a delicate pendulum swinging from side to side. If it swings toward us and stops, I'm afraid we're all lost."

She spoke lightly again, with her sick air of gaiety.

"Not you, I hope," Emmy said quickly. And to herself she thought, And not the doctor — and not Mark.

She felt suddenly so constricted, so overladen by all that had been done for her, that tears rushed to her eyes. These things she could never throw away. The inexplicable generosity, which even her own generosity couldn't quite bear or understand.

"Do you want anything before I go?"

"No, thank you."

"Good night, then."

The Countess held out her hand and Emmy caught it impulsively and kissed it.

The Countess drew it quickly away. Not because Emmy was another woman and her social equal, but because in her rigid state she was afraid of the entirely natural expression of a still flexible being.

"Good night," she said again.

Flushed with embarrassment, she picked up the tray and went out.

Chapter XXV

MARK sat on the edge of the bed and every now and then leaned back on the pillow and slept for a few moments. As he woke his first gesture was always to lift his hand and look at his wrist watch. Once or twice he got up and leaned out of his window, breathing in the cold night air. Over the peaked roofs near him he could see the bulk of the larger hotel where he supposed the General was staying. All through the night there was a square of light shining in it, and he was sure it came from the General's room.

It didn't seem possible to him that the General could be asleep. He imagined him sitting also on the edge of the bed, his great blond head sagged forward and his monocle dropped from his eye. And somewhere outside the blind image of the man he saw his mind, a separate thing running like a little dog, back and forth. He saw it nosing out the scent, getting always a little nearer and a little nearer, until finally it was ready to set up a howling outside a closed door.

He followed the General's mind back and forth on its hunt. He saw all the scraps as it nosed them and turned them over, and he saw how these scraps gradually fitted together and made a whole. . . .

"What's that American doing in town?" (Fritz said the whole village would be talking about it tonight.) "Why, he came to bury his mother. He and Fritz Keller buried her at three this afternoon. They say she was a criminal of some sort."

So she's dead already, is she? And he buried her today? Then he has known everything that's been going on. He and this Fritz — "An old servant, you say?"

"Oh, but Mr. Preysing was here for lunch." All that laughter at the table. "Mr. Preysing, you're a scream!" "I knew a tarantula once who kept a lady." "You take a great deal from me, Mr. Preysing."

I'll telephone up to town as soon as it's light. I'll telephone and see what really happened there.

"But she wasn't executed, General. She died suddenly in the middle of the night."

"Oh? And who was with her?"

"Doctor Ditten was with her. She was his special case. He operated on her and saved her life a short time before."

Ditten? The fellow with the brusque, independent manner; trades on his uncle's position? Ruby's protégé. She used to give him milk and cakes in the country when he was a staring, blue-eyed child. *He'd do anything for Ruby.*

"Hold Ditten, will you, till I make a few more inquiries."

There was a strange-looking wagon, like a delivery wagon, turning in the drive . . .

"I'm afraid I have a headache and you'll both have to leave. Let's make an excursion somewhere tomorrow. Be gone all day. Mr. Preysing has to stay here. He can't possibly come with us."

Mark went over all this, back and forth, adding a bit here and there, working on it as carefully as though he were the hunter and not the hunted.

If I only had the passport now we could go at once.

But Fritz can't be working at it all night. He may have had engine trouble or an accident. He may not even be there. The man who sells the passports may be gone. He may have been arrested. Even if everything goes smoothly he can't possibly get back till sometime in the morning. Probably ten o'clock . . . And that's too late now.

Then he began to push forward into the day that was coming. He saw the doctor, drinking coffee before the little iron stove in his big room full of chilly morning light, the light of the morning that hadn't broken yet. Downstairs the bell jangling suddenly. "It's our bell, sir." The old servant looking at him — "Who can it be this early?" And the doctor's small blue eyes suddenly full of cold and obstinate courage.

Fritz stepping off the train, his old Homburg sagging down over his ears, his shabby coat pulled up against the raw mountain air. In his inner pocket the false passport. "Are you Fritz Keller?" The preoccupied, sour look suddenly turning blank. "Come along with us."

Finally, the Countess, in a white robe with a red cord around her waist like a medieval penitent. "Don't go upstairs. There's no one up there. I forbid you to go!"

But if I had the passport now, we could still get away. There'd be no one there. The upstairs room would be empty. "But, my darling, you see you've imagined the whole thing — surely you know I love only you."

That would leave her behind. Can I really leave her behind? Aren't some things worse than prison and torture and execution? No, by God, there are no things worse. Let her take what's coming to her. She had him for years. She can go on having him.

What time is it now? Four o'clock.

If I don't get out in a few hours it's too late.

What can I do? Get her and climb over the mountains in the dark? She can barely walk.

I've ruined everyone: the doctor, Fritz, the Countess, and myself. And Emmy worst of all. It will be a hundred times worse for her now. Better kill ourselves than go through what we'll have to go through. Better blow our brains out now.

But I should have killed him last night there in the snow. Him and his dummy driver with him. Perhaps I could have done it. It was so essential that I might have done it.

A sudden sleep lasted only a few seconds, or perhaps half an hour. Then he started up. Someone was moving gently on tiptoe outside his door.

He's come for me.

He lay still, and a sick relief came over him. It was over at last. Now there was nothing he could do.

He heard voices, two low voices murmuring. Then the steps tiptoeing past again.

The inner walls of the hotel were thin partitions, the doors pine boards with wide cracks. In the room next to his own he heard someone moving. A splash of water. Finally a loud yawn in a descending scale.

Someone was getting up early. That was all. A man next to him was shaving. The footsteps had been the clerk giving him an early call. He was a skier perhaps. A man who wanted to make an excursion, or catch a train.

Mark got up. He went to the window again and looked into a white well of mist. He couldn't see the houses or the hotel or the square of light.

It was nearly five o'clock.

He opened his door, went to the head of the stairs and looked down. From the office below came a dim light.

He went downstairs to the office and found the little clerk who had let him in the night before. He was sitting behind the desk, his head against the wall, dozing, with his mouth open. He heard Mark and started awake, his eyes sleepy but surprised when he saw who it was.

[394]

"You wakened me," Mark said, "with all your tramping up and down the stairs."

"But I'm sorry sir. I apologize. I went as quietly as I could — "

He went on stammering and Mark said, "I sleep badly. Anything wakes me."

He began to walk up and down the little office, his hands in his pockets, and the clerk watched him anxiously. He stood up behind his desk, not knowing what to do about it.

On the wall were brilliant railroad and tourist posters, snowy crags, castles, and ski slopes. The clerk's head was in the middle of a baroque church.

Mark stopped suddenly. "Since I'm up I might as well make an excursion. Can I hire a car this early? Where could I go for a day's excursion?"

The clerk began to hunt with an air of haste and efficiency among the travel folders lying in pigeonholes and on his desk.

"You can go here — or here," he said, shuffling them out for Mark to look at. "Here's the most beautiful baroque church in the country. Here's the village which is the most famous in the world, if you except Nazareth and Bethlehem."

He was anxious to please. The General, Mark saw, had given him great prestige by his visit of the night before, by his gracious call to take him dining with the Countess. What if his mother was a criminal? Many in high places came to grief in these days.

This last glimmer of his prestige, so soon to vanish, Mark made the most of.

"You get me a car," he said; "I'll decide where to go later. I can't go back and go to sleep now. Send up some hot water, and some coffee and rolls."

He went toward the stairs. He thought, at least I won't be here when he comes. At least I can go and get her and take her to another hotel. It will hold him off for a little while longer. Then as he began to climb he had a moment of vertigo and of hallucination. He saw himself and Emmy, the doctor, Fritz, and the Countess, all falling together in the Miltonic chute that Rubens painted, and as they fell they turned also into stone and scales and green corruption. Because they were weak, and the offense of weakness, he saw at last, was unforgivable. But the General and the Commissioner and the soldiers in the little café, the landlady of the Pension Eden, all the half-seen and half-known other ones, the strong ones, the insignificant ones, leaned above them, suddenly brilliant and transfigured in triumph. It was so monstrous and so inevitable in its complete realization that it was the lowest moment he had ever felt. As his hand moved along the stair rail, touching the rough, fresh pine, he thought that if he ever lived to see anyone else make that gesture he would shudder, certain that unspoken horrors must fill his mind.

The clerk hurried after him with hot water. He shaved, but before he had finished the clerk was back with hot coffee and rolls. He had added butter and jam as an appeasement. Mark ate hungrily. Next door he heard the unseen man clicking his own cup as he drank his coffee, and suddenly Mark felt better again and not so afraid. He felt only extraordinarily nervous. Through his open door he could hear the clerk telephoning about the car.

The other man finished his breakfast and went downstairs. Mark heard him talking to the clerk. Presently he went out.

It was still dark outside and the mist shrouded everything. It seemed to Mark kindly, because it gave him a feeling of shelter. It was a half-light that would hold back for a time the full glare of day.

He took his overcoat and hat and went downstairs again. The clerk was standing at the door looking out.

"What's the matter," Mark said. "Can't you get a car?" This was like waiting for Fritz at the little café.

"Oh, yes, sir. Gertner's coming. His wife says he'll be here right away."

If Fritz would only turn up in the wagon as he had before! Fritz and the passport. He walked up and down the office, looking at the travel posters.

"Why doesn't he come?" he asked.

"He has to have his breakfast. People don't usually start this early without leaving word. It would have been better to order it the night before."

"I wouldn't have ordered it at all if you hadn't wakened me."

"He'll be here in a minute, sir."

But the car didn't come. Mark kept looking at his wrist.

"Call him again," he said finally.

"He's coming as soon as he can, sir. He's got the best car here. I didn't want to get just any car."

Not for the General's pal, Mark thought.

Finally he heard it coming down the street. It filled the morning cold and stillness with its warm, purring sound.

"Here it is, sir." The clerk was much relieved.

Mark went to the door and saw a rather old but once luxurious limousine. The driver was red-faced still from sleep but he looked robust and exceptionally cheerful. He had the face of a sly, garrulous man. He'd been told already that the eccentric foreigner who couldn't sleep wanted him for the day.

Mark got in.

[397]

"I'll be back sometime tonight," he told the clerk.

"Where do you want to go, sir?" the driver asked.

"I don't know," Mark said. Then he told him to drive to the big resort town first, where he'd have a good hot breakfast and decide on what he wanted to do. They drove off slowly in the mist.

"This will clear right up as soon as the sun rises," the driver told him.

Mark asked him about the excursions he usually made and where was a good place to go. "I hate excursions," he said. "I never can make up my mind where to go or what to do."

The driver clicked his tongue sympathetically. He had heard, too, perhaps, about the funeral. "It's sad to travel alone," he said.

"Yes, it is," Mark agreed.

He kept his face to the window, trying to see out in the mist. He saw a letter-box he thought he had noticed when he came from the Countess' house. In a few moments hers would appear.

"There's a lady," he said, "who promised to make an excursion with me. I don't know whether she'd think it too early to start." He spoke as if to himself.

The driver said, "Ah, do you mean one of the Countess' young ladies?"

"No, a guest of the Countess."

"The Countess used to have a lot of guests." The driver turned so that Mark saw his crimson profile and one sly blue eye. "Now she has very few."

"Turn in there," Mark said, "I'll see if I can persuade her to go."

The driver smiled rather impertinently.

The little chalet with the bird perched on it rose in a swirl of mist. The car turned in sharply. They went slowly

[398]

along the driveway, up the little hill, past the evergreens, with no snow on them now.

And here was her house again, as it had stood yesterday against the upward spears of pines. But now it was a drowned house, drowned in white mist, the world around it all whiteness. And though the house looked dark at first, as he got out he saw a dim glow, as though somewhere inside a light was burning.

He stood before the door, but he did not need to knock. It opened at once and he saw her white face and her white robe in the gloom of the hallway. She stretched out her cold hand to him and drew him in. The door shut behind him. As she drew him she retreated, and before he could clasp her she had slipped away and flitted to the foot of the stairs. There she turned on a light in the hall.

"I heard the car," she said. "I'd come down to the kitchen to get her some hot coffee."

"I had to come for her," he said. Then seeing her white figure, so solitary, at the foot of the rising stairs, he said, like a plea for forgiveness, "I've got to get her away."

"Oh, yes. I know you must. I was afraid all night."

"So was I."

She went up and he followed her. In the upper hall she turned on another light. She took a key from her pocket and unlocked the door of Emmy's room. The bed light was still on but Emmy lay sound asleep, her arm across her eyes. She didn't wake when they came in.

Mark touched her on the shoulder and she flung back her arm and her eyes opened.

"Mark!" she cried.

He bent over and kissed her. "We've got to go now, darling," he said. "Can you get up, do you think?"

She looked at both of them, her immense eyes making a glistening light of their own in the softly lighted room.

[399]

"Of course," she said.

"I'm getting her some hot coffee," the Countess said, "before the servants get up." She turned to the door. "Wait a moment," she said, "What will you put on? I must get you some of my clothes. You can't wear those shoes. And you must have a hat. With a veil, perhaps. The fur coat will do."

She went to her own room and opened the wardrobe doors, got out a hat with a veil that wound around the head and under the chin, chose a woolen dress, a pair of oxfords.

She took them back. "Put these on," she said. "You must look like a traveler, and it won't hurt if you look elegant. These are French clothes."

Then she ran downstairs, took the coffee from the stove where it was boiling, got the milk and the hot rolls. When she carried them upstairs Emmy was already dressed. She was sitting before the dressing table, her hair still down her back. The Countess put the tray beside her on a little table.

"It's so hard to do my hair," Emmy said. She began to eat the rolls and drink the coffee.

Mark stood by the window watching her. His face was so pale his eyes seemed like black smears.

When Emmy had finished the Countess said, "I'll help you with your hair." She lifted Emmy's heavy braids.

Mark said in a flat voice, "You know she has no passport."

The Countess let the braids fall. "He hasn't come back with it?"

"No."

"Then you can't get out."

"What's this?" said Emmy.

Neither of them dared to answer her.

Then Mark, looking at the Countess, said, "We
to get out, because of the General."

The Countess put her hands on the back of a ch
steady herself. "Yes, the General. But where will you

"I don't know but we must leave here. He mustn't
her in your house."

"But you can't leave the country."

"Not without a passport."

"Then what will you do?"

"We'll go somewhere. I thought I'd leave her in a hotel
She must not be found here. I'll come back and meet Fritz
and get the passport. I'll take it back to her if I can, or
I'll mail it to her wherever she is."

They talked over Emmy's head. Emmy sat quite still,
her hair down her back, looking in the glass.

"You see, it's the General," Mark said again.

The Countess nodded. "Then it's no good to run away,"
she said at last, "unless you run far enough."

Suddenly for all of them it was intolerable. It had gone
on too long. They had been too frightened. They had
endured too much. It would be better to give up. No one
could do any more.

The Countess leaned on the back of Emmy's chair and
thought, I can't help them. I'm useless. I'm dead. Not to
help them now is death.

Leaning on the chair her will and her senses seemed to
pass into a long swoon of forgetfulness.

She opened her eyes and saw her face in the glass and
below it Emmy's face. But it seemed dimly like the face
of someone else. It was as though someone had opened
a door for her and whispered in her ear: Come this way.

She said slowly, "Why, I'll get you a passport."

She went out of the room and walked down the stairs
to the hall below. She crossed the gallery into the other

section of the house, where the girls slept. Their rooms opened off a corridor filled with gay flower prints. The windows looked into the court on the other side of which were the servants' quarters. She looked at all the doors carefully to be sure she had the right one, then opened it and stepped inside. She switched on a table lamp.

"Suzanne," she said in a low voice.

The French girl was too sleepy to be surprised at seeing the Countess by her bed.

"Suzanne," the Countess said, "are you awake? Can you hear what I say?"

"Yes, Madame."

"I didn't frighten you?"

"No. I'm not frightened. What is it?" Her black eyes grew suddenly alert. She sat up stiffly in her bed, waiting to hear.

"Suzanne, I have to ask a great favor. I ask it because I must. If you can't do it promise me you'll never speak of it."

Suzanne answered composedly, "What is it?"

"I want you to lend me your passport."

"My passport?"

"Yes. Only to lend it. It will be mailed back to you shortly. If it isn't you can always say it was lost or stolen. Your consulate will make no trouble about issuing another."

"My passport?" she repeated.

The Countess suddenly feared she didn't understand. "It's to help someone very unfortunate," she said, "someone who looks a little like you and might be able to use it."

Suzanne stared ahead of her and knitted her black brows. The Countess thought, But she doesn't look like her at all: why did I think so?

She said desperately, "Suzanne, you remember young Mannheim, don't you?"

"Yes?" Suzanne turned, her eyes full of a wild question. "Where is he? Has anything happened to him?"

The Countess said, "He's dead. He shot himself."

The girl's eyes grew slowly dim. Then she drew up her knees and leaned against them. The Countess heard her say, "I was afraid he would." She clasped the back of her head in her hands, and the Countess had room in her heart to pity her. Then she leaned over and touched her shoulder. "You'll let me have the passport?"

"Yes. Take it." Suzanne, without lifting her head, pointed to her purse lying on the dressing table.

The Countess got the purse and opened it. She found the passport and held it close to the light. The photograph was of a staring, black-eyed woman with a large nose, and hair cut in bangs drawn tight back over the ears. In the ears were earrings of a queer design, like starfish.

"May I have the earrings?" the Countess asked.

Suzanne jumped out of bed and went to her dressing-table drawer. She was in a thin chiffon nightgown and the Countess saw her smart, rather ugly, long body, already with something prematurely old-maidish in its lines. She was shivering with cold and excitement. "Here they are," she said. She pushed them into the Countess' hand.

"Thank you, Suzanne. And lend me some lipstick too, some mascara. I haven't any." Suzanne gathered them from the drawer and gave them to her. "Get back to bed now. You'll catch cold."

She went to the door. "I'm in a terrible hurry," she said. "I must go. But you've done a good thing, Suzanne. You've helped someone you'd want to help."

Suzanne watched her from the dressing table, but she said nothing.

The Countess closed the door behind her and ran lightly back along the corridor, across the gallery, upstairs, and into the room where Emmy sat. She saw Mark standing by her.

"Here," she said. She laid the passport down before Emmy. "Here's your passport."

Neither of them seemed to understand.

"And the earrings too," the Countess said, "and rouge and mascara. See? That's all you need."

It was the happiest moment of her life. Now she had saved them. And at the moment when they had given up in despair.

But they didn't realize yet the simplicity and perfection of what she had done. Emmy only picked up the earrings wonderingly. Mark examined the photograph.

"It's that French girl," he said, without excitement.

He held it out for Emmy to see. She glanced at it and then at the earrings again, and the lipstick and mascara. She looked in the mirror at the Countess' pale and radiant face, and suddenly she smiled.

"Can you look like that?" the Countess asked.

"I can look like anything."

The Countess got her big sewing scissors and cut a bang of Emmy's hair, drew the rest back into a knot high on her head, put on the hat, and wound the veil under her chin to hide the throat. Emmy, with cold cream, powder, and lipstick, carefully made up her face, changed the shape of her mouth. "If I had some tweezers I could change my eyebrows, too, but they'll have to do," she said. Then she sat in front of the mirror, and holding the passport in one hand tilted her head backward and looked from under her brows, lifted an eyebrow as though she were skeptical of the whole proceeding.

It was so exactly Suzanne's attitude and expression it made the Countess gasp.

Mark still wasn't impressed. "It's pretty good," he said,

"but just the same, no one would take you for that French girl."

"They don't have to," Emmy said, "they only have to believe that this picture is a bad one of me. And they mustn't look too closely. That's a chance we'll have to take."

"You must have some luggage," the Countess cried. She moved about as swiftly as a swallow. She was so full of happiness she wanted to sing. She ran into her own room next door and got her handbag and another bag from a closet. The crowns, she thought, won't show under the covers.

She threw in underwear, stockings, a silk blouse, soap, a dressing gown and slippers. "These will do," she said. She brought them back. Mark looked at her and saw her face brilliant with energy and delight. Every movement was vivid. He hardly knew her.

"Now, if you'll take my advice," she said, "you'll drive straight back to town. Who have you got, by the way?"

"A fellow named Gertner."

"Oh, I know Gertner. His daughter Lili was my parlormaid once, and he drove my car for a time, when I had one. Well, you just let him leave you at a hotel. Be as mysterious as you like and pay him for a full day. He'll only think it's a clandestine love affair. He's got that kind of imagination. I had a lot of bother with Gertner. He got Juli's sister into trouble. Yes, you must make it seem to be an escapade."

Emmy listened intently, nodding her head. Her imagination seized everything, already was prepared to take her role. But Mark was heavy and saw nothing. "Then what?" he said, not as a question but as an ironical disclaimer.

"Then take a taxi at once to the airport. You can get the eight o'clock plane to Zurich if there's room in it. I

[405]

took that plane myself once. It's just about an hour's trip. If not, take the first one going anywhere out of the country. Be very bold about whatever you do. With these people, and certainly in the circumstances, it's the only way."

She had never before said "these people," and now she didn't notice she had said it.

"You should be in Zurich by nine," she said. "Just think of it! At nine o'clock you're free."

Mark's heart shook at the word.

But he couldn't believe it. He felt bogged down, not only by distrust but by the final weight of details. "What about my hotel bill?" he said childishly. "I left my things there, you know. Even if I leave money to pay them, won't they suspect you of taking part in something queer, won't they start one of their damned inquiries?"

"Oh, they don't inquire about everything." The Countess spoke as tolerantly as to a child. "I'll pay your hotel bill. Don't object! You can send me the money when you want. I'll just say you didn't like the place and decided to go elsewhere, and I'll have your luggage forwarded."

"Oh, the luggage doesn't matter."

"Then, I'll want to be sure you got away. I must be sure. So you'll telegraph me the moment you land?"

"The minute we land." Emmy answered before he could.

The women looked at each other as though to say, "How gay and how lovely to be planning these things!"

"You can telegraph right from the airport," the Countess said. "You might say 'Changed plans. So-and-so and I leaving for Paris. Please forward luggage.' Something like that. I could show it to the hotel."

She took Emmy's elbows and lifted her up, helped her on with the fur coat, found her purse. "Now you must

[406]

really get off," she said. "You've got to hurry to be in town before eight o'clock."

She gave Emmy a last look, rearranged her veil a bit, and stuffed the passport in her purse. Mark picked up the bags.

The swing of her voice and her unhesitating movements carried them to the door, to the hall, and down the stairs. But Mark went with feet of lead. He was leaving her, with her eyes brilliant, her voice sure, and her whole body dizzy with triumph. But there was still the General.

He was silent as she hurried to the front door. He wanted to hold her back, say something to her, but she gave him no chance. She flung open the front door and called gaily to the driver, "Good morning, Hans. Come and get some bags."

Gertner jumped out and came up the walk smiling. "Good morning, gracious lady."

"Take my friend's bags," she said. "Mr. Preysing is driving her up to town."

Mark handed him the bags.

"How is Lili?" the Countess asked.

"Oh, very well, thank you, gracious lady. Very well."

"Tell her I have a present for the baby. She must come some day soon and get it."

How can she be like this, he thought; how can she be so happy?

She caught Emmy by the shoulders and kissed her on both cheeks. "*Au revoir, ma chérie!*" she said effusively. "*Bonne chance. N'oubliez pas le télégramme.*"

"*Au revoir, et mille remerciements,*" cried Emmy.

They both laughed as though they were sharing a gay conspiracy and some guilt and a little mockery. Emmy's acting was perfect, but it was no more perfect than that

[407]

of the Countess. Gertner gave them a shrewd, complaisant look and picked up the bags.

Mark took Emmy sharply by the arm and went down the walk with her to the car. For a second he had thought, I'll let her go alone, but the few steps to the car showed him she could never get away by herself. Gertner, stowing the bags, didn't see, but her steps faltered, her face was suddenly white with strain under the rouge and powder.

He half lifted her into the car. "I'll be all right," she whispered. "It's just at first." She leaned her head back on the seat and closed her eyes.

"Ready?" Gertner asked.

"Just a moment."

Mark turned and walked back to the door. The Countess was standing just inside, her white woolen robe drawn close against the cold. He drew the door half-to behind him and stood with her in the little vestibule.

"I can't leave you here," he said. "Come with us. We'll wait."

"I can't come. Not now."

"Why not? You've got a passport. Tell the girls anything."

"Oh, no."

"It's dangerous for you to stay."

All the light left her face. She looked at him with wide-open eyes that saw him as a small figure in a big, empty space.

"I can't come," she repeated.

"You mean you can't leave him."

"I mean if I leave now he'd never rest till he'd uncovered it. And then the others would suffer too. Those others who helped you. It wouldn't be fair."

"But you're afraid now."

"No, I'm not."

"Then you see something you won't tell me. What is it?"

"Nothing. Nothing."

But she did see something, though perhaps she hardly knew what she saw. With a stab of pain he thought, It's a fey look.

"Will you come later?"

"Oh, yes. I'll come later."

"No, you'll never come. You're a prisoner, too. More than she was. You can't get away."

"I can get away."

He said despairingly, "You saved me, and I can't save you."

"But I'll come," she said. Her face, swanlike and mysterious, lifted to his and he kissed her. "Oh, my darling, good-by."

He turned from her and pushed the door open. He ran down the path.

Emmy was leaning forward, her face pressed against the window of the car. As he opened the door she stayed his hand, holding the door open to look out.

The sun was coming up behind the mist, the world was still white but opaque and full of hidden light. Of the country Emmy loved so much she could see only a peaked house, the black points of pine trees; and under the crusts of melting snow by the path, the brown dried stalks of last year's flowers. Tears ran down her powdered cheeks. "Oh, it's so beautiful," she said; "it's so beautiful."

Mark got in beside her and begged her without words to forgive him because for an instant he had almost hated her. He drew her head back against his shoulder and the driver started the car.

They rolled down the drive and out into the road. No

use looking back to see the house. The mist hid it and he knew the door was closed.

Before they reached the resort town the mist began to lift and in half an hour the road, the houses, the pine trees, were clear and distinct and glistening with moisture. But Emmy didn't open her eyes to look again, and he saw nothing but the sun flashing on the windshields of a few passing cars.

He knew that it was all over. He would never see the Countess again. And presently, in the apathy of a thing already over but never to be entirely recovered from, he would pass with Emmy through the locked iron gates. And after so much intolerable anguish their passage would be as effortless and gentle as a peaceful death.

Chapter XXVI

She stood in the vestibule, hearing the door of the car slam and the engine starting and the crackling sound of wheels moving over crusty, melting ice. Then it was quiet again.

Gradually, as the car didn't come back, as no sound came, she knew they were gone.

But she remained standing there until she shook with cold. What am I waiting for, she thought. Oh, the telegram. The telegram from Zurich. But that will be hours yet. At the earliest I wouldn't get it till nine-thirty. At the very earliest. In the meantime I have a thousand things to do.

She ran upstairs and snatched the dishes that had been left in Emmy's room and took them down to the kitchen, washed them hastily and put them away. She was just climbing the stairs again when she heard her servants coming across the gallery to the kitchen. She went to the room where Emmy had been and straightened it up. She couldn't remember when she had made a bed and she made this one awkwardly and replaced little things around the room that had been moved. Presently it looked exactly as it had before. It was as though Mark and Emmy had never been there. If the General were now to walk in the door he could look at the couch and never see that Mark had once slept there, and the mirror would hold no trace of Emmy's face, peering into it with the sudden face of

Suzanne. The room was so empty of them, it told her they had got safely away. She took a last look to assure herself, went out, and locked the door.

As she went down the hall to her own room the house seemed queer to her. For a time she had thought of it so intensely as a shelter for them that now it had an empty, purposeless air. She got into her bed to wait for breakfast. Sitting there against her pillows she tried to imagine what the house would be like when she left it. Because she had no doubt that she would be leaving it soon.

I'll have to arrange to sell it, she thought. But no, that's no good. I couldn't take the money. (Emmy Ritter tried to sell a house!) I'll have to rent it. I can probably manage that somehow, though it's pretty big. It costs a great deal to heat it.

Then there are the servants. I can't turn them loose on the world. I must especially look out for Juli. Perhaps I can manage to take Juli with me. I took her with me before — to New York.

But take her where? Where am I going? Where will I be at home now? What house will shelter me? And how will I live? There won't be any money.

Of course I can sell things. There's still lots of furniture and there are the porcelains and some of the books and pictures. The jewelry is all gone. All the best things are gone.

But like the house, which I can't sell and can't even rent, I can't sell my things because I can't use the money. I can't get it away.

She was still too swept onward to be discouraged. There are ways of doing everything, she thought. I must see that old servant of theirs. Fritz, they called him. He's sure to come back with the passport. He'll come straight here. He looked like a capable man, and I'll ask his advice. How

[412]

strange to depend finally on a disagreeable old servant!

What was that dark thing I saw, or thought I saw, just as they were leaving? It was so awful for a moment. Well, I can't quite remember it. After nine o'clock I don't need to remember it.

When Juli came with the coffee she found the Countess wide-awake, with a strange, dreamy look on her face.

"Good morning, gracious lady," said Juli. The curtains were already drawn back and the sun was beginning to shine on the melting snow. "It's a lovely day," Juli said tentatively. She pretended not to watch the Countess. She had known all about her and the General for many years, and she could tell by a glimpse of the Countess' face whether things had gone well or badly between them. This morning she decided the Countess was happy. She would go downstairs and tell Kathe they had made up their quarrel.

The Countess sipped her coffee and the noises of her household began around her. She couldn't remember what the girls were planning this morning but it didn't matter. Some probably would have lessons from the old professor who came from a near-by village where he lived. Some of the more expert might still go for skiing to the higher slopes, where the snow might be firm enough.

She thought of Suzanne and wondered what Suzanne would do today. Yesterday she had thought of Suzanne as that disagreeable French girl. Now she was bound to Suzanne, less by obligation than by understanding of her. She didn't like to think of Suzanne and Leo. It was such a fruitless grief. Leo had not even been able to take from Suzanne what consolation there was for him. The sadness of it turned her mind again to the moment in the vestibule. Something she had seen then, a glimpse of barrenness and waste places . . . No, it wasn't to be like that. Because, she thought, I've thrown all that away. I'm starting all over. I have a new life. Or I will, at nine o'clock.

She jumped out of bed and left her door open so that she could hear the golden clock. She took her bath slowly and dressed. Instead of putting on the day dirndl, or one of the pretty little suits of the country, she took out a sweater and tweed skirt. She put these on and took Suzanne's lipstick and rouged her lips. She looked, in the sweater and with the flash of color at the lips, ten years younger.

She began to look through her bureau drawers and to see all that had accumulated in them and to wonder how she would begin to throw things away. She looked at her clothes and decided she would give them all to Juli. Except for a few to Kathe. She didn't want to keep any of them.

And then her desk was full of bills and papers of all kinds. Letters — those must be gone over and thrown away. Letters meant friends. They would have to be thrown away too, just like the sheets of paper. But it's harder to discard people. Do I love my friends very much? she thought. Could I really not do without them? I've had some of them a long time. Perhaps that's all there is to most of them — long association, things shared. But if I don't want the things we shared? The moment I don't want those things any more, then I'm another person. And they wouldn't love me. Most of them would hate me for changing. The moment I changed I lost them, whether I wanted to or not. But that's all right too. They'll be easier to lose than the things and the places I love so much, the little nooks and niches that I've made myself, the dear possessions I've had, and the special quality about them that no one sees but me.

Then there's Kurt. But I won't think of him now at all.

She rushed her mind away from him and turned feverishly again to her house and her possessions.

[414]

It would take days and days to clean things out of her various desks alone. It would be weeks and weeks, she thought, before she could leave this place. What would Emmy Ritter do if she decided to leave as I am leaving? She would just get up and walk out! But then I can too. Just the same, there are a few things I *must* keep. I'll make a little list of them.

She sat down at her desk, took up a pencil and paper. The golden clock downstairs struck eight, and the little tune rang out clearly.

Is it possible that over two hours have gone since they left? If they got to town without accident then they are at the airport now and boarding the plane (Oh, I must keep the clock! She put it down at the head of her list.) Then she began to imagine them getting into the plane. First they would show the passport, and there was sure to be no trouble about that. Who really examines a passport picture? The last one she had taken looked less like her than Suzanne's did like Emmy Ritter. And no one was on the lookout for Emmy Ritter. Not yet. No, they'd certainly board the plane. But what if there was no place in the plane? She tried to imagine a setback but couldn't. It was certain they were on the plane.

Now they must be taking off. She remembered the curious realization of the earth just not there any more. Suddenly the damp, brown fields slowly sink and turn and the clusters of red roofs lie like little pebbles. And then one sees the forests far below, like a fell of coarse fur. Then the mountains come up, but so far below that their sharpness and terror and beauty are lost, and they are only curious and a childish, almost pedagogical simplification. And are those lakes or only snowy meadows? How people do exaggerate the beauties of air travel! They are only carried away by newness, by the mystical conquests of the combustion engine. Still, the loss of that line to the earth, which makes looking from a mountain top so much better than looking from a plane, and the speed that destroys all delicacy of vision, the thunderous noise, do give a feeling of escape. Yes, a plane is made purely for escape and those two are at this moment escaping in one.

Suddenly she thought: But if they should crash — If the engine fails, if the mists hide the higher peaks and they fly too low — She imagined a searing sheet of flame, red and black. But that was impossible too, because already she was with them as they landed. The earth came up to meet them and she felt with them the slight shock of landing. Then they stepped out and she knew the quiet, the smallness they felt, the wavering feet.

First we must send the telegram. But are we here? Is this really Switzerland? You're sure it's Zurich? Where can we send a telegram? I must buy a toothbrush. Let's go to a hotel. Let's take a drive. Let's sit on a sunny terrace and have a drink. Let's talk to people. Why not go on to Italy, or Africa? Let's never stop flying.

But she had outstripped them. It was only eight-fifteen.

Now as to this list. First there's the clock. Then there's my little porcelain of Flora, and the yellow stove of course . . .

Some of the girls passed below the window carrying skis on their shoulders. Now the downstairs was free.

She went downstairs. The house was quiet but there was a girl, Sully probably, practising piano in the music room. She was playing the Forest Pieces of Schumann. The doorbell rang, and it was the old professor come to give his lessons. He was shown into the writing room and two of the girls came running down the stairs and joined him.

She sat down in her library to wait for the telegram. It couldn't be very long now. She leaned her head back. All her porcelains, the shepherdesses, the masked comedians, the hussars, hung around her in suspended motion. Nothing seemed to move but the gilded hands of the clock just outside. Presently it struck nine and played its little notes, but she didn't hear it. She was asleep.

She didn't even hear the doorbell when it rang soon after. Juli had to touch her shoulder to make her wake and to say to her, "The General is here."

"Of course," she stammered, "I'll come."

Sully was still practising in the music room. Her notes had the eerie melancholy of a piano played at a little distance.

She went into the drawing room and saw Kurt standing by the window with his back to her. The sun was shining now, and the melting snow made a dazzling square against which he was a black pillar.

He did not turn around until she said "Kurt," and when he turned she saw at once that he knew. Even though his face was dusky against the snow glare, she saw that he knew.

"Sit down, Kurt," she said. She dropped into a sofa and rested her arms on a little marquetry table where the porcelain statue of Flora stood holding a wreath of delicate flowers. Kurt came slowly, so slowly she could not tell whether it was with reluctance or intense deliberation, and drew up a chair to sit across from her with the table between. He was giving them both time, and she used hers to shake off the weakness of sleep and to draw up every power against him.

Here they waited now, with a frail table and a gay porcelain between them, at the mercy of his anger which she had known so often before. And again she was afraid. Not of what she already knew but of what was still unknown in him. The final direction of his anger, the long plunge of it, and where at last it would leave them both.

"Are you ready to take the trip?" she said. "I dressed for it."

"We're not going," he said. He looked at her but she found it impossible to look at him. And yet it was a little better now they had begun to talk. She turned the Flora from side to side as though she were examining it for the first time.

"What do you want to do, then?"

"To talk to you."

"All right. What shall we talk about?"

"I must tell you some things," he said; "and then there are some things you must tell me."

"What are they?"

Not looking at him she knew he twisted his monocle into his eye, that his hand, so small and delicate for his great size, shook as he lifted it. She knew the vein pulsed sickly in his forehead and that in the whites of his eyes the fine veins made a network. He sat half-turned from her, one elbow on the table, staring at her, and he suddenly sighed, a sharp, quick sigh. That meant the worst for both of them. He sighed because, exacting, brutal, sentimental as he was, he had been forced at last into the worst he could imagine.

"I must tell you," he said heavily, "that this morning I telephoned into town and I learned that Madame Ritter died suddenly in prison Tuesday night."

"How sad!" she exclaimed.

"It was not sad for her son, was it? He was very happy indeed all the next day."

"Perhaps he didn't know."

"He buried her himself."

"Oh! Then he must have thought she was better off."

"Ruby, stop these lies. They're no good. You know all I'm telling you. But I must go on telling you, just the same."

"To torment me?"

"Perhaps. You haven't hesitated to torment me."

"I don't know what you're talking about."

"You do know. And you've known all along. What a fool you made of me! I remember your first question to me about this woman, this Emmy Ritter — you looking so innocently at a book about her house. Already you'd seen the son."

"I met him quite by chance that day at the lake. It was the first time."

"I'm not at all sure it was by chance. And I'm still less sure it was the first time. But my questions come later. First I'll tell you. The day I was occupied with the Marshal, you spent with young Preysing. You went to the concert with him."

She nodded, still not able to look at him. She was hardly listening to what he said, but rather to the quality of his voice. There was something new in it. It wasn't just his angry voice, purring and sarcastic, shouting at her finally with a tinge of hysteria in it. It was low and heavy with poignant regret and sadness.

"And after the concert you met — also I suppose 'by accident' — your protégé Doctor Ditten, the young man you knew when he was a child and have befriended ever since."

She was surprised by this. "Ditten? Why, what's important about that? I met him by accident."

"There are too many accidents, Ruby. Too many coincidences. For instance, this one: that Doctor Ditten was the man who attended Madame Ritter and made out her death certificate."

"What!" Her horror was so genuine that even he believed in it for a moment. She looked straight into his eyes, blankly, forgetting he was there. "What! I don't believe that."

"Then Preysing has made more of a fool of you than I thought." But his voice was a shade lighter, it showed his relief at any possibility of her innocence.

But she wasn't concerned at this moment with his belief in her innocence. So it was Ditten who had sent Emmy out alive! And now Kurt would crack him like a nutshell. Why hadn't they told her about Ditten, Mark and Emmy? Because the fewer who knew it the safer he would be? Only now Kurt, the one who must not know, did know.

"Then there's the matter of the servant. An old servant of the Ritters', named Fritz Keller, who lives here in the village . . . It was he who claimed the body and brought it down here to bury. He turns out to have been a very faithful servant indeed. He even testified at her trial."

"Well, what of it?" She tried with all her strength to speak indifferently. "Madame Ritter is attended by young Ditten, and dies. Her servant and her son bury her. What's wrong?"

"When I came here yesterday I was sure something was wrong," he said. "My whole instinct warned me. But I couldn't guess what it was for several reasons. I saw you and the young man must be in love. I thought you were trying to hide it from me. Then later I saw you gazing into each other's eyes and I was nearly blind with jealousy. But I did see that probably you would try to help him. Only I didn't know how you, with your feeble character, could possibly do that. And also I didn't know that the mother was supposed to have been buried that afternoon. As soon as I found that out, the whole behavior of Preysing seemed monstrous, incredible, even stupid. Until — quite suddenly it became clear. *She wasn't dead at all.*"

Of course he had to guess. It was too obvious. But *when* had he guessed? Had he already telephoned to town? Were they stopped at the airport? If they had got away he had no proof, and the rest of them could lie themselves out of it.

"You see, once I knew she was alive, everything was explained: the young man's strange air of unconcern, or rather his concern with other things, the disloyalty that I had felt slowly building up in you. It became clearly a worse disloyalty than I feared. It had made you the complete tool of that scoundrel, and made you betray Ditten into a folly that's going to cost him his life. And once I knew she was alive, I even saw why it was that the two of you so obviously didn't want to be together. You tried to get rid of him today. So transparently — My poor Ruby! The excursion — It was to have kept me out of the way while he was free."

No use talking to him. The less she said now the better. It was no longer a question of what he knew. It was what he had done or was going to do. It was what he had now become, either a man who hated her, or a man who still loved her. She sat stupidly turning the Flora about with hands slippery with sweat.

"There is also that wagon coming in yesterday morning," he said. "Ruby, Madame Ritter is in this house, isn't she?"

"Certainly not," she said. "Would you like to look?" Then she smiled, remembering the clean, empty room upstairs. "Really, Kurt — What a story! I had no idea you could imagine all this."

He looked at her so steadily that she felt abashed. "Don't, Ruby," he said. "It's useless. She is here."

"But she's not," she said more eagerly. "No one is here. The poor woman is in her grave and even Mr. Preysing seems to have gone off for the day. He passed by early this morning."

"I know he's left his hotel. But his bags are there. His bill is unpaid."

"Oh, then he'll certainly be back and you can question him yourself if you like. But perhaps you frightened him away. You were horrid to him. He may not come back."

He leaned toward her and said, "Ruby, is it true there is no one in your house?"

"Yes."

"Then I must call the police at once."

"Police! What for?" She threw out her hand and caught his arm as he started to get up. "What for, Kurt?" she cried, but her voice rang unafraid. Had he really not yet called the police? Then they must have got away.

He sat down again, heavily, and she saw how sick he was — how all his great bulk trembled. "Why have you done this to us?" he said. "How could you do it? Don't you see I wanted to keep you out of the worst of it? I didn't want her found in your house. That's why I didn't telephone the police at once. I hoped if I gave him a little time he would come and take her somewhere else. It seems he has done it, so now I must phone and have every road, every hotel, every station, every port and airport watched."

He hadn't telephoned yet. But what if there was no space on the plane . . .

"They can't get away. It's not possible. For one thing the woman has no papers. Don't try to save them. Don't try to save Ditten either. I must have him arrested. And that servant."

"And me?" she asked.

"And you." He put his elbows on the table and buried his face in his hands.

"What a hero!" she said lightly. (Perhaps they were

already in the plane.) "But you don't have to be a hero. There's nothing to be heroic about. No one's here. No one's anywhere. The young man has left. It's silly to take Ditten and the old servant. You couldn't prove anything and you'd only make a fool of yourself."

He said nothing and she couldn't see his face. Only his delicate hands and his big gold signet ring.

"Kurt, you know you hate to be made a fool of. After all, I really can't let you. You'd call up the police and they'd all laugh at you. Rudi would love a joke like that on you. He would say, 'Well, where *is* the woman?' You can't produce her, can you? Let's forget it all, shall we? Let me give you some coffee. We'll have our excursion. What time is it, anyway?"

She raised herself to look out at the clock in the hall, but she never got that far, for he said, "I will have the coffin exhumed."

She sank back and he took his hands down and said, "Oh, your face, Ruby! It tells everything. I don't even need to do it. But I *will*."

The shock of that passed and she watched him, knowing that everything now hung on what she could do with him. He was the only one who knew, and if she could control his knowledge they were safe. Whether they caught the first plane or not, they were safe. And so were Ditten and old Fritz. And she also would be safe, and her own new life, clean of all these horrors and clean of Kurt himself, could begin again. But they couldn't be free of him unless she was able to use all she knew of him to seduce him. What did she know of him? Mostly his love and his anger, his sickness of body and spirit. Many times she had drawn him back from the brink of a darkness waiting for both of them! Now she must draw him back again, if she could.

[423]

"Ruby," he muttered, "if you had only been clever, if you had only kept yourself clear in this. You shouldn't have let them bring that woman here. I don't care now for your lying. I don't care that you cheated me. I only wish you'd been clever."

"Well, I wasn't," she said. "That can't be helped now. What is going to happen to me?"

"I don't know."

"Will I be arrested?"

He leaned his head in his hands again and she heard him breathing like a tired cart-horse straining up a hill. He said again, "Why did you do this?" Then he added in a low, ashamed voice, "You must go away at once. At first it won't come out that you're involved, and luckily she won't be found in your house. Go while you can. You'd better go at once."

Her whole body seemed suddenly to stream upward like a volatile essence. Oh, to be free! "But if I go," she said, "you'll go through with it just the same? You'll catch them if you can? You'll arrest Ditten and the old man?"

"I have no choice."

"Why should I go then? To save myself, or to spare you?"

"If you must have it so — to spare me. You know, Ruby, I loved you."

"Don't speak of love," she said gently. "For fifteen years I've known your love. Do you think I really care what happens to me?"

He looked up at her with outraged, bloodshot eyes, and she saw what she was doing now. By instinct rather than plan, she wasn't drawing him back from the worst but pushing him toward it, and herself with him. Perhaps that was the only way. And strangely she saw that whatever else was happening now, it was also the climax of their years

[424]

together. They were drawing closer and closer. Emmy and Mark, the others, were far outside. It was she and Kurt going down into a darkness together.

"You're trying to hurt me mortally," he said. "You know you can do it. Even after the awful blows you've given me you can still hurt me. Well, go ahead. Spoil everything we've had."

"You've spoiled it," she said, "you've made it dirty and cruel and mean."

"Hush!" he cried. "It's dead then, since you say it is. Leave it alone. But I came here hoping against hope to save you."

"Everyone wants to save someone else," she said mockingly, "and now you want to be heroic too. You've always wanted to be a sort of God, haven't you? Oh, I can see you being God. Pulling your wretched Ruby out of the mire. Then I would grovel and say, 'Forgive me! I love no one but you.' "

"Do you think I want to turn you over to them?"

"No. But if you arrest the others you'll have to. Because I'll be right here."

"If you won't go then you must keep your mouth shut. You mustn't say anything."

"Oh, but I will. I'll say everything. Imagine what it will be like, Kurt. First there'll be the trial. All of us there together." She spoke in a low voice, leaning over so that her head almost touched his, and his glassy blue eyes were close to hers. The monocle had dropped and he hadn't noticed it. She smelled the dye in his uniform, brought out by the heat in his body. He sat as though he were bound, a great, laboring animal breathing with terror, bound too tightly to stir.

"Just imagine, Kurt, how we'll stand there. How they will stare at us! You'll be there, of course. 'That's the man who turned his mistress over to the police,' they'll say. 'What a patriot!' 'And there's the woman who betrayed him for the sake of a nobody.'

"You think I'm so shy and timid, don't you? But I won't be. I'll say everything I can think of. I'll say you did it from jealousy. I'll say you're a half-mad, sick creature, not fit to be on your feet.

"I'll insult them, too. I'll tell them I loathe the country and everyone in it. That I'd betray it over and over if I had the chance. I'll make them be cruel to me, do fearful things to me. And you'll have to see it."

He reached across and seized her arm and shook it till long arrows of pain sprang from his fingers. His fingers were rigid and couldn't let go of her. "Keep still!" he cried. "You're crazy. Keep still!"

"Yes, I am. But it's because I've always been afraid of you. I've always known you had a kind of madness and blackness in you. Well, now you can let it go. Now you can get what you always wanted. You suffered because the world wouldn't let you be great enough, Godlike enough. Now you can be God at last; a funny, smoked, black image of a god out of the past, out of the night of everything old and ugly."

"Ruby!" He let go of her arm and she could hear his breath whistle in his throat.

"Be God," she said gently, "be God at last."

With great slowness and caution he put his hands on the table and raised himself out of his chair. He stood leaning over her, supported by his hands.

"You'll do what you must," he said. Each word came like a stone dropped. "And I'll do what I must."

She looked up at him and saw with great lucidity what she had done to him. Also she saw that at last he, unlike herself, had been able to see an issue more important than themselves. And because of this, though all she had said was true, there remained a glimmer of something noble in him. Something to remind her of what he was when she first knew him . . . when she hadn't seen him as a great, arrogant lord in his own land, or even a lover who would bring disaster or happiness, but simply as a man struggling to recover from awful wounds of body and spirit, clinging in despair to the one thing that seemed to him unbroken in chaos: the integrity of his people and his race.

His grip on the table slowly relaxed and slowly he fell forward, the table and the little Flora crackling under him as he fell. She sat on the couch watching, without a cry or a movement, till he lay huddled at her feet.

Then suddenly she screamed, "Juli!"

Juli came running from across the hall and it was she who kneeled down by him and lifted his red, swollen head and tore open the collar of his tunic.

"Is he dead?" she asked.

"No, no," Juli assured her. "He's quite alive, God be thanked. It's a stroke."

"I always thought he'd have one," she said.

She saw against his neck the little gold medal she had once given him, hanging by a thread of gold. His breathing was ugly and stertorous now and filled the room, but through it the golden clock in the hall struck ten and played the first four bars of *Voi che sapete*.

He'll be sick a long time, she thought, looking at the medal caught in the pale hair at the base of his neck. . . . I brought that to him from Rome.

Now that's over. But how Kurt will hate being sick!

Juli put a cushion under his head and ran to the closet beneath the stairs to telephone a doctor.

On the landing the door opened and the professor said, "Did anyone call?" Hearing no answer he closed the door.

The bell rang and Kathe opened the front door. She spoke to someone, then closed it. She came and stood in the drawing room, struck dumb with curiosity and horror. "A telegram," she whispered, holding it out in her hand.

In the music room Sully played "The Bird Is Prophet." The Countess held out her hand for the telegram.

I'll have to take him to Italy, she thought. He needs a long rest. He needs the sun.

She seemed to see the years ahead: Herself a trembling old woman, sitting on a terrace in the sun; and beside her a sick and querulous old man. Someone was saying, "There's the painter, the famous one." And the man who passed could by no means recognize her, nor indeed could she really recognize him.

This, she thought, is what I actually saw in the vestibule, just as he was leaving. And curiously she found a consolation in it, as soft gray twilight began to settle over her.